The
COST

REVIEWS for **I CHOOSE PAIN**

"I'm losing too much sleep at night reading this book! I love the character development and the way it is told from the four different voices!" - I. Jackson

"From the moment I turned the first page I was hooked. I loved the way the author introduced the friends and let us into their life. Relationships are tough and filled with a host of emotions. I can relate. The author did a good job of telling the story and left me wanting more." - E. Porter

"'I Choose Pain' is a fantastic novel! This story had me hooked from beginning to end. Beautifully written with tales of a friendship that is relatable & entertaining throughout. You will not regret making this purchase." - M. Colyer

"What wonderful explanations and reliving of the lives and attitudes of same gender loving brothers of color over many years! Stories interwoven intricately developing characters known so well. Hurts and fears, friendships, and discoveries, supported by heart retching naked truths. I Choose Pain is therapy sessions told over many years. Exciting and worth the read." - A. Head

"From page one, the characters in this book had my full attention. It was so superbly written, and such detail was given that I felt like I knew every one of the four main friends personally. The story line and plot kept me guessing all the way and wanting more. I can clearly see this story as a movie. Also, the author's written voice reminds me a lot of E. Lynn Harris, the critically acclaimed author. However, Eros da Artiste is a younger, hipper version who leaves nothing unsaid. This book far exceeded my expectations. Grab a copy, curl up on a couch and dive in." - K. Webber

The
COST

A Novel by

EROS DA ARTISTE

The Library of Congress has established a record for this title.

Paperback ISBN: 978-0-578-68484-0

Printed in the U.S.A.
0   1   2   3

DISCLAIMER
The self-help practices and ideas conveyed in this book are not a substitute for professionally administered mental care. If you are suffering from depression, hopelessness, or thoughts of suicide, please call

1-800-273-TALK / 1-800-273-8255

BIOGRAPHY

The eclectic Eros da Artiste is a unique Renaissance Man. He is a singer, songwriter, actor, theatrical music director, musician, digital painter, and visual artist. He resides in Baltimore, MD, by way of San Antonio, TX.

The Cost is his second literary work, a sequel to his debut novel, **I Choose Pain**. With this sophomore effort, he hopes to shed light on different topics many tend to shy away from, as well as remind the readers of all persuasions that we all are called upon to make a difference in this world and that we must come and work together to find creative and productive ways to coexist and love one another.

FROM THE AUTHOR

As I sit at my desk to type these words, I reflect on this crazy journey I call life. It is filled with twists and turns, as well as hills and valleys. When I was a child, I never envisioned writing a novel that speaks to and about the lives of gay, bisexual, lesbian, or transgender individuals. Back then, the rainbow scared me, and my fear was based on the black and white morality laws I was taught in church and in my family, as well as the unknown facts concerning the desire growing inside of me.

To be transparent, I was one of those kids that knew he was attracted to the same sex but wanted to be liked. I had a faulted thought process, as well as a huge inferiority complex. Because I was diagnosed with autism at age two, I felt that I was incompetent and nothing I did was good enough. When I discovered I had talents, I used them all to gain friends and associates, and for a little while, I did. I wanted to be accepted, like any kid. And if I could not be accepted, then I would fade in the background, praying that I wouldn't call any attention to myself and earn ridicule of my peers.

Being gay is something that I never wanted to be because it went against the Biblical and familial teachings that I was raised to cling to. I remember one occasion when a classmate of mine was subject to an exorcism of sorts. He was gay and the church was not inclusive or affirming. In fact, the ongoing dogma was that those who were gay were sinners of the worst kind. So, the church did what many have done since the beginning. They tried to "pray the gay away". No one thought to ask my classmate of his story, which was that he was molested and raped by his own older brothers and sisters.

I knew that pain because I was molested at different points of my life, starting at age five. But after seeing him go through that, I decided to keep my existence as a gay teenager a secret. Armed with that decision, I ran from what I was for years, creating clever ruses and maneuvers to mask the growing attraction with the same sex. Even when I tested positive for HIV at age twenty-four, I still felt it increasingly difficult to accept who I was, or to claim our community as family.

However, it was during that time that I began the first novel, while playing for churches and going to grad school at Morgan State University. Throughout twelve years, I wrote-then stopped- then wrote again. I knew the story needed to be told, but I was afraid of the backlash and rebukes I would get from the religious institutions that I held in high regard and served for so many years. It was not until I got fired from a church that I decided to finish the book and deal with the repercussions.

Yet, even after the book was finished, I STILL could not be content with being a gay man. Then one day, a light came on and I said to myself that, as a black man approaching age forty, I did not want to spend my life hiding from and lying about who I was. If I was going to write a book championing us as a community, then I had to embrace the part of me that my family, the church, my peers, and others told me was evil, abominable, and horrid… but I had seen as beautiful, magical, and filled with love.

When I released the first book, **I Choose Pain**, I thought to myself, "Well, you wrote a book. Now you can cross this off your bucket list." The process was therapeutic, cleansing, and purposeful. But there was a call deep within me to tell more of the story of Lionel and his crew, as well as why his mother harbored so much bitterness. And quite a few readers have asked me to continue the story of Lionel, so this is my grateful answer to them.

Through examining different accounts of the lives we lead as LGBTQIA individuals, I have learned two things. One: Being gay is no choice. No one chooses to be maligned from the pulpit or ostracized by a homophobic society. Two: The LGBTQIA community involves EVERYONE who has the capability to love and not judge. Every person from each facet of our community is important, and it is my dream that we can see each other's worth enough to band together and minimize hate-driven brutality and refute religious rhetoric against our rainbow family.

The book you are about to read may trigger emotions concerning areas in your life that are wracked with great pain. But I ask that you remain open to what you read. This book at times will take the church folk to task, but it is not meant to injure; it is simply to encourage them to become better informed and find compassion to love- or at least be honest and not hide behind religion to justify their disdain. As I have said in the disclaimer of the first book, the faith themes in this book are not meant to slight or disparage any other personal creed. I hold with the belief that we all have different paths that lead to fulfillment and peace. I also believe that whether you are a Christian, Muslim, Buddhist, Agnostic, or Atheist, there has been a point when you had to call on a supernatural strength to bring you through hardships, even if that meant simply looking inside yourself to discover a power you didn't know you mortally possessed.

As you read this book, it is my hope that you laugh, cry, and feel the romance and the friendship involved. I also hope that you can identify and hold fast to those people in your life that love, support, and affirm you.

May the hopeless find hope again.

May the depressed find their joy.

May the lonely drifters in life find their way to peace and harmony.

Most importantly, may the hated soul find love to give to themselves and others.

Enjoy the book… and you have my love always.

Eros da Artiste

ACKNOWLEDGEMENTS

There are so many to thank that I cannot name them all for fear that I will forget someone. So, I will keep it brief.
I would like to thank:

My Lord and Savior, Jesus Christ, for loving and sustaining me and for bestowing upon me many artistic gifts, including the gift of literature to speak of the struggles we suffer as a community,

I would like to acknowledge the following organizations for your invaluable assistance over the years: *The Adodi Brotherhood, Big Boy Pride Family, SGL Cruise Family, S.O.U.L. Gay Straight Alliance at Morgan State University, Iron Crow Theatre, and The Pride Center of Maryland.*

I would like to acknowledge these following people for being such wonderful people in my life and letting me know that it is OK to be myself:

My Baltimore Crew and friends- Gerrell Ross, Quae Simpson, Marla McKinney, Timoth Copney-Welton, Nicholas Miles, Asia-Lige Arnold, Danielle Harrow, K. Carter, Vincent Dion Stringer, and Brandon Shaw-McKnight.

My San Antonio Crew- Angelique Black, Stacy Black, J. Wilson, G. Williams, K. Webber, A. McKinney, D. Salone, Elonda Russ, and the Russ Family.

My friends in Atlanta: Ian Jackson, Jamal Guiden, Ernest Duncan, Chandler Moore, Keith Sibley, Mark Dupree, Claude Everett, Lee Hayes (the author of the heart stopping **Passion Marks** Series as well as the Web Series, **BAIT.** It is FABULOUS!), and George Daigle.

My friends in Washington, DC: Mary Davis, Charles Jackson, Rayceen Pendarvis, Gregg Mims, Donald Beasley, and Marcel Emerson (Author of **The Library**.)

A dear author friend of mine in Las Vegas: Chanel Hardy. Thank you for your encouragement and your help with I CHOOSE PAIN.

Much thanks go to every supporter, well-wisher, and reader of both books. I hope you prosper and forever be in good health.

TO BE REMEMBERED

Mother:

I am grateful that you were nothing like the mother in this book. Although you disapproved of my life as a gay man, you never let your disapproval cloud your love and affection for me. I still remember your words, "Good, better, best. Never let it rest 'til your good is better and your better is best.I pray that you are resting in God's power and peace. I love you and miss you much.

My dear brother, roomie, and friend, A.D.

You said that you saw big things for me when you met me shortly after I moved to San Antonio. Well, look at what done happened! Not a day goes by where I don't look at your picture and miss our heart-to-heart conversations on the balcony or over those fabulous dinners you used to cook. I miss those times, and I miss you. Rest in power. I love you.

DEDICATION TO OUR FALLEN

This book is dedicated in memory of Torrance "Miss Whoochie" Cheeves as well as countless LGBT individuals that have been murdered by way of hate. May they all find peace.

It is also dedicated to the lives of Armaud Arbery, Breonna Taylor, and George Floyd, as well as so many others whose lives were cut short due to a racist system that allows police officers to shoot and kill, instead of doing what they were supposed to do: protect and serve.

Final dedication goes to the millions of lives that were lost during the 2020 - 2021 Pandemic. Gone too soon.

May your spirits live on.

TABLE OF CONTENTS

Hate… it has caused a lot of problems in the world… but has not solved one yet.

-Maya Angelou

There is a cost for relying wholly on a crutch… whether it is literal or figurative. It will kill your spirit if you lean on it too long.

-Eros Da Artiste

You are Cordially Invited To
Witness the Marriage Ceremony of

LIONEL SHEDRICK DAVIS

and

JOSEPH STANLEY THOMPSON III

February 23rd, 2021
5:30pm
On the Regality Vessel of
FunTown Cruise Lines

Please RSVP

A Wedding…

"We are gathered here on this ship to unite these two beautiful men in matrimony, Lionel Shedrick Davis and Joseph Stanley Thompson III. In learning more about these two individuals, I can say that it is exceedingly rare for me to perform a ceremony involving newlyweds who have been friends since they were born. I suppose to anyone looking at these two for the first time, it would seem like they had been married long before now; but Lionel and Joseph have decided to make it official on this beautiful day."

We are here on this Rainbow Pride cruise in front of Reverend John Kelvin Washington, getting ready to tie the knot. My brothers, A.D. and Dean, are standing with us. My sister Brenda is standing beside Jojo with her husband, Mercer, and they both have bright grins on their faces. Garrett Peterson and his sister, Rachel, are sitting with their mother, Eunetta, on the front row. Peep and Jimmy are sitting behind them, with my youngest brother Roland sitting beside them. A family chain bound by love. One flaw in the chain is the absence of the fourth original member of The Fellas, Corey. I stand holding Jojo's hands and a tear runs down my cheek. I look at the man I'm about to marry and I see a tear in his eye that matches mine. We look at the empty seat where Corey would have sat. I feel certain sadness. Corey should be here! I look at A.D. and he places his hand on my shoulder in understanding.

"Marriage is a sacred trust in the covenant of love between two people, and it should not be taken lightly. Therefore, if there is anyone who can exhibit justification as to why these two should not be joined in marriage, let them speak now or forever hold their peace." There is silence, then A.D. exclaims. "Can we go 'head n' git you two married already? I'm hungria dan a fat gal on Slim Fas'." Everybody laughs and I see Jojo cracking a huge smile. My palms are sweaty as hell. I can barely hear Reverend Washington as he says the words, "Do you, Lionel Shedrick Davis, take Joseph Stanley Thompson to be your partner in life, to love and be loved, to protect and be protected, to honor and be honored, and forsaking all others for as long as you both shall live?"

Do I?
  Can I?
    Will I?

Stop!

Let's Press Rewind, shall we?

PART I:

ACHILLE'S HEEL

<u>Chapter One</u>
WE GATHER TOGETHER

"Lionel..."

"Lionel..."

I hear a voice call my name. I awaken from my night's sleep to encounter the sweet face of my lover, Jojo. His eyes are shining brighter than the morning sun pouring from the windows. His dark chocolate skin glistens with the residue of freshly applied face cream by Naambi. My eyes travel down to his full deep pink lips, puckered with amusement.

"Lionel, wake up. We have to get dinner started before this afternoon. You know, everyone's coming at three," Jojo beckons.

"It can wait. Come over here and give me some Thanksgiving candy," I say as I pull him to me and kiss him on his lips. After that deep long smooch, Jojo pulls back, "Alright now. We don't need to be starting something we can't finish. I still got to get the turkey in the oven, the stuffing made, the pies baked, and the collard greens on the stove. And you have to bake the ham, the pineapple and German Chocolate cakes, and the sweet potato casserole."

"I don't think you have to worry about the pies. Peep said he was bringing some."

"I know. We talked about it. I'm doing the coconut and pecan pies, and he's doing the sweet potato and pumpkin pies."

"What about the ambrosia salad?"

"I did that last night while you were watching the game. Did you make the potato salad?"

"Yeah. It's on the bottom shelf of the fridge."

"And I know you cooked those damned ox-tails. Ugh! I smelt them when I came over last night."

"Why you messing with my oxtails, baby?"

"Them things are disgusting."

"You just don't know what you are missing."

"I'm glad I don't," Jojo says with a laugh. "Who all is coming over, baby?"

"Peep and Jimmy, Corey, and A.D."

"Garrett's not coming?"

"He may stop in later with Rachel. He has Thanksgiving with his own family, you know."

"Oh ok."

"You do know that Peep is going to want to take over the kitchen. He did that last year."

"Yeah, but hopefully, everything that we would've cooked will send a clue for him to take it easy."

I roll my eyes. "You know that's not going to happen. He's either going to micromanage what we are cooking or bring some of his own food."

"Yeah, that's true. Besides A.D., who else is coming from your family?"

"Dean is coming. And baby, I asked for Nate to come over."

"Jesus, why?" Jojo whines as he sits straight. "You already know that him and Corey go at it all the time. I'm glad that y'all are friends, but I think those two enjoy opening and pouring salt into each other's wounds."

"I know baby. But remember, this is been a rough month for Nate with his father dying. He was really close to his dad. He could use some people around him right now."

"Ok. Well, I guess we can put up with their bickering for one day," Jojo assents as he gets up from the bed.

"Hey," I call to him.

"What?"

"Where are you going?"

"Downstairs to season and roast the turkey."

"Let it wait, baby," I say as I look over at my clock. It is now 7:56am. "The folks won't be over here until after three. Except Dean, you know that everyone coming is on CP time." I move my body to face his standing form, as I caress my left nipple seductively. "Now, you mentioned something about not starting something we can't finish. How about we start it and go halfway? We can finish when everybody goes home."

"You know good and well that shit is not going to happen," Jojo says. "We are both like those potato chips. We can't eat just one! But I will give you this." He straddles my body and gives me a long kiss, wet and moist, with his long tongue exploring my mouth. I respond to his kiss with the same fervent heat as when we kissed a year ago, cementing our love and commitment to be in a partnership as we sailed on a Caribbean cruise.

Jojo, formally named Joseph Stanley Thompson III, is my childhood friend and my soon to be partner. We decided to become an item on July 16th, 2018 after a lengthy delay on my part. I stalled on him because I didn't want to place our friendship in jeopardy. It was he that convinced me that this would only make our friendship stronger. He told me that it was only natural for us to become an item, since we had been friends for so long and knew each other so well. I proposed to him on a cruise ship after hearing a song my best friend Corey wrote called "Love Makes Me Beautiful." We have a long engagement going to see if we are ready to be married. To help us even more, we had been going to pre-marital counseling with Rev. Washington, and those sessions prove fruitful most times. After five months of counseling, we decided to go ahead and set the date for marriage, which is what we plan to share with our friends during dinner tonight.

I am attracted to his mind as well as his body. I remember thinking that he was a bit unlearned, but our relationship has caused me to see him differently. The more he talks, the more attracted I am and eager to learn more. Through his intelligence, Joseph never fails to open my eyes to different points of view and show me that the world is bigger than my oftentimes tunneled thinking.

I mentioned that I was attracted to his body. And what an attraction it is, especially as he straddles me now! He stands 5'11, with his wavy cropped hair protected under a stocking cap, a practice undertaken every night since he was thirteen. He also has a thick muscular ebony physique and abundant hair covering his chest and tapering to a line leading to his groin where his sex protrudes, a wiry, hard, and black shiny phallic wonder with a fleshy deep pink head on the top.

Without even knowing it, he is teaching me things about him that eluded me as platonic friends. I'm learning so much that I know he's happy by the way he smiles.

I know he likes sleeping on his right side.

I am in tune with his slow and relaxed breathing as he sleeps.

I am mesmerized by his enormous and beautiful eyes as he asks the question, "Do you love me?" *(Yes!)*

I know how his breath quickens when he is angry. *(I sometimes start mock fights just to get him riled up… because the sex afterwards is out of this world!)*

"Lionel."

"Huh? W-what?"

"What are you smiling about?"

"Am I smiling?"

"Yes. You are smiling big-time, and your eyes are twinkling."

"I'm thinking about how beautiful you are and how much I love you."

"You still love me?"

"Of course, I love you. Did you ever doubt that?"

"No, not really. I'm just amazed."

"What do you have to be so awestruck about?"

"That I've wanted you for all these years, and I finally got you."

We kiss again. I roll him on his back to straddle *him.* Our lips connect as if they are magnetized. Our breathing becomes labored and sweat begins emerging from our skins. Just when we are about to get hot and heavy, my cell phone rings.

"Aw shit!" we say in unison. I grab the phone from the nightstand. "Hello?"

"Climb up out the 'ass-pussy' and come up for air for a minute," Corey's voice bellows over the phone lines.

"What in the hell are you talking about?" I say, giving Jojo a kiss afterward.

"Oh, so Lionel wants to play dumb so early in the morning. I know Jojo's ass is over there and y'all are giving each other reasons to be thankful in your own special way. I'm surprised that you haven't moved in together yet."

"All in good time. What's going on?" I ask Corey as Jojo gets up, puts his clothes on, and sits in my armchair to pull on his socks. I stand to wedge the phone between my ear and shoulder so I can pull on my boxers.

"Nothing much. I just wanted to make sure we are not cooking the same things. I'm going to bake my monkey bread and sweet potato pies."

"Bring the monkey bread because Jojo and Peep are baking the pies," I suggested.

"OK, I'm also bringing my mustard greens."

"Well, we already have collards. But if you want to bring them, it'll give us some variety."

"OK. Now, I know that you invited Nate for dinner, and for the sake of him losing his father, I'm willing to keep the peace."

"Thank you… because we don't need any blood on the floor."

"Trust, if there was going to be any bloodshed, it would be his. But I will pack my razor away for today."

"That's all we ask."

"I also have news to share with everyone"

"What news?"

"Nothing that I would let slip over the phone. This is more like a dinner conversation."

"I bet I know what it is."

"Careful, Miss Cleo. You might lose that bet. I'm gonna let you keep guessing while I put this monkey bread in the oven. Three-thirty, right?"

"Close. Three o'clock sharp," I say as I shake my head and snicker. This boy is going to be late to his own homegoing.

"All right, I'll see you then. Kiss!"

"Kiss." I press the end button.

"Well, what did Corey want?" Jojo asks, his large eyes widening questioningly.

"He wanted to know what we were cooking so he would not be bringing the same things."

"Smart thinking," Jojo muses.

"He also said he had some news for us."

"And I bet you my bottom dollar that I know what it is."

"What is it then, Mr. Clairvoyant?" I tease as I rise from the bed to embrace him.

"Garrett popped the question. They are getting ready to ring the wedding bells, baby," Jojo says, with his arms around me and hands clasped at the small of my back.

"That thought did cross my mind, but maybe it's something else."

"Well, I guess we won't know until tonight," Jojo says as he clutches my ass.

"Alright now, what happened to us not starting something we can't finish?"

"That is a privilege reserved for Joseph Stanley Thompson the Third."

"Oh, so you can grab my ass, but I can't kiss you like I want to?"

"Correct."

"I betcha I can!"

"I betcha you can't!" He says as he tears away from me, laughing and racing through the door. A challenge!

We race down the stairs and into the kitchen where he takes my flour pot and throws some flour at me! I open my cabinet to retrieve the spare bag and throw some at him! After a few seconds of this merriment, I do the one thing he cannot fight against: I wrap my arms around him and squeeze.

"No fair!" Jojo says, grinning.

"You grabbed my ass, then refused to give me yours. THAT wasn't fair!"

I smile into his eyes as he wholesomely beams into mine. Then, as we have many times before, we feel the spark of primal magnetism that pulls romantic kindred souls together. We kiss the kiss of abandon.

The kiss of promise...

The kiss of heat!

When we finish our kiss, we pull back from each other, tittering nervously. I look at the flour strewn about the floor.

"I guess I had better clean this up, so we can cook."

"Naw, baby. I'll clean this up. You go upstairs and shower."

My cell phone rings again, "Hello."

"Hey Lionel."

"Oh, Nate! What's going on?"

"Nothing much. You got a minute?"

"Sure. Hold on." I push the mute button. "Jojo, you mind if I talk to Nate a minute. I feel like this might be kinda heavy."

Jojo looks less than thrilled. But he says, "Ok, baby. I'll start the turkey."

"Are you alright?"

"Why do you ask?"

"You had a funny look on your face."

"Go ahead and talk with Nate. We will discuss the look while prepping the food."

"Count on it," I say, puzzled. I run up to my bedroom and close the door.

"What's going on, Nate?"

"I've been thinking that maybe I should forgo the dinner."

"Why?"

"For two reasons. One, I don't want to make things awkward between you and your friends, particularly you and Joseph. I mean, we *are* ex-boyfriends."

"Point understood," I say as I slip back out of my boxers to shower once we get off the phone. "But we are just friends now. So, it shouldn't be a problem. Second reason?"

"The second reason is I don't know if I am ready to interact with people yet. It was rough at Dad's funeral, having to talk with folks and hear them saying, 'I know how you feel' and 'God knows best'. Makes me want to scream."

"That I believe is a more understandable reason. When you are grieving, you need space. But what are you going to eat?"

"I'll probably go to Hibachi Grill and pig out."

"Oh no! If you are planning to do that, then I am insisting that you come. If you want to be sad, be sad. But be among people who have gone through this. And if you need space, you can go out on the deck and chill."

A long hush comes over the line. I can tell he is thinking it over. After a few seconds, he says, "Ok, I'll come. But I have to ask you one thing."

"What's that?"

"Keep Corey away from me. I'm in no mood for him coming for me and shading me."

"Don't worry about that. Besides, he promised up and down that he was going to be cool."

"Ok, should I bring anything?"

"A bottle of wine, preferably D'Astieno. That is Jojo and Peep's favorite wine. I think that will thaw the ice between you three."

"You got it. Anything else?"

"Well, if you want to travel on the right foot with Corey, get a bottle of Primo Mazzo's Strawberry Moscato. He absolutely loves that."

"Ok. Three o'clock, right?"

"Yes."

"Ok, see you then."

"Cool, bye."

I press END on my cell and go to the window to stare out over the pristine pavement of Bolton Street. The guy I hung up with is Nathan Pierce. He was my ex-boyfriend before I committed to Jojo. We busted up when he cheated on me with my co-worker, Shawn. Over time, we decided to patch things up and try being friends. I believe, however, that Jojo thinks there is still a part of me that wants to be with Nate. Maybe that's what the look was about. I ponder all of this as I go to the bathroom to shower, then trip down the back stairs to the kitchen. The flour is swept from the floor and Jojo is cutting up vegetables. His high and round ass stretches the seat of the nylon shorts he wears, his hairy and thick ebony legs an absolute heavenly vision.

"Ok, Jojo. Do you want to tell me what that look was about?"

Jojo pauses and turns around, "Well, I just feel awkward whenever Nate calls. He was your ex-boyfriend."

"'Ex' being the operative word."

"I know. I guess I'm a little scared."

"Of what? Me getting back with him?"

Jojo shrugs his shoulders and turns back around to continue dicing the vegetables. I go to him and take the knife from his hand. I turn him gently around to face me and wrap my arms around him. All I want to do right now is take that worried look off his face.

"Jojo, when I said yes to you, I did not see Nate. I saw you and I am committed to this. I am marrying the one I wanna be with. And you know who that is?"

"Who?"

"The very one I'm holding right now."

"Are you sure?"

"Of course, I'm sure. Jojo, you are the one I want, not Nate."

Jojo smiles and nods his head. "I'm sorry. I don't mean to be suspicious. I just don't want to end up losing you."

"Baby, you got me for life, and I mean that."

The look in his eyes is childlike and full of wonder. Lost in the rosy magic we have learned to create so well, we let the ribbons of love wrap around us to bind us together as one.

*****

We are all seated around the table in my dining room, just laughing and chomping down food. This spread is fabulous! My baby and friends sure can cook! We have the standard fare. You know... Turkey, yams, cornbread dressing, collard greens, macaroni and cheese, and ambrosia salad, all prepared by my baby. But Jimmy and Peep decided to collaborate and pull from their late relatives' recipe books. Peep brought over some apple turnovers, black-eyed peas, and neckbones. Jimmy brought chitlins, barbequed ribs, okra, and loaded cranberry sauce. Corey brought the monkey bread, the mustard greens, lemon meringue pie, cole slaw, and some good old-fashioned North Carolina barbeque from Scott's. Throw in my ham, oxtails, casserole. cake, and potato salad and the wine Nate brought, and we got ourselves a feast fit for Henry the Eighth!

Gazing around the table, my heart is filled with deep gratitude because I am spending Thanksgiving with an array of beautiful black men that God blessed me to have in my extended and blood family.

Heading the table is my oldest brother, Andrew Martin Davis. Our mother nicknamed him Andre and we followed suit. But he hated it because it was the name of a childhood rival. So, he came to us one day, telling me that he wanted to be called A.D. He has really come a long way from where he was. Very streetwise and gruff, he knows the allure of fast money, drugs, and the streets. But during a stint in prison, he, as Charles Dickens would say in *Oliver Twist* concerning the character Charley Bates, "fell into a train of reflection" and decided to go straight by getting his High School Diploma while on lockdown. He used to drive trucks to and from different parts of the eastern region. But shortly after he relocated to Baltimore, he switched to working for Thurgood Marshall as a TSA Agent. I asked him why he switched, and he told me that he liked the pace and that he used to work as one in Birmingham before he was persuaded to work for BG Trucking. The perk for me was that he always had stories about the passengers that he would tell me, making me laugh my ass off. When he is not working, he is taking classes at Baltimore City Community College to get his degree in criminal justice. He WAS going to become a registered nurse. He even took on a few classes and was pulling high marks. That only lasted one semester because it slowly dawned on him that he'd have to change bedpans and sometimes clean up a patient who shits in the bed. He said "If A.D.'s go'n clean up any shit, it's duh BULLshit bein' pushed in dis fucked-up system dat be slicin' and dicin' us Black folk. An' we don' even git a fuckin' Ban'-Aid when dey do it!" Humph… That's my grouchy but loving brother! Now…he *is* heterosexual (At least I think he is). But he has learned to embrace me and my friends and will stomp the shit out of anybody who even looks at us cross eyed, especially his new buddy and my best friend, Corey.

Sitting across from me is my fussy, dapper twin brother, Dean Anthony Davis. He is an egghead and math-whiz if you have ever seen one: A first-rate Calculus professor at Virginia Union University and part-time accountant living in Richmond. Dean and I are twin brothers, but we are as different as night and day. He is quiet and meditative whereas I am outgoing (more or less). He is the type that would tell you a whole story just by looking at you a certain way while I would just say what I'm thinking. Though he is open-minded about most things, Dean is also the type that insists on doing everything by the book, with the smallest of deviations. "Instructions and formulas were made to be followed," he would always say. He did not always share my evolving view that spontaneity only made life more interesting, but he was always supportive of my life and choices therein, just as my late father would've been.

Next to him is my ex-boyfriend, Nate. He is just picking at his food. No doubt, he is thinking about his father. His handsome ebony face holds a drawn, melancholy look. His strong and massive shoulders are slumped, forcing his tall body to slouch. Maybe he was right. Him coming for Thanksgiving was probably too soon. He is still grieving. On the other hand, he didn't need to be in that house by himself. I continue my gaze around the table.

Corey, as loud and expressive as always, is sitting on the other side of Dean. His handsome butterscotch face is lit up with mischief and life as he chatters on and on, occasionally trading witty rejoinders and sarcastic barbs with Peep. He is extremely attractive with his six-foot frame underneath sinewy, slim, and toned skin. Corey and Peep are Jojo and my best friends and we have been friends ever since we met as freshmen attending Morgan State University. That was eighteen years ago, and it sometimes amazes me that we have remained this close for so long. Corey is short for Cordell, as in Cordell Rodgerick James Kennedy. He is now music professor at Howard University. He left Towson U. because he felt he needed a change in scenery. He is still Minister of music at Unity and Love Community Church, where we all attend services. It is nothing short of glorious to watch his right hand grace the keys of the B3 organ, while simultaneously pedaling a strong bass line and directing the choir with his left. Corey has a story like no other. He fought through so many personal demons that tormented him constantly… and he STILL stood up smiling. He is also the type that pulls no punches and will not hesitate to start throwing blows. He has calmed considerably since going to therapy, though. In many ways, he and my brother A.D. are a lot alike. Maybe that's why they get along so well. Recently, he teamed up with Darrell Alston, a pop star whose music went big in the international circles around the late 2010s. He fell in love with Corey's songwriting abilities ever since the night on the cruise, when he heard the song Corey wrote for

Jojo and me as a birthday present. He called Corey and they recorded the song. Afterwards, they began writing hits together that yielded phenomenal results.

Felipe Alexander Walker-Hartfield, otherwise known as Peep, is financial advisor at SunTrust Bank and certified personal trainer at Lifetouch Fitness Center. In the last extended entry concerning my life, I shared the story of how he got that nickname. In this entry, let it suffice to say that the nickname started with me and believe me when I say that he got that name honest. Peep is achingly gorgeous. His 6'1 frame is packed with golden brown muscle. With his hair cut in a two-toned brown and blond curly fade and his body clad in a wool form-fitting red sweater and blue jeans, he looks as though he is preparing for a photo shoot. Peep is incredibly stylish. There is no well-known designer that he does not know about. He keeps up with the fashion industries that sell clothing from Milan to Paris, and the latest trends usually find their way into his closet. He hails from Los Angeles by way of San Antonio and stuck with Baltimore, like we all did after graduating from Morgan.

Seated beside him is his gorgeous hunky husband, Jimmy Hartfield. I've always teased Peep that he must have sent the Creator a specific list of what he wanted in a man. When we were students and roommates at Morgan, we would trade wish lists on what we wanted. He said he wanted a faithful and loving man with mixed heritage who was tall, hairy, and had a bulky build. Well, he got all that and then some. With Jimmy's smoldering good looks, his full-throated deep voice, his child-like grey eyes, and his completely hairy body, he captures attention wherever he goes. He is a Baltimore native, a cum laude graduate of Towson U. with a Master's in Kinesiotherapy, and a registered nurse at Saint Agnes Hospital. Both my friend, Garrett, and he became A.D.'s "rolling aces" when he moved up here. Recently, he lost his mother to Diabetes, so all of us became his support system.

This is my beautiful family- some blood and some water. But all of them are near and dear to me.

"So, Corey," I say, while scooping up a forkful of greens. "You said you had news."

"Yeah. One wonders what it is," Jojo follows.

"And what special person it involves," Peep digs.

"What in the hell are you talking about?" Corey asks incredulously.

"You and your boyfriend, 'Zaaaaaach'!" Jojo teases.

"What about him?"

"Do I really have to spell it out for you? Bells, preacher, flowers, cake… Get the picture?"

"Say wha-," Corey begins. Then a look of understanding crosses his face. "Oh, is that what you think my news is?"

"Well, what else could it be?" I ask.

"Yeah, you and Garrett have really been getting close lately," Jimmy observes.

"Ah, well. As much as I hate to disappoint you loves, that is not the news I am speaking of," Corey informs.

"Well, whut is it? Hur' up and git to it so I can git back tuh muh eatin'," A.D. says.

"The news is… I am going on a world tour with Darrell Alston."

"Shet up!" A.D. exclaims. "Fuh realz?"

"For reals. Darrell called two nights ago and told me that his manager scheduled it. Since half of the songs on his latest album were written by me, he wants me to come on tour to perform them with him."

"That is great!" Jojo exclaims happily.

"What is the money gonna be like?" Peep asks.

"I kinda want to know the answer to that question myself," Dean trails.

"The money is pretty decent, with airfare and accommodations included… and five hundred per show."

"Well, shit. That ain't nothing to sneeze at." Dean says.

"Who you tellin'," Corey beams at Dean.

"How many shows?".

"It's a three-month tour covering Venice, Okinawa, Hamburg, Barcelona, Argentina, and some parts of Africa. We are doing four shows per week, not counting the two weeks off."

"Did you say Barcelona?" I gush.

"Yes, Barcelona."

"Ugh, I despise you! And I want an authentic painting from there. My bathroom wall is bare!"

"Despise me, then demand an item. Mmm…"

"You know that is the one place that has a culture I want to experience before I croak."

"Ok, I'll snag you a painting. What do you want?"

"'Rainbow Paradise' by Nicolau Rastovich. I have the money to give you before you go… And I am happy for you."

"Me too. But for Chrissakes, that's a lot of shows. Are you sure you can handle that?" Peep asks, concern in his voice.

"Of course, I can."

"Have you ever been on a tour before?" Jojo asks.

"Yeah. Peep, I know you remember when we both used to go with the choir."

"But that was only for a week or two. We're talking about three months here," Peep reminds.

"Well, there's a first time for everything. Garrett and I talked about it last night. This is an opportunity to get my music to other countries besides Japan. I can't pass it up."

After a hush, Peep says, "I guess you're right, but you are gonna be gone for such a long time."

"Don't tell me you're gonna miss me," Corey replies, laughing. "It's going to be fine. Besides, I think this is what Miss Schumacher and Pop Kennedy would want me to do… Irene too."

There is complete silence as we remember Jimmy's late mother, Irene. She was so full of life. She took chances and learned lessons from each one.

At length, Jimmy says, "What are ya'll lookin' so down about? It's three months, not three years. He'll be back, and we'll celebrate him when he does."

A.D. sits up straight and says, "I'm feelin' yuh, bruh. Ya'll, let's toast tuh dat. To Corey slayin' 'em worl'wide!" We all raise our glasses and clink them.

"Maybe the next news will involve some 'I do's'," Jojo jokes.

"All in good time. Speaking of 'I do's', when are you two going to say yours?" Corey queries, nodding at both of us.

"Well, it looks like we got news of our own," I say, grabbing Jojo's hand. "Is that so?"

"Yes," Jojo informs. "We decided that we are going to get hitched on the Rainbow Pride Cruise next year!"

"Yeah," I follow. "Since I proposed on the ship, we thought it befitting to marry in the same ambience."

"I couldn't agree more," Jimmy concurs.

"We want all of ya'll to be there. So, start saving up your money, you got eight months."

Nate suddenly stands up with tears in his eyes, "Excuse me." He rushes out of the dining room and crosses the kitchen to exit the back door. We sit silently for a second, then I volunteer to go talk to him. Jojo cast me a questioning look, which I meet with my eyes to assure him that all will be well. And yet, I couldn't help but feel regret for two reasons. One is because I didn't listen to Nate when he said that this was still fresh for him. He needed time to heal. The other reason is because sometimes when you are going through grief, the last thing you want to hear is everybody else's good news, especially when some of it involves your ex getting married to someone else.

Chapter Two
REPLAYING OLD TAPES

"Nate?" I call softly as I step out onto the back deck, where Nate is standing and smoking a freshly lit cigarette. "You alright?"

"Yeah," Nate says, after a pause. "I'm fine. I just needed some air. I'm sorry. I didn't mean to have you come out here."

I walk across the deck to lean against the bannister. I let a few seconds pass while inhaling the scents of marinara sauce and pizza dough coming from Mama Rossati's Italian restaurant. Afterwards, I say, "I should be the one apologizing."

"For what?"

"Well, you told me that you were still grieving, and I should've left you alone. I just didn't want you to be by yourself today."

"Nah, you alright. It's just gonna take some time to move past this."

"Believe me, I know. I felt the same when I lost my father. I loved him just as much as you obviously loved yours."

Nate turns around to stare at the back-parking slab. "With Mama dying shortly after birthing me and my real dad getting killed, he took me in and raised me as one of his own. He was dating my mother after losing his wife. Rumor had it that they were sweethearts at City College. When she died, he made room for me in his life, even though he was raising his own blood son alone." Nate lets out a huge gush of air. After a beat, he questions gravely, "How could someone that young and vital just pass at the age of fifty-nine? Joe Pierce had the heart of a lion. He trained me with the weights. He worked for years as a construction worker. Well built.

Healthy. With someone like that, you would never imagine death being around the corner, waiting with a heart attack to take him down."

I want to tell him that even the healthiest of people have an expiration date. However, I find that the best way to be there for someone grieving is to just listen. Nate heaves another huge sigh. His next words are so low that I strain to hear them.

"I don't know if I can get used to this."

"Get used to what?"

"The knowledge that I'm going to have to live out the rest of my life without my parents."

"Well, Nate. That's what I'm doing."

"Oh, please. You still got your mother."

"No, I don't."

"What do you mean you don't?"

"Because my mother disowned me when I told her I was gay."

Nate turns around, shocked. After a pause, he says, "When did this happen?"

"Shortly after we broke up."

"Wow, I didn't know. I always thought your mom was ok with you being gay. Otherwise, you wouldn't be marrying Jojo."

"Surprising, isn't it?"

Nate reflects, then says in an offhand way, "Then again, how could I know? You never told me anything about your family or your past. Every time I asked you, you would close up."

"I didn't want to involve you in all that. But, that's not important. The point is that you are not the first or the last to have lost both his parents."

"I know that."

"Look at it this way. At least you had a father who loved you, blood or not. Imagine those kids who have to go through their whole lives not even having parents and are being tossed from one foster home to the next." Even as I say this, Corey pops in my head. Maybe he could put aside his dislike of Nate enough to dispense more wisdom than I could. "Wait right here," I tell him.

I rush back inside and make my way into the dining room. "Corey, can you come into the kitchen for a minute," I say, amid the conversation.

"Is everything OK?" Jojo says.

"Yeah, I just need to speak with Corey about something."

"OK," Corey assents, looking puzzled. He gets up and follows me into the kitchen where I lean against the counter.

"What's going on?" Corey says.

"Now, Corey," I begin. "I am about to ask you to do me a huge favor."

"The nature of the favor will determine whether I do it."

"Do you always have to be such a smart ass?" I joke.

"I can't help it. I'm naturally brilliant!" Corey retorts, laughing.

I take a deep breath and exhale, "I need you to talk with Nate."

"How is it that you ask me for the one thing I won't do?"

"Oh, give me a break, Corey. I just need you to talk to him."

"Absolutely not! What could we possibly have to talk about? I said I wouldn't get into it with him. Isn't that enough?"

"Look, he is depressed. He has no parents at all, and I felt that if anybody would understand his feelings, it's you. Out of all of us, you are the only one who was adopted like he was."

"He was adopted?" Corey asks disbelievingly.

"Yes. Now, do you see why I need you to do this? Who knows, maybe ya'll can bury the hatchet already."

"I don't know…" Corey says doubtingly.

"Come on, I'll go out there with you," I encourage, steering him outside.

Upon hearing us come out, Nate turns and sees Corey. He tenses and his left jaw begins jumping as he growls, "What did you bring him out here for?"

"Please, Nate, just hear me out. Corey has been through exactly what you are going through. Maybe ya'll can talk about it."

"Nah, I'm alright. I don't need any help." With that, Nate turns back around to gaze at the darkening sky. Corey makes a move to go back inside but I stop him and gesture to Nate. Corey reluctantly sidles up to him.

"I… uh… I want to thank you for bringing the Moscato."

Nate turns in surprise. He glances at Corey, then resumes his skyward gaze. Haltingly, he says, "You're welcome."

Corey gazes up with him, as if trying to decipher the vision Nate sees in the heavens. Minutes pass. Then Corey faces Nate as he props his elbow on the railing and says, "Listen, Nate. We don't always agree. No mistake about that. But I can relate to your pain."

"Oh, gimme a break. Look, I don't need your sympathy."

"And I'm not offering any. You are not the only one who lost his parents and had to make do with fosters. Been there, done that, bought the T-shirt."

Nate then turns and looks at him, speechless. Corey glances back at him. "Shocked?"

"Well, yeah. I mean I didn't know…"

"How could you know? We don't talk."

Silence. Then Nate asks, turning to lean against the railing of the balcony, "Were your foster parents good to you?"

"Well, they were years apart, but yes. Both were very good to me."

Nate looks at both of us, confused. Corey caught the look and said in understanding, "I was raised by an older lady when I was a toddler and by a pastor when I was a teenager."

"What happened in between?"

Corey takes a deep breath and says, "I lived in an orphanage."

"For real?"

"Yeah."

"What was it like?"

Corey gets quiet and looks down. I take that as my cue to jump in. "Corey doesn't really like to talk about what happened."

"Why? What went on?"

The silence is deafening. Then Corey says, turning around to gaze over the balcony, "I was a black kid in an orphanage run by white pedophilic racists who beat and messed with kids of any color. Fill in the blank and there you have it."

Nate stares at Corey as if looking at him for the first time. Then, shocking me and Corey, he places his hand on Corey's shoulder.

Corey, totally disarmed, struggles to regain composure. He then says, "Look, I just want to let you know that you're not by yourself on this. When I lost both my foster parents, I didn't think I would ever find myself again, especially after all the shit that happened. But I'm getting there. Little by little… And you will, too."

As I watch my friend and my ex converse in a semi-affable tone, I am engulfed with a feeling of contentment. In the years that these two men have known each other, they were always at odds. It feels good to see them comforting each other: Corey by way of his words and Nate through his gesture of understanding.

I excuse myself and return to the dining room. The conversation stops as I enter.

"Is everything OK?" Dean asks.

"Yeah."

"Where's Corey?" Peep follows.

"Out back talking to Nate."

"Will wonders never cease? Those two hate each other."

"Well, with both being adopted and losing fathers they came to love, that gives them common ground- hopefully enough to call a truce."

"Fingers crossed," Jojo says hopefully. After thirty minutes, Corey and Nate rejoin us at the dinner table. *Hmmm…* Nate looks a lot more at ease so whatever was discussed must have been fruitful.

The doorbell rings and I go to answer it. When I open it, Garrett, Rachel, and Mike Jr. walk in. We exchange big bear hugs.

I met Garrett last May through a phone conversation. He got my number from Peep and we began talking. Initially, I was very attracted to him sexually. Who wouldn't be? He has long dreadlocks, coal black skin, brownish black lips, large inquisitive eyes, glacier white teeth, and a tall muscular frame that became more diesel ever since Peep started training him. Frequent association and conversation softened the attraction to another close platonic bond. Garrett had much more to offer me through his friendship. He caused me to look at things from a broader, practical point of view and played Devil's advocate to show me that life was not always the black and white I was taught to believe it was. His heart belongs to Corey though. They met in the orphanage and fell in love as kids. Time separated them for twenty-four years, but fate brought them back together on the cruise last year. Since that time, they have been inseparable.

Rachel is Garrett's adoptive sister and she is beautiful! If I ever did the dames, Rachel would be the type I would go for. She is a blend of sass, brass, crass, and class! She has flawless honey brown skin with full lips and huge doe-like eyes. Her brownish red hair is fluffed into a medium sized, perfectly shaped Afro. She also has a figure that a Broadway dancer would envy. Standing beside her is her little boy, Mike Jr. He has his abundant curly hair fluffed out like a halo and his skin looks as though he was bathed in butterscotch and caramel. He beams a big, bright smile as he gazes at me with his mother's eyes shining from that chipmunk face. He is like a jitterbug with his boundless energy. His innocent and youthful way of looking at life is what made me like him. He reminded me of me when I was his age… before I became jaded by my mother's disapproval. Rachel and Mike Jr. have gone through a lot. She separated from her abusive ex-husband, Samuel Kincaid, and has been seeing A.D. Their relationship is sometimes challenging, but the love they share is blissfully evident.

"Hey man. Ya'll ate up the food yet?"

"Blueberry, didn't you eat enough at Mama's house? I swear you got a bottomless pit for a stomach," Rachel teases lightly.

"When are you ever going to stop calling me Blueberry?"

"When both of us are dead and gone."

"Don't mind them, Mr. Lionel. They been teasing each other all day!" Mike Jr. says as he hugs my waist.

"Oh, I ain't worried about your mama and uncle. How is Eunetta, Rachel?"

"Oh, she is fine. She asked about you and The Fellas. How is your family? Is A.D. here?" she says as she smiles sweetly.

"You would be asking about him. Could it be you're falling in loooove?" Garrett teases, singing out the last phrase. She swats at him playfully.

"Oh, shut up, Blueberry. I know *you* ain't talking with you being all up in Corey's business, or should I say, 'Simon's'."

"You see what I mean?" Mike Jr. looks up with another big, beautiful smile.

"I do, Jitterbug. I do," I say, calling him by the nickname I gave him. I then look at Rachel and Garrett and inform, "The food, and your loves, are in the dining room and there's plenty left. Go on in there and have a good time!"

"Thank you, Lionel. But Mike Jr. and I are not staying too long," Rachel says. "I just came by with Garrett to wish ya'll a Happy Thanksgiving. Plus, Junior wanted to see y'all. We are going home, and this little champ is getting a bath and going to bed."

"Aw, Mama! Come on! Why?"

"Because I said so."

"I don't even have school tomorrow."

"Doesn't matter. You are still going to bed, my little man!" Rachel chides Mike Jr.

Mike Jr. begins pouting but pulls his lip in quickly when Rachel gives him that kid-feared stern look. "Boy, fix your face. Don't be showing out in front of folks. Mama said you need to get some sleep. Besides, you want to get up early to play XBOX, don't you?"

Mike Jr. brightens and nods. I say, "Well, you can at least get a big plate for you and Jitterbug. I think there is some sweet potato pie and German Chocolate cake in there!" I finish my statement looking at Mike Jr. with a Cheshire cat grin. He jumps up and down.

Rachel purses her lips playfully, then says to Garrett, "See, this is the reason he wanted to come over here. He knew he'd get more sweets."

"Pleeeeeeeeeease?" Mike Jr. says, looking up at her with a sweet expression. No way she could resist that face!

"Oh, all right!" Rachel says, bending down to kiss him on his forehead. "You spoiled curly-head rascal. Get on in there!"

They proceed into the dining room. A.D. stands up to hug Rachel and slap Mike Jr. five. Of course, the first thing Garrett does is make a beeline to Corey to give him a wet sloppy kiss.

"Jesus, man," Peep says. "Get a room!"

"You know what?" Corey counters. "Give me another one just because he said that."

Garrett obliges while Peep makes a gagging motion. Then we all sit, and the conversation and wine flow once more.

*****

All my family are stuffed to the gills and knocked out on my living room floor like beached whales. As I load the dishwasher with the dirty plates and store the leftovers in the fridge, I think of how blessed I am. Around this time last year, I wasn't sure if I would be able to enjoy a Thanksgiving with my family. I mean, I had my words with Mama, and she rejected me yet again through her silence and by shattering a gift I bought her to mend the bridges. It was a beautiful gift too. A shimmering crystal snow globe with a figurine of mother and son walking through the snow. After I spoke my truth and turned to leave, she threw the snow globe against the wall. After that, the last time I saw her was when I went to the family reunion this summer at the request of my siblings. I guess I was thinking yet again that Mama would be more accepting or that time would have mellowed her out. I spoke to her, but she just stared resentfully at me, like she wanted to erase me off the face of the earth. I took it as a symbol that we were done and not a word has been spoken between us since.

I do wonder how she spent her Thanksgiving, and while doing so, a pang of guilt enters me. She didn't have much family to celebrate with. Gramps died when I was seventeen and Granny recently passed in February. I heard that Mama was in glee because with her being the only surviving next of kin and her uncle Larry being in a rest home, Granny's house was left to her. Rhonda is locked up for possession of a controlled substance. Roland is with his fiancé in Orlando. Dean and A.D. are up here with me. So that leaves Brenda. She said she would make the trip to see her since she and her husband, Dr. Mercer C. Odom Jr., lived in Atlanta. This is a switch because they usually travel to Bismarck, North Dakota to visit his parents for the holidays. I wonder how she made out with Mama.

"Need any help, Li'nel?" I turn around to see A.D. standing in the doorway.

"Nah, I got it."

After a stretch of silence, A.D. says, "Yuh know, I talked wit' Mama not too long ago."

My breath becomes still as I freeze and wait for him to continue.

"I talked wit' duh docta' too. 'E dropped me a bitta bad news... They think duh cancer's back."

I resume loading the fridge. But I cannot say anything.

On my way across the kitchen to put the turkey in the fridge, A.D. blocks my path. He takes the turkey from my hands and puts it on the counter.

"Listen, Li'nel. We gotta talk 'bout dis."

"A.D., there's nothing to talk about."

"Ok, you don' have tuh talk. But I am pullin' rank as yo' big bruh, and I'm tellin' yuh tuh listen!"

I stand there, looking at him. At that moment, I see my father's resolute face on A.D.'s body. It was the face he gave us when he meant business. It was the face he used when he had something heavy to lay on us; and if there was anything that would stop me in my tracks and force me to pay attention, it was that face. We both sit down at the kitchen table.

"Li'nel, I know 'bout all da shit Mama can cause betta' dan you. She put us thru hell. I had muh own days win I jes' didn' wanna be bothered cuz of rememberin' all duh shit she pulled all dem years. But no mattuh how mean she is, we caint ditch duh fact dat she is still our mama."

"But she's not *mine*, A.D. She made that clear. For me to get along with her and be her 'son', it would mean disowning myself as a person. She wants me to say that I'm not gay and that she's right. She wants me to dump Jojo as a friend alnd fiancé. What's driving her up the wall is that she can't beat me into submission like she did when we were kids."

"Listen, you is you an' ain't nothin' gone change dat. But, did yuh evuh stop tuh think where all 'er shit is comin' from?"

"I tried asking her that when I called last year on Mother's Day. She just said, 'That's just how I feel'."

"Nah, bruh. I think it's a lot deepuh' den dat. Yuh know, I been readin' up on it fo' one uh muh classes an' dey say dat win folks be lashin' out, dere's shit in duh pas' dat dey ain't gotta handle on. An' it ain't gone git no betta, unless duh person start makin' some changes."

"I know that."

A.D. takes a deep breath, then looks at me saying, "Life is showt, dude. We ain't got dat much time on dis' earth. And death might be comin' tuh knock on Mama's doe' before it gits tuh any of us. I know yuh said dat yuh forgive 'er, but I kin tell yuh still holdin' on tuh somethin' yuh need tuh let go of. An' it's makin' yuh self-destruc'. Yuh know wut 'm sayin'?" A.D. asks, looking at me with a stern, knowing gaze. *What in the hell is he getting at?*

"A.D., I'm not holding on to anything. How *could* I if I am choosing to eliminate all the bullshit in my life? Right now, Lynetta Davis is at the top of that list."

A.D. pushes back from the table and stands up. "Den yuh might as well let Mama keep da switch in 'er hands, cuz she still punkin' yo ass and making yuh bitta as fuck."

I snap, standing up, "I am not bitter. I just can't forget what she did to me. She scarred me for life, A.D. Both when we were kids and as adults. Those scars are never going to go away."

"Li'nel, listen to yuh big bruh," he says, putting his hands caringly on my shoulders. "The longa' yuh keep focusin' on dem scars, de mo bitta' yuh git. An' de mo bitta' yuh git, de easiuh duh chance dat yuh might fuck up thangs 'tween you an' Joe, duh fellas, an' duh family dat do support yuh. I ain't tellin' yuh wut I done heard. I'm tellin' yuh wut I know."

*****

A.D.'s words stayed with me that night after everyone except Jojo went home. As I hold my lover, two questions race through my mind. *Have I truly forgiven Mama? Have I truly let go of the hurt?* That was the reason for the talk in the hospital in the first place. To find peace. I guess it is true what they say: the road to peace is not always peaceful. There are a few bumps, bruises, and lessons along the way.

My phone rings. "Hello?"

"Hey Lion. Just letting you know that I got home." It is Corey. I creep out of the bedroom so that I don't disturb Jojo's slumber.

"Cool, and thank you for talking to Nate," I say as I descend the stairs to my living room.

"No sweat."

"Did ya'll talk about anything else?"

"Well, we did decide at least to coexist without baring claws and teeth for now. I might learn to like him… a little!" Corey jokes.

"That's good," I sigh, remembering my conversation with A.D.

Corey's voice fills with concern, "Are you alright?"

"Yeah, I'm fine. Why do you ask?"

"Well, when you were seeing everyone out, you seemed bothered about something."

"I was."

"Do you want to talk about it?"

"Not really."

"Oh… Well, OK."

I take a deep breath. Then, a thought passes through my mind. *If you cannot confide in friends, who can you confide in.* I sit in my chair.

"I had a small conversation with A.D."

"Yeah?"

"Yeah. He told me that doctors are fearing return of Mama's cancer."

"No shitting."

"And, if I know Lynetta Davis, she's either not cooperating with the doctors or not participating in chemo like she should."

"Those things will definitely cause cancer to rebound."

"Yeah."

Silence.

"Am I crazy, or is there something else heavy on your mind?"

Exhale. "There is."

Pause.

"A.D. said something today that has me thinking."

"What about?"

"Well, I am sure I have forgiven Mama for all the shit that happened. But he is saying that I may be still holding grudges."

There is a long hush in the air.

"Corey?"

"Yeah, I'm still here."

"Why the silence?"

"I'm sorry, Lion. I'm just thinking."

"Thinking what?"

"Well, A.D.'s not the only one that can sense the grudges. I've peeped them too, and so have Jojo and Peep sometimes."

"What?"

"Yeah. And I think it's the reason why many times you have all this anger that creeps into your voice when the smallest things rile you up. It's why you haven't stopped taking Alprolozine to help you to sleep. Now, I believe you need medication, but the problem came when you stopped going to Dr. Banneker because he wouldn't give you anything more than the Doxepin to help you sleep. He was actually trying little by little to wean you off Doxepin."

"Now wait a minute…"

"No, you wait a minute. No need to get pissy with me. I'm not jumping down your back. I am just telling you what you told me when you stopped going. I asked Dr. Lofton who he recommended, at your request. But you couldn't wait. You went out and found this Dr. Williams character and made him your new shrink so you could get him to write you a prescription for a stronger drug without asking any questions."

"I need something to help me sleep and control my anxiety, Corey."

"As far as sleep, you can always go herbal. Try St. John's Wort or tea. Speaking on the anxiety, you do know that Dr. Banneker would have put you on something with less side effects and dependence factors, right? I think you ought to go back to him and ease up on the Alprolozine if he can't stop you from taking them altogether. Sometimes they slow you down and I've noticed it. That medicine is dangerous, from what I've read. I'm scared that you are going to overdose on those pills and end up in a coma."

I didn't know Corey was tracking my pill popping. I try to keep information like my meds to myself. The only one that knows about it is Jojo. When he sleeps over, he sees me taking a pill and there have been times when I took two because of particularly stressful situations. But I got it under control. I start to feel anger at Jojo for telling Corey, but I dismiss it because I know he did it out of concern. This is the sore spot in the relationship between Jojo and me. On and off, he has been telling me since I started the Doxepin how much he hated my need for it, but he has since learned to live with it. When I started taking this new drug, he began to be a non-stop source of irritating reproach.

"Corey, you haven't just met me today. You know I'm always careful."

"When did you start going to Dr. Williams?"

"A month ago."

"Well, I don't like him."

"What do you mean?"

"I don't like the care you're getting from him. I saw him when I came to pick you up that day when your truck was in the shop. There's a look he has that says, 'I don't care about this man's issues. I care about my ninety an hour.'

I consider his words. There is a little truth to what Corey is saying. When I show up for my appointments, there is an empty look on his face. He just doodles on his pad and steals looks at his desk clock. The last time I went, we just sat there until he said, "Your time is up". The questions he asks are not as probing as Dr. Banneker's. It's usually questions he asks to remind him of rudimentary shit I went over with him in our first meeting, which he would know the answers to if he looked at the pad he's always writing on. I've always assumed that what he was scribbling about had to do with our sessions, but perhaps not.

"Why would he be in the mental health field if he didn't care?" I ask, rhetorically.

"Lion, I got a psych friend who gave me the low down on some of these shrinks. And he said it like this, 'There are those that care and those that don't'. Some of these doctors write prescriptions for people just to test how the meds work, and others write them assuming that 'one med fits all'. You are a patient, not a guinea pig. Honestly, when you were going to see Dr. Banneker, you were making a lot of progress. But now with these new pills and this new jackleg shrink, you are taking a giant step backwards. You've been getting dizzy spells, headaches, and upset stomach pains. When anyone mentions your mother's name, you go into a completely dark place. You clearly have this dangerous look on your face that says, 'I don't want to talk about this shit.' And we are not going to even talk about your unpredictable mood swings."

"I'm doing fine, Corey."

Silence. Then Corey says, "OK, fine."

There is a another hush over the line. Then Corey says, "Are you still writing?"

"On occasion, when I have something on my heart to put on paper."

"What feelings do you have when you write?"

"The feelings vary. Sometimes I'm happy, sometimes I'm sad, and sometimes I'm just mad as hell."

"When you are mad, what do you write about?"

Sarcastically, I respond, "What else can I write about? I write about Mama. I mean, the children she beat on for years are the same ones who paid for her operation, and she is still just as mean and twice as nasty as she ever was."

"You write that in your journal?"

"Yeah."

"OK, I'm going to ask you a question. I'm not trying to be facetious because I believe it is good for you to write your emotions. This way, you can get every hurt out. But what good is it doing you in there?"

"What do you mean?"

"I mean, why confine your feelings to pages that you lock away when the person that hurt you the most needs to hear your anger?"

"I expressed that already. Remember?"

"Then you should be over it now, right?"

"I AM over it!"

"Then why are you still writing about it? And getting on the defensive when someone mentions their concerns?"

I can't answer that question.

"I am not trying to preach you a sermon, but I will say this; you can't appreciate new music by replaying old tapes."

"Talk plain, Corey. What are you saying?"

"I'm saying that if you don't overcome this and leave it in the past where it belongs, your future is going to suffer."

"Look Corey, I..."

"Just let me finish. Now, you told your mother how you felt about what she did to you, to your father, and to your brothers and Brenda. That's step number one. Bravo for taking that step. But now we're at step number two, which includes being able to let the wounds heal by leaving the scabs alone. Your brooding over your mother's past bullshit is like picking at the wound. Now, I suggest that instead of writing it in your journal, write it to your mother and mail it. Only this time, let your words come from a place of love for the woman that gave birth to you."

"I don't know."

"Lionel, from what you told me, your mama is getting ready to check out of here. Are you really going to let her go without killing all the anger you have with her?"

"I guess not," I acquiesce, after a long moment of thought. "But how I do approach this? I haven't seen her since the family reunion- and THAT went up in smoke."

"I'm sure that an idea will present itself. Besides, it's been a year. That coupled with the diagnosis, she might be in a better position to listen to you than she was before. And with that letter, she will have no choice but to read your words, especially if she wants to leave here peacefully."

"I hear you."

"OK. Well, let me get off this phone. Garrett is over here trying to get my attention. I'll collect my dollar from you next time I see you."

"Cool. Well, take care of your man. We'll talk soon."

"OK baby. Kiss."

"Kiss."

As I hang up the phone, I bathe in the silence of the room, broken only by the sound of the clock ticking the seconds away. My mind is filled with confusion. *I thought I put all that shit with Mama behind me,* I think to myself. *Maybe I haven't if my friends and brother feel the need to call me out on it.*

I admit that Corey was right about Dr. Banneker trying to wean me off the Doxepin. In fact, that was an ongoing dispute between us. He told me that the Doxepin was reported to the FDA for having high toxicity levels and suggested another med, but I wouldn't go for it because I felt fine. He then began lowering the dosage little by little based on the progress I was making. I mean, yes. I was happy and contented, but there were still some nights when I couldn't sleep thinking about the pressures I faced at the office. I had crazy dreams when I did go to sleep and the tossing and turning affected my alertness the next day. I told him that I needed the regular dosage to help me sleep and calm me down, but he told me discreetly that I was beginning to show signs of dependence on it.

But I wasn't! I just needed to mellow out and the lower dosage wasn't helping. I told him this, but he calmly stated that he could no longer give me that dosage because it would do more harm than good. I said nothing at that time but made a mental note to find another shrink. I called him a week later to tell him that I felt we had come to a parting of ways. I enlisted Corey's help to find another shrink and he, after trying in vain to get me to reconsider, reluctantly agreed to talk to Dr. Lofton. I waited three days but after receiving no word, I went online to hunt one up for myself. Hence, we segue into therapy with Dr. Oscall P. Williams.

Dr. Williams is a tall, attractive, pale man with a pinched face, shrewd grayish-green eyes, and lean frame with contours that his expensively tailored suits can barely conceal. He has a slight arrogance about him, but I chose him because he had impressive credentials and performed groundbreaking research of the subject of mental health and depression. Additionally, his website specified that his practice was LGBTQ affirming.

I asked him about the Doxepin, but he too told me that the Doxepin had been getting the bum rap. He didn't specify why but he put me on a new prescription fresh out of the lab, Alprolozine. He told me to take the one hundred milligrams to sleep and the twenty-five for my anxiety occurrences. It didn't take long to feel the effects of the pills once I began taking them. I started sleeping like a baby and sailing through my day.

But when did the hard feelings for Mama resurface? I think to myself. *When?*

The Cost

Suddenly, the memory is depicted vividly in my brain. It started two weeks after the switch of doctors and meds. Brenda called to ask if I was going home for Thanksgiving. When I said no, she told me that I should because Mama was beginning to get sick again and the doctors gave her six months to live. I can't explain it, but the memory of her silent contempt in that hospital bed and the letter implicating her role in my father's murder caused my anger to brim and boil over like scalding lava from a Hawaiian volcano. I kept a lid on it as I calmly told Brenda that I already had plans that I couldn't cancel, said good night, and got off the phone.

See? I'm handling my anger. Maybe not in the way my friends and family would approve of, but I AM handling it! As for Dr. Williams, he is NOT that bad. I can deal with his aloof approach regarding my care. That's how shrinks are. Besides, I don't need him to analyze my emotions. Thanks to Dr. Banneker, I can do that myself. I just need a professional ear to bend, a bitch session every now and then, and pills to help me sleep as well as keep my sanity.

These pills are a godsend and a comfort, especially when dealing with either crazy assed clients with bogus bullshit I have to help peddle as usable merchandise or childhood memories of an evil, hard-hearted battle-ax that loosely holds the term "Mother", but deigns to live up to the distinction attached to the title.

"Lionel," I hear Jojo call.

"Coming, Baby."

Chapter Three
CONSEQUENCES AND RESERVATIONS

"I'm sorry, but this concept is not grabbing me."

"But Vivian, this is the direction you instructed for us to go in," my boss, Mr. Floyd Alexander, reminds her as he struggles to retain his pleasant expression.

"It may be, but it was executed all wrong."

"Miss Harrington, with all due respect, we have been down this road four times already. Lest we forget, we had an advertising layout all prepared for you when you came, tailored to what you said you wanted. At first, you said you were fine with the ideas. But suddenly, you said that it wouldn't work. So, we listened to more of your ideas and the art department tried each time to implement them by drafting a new storyboard for each request. You kept changing the idea each time," I say, trying to keep my restraint as well.

"Mr. Davis, need I remind you that VaVoom appointed me to oversee the artistic particulars of this campaign. Therefore, I have the right to voice specifications as to what will be suitable- and this is not it. The plain truth is that you have misunderstood my directions," she says in a nasal, grating voice.

What a rotten, condescending bitch! I think to myself as I look at Floyd. Catching my expression, he comes from behind his desk and stands in front of us. Clasping his hands together, he says, "I'm sorry, Vivian, that this layout did not coincide with your specifications. But it just means that we have to go back to the drawing board. Why don't we take the rest of the day to reassess the direction you would like to go in and reconvene Monday morning? I'm sure Mr. Davis, the art and media department, and I can revamp the concept to reflect a campaign that you will be pleased with." I give him a dirty look which he returns with a gentle, yet firm expression. *Damn this woman!*

She stands in a huff and wraps her luxurious white fox stole around the shoulders. I'd like to take it and wring her neck with it. She says, "Keep in mind, we do not have time to waste. VaVoom must have this perfume advertised on billboards, magazines, and television commercials by May. And VaVoom is paying three million for the correct execution of this campaign. Are we clear on that?"

"Crystal," Floyd and I mumble simultaneously.

She turns on the heel of her Jimmy Choo stiletto and struts haughtily out the door.

The shit I have to deal with on my job nowadays is making my brain scream for mercy. A new account was dropped on my desk and you have no idea how much I wish it wasn't. This time, we are working with VaVoom Perfumes & Cosmetics Incorporated, a company based in Beverly Hills, California. A chemist came up with a scent in her basement and patented it, naming the fragrance "Enchantress". She signed with VaVoom and they, through mass manufacturing and distribution, made the perfume a regional success in the first year. They then used aggressive marketing to expand the knowledge of both the perfume and the company throughout the west coast. Through the profit of these efforts, the chemist and distributor's pockets got fat. They came to Robertson & Moore to see if they could work that same magic on the east coast. The catch is that we have to deal with the "glamourous" tycoon, Vivian Harrington. If that wasn't bad enough, they didn't want to use the model we prepared to sign on to the project. Instead, they used their own model as the face of the franchise, Bianca Harrington, the spoiled niece of this hateful woman.

From the day Bianca walked through the doors of the firm, she started dishing out the drama. It began when she demanded us to have her dressing room painted powder puff pink with baby blue crown molding. When asked the reason, she said haughtily, "Artistic models shouldn't have to explain inspiration." There are many days when I want to tell "Miss It Girl" where to put her inspiration… as well as rip that unsightly wart off her back and make her eat it. Not only is this arrogant shrew demanding. She is also incredibly rude, inexcusably late, and insufferably dumb. I wish the company would have grown a pair and used the model we intended to sign on to the campaign. We would be much better off, and Floyd wouldn't have to keep a bottle of Pepto Bismol as well as Tylenol on his desk to prepare for every downhill meeting.

After breathing a sigh of relief, Floyd suggested that we go to Sorbet's for lunch and to clear our heads a bit. I must admit, I love working for him. Floyd Alexander is one cool cat, hardly ever fazed. When he walks, he exudes the quiet confidence of an African king. When it comes to business, he knows his shit. He is also quite the looker! Sexy as hell! His six-five, bald-headed, plum black, stocky, muscular majesty captivates you whenever he enters the room. His skin looks as sleek as oiled rubber, without a line or wrinkle to betray his age. And he is almost seventy!

When I first came to the company, he was the senior marketing executive of Robertson and Moore, but his education, rapier thinking, and impeccable work ethic caused him to breeze through the ranks when Raymond C. Moore died and the co-founder, Manford G. Robertson, promoted him to Senior Vice-President soon after. Once he got the position, he started grooming me for the position that I now hold.

"I can't stand that woman… and her niece is even worse," I spit out.

"I feel you, but she *is* a multi-million-dollar client."

"With all due respect, Floyd, is her money worth all of us getting ulcers and having to be sent to the nut house?"

"Look, it's just for a few months."

"Floyd, there is only so much Pepto-Bismol and Tylenol you can swallow without getting sicker. We have been dealing with her nonsense for weeks now. Remember, we had to work through Christmas to satisfy one of her tacky assed ideas. Now it is January, and we still haven't chosen a concept because of her."

"I understand. But just be patient. Whether we stick with her or part ways, I must handle this delicately."

I raise my hands in concession. The waiter comes and takes our orders. After he leaves our table, Floyd asks, "So, you know the annual company getaway is in May, right?"

"I am aware of that."

"Can you come this year? It will be a good time to rub shoulders with the higher-ups. The added bonus is that it's on Myrtle Beach."

I laugh out, "Floyd, you ask me that every year and every year I say no."

"True."

"So, what makes you think I'm going to say yes this year? My vacations and getaways are set aside for leisure and enjoying my friends. Now, office parties and company dinners are the times when I am best at rubbing shoulders and pressing palms."

"Lionel, Have I not taught you anything yet? Big business does not just happen in the board room or over lunch at a swanky restaurant like Sorbet's. Sometimes it's done at a beach while parasailing or on a yacht over cocktails. We have been through this. You may think you can make it through merit alone but, like I told you when you first came on, it's about who you know and what you have done for them lately. I'd like to introduce you as one of Robertson and Moore's top guys to handle the campaigns of prospective clients. How can I do that if the top guy isn't there?"

I consider what he is saying. In the eleven years I had been working at Robertson and Moore, I managed to avoid going on these company getaways. Maybe it's because of what my business professor at Morgan, Mr. French, told me. He said, "Davis, Company getaways can sometimes spell trouble. You see a whole lot of bullshit best left behind closed doors. Now I'm not going to be your moral conscience and tell you not to go, but I will say watch yourself in those settings." I figured that the best way to safeguard my career is to just say no.

"Will my job be in jeopardy if I don't go?"

"No, but I will say that being there gives you a chance to have one up on your competition for future promotions."

I think about that. My competition is Shawn Tolbert, a fellow marketing executive. If there was anybody I disliked more in this firm, it is Shawn. He came in under my wing three years ago as an intern. Being that he was a Morgan alum and had an eye for marketing strategies and concepts, I decided to vouch for him. Big mistake, because, according to office lore, he didn't breeze his way up through merit alone. He got it by bobbing for the Junior V.P.'s apples- if you catch my meaning. He is smart, I'll give him that. He has ideas out of this world but the concept of doing his own share of the work hasn't made it to his head yet. He schmoozes his way into promotions. The people around him do most of the work. Then, at the tail-end of it all, he implements an elementary idea that a mere child would write off as common sense. If the work is praised, he hogs all the credit. If the work is criticized, he finds a way to clear himself while everyone else takes the critique.

We started out as casual acquaintances, but that camaraderie turned sour quickly. One reason is because he lacks authenticity. When I come into the office with an item or an idea, Shawn will not rest until he copies it… That is, if he can't top it. Another reason is because he couldn't keep his hands off my ex-boyfriend, Nate. I caught them in my bed fucking. As I have said before, I forgive Nate. But Shawn, I handle him with friendly caution because he is the type that will smile in your face, then lay in the cut plotting shit behind your back.

Maybe I need to consider making the getaway. I *am* trying to move up in the company and this may be the best way to do it.

"Ok, I'll think about going,"

"That's all I ask." Floyd says, raising his coffee cup to his lips. After taking a sip, he puts the cup down and asks with a sly look, "So, how are plans with the wedding?"

I look at him in shock. Ordinarily, I try to keep my business and personal life separate. "How do you know about that?"

"It's a small world. We have mutual friends in different circles, one being a part of the Rainbow Pride cruise you took October before last."

Now I'm wondering who the blabbermouth was. I just look at him as he reads my mind.

"I'm friends with one of the organizers and he told me that a couple got engaged on the ship. When I asked who, he told me your name."

I relax. "Well, we haven't started charting the specifics yet, but we plan on getting married on the next cruise."

"Are you sure you want to do this?"

"Why wouldn't I?"

Floyd sits back, his face pensive. After a moment, he says, "Look, have I ever steered you wrong?"

"No…"

"You've always been able to trust me, right?"

"Yeah… Wait a minute. What are you trying to tell me?"

Floyd looks me in the eye and says, "Listen, Lionel. I am happy about your upcoming marriage and the love you have found, but I want you to be careful and consider your career. Now, the LGBTQ community has come a long way. But corporate America is still very homophobic, and it doesn't care how smart or brilliant you are. More business goes to men who are married to women. People tend to talk contracts with guys who spit out football stats and can do the dozens. Quite a few clients are judgmental churchgoers that look at mannerisms before hearing a pitch. Take it from me. Being a black, gay man is hard in corporate America and marrying another man is not going to make it any easier."

My face feels hot. There is a fire that flames in the pit of my stomach. "Floyd, if I didn't know you any better, I would think you are telling me not to marry Joseph because of what other people might say."

"No, but I am telling you to be mindful. I'm not saying, 'Marry Joseph and you are fired'. I'm just giving you advice. Progress can potentially be halted in this business if male clients cannot accept doing business with a man who is in a same sex marriage."

I rise to my feet and raise my voice, "Now, you listen to me! They are not accepting me! They are accepting the work that I bring! My brains and work are what got me here and those things will keep me here. You really have a lot of nerve to come at me like that!"

Floyd precisely puts his napkin down. Then he temples his hands and looks dead ahead.

"First of all, sit your ass down," he says, calm as a puddle.

I comply.

"Second, take the bass out of your voice. And third, pick your face up off the floor."

I slouch, feeling like a piece of chewed string. Then he says with quiet authority and control, "Now you missed the whole point of what I'm trying to say. To begin with, yes… it was your brains and work that got you here, but let's not forget that I was there grooming you. Your eyes were shining with bright ideas, yet your mind didn't know shit from shinola about how to execute them. Now you are at the top of your game and I want to keep you there. But every now and then, you need a nasty dose of sulfur and molasses, and you need to take it from someone who has already been down this road. Are you following me?"

"Whatever…"

"Don't give me that whatever bullshit. You know exactly what I'm talking about. To coin a phrase from the young bloods, I'm going to keep it "one hundred" and tell you something that corporate America won't. You are a black, gay man who is about to marry another man. That's three strikes. The odds are against you, but this is where you have to work three times as hard to prove that you can beat every last one."

He sits back and sips his coffee. Then he continues, "You know, I came up in a time where two men didn't get married… they just lived together in private because they knew that they would be axed if they came out. This was before the kids were shouting about the right to same sex civil unions. Now, living in private with your man might seem weak to you, but we called it survival and wisdom. Things may have changed, but they haven't changed all that much. If given info about you and Joseph, a great deal of the business world filled with straight, all-American white men will only see one thing. Now, you love him enough to marry him. That's wonderful and I wish you all the best, really. But I wouldn't be doing my job as your mentor, boss, and friend if I did not tell you that there are dangers to look at as well."

I ponder over what he is saying. Trepidation grips me. I hadn't thought of the possibility that my career would suffer. Floyd sees the look and slaps the back of my hand playfully, saying, "Now, don't be looking all like that. You know I will take the bat for you because I believe in what you bring to the table. Remember, I'm going to stay in your corner. You are one of half the people in this firm that hasn't tried to fuck, suck, backbite, schmooze, or sabotage others to get ahead. Your integrity is going to keep you in a good position, maybe to even move up to my job when I retire. But I gotta tell you. If you go into this marriage, you need to go with your eyes wide open and be smart about your disclosure thereabout… because this is our reality."

*****

My mind is unsettled as I walk into my house and shed my coat. I sit in my favorite chair and I meditate in the silence of my home. This is a tough situation and I am feeling the same fear that I felt before agreeing to get into a relationship with Jojo. God, what am I going to do? I replay the conversation I had with Floyd. Of course, I'm still a bit pissed. But my anger is no longer directed at Floyd; it is at the homophobia in my line of work. I witnessed the gay shaming… particularly coming from one churchgoing client who owned a chain of barber shops. He wouldn't deal with one of our resident executives because of his "faggot shit". In fact, he ranted and raved about how much he hated gays. Hmmm… I guess he missed the memo when Jesus said, "Love thy neighbor."

I look up the stairs in the direction of my bedroom. My pills are up there. I contemplate taking one because my anxiety is beginning to take flight, but for some reason, I abstain. Instead, I opt to sit back and meditate on what to do.

It is thirty minutes later and I'm still sitting in this chair, more at odds than before. Hm… this is strange. Usually, I can solve the biggest problems sitting in this chair but I'm drawing a blank today. I look back upstairs and prepare myself to get a pill when the landline phone rings loudly beside me, startling me. I pick up the receiver.

"Hello?"

"Hey Blackjack, what's poppin'?" I smile to myself. It is Garrett.

"I'm hanging in there, Spades. How's life?" To explain the nicknames, we coined them for each other after we went to a casino one night on the cruise in 2018. Blackjack was my game and Spades was his. Afterwards, whenever we greeted each other, we used those names.

"I can't call it. Like the song says, I just live it from day to day."

I chuckle. Something about his playful tone is causing the day's troubles to lessen a little.

"I hear you. What'cha got goin' on today?"

"Dinner with Corey."

"Any place special?"

"Yeah, this soul food place off Belair Rd."

"Teresa's?"

"Yes. You've been?"

"Yeah. I went there with A.D. You're gonna love it. The food is slamming. They serve good 'Mama draws in it' type of food."

"Like fried chicken, yams, collards and shit?"

"Yep. Almost everything we had for Thanksgiving."

"Oh, we 'bouts tuh git our grub on!" Garrett says, laughing as I chuckle. *Ok, somebody's been hanging with A.D. a lot. I'm starting to hear his dialect coming from Garrett.*

We talk for almost an hour. During the conversation, he told me that Sam, Rachel's ex-husband, went over to her house to start shit over the divorce papers he received by mail. As soon as Rachel heard him banging on the door, she checked to make sure the doors were locked, grabbed Mike Jr., and told him to stay quiet. The silence only made him angrier, angry enough to start repeatedly kicking the door so hard that it splintered from the inside. Luckily, A.D. and their cousin Melba came in through the back door while he was ranting and raving. A.D. took one look at what was going on, and, without saying a word to Rachel or Mike Jr., he gestured from Melba to give him her gun, made sure it was loaded, opened the door, and pointed it at Sam's eye. He then said, "If I shot'cha in yuh right eye, do yuh think you'd be able tuh see outta yuh left?" After that, Sam's punk ass got in his car and drove off.

"Damn! It was a good thing both he and Melba showed up."

"Who you telling?" Garrett says jokingly. An uneasy silence hovers in the air. Then he speaks again, "Uh-oh! You got something rattling around in ya brain, what is it?"

I share with him my conversation with my boss and the concerns I had. After a long pause, Garrett says, "Well, he does have valid points."

"How so?"

"Well, like he said, there is never going to be a day when us gays are gonna be FULLY seen for what we offer."

"It could happen. What makes you say that?"

"Just seeing what the 'out' brothers have to go through on my own job is testament enough. And I'm talking brilliant, college-educated, ambitious go-getters who are always relegated to the back. And if you are Black, you are pushed three times as behind as everybody else. The deal is you just have to protect your shit. There are a select few at my job that know my 'Modus Operandi' and I keep my business on lock even with them. Because half of them is gonna wanna try me."

"Try you?" I query, puzzled.

"You know… climb the pole and slide down," he says in a hinting voice.

"OOOOh! Now I get it. What about the other half?"

"The other half, mostly the dames, swear up and down that they are not homophobic, but wait until there is an office party. Their paranoid asses stick to their husband's sides like flies to shit."

"Sad commentary, but true."

After we both meditate a few seconds, Garrett asks, "Have you talked to Jojo about the conversation?"

"No."

"Maybe you should."

"Maybe not."

"Why not?"

"We had been working hard and learning enough about each other to even entertain the thought of marriage. This might cause him to regress… perhaps call off the engagement. We've already had our bouts as to my uncertainty in getting deeper with him. I want to prove to him that I'm all in."

"If you want to prove that, then you owe it to yourself and him to start the marriage in honesty and reality. Even though it may hurt and there may be consequences, he needs to know your uncertainties, so he realizes what he's dealing with."

"I guess."

"Besides, in the couple of years that I've known you, you always tended to over-analyze things. I think you are doing that now. He might be having the same concerns. You never know. Look, just think about it."

"I will."

There is a silence, after which Garrett asks, "Other than that, is everything else cool?"

"Of course, Spades. Why do you ask?"

"Well, you've been crossing my mind a lot lately, so I'm just asking."

"Oh, I'm doing alright," I assure.

"Cool, well lemme git ready fuh muh date! It's almost seven thirty."

"You know, I can tell you and A.D. have been hanging out a lot."

"What makes you say that?"

"Because you are picking up his lingo," I say, laughing.

"Bye, Blackjack!" Garrett retorts. I hang up the receiver.

I'm going to take a little walk. I think to myself as I rise from my chair. I go upstairs to my bedroom and change from my work garb to my red cashmere turtleneck, black fitted jeans, and burgundy winter coat. I sit on my bed and put on my heavy winter socks as well as my boots, then I grab my white toboggan, scarf, and keys as I head out the door. As I pace the sidewalk on Bolton Street, those tormenting thoughts start to stampede into my mind again. *Have I really thought this through? What damage is my marriage going to do to my career? I worked hard to get where I am... and as much as I love Jojo, I don't want to lose everything I worked for.*

Before long, I find myself on Madison Avenue, the street Jojo lives on. *Hmm... I wonder if Jojo is home. Maybe I should follow Garrett's advice and talk to him about this. After all, the conversation is bound to come up anyway.* I pull out my cell and text him.

Hey Jojo.

Hey babe.

Are you at home?

Yeah.

What are you doing?

Just sitting around reading.

Come outside.

???

Just come out, please.

As I shiver from the cold and exhale nervously, I see Jojo descending his stoop. He spots me, beams a beautiful smile, and comes towards me. "Well, this is a sexy surprise. What are you doing all the way over here?" he says, as he hugs and kisses me tenderly.

"I just had an impulse to take a little walk. I needed to clear my head."

Jojo steps back and searches my eyes. "What's wrong?"

"Nothing I can't handle."

"Lionel, we are almost forty years old and you haven't learned how to front yet. Besides, I know you didn't just walk all the way up here for your health," he jokes sarcastically.

I don't say anything but something on my face betrays my feelings. Jojo sees this and grabs my arm, saying, "Come on inside."

We walk up the stoop and through the door. He takes my coat, boots, toboggan, and scarf and instructs me to sit down while he makes hot cocoa to warm me up. As I comply, I take in the warm space that is Jojo's living room, tastefully decorated in colors of brown, white, and rust. It is illumined only by the light of the fire in the fireplace. I am sitting on a rich brown leather sofa with patterned orange and white throw pillows. Two mahogany end tables with gold lamps grace the sides of the sofa. A plush rug with a brown and rust mosaic pattern lies underneath a polished mahogany coffee table and two rust Queen Anne chairs are positioned on either short side of the table, facing each other. There are Black themed paintings on the walls. One in particular stood out for me. It depicted two men crying, with one comforting the other. Underneath, it says, "Brother, Let Me Cry with You."

Jojo steps into the room with two mugs of hot chocolate on a serving tray. "I know you like your hot chocolate loaded with marshmallows." I thank him as I take the mug and sip the contents. Jojo just sits there and looks at me. When I lower the mug from my lips, Jojo says, "So, what's the problem? It must be pretty big for you to stroll down my way on a freezing night like this."

I take a deep breath and ask, "Jojo, do you have any reservations about us getting married."

Jojo clears his throat while sitting up straighter. Then he says, "I have a few. I mean, we are two men marrying each other. We are going against the grain."

"Do you ever think that this might put a wrench in your career?"

"Shortly after the announcement, I thought about it constantly," Jojo says, picking up the mug and sipping the hot creamy liquid. After registering the sweet taste, he goes on. "But in thinking about it, I believe that I'm in somewhat of a safe position. Everybody at the office knows I'm gay and my sexuality doesn't keep me from doing my job. The truth is, as long as the firm deals with money, all they care about is whether the books are in order."

"That's what I was thinking as far as my job. But Floyd sat me down and talked to me because he heard that we were getting married. The conversation had me thinking about how homophobic my line of work can be. It took a lot of work to get where I am, and I don't want to fuck that up." I say all of this haltingly, afraid of how Jojo will take it. But when I look in Jojo's eyes, all I see is a look of empathy.

Jojo carefully says, "Well, your job situation is different. You are in clients' faces and selling their product to the masses. Therefore, you are the mediator for the big boys of the company and the clients they are trying to sign. There's a certain persona that you have to adopt. But I believe that there is a way that you can do it without lying about who you are."

"Oh yeah, how's that?"

"The way you've been doing, keeping everything in perspective. Let business be business and don't bring personal life into it, including our marriage."

"That wouldn't be fair to you."

"How? All you are doing is shooting the shit and using the gift of gab to get their signatures. They are not going to ask who you are married to or if you are gay."

"And what if they do?"

"Then answer them with a question, 'Is there a particular reason why you are asking?' If you think the reason is valid, then tell them but be short and to the point about it. They don't need to know all your business. Besides, anybody asking too many questions about your personal life is too damned nosy. They either want some dick or trying to dig up dirt. Did Floyd say that he'd fire you if you marry me?"

"No. He just said to be careful."

"Well, there you go. The way I see it, Floyd heard we were getting hitched and wanted to tell you that he's happy for you but watch who you tell your shit to."

*****

Two hours later, we are lying side by side on the rug. Humorously, we share our experiences in the workplace and how hard it is to be gay in a business setting.

"So, there was this one time when I had to go to the bathroom, and Marvin Rigsby was at one of the urinals. You remember him, right?" Jojo asks.

"Yeah."

"Well, the only urinal that was free was the one right next to him. I step up to it and pull my dick out to piss. He just side-eyes me and turns up his nose. Then he angles his body so that his back is to me."

"No shitting."

"Yeah. I mean, what in the hell was he thinking I was going to do, turn him around and give him a blow with the three other guys watching?"

"Please. If the other guys weren't in there, he would have pulled it out and had you to suck it right then and there."

"Right."

"These fronting assholes give me a headache just thinking about them. And what's worse is dealing with these married women who are so insecure that they can't let their man out of their sight or anywhere near a gay man. There's this chick named Andrea in the accounting department whose husband brings her lunch sometimes. For some reason, she always feels the need to grip on him every time they are in the break room with one of the more flamboyant employees, Michael; giving him this "don't even think about it" look."

"Talk about insecure… and paranoid."

"That's what I'm saying. Michael was dying to tell her that she can have him."

Jojo chuckles, then looks out the window. A childlike glow lights up his face. I follow his gaze to see beautiful flurries floating from the leaden sky. We look at each other and in wordless agreement, decide to bundle up and go out to the back slab and partake in the enchantment of the snow. *It is so magical.* I think to myself. I look up and shiver as the snowflakes melt on my face. I lower my eyes to witness my one and only twirling around, filled with laughter that only a child or youthful heart can possess. He stops and looks at me, his bright smile causing his face to glow between his beige knit toboggan and matching scarf. I feel my face muscles stretch into a grin. Jojo begins to dance in the snow. At this moment, looking at Jojo swaying without a care in the world, I feel magic. My heart feels as though it is going to burst with love for him.

He stops dancing and suddenly runs towards me, hurling himself into my open arms. I pick him up and spin slowly around. The beauty of this moment is making me drunk with pleasure. As I lower him down, I hear a sweet melody with a beautiful refrain, and I hold him close as we sway in abandon to the song of love that we hear in our hearts.

Chapter Four
"I DON'T NEED TO HEAR THIS"

March is finally here. The snows of a blustering cold Baltimore winter finally began to lift, leaving a residue of coolness to soon evaporate in preparation for the spring. I am an avid lover of all the seasons but if I had to choose from among them, I'd pick spring. There is just something uplifting about the snows melting away and shy tiny buds blossoming into enormous and gloriously hued flowers.

The spring not only dominates the pastoral scenes of Earth. It also sends the marketing department of Robertson and Moore into a frenzy. On a busy day, you can expect to hear these questions. *What colors are being used this spring? How can we make this spring's marketing strategy more lucrative than last year's?* And of course, this also means traveling from coast to coast with Floyd and fellow executives. We have to do this to court prospective multi-million-dollar clients and coax them into signing with us.

Speaking of such, Vivian and Bianca Harrington finally agreed on a concept I drafted for the Va-Voom campaign. I swear, I did try to incorporate Miss Harrington's ideas but whenever I attempted to do so, the concept seemed plastic and artificial. There was just no verve... no gusto. Plus, from a marketing standpoint, her ideas would cause a perpetual standstill in perfume sales. Now, don't get me wrong. She had some good concepts, but they were somewhat outdated. To be fair, they were a lot better than the first one she came up with. I'm talking straight pink and blue with some empty-headed chick blowing bubble gum. Anyway, I sat down with her, as well as Floyd, to explain why the ideas wouldn't work. Prior to the meeting, I spoke with our Art Director, Marianne Dewitt, and as I dictated my notion, she drafted a new and popping storyboard concept. I don't know if Miss Harrington had several martinis before she came to the meeting but, to my utter surprise, she consented to listen to the idea.

With this campaign, I decided to go avant-garde. It begins in a ballroom with two tuxedoed male dancers doing the merengue. Then Bianca glides down the staircase wearing an eclectically designed pink satin gown with feathers by Moret Giordana, her hair wrapped and teased to look windblown, yet with overwhelming elegance. She dances with one dancer and he sniffs her shoulder. Intoxicated by her scent, he dances even more passionately. As he dips her, she reaches her hand out to the other dancer and he pulls her away to dance with her also. Of course, none of this is making the first dancer happy. With their tempers heightened towards each other, they stand toe to toe, ready to fight. With gloved hands, Bianca pushes her way through to stand between them. She caresses one, then the other. Afterwards she shoves them both away and struts back to the grand staircase. She turns with the perfume bottle in her hand as she winks at the camera. As the camera freezes, the word "Enchantress" appears diagonally across the right bottom corner.

After hearing the concept on Tuesday, Vivian arrogantly nodded and said, "Surprisingly… adequate. We may proceed. Messenger the contract to VaVoom's legal counsel. He will look it over and get back to you within seventy-two hours." After two days of biting our nails and waiting anxiously, the attorney assured Vivian that the contract was on the up-and-up. Vivian and Bianca signed the contract and we begin shooting again next week. May God help the camera people and director because they are going to go through hell!

The Fellas and I are at the gym exercising and talking trash. Jojo is doing squats, Corey is on the row machine, and Peep and I are lifting weights. I'm noticing that Peep is bothered about something. *What's up with him?* I make a mental note to ask him later. Corey, bubbly as ever, is just gabbing away while Jojo listens intently with his characteristic sweet smile.

"So, the contracts for the tour arrived. I had my lawyer look them over."

"All is well, I hope?" Jojo asks breathlessly.

"Yeah, everything is legit. Now, I just need to get to Mondawmin to get something important."

"Ewww! Mondawmin? I hope you are not getting any clothes," Peep asks with disdain, upon hearing the name of the bald-headed stepchild of malls in Baltimore. You see, Mondawmin Mall has always had a bad reputation in Baltimore because of the crime and the so-called "type of people" who shop there. I kinda like Mondawmin though. I call it "the mall of the people" because almost ninety five percent of the patronage are Black. They have good stores with awesome deals whenever I shop there. I don't go very often though. I mean, would you want to frequent a place where they have girls fighting over a fucking chicken sandwich?

"No. I saw a luggage set that I liked, and I ordered it online. The store called and said that it came in yesterday," Corey informs, stepping off the row machine and taking a seat on the weight bench.

Peep wrinkles his nose as he complains, "I don't know why you and Lionel like shopping in that mall. You need a Glock and a Kevlar vest to be in there for even a few minutes."

"Well," I counter. "I go for the holiday deals and clearance sales."

"And every now and then, it would be nice to be at a place where white clerks are not tailing you on the sly because they are afraid you are going to steal any of their tacky shit," Corey says, bolstering our position. His expression changes, becoming more wistful and thoughtful. He says, "But maybe you are right. Mondawmin is in a rough neighborhood, like I'm in now."

"Oh please, Corey. Your neighborhood is two steps away from Heaven's front gate," Peep laughs out.

"That was the case when I bought the house but, over the years, a seedier element of people is beginning to take root. I'm talking Penn Ave Counts, hookers, and creeps. I saw one before coming to the gym today. I was walking my last piano student out and I saw this thug eyeballing me."

"Eyeballing you?" Jojo echoes in alarm.

"Yeah, and the look he gave me was creepy as hell."

"Well, here's hoping that he'll move someplace else," I reason as I look at my watch. It is four fifteen. I place the barbell back on the rack and grab my gym bag. "I have to get going. I have a five o'clock appointment with Dr. Williams," I inform.

It is kind of hard to miss the looks of concern coming from my friends' eyes. There is a long stretch of silence, broken by Peep saying while lifting, "I am still lost as to why you left Dr. Banneker."

"I don't want to get into it," I say.

"You don't have to, baby. All we are saying is that you seemed to improve a great deal when you went to him. You were thinking a lot clearer and he wasn't trying to push pills down your throat," Jojo responds mid-squat. I look at him, annoyed.

"Really Jojo? This shit again?" I mutter.

"Yes, this shit again," Jojo retorts fiercely as he comes up from the squat and steps in front of me. "Lion, I don't like that Dr. Williams character."

"And I can't say that I like him either," Peep says. "There is something completely off about him."

"Peep, he is a shrink. If you ask me, I think there is something off about all shrinks. They would have to be a little off their rockers to want to climb into people's heads."

"That may be true. But this 'Dr. Williams' dude strikes me as someone who has mental issues of his own." Peep pants out as he drops the barbell and sits down on the floor. Catching his breath, Peep continues urgently, "And I don't think he takes the well-being of his clients seriously, like he should. I know this because last week a friend of mine at the club told me about the shitty deal that she got from him before she had the good sense to drop him. According to her, he half listens, has no filter when prescribing meds, and does not follow up with his patients. Why go through the process of medical school and taking the Hippocratic oath if you are not going to abide by it? And I happened to tune in to local talk show that featured him on TV. There is a look in his eyes that clearly spells, 'I don't care!' I personally don't think he should be offering mental therapy to anybody, let alone prescribing pills if he's not going to double check the chemical properties they contain."

"Peep's got a huge point," Corey firmly pipes in. "And we have already had this discussion. Look Lionel, Pop Kennedy used to tell me this all the time. 'Good things come in three.' And for your own good, all three of your friends are trying to tell you that this shrink is incompetent, nonchalant about your care, and just in it for a paycheck. With all the money you're paying him, you should have the best care possible, not just someone who thinks a loaded pill is the answer for everything!"

Them being all up in my business is really beginning to aggravate me. It is making me hot in the face and loose in my angered vocal delivery as I utter these words, "I really do not need to hear this right now. Besides, last time I checked, it is MY insurance and money that pays the doctor's bill. And it is MY mind he's climbing into. I ought to know what's best for me since it's MY goddamned body!"

"Now, you wait a minute," Peep says, bounding up and advancing towards me. Corey steps in front of him to calm him down. I see a scarlet flush staining Peep's face as he struggles to maintain his control. "All we are trying to do is help you. It is your entitlement to choose your doctors, but it is more important to have psychiatric care that benefits you mentally. And judging from these periodic outbursts of yours, that is exactly what you are not getting."

I turn away from him, saying, "I don't have time for this shit." In a flash,

Jojo jumps in my path. Corey and Peep move to stand in front of me as well.

"Look, Lionel," he begins, disarming me with his huge caring eyes. "We are not trying to tell you what to do. We just notice things concerning you and this Williams character that do not add up. We are just concerned about you. And Peep is right. Lately, your temper has been hard to deal with."

Peep follows, with calmed concern. "And lest you forget, we all have dealt with you at your angriest, and you have a right to be angry with all the shit that's happened to you. But if you are getting therapy, your anger is supposed to be redirected toward being productive, not destructive."

"So, what am I supposed to do?" I ask. "Switch doctors again?"

Jojo reasons, "That is up to you. But do me a favor. When you go into his office today and you tell him what's going on with you, watch his face. Shrinks have been trained to show no emotion, but there is an element of caring to be found in their demeanor if you look hard enough. If you can't find it in him, then you know what you got."

Corey follows, "And while you're at it, you oughta keep track of the time you spend with him. You are guaranteed at least an hour in his office because that's what you are expected to pay him for. But if he tries to end the time early and still insist full payment, I'd drop his ass like a red-hot plate."

"Cool, I got it. I'm gone," I say impatiently as I veer past them and cross the gym lobby to exit the glass double doors. I know that they are just looking out for me and I feel a bit guilty for my episode. But I really wish they would give me credit for having a few smarts in my head. Nowadays, it seems like every time we see each other, we get into it about one of the following subjects: my doctor switch, my alleged anger, or my taking these pills. Sometimes, like today for example, they harp on all of them at once and it is working my last good nerve.

*****

Two hours later as I am parked in front of my house, I recount the appointment with Dr. Williams while considering what The Fellas told me… and concluding that they were right. Throughout the time that I was venting my frustrations, he just sat there with a bored, slightly condescending look on his face, even when he had his nose buried in his notes. It was like he was saying, "I'm doing YOU a favor by being here listening to your bullshit."

Two unpleasant memories flash in my head. The first occurrence was two weeks ago. I was having the truck detailed and Jojo came to pick me up. We shared a kiss and from the corner of my eye, I noticed that Dr. Williams had this look of apparent disdain when staring at Jojo, then me. The second occurrence depicts our initial appointment. When I told him I was gay, he had this pretentious façade that Stevie Wonder could see through. I got the feeling then that he was homophobic. That would explain the indifference.

My mind deliberates over the two facts that sum everything up. He obviously is not LGBTQ friendly like his website said and he's inattentive in our sessions. So, what am I still doing with him? *Oh Lionel, who are you kidding!* My mind says. *You know you're in it for the pills.*

Corey was right about his cutting the time and demanding full payment. When he indicated that my time was up, I looked at my watch. It was five forty-one. I pointed this out and he mentioned that he had to cut the appointment short because he had a speaking engagement at seven. I nonchalantly said, "Ok. So, same time next week?"

"Yes."

"Am I still paying ninety dollars for today?"

"Of course."

I remember feeling puzzled. "Funny how it's still ninety when I wasn't here for an hour, don't you think?"

He then looked at me with a snide, sneering look as he sat back and folded his arms. *Defensive posture.* "The cost is indicative of how important your mental care is."

"What does that even mean?"

"It means that the minutes you are given are not as important as the ongoing care we are striving to provide for you."

"But even the 'ongoing care' is spotty at best. I call the office when I'm ten days shy of having no meds and it takes forever for you to call the prescription in. And it is hard to put a message in because your voicemail is always full. When it's not and I can leave a message, I rarely get a call back"

He said coldly, "Mr. Davis, you are not the only psychiatric patient I have. I deal with twenty patients every week and many of them require my constant attention."

I made my voice just as cold as his. "Be that as it may, I am still a patient in need of care, and I came to you because I felt that you were capable of providing it. I also feel that it is bad business for you to make your patients pay for *your* poor time scheduling. I bet my bottom buck that the Maryland Psychiatric Society may feel the same way if I decided to tell them about the care I'm receiving. Do you see where I'm at?" I finish my declaration by standing, placing my palms flat on his desk, and leaning over it to stare him down.

He obviously saw exactly where I was going because he turned off the bitch switch. He said, "My apologies, Mr. Davis, for not making myself more available to you. I hope you know that my intentions are to see that you get the best care possible." After he said this, he discounted my rate to sixty-nine bucks.

I mull all this over as I exit the truck and walk into my house. While closing and locking the door and sitting in my chair, my mind drifts to The Fellas. We have unfinished business. I have to call them. I pull out my cell phone and start to call Peep first when it buzzes loudly, displaying his name on the screen. I answer, "Peep, I was just getting ready to call you."

"You were?"

"Yeah, I wanted to say I was sorry for what I said earlier and for leaving the way I did," I express apologetically as I rise to hang up my keys.

"And I was calling for the same reason. I should have kept my mouth shut about Dr. Williams. I don't know him apart from what my friend said about him… I am just concerned about you, that's all."

"I know. But Peep, you don't have to worry about me. I can take care of myself."

"But Lionel…"

"Listen, Peep. We just got through apologizing to each other for one dispute. Let's not start another."

Peep concedes, "Ok."

"Now, what's going on with you? You looked a bit bothered earlier," I say as I sit down on the chaise.

There is silence on his end. Then he says, "It's Granny's birthday today. She would've turned eighty-one years old."

"Oh, Peep… I forgot about that. How are you holding up?"

After a beat, Peep says, "Around this time, those feelings start returning. I start thinking about what I could have done…"

"Peep, don't do this to yourself. Death happens and there's nothing you can do about it. And remember, in that letter, your grandma said that it was her pleasure to do what she could to see that you grew up successful and that you felt supported and loved."

"My mind knows that," Peep says with tears in his voice. "But my heart is still grieving. I loved my grandparents dearly. Hell, I am thinking that even though they raised me up in that homophobic church, maybe they would've understood and still loved me if I had told them I was gay."

"They never had ANY clues?"

"My granddad didn't, but Granny did. A month before I left for Morgan, my neighbor came over, saying that he had something to tell me. His name was Jerry Blackstone and he lived a few houses away from us. He was my best friend... and one of the few people I could talk to about anything. Well, almost anything. I never told him about my sexuality. It just never came up."

"What happened when he came over?" I ask, intrigued.

"Whatever he was going to tell me never made it out of his mouth. He stammered saying that he had felt something special about our friendship. He got really quiet and before I knew it, he cupped my head and kissed me on my lips."

"Shut up!"

"Yeah."

"Then what?"

"You want ALL the details?"

"Damn straight. No pun intended," I say with a laugh.

Peep chuckles. "Well, I never told him this, but I felt the same way about him too. I remember watching him read his books on the bus, with thick, round glasses and curly hair. He was the type that most people called nerdy, but I was insanely attracted to him. He had smooth olive brown skin and a tall slim body with nice huge and hairy legs. It drove me nuts to see him dressed in his shorts. And his eyes? Oh... adorable! Anyways, when he finished his kiss, I stroked his cheek and if you could've seen the look of pure heaven on his face when I did that! Of course, *that* was the time that Granny chose to step in the room to put my clean clothes in the drawers. When she saw my hand on his cheek and the look he had on his face, she stopped and gave me a funny look, then turned around and walked out."

"Wow! What happened after that?"

"At dinner, she asked me if I was gay and she didn't have any contempt on her face. She prefaced the question with telling me that I was her grandson and no matter how I answered, she loved me... But I lied and said I was straight."

"Why didn't you just tell her?"

"I was scared. All I thought about was how manly Granddad was, how I always wanted to be just like him, and how she adored him. In my teenaged thought process, my admitting to being gay meant admitting that I wasn't half the man he was."

"But she said she'd love you no matter what."

"Yeah, but at that time, when you're a kid listening to sermons of hellfire reserved for gays, that is the last thing you would admit to."

There is another silence. Then I break it, asking, "Did you and Jerry ever talk about your attraction?"

"Yes. Later that night, he snuck back over to my house after Granny went to sleep. He climbed up the tree to my window and tapped on it. When I opened the curtains, I saw him smiling this sweet smile. I let him in, and we talked. He told me that he was attracted to me ever since junior high, and I told him that my attraction started when we were freshmen in high school." Peep stops to catch his breath. I am on the edge of my seat!

"Well?"

"Well, what?"

"Well, what happened then?"

"What do you think happened? Sex. Hot, butt naked sex that we had to keep quiet so we wouldn't wake Granny."

"Oh my God!" I exclaim. Then my voice lowers to a secretive tone. "I'm almost scared to ask."

"Ask what?"

"How was it?"

"You are one nosy ass bitch!"

"Come on, Peep. You already know that I'm going to demand the juicy details."

"I know this," Peep replies with a snort.

"So? Are you gonna tell me?"

"Bay-BAAAY! That boy had dick that made me sore for days, and did he know how to use it or what!"

"Mmmm… Now I see why you love Jimmy so much."

"Why is that?"

"Because this Jerry sounds like a younger version of Jimmy."

Peep ponders, "Mmmm… I hadn't thought of that."

"Have you heard from him since?"

"Naw. Rumor had it that he got married to some chick. They moved to

Oakland and pumped out three young'uns."

"Do you think about him often?"

I hear a beep and I look at the screen. It's Brenda.

"Sometimes. But on those times, I throw my big ass on Jimmy and he chases away the memory very well! Hah-HAH!"

As I laugh, there is another beep on the line. "Oh Peep, I'm sorry. This is Brenda calling. Hold on."

"No, I have some numbers to crunch. I need to finish and get Jimmy's dinner on the table. Call me later and tell Brenda I said hello."

"Ok." I click over. Immediately, I hear sobs and I jump to my feet. *Oh my God! What's happened?*

"Brenda? What's wrong?"

"Lionel... Mama is..." she starts, but the tears break off her statement. She resumes crying even louder than before.

A feeling of dread chills me from my shoulders to my toes. "Brenda, please calm down. You're scaring me." But all I hear are sobs of anguish, sobs that make my own eyes begin to shed tears as I pace the floor. "BRENDA! TELL ME WHAT'S GOING ON!"

Suddenly, I hear Roland's voice, which is audibly shaken, "Lionel, you need to get to Atlanta. We're at the hospital."

"Hospital?"

"Yeah."

"What happened?"

The long hush on the line is unbearable. It is coupled by Brenda's hysteria. Roland says the words, "Lionel, Mama is gone. She died ten minutes ago."

I feel a numbness creep through my body, like water poured in a glass full of ice. I fall onto my chair, trying to breathe. *I can't breathe!*

"Lionel..."

I can't move... Oh God in Heaven! I can't move!

"Lionel..."

I am completely immobilized by the words I just heard. I take in a short sharp breath, forcing air into my lungs. *Goddammit, Mama!* The sadness of the news petrifies me. Suddenly, I catch sight of the scar on my calf, inflicted by my mother's paddle. Red hot anger floods my face and chest as I slowly resume movement.

"Lionel, are you there?"

In a voice I barely recognized as my own, I croak out coldly, "I'm here."

"When can you get back here?"

Silence blankets the room. I don't want to go anywhere near Yeti or Mama's corpse. Everything in me is telling me to say, *Never. Let the woman rot.* But I need to be there for the rest of my family. So, despite my anger, I say, "I'll be on the plane tomorrow... Did you call A.D.?"

"No, not yet. I was hoping that since you both live in Baltimore, you would tell him."

"I'll tell him."

"Ok, and I'll call Dean."

"Ok."

I hang up the phone and call A.D. When he answers, I tell him the news quickly, stunning him into shocked silence. When he recovers, he asks, "When yuh leavin' tuh git down dere?"

"Thinking of going tomorrow."

"Ok, I'ma git us two tickits on Soufwest. We might needta leave layta in de moanin'."

"Fine," I say curtly.

"You a'ight?"

"Yeah. Why wouldn't I be?"

Moments pass, then A.D. says, "Li'nel, I usedta wish for dis day tuh come. But now dat it's 'ere, I'm los' as fuck."

"That's the difference between you and me. I'm glad she's gone. She left here carrying the same evil shit that she put out."

"Li'nel, dat ain't no way tuh be talkin'. I know she wuz…"

"I'm sorry," I say, interrupting him. "I gotta go. See you tomorrow."

As I abruptly click the phone off, my thoughts travel back to the conversation (or the monologue) I had with Mama in the hospital. Reflecting back, I believe it was her silence that hurt me more than the shard that cut my cheek. Call me crazy, but I guess I was expecting for her to take that opportunity to explain why she killed Dad and why she was so evil toward me and A.D.

I recall telling Dr. Banneker that I didn't get abused worse than A.D., but I didn't tell the whole truth. I got it just as bad, if not worse. Maybe it was because of my friendship with Jojo or the closeness I shared with my father. Whatever the reason, those beatings scarred me for life.

I remember one time when I was thirteen years old. Dad was gone on one of his business trips that lasted a month long. She was "cleaning" my room and she found a book I checked out from the library. It was called *An Existence Unseen*. She opened it and started tripping over what she read. She read only a few lines into the book before she started yelling my name.

The moment I came into the room, I felt her hand savagely hit me across the face. Then she asked me, *"What in the hell are you doing reading this kind of shit?"* I didn't answer her back. By now, I was completely aware of what was coming. The long cherry switch she had at her side confirmed it. She raised her hand to hit me again and I put my arm up to ward her off, which made her angrier. I quickly said, *"I was just reading it."*

"Why are you 'just reading' trash like this?"

"It was for a class project. The teacher asked us to report on a book of current events."

"What kind of teacher would allow you to read and report about this sick smut?"

I remained silent.

"You won't answer me, huh? Ok. Then I'm going down to that school to talk with the principal about why he would hire someone without the sense to keep this depraved shit from the hands of children."

At that moment, I saw a vision of my English teacher, Ms. Sawyer, getting fired. *An Existence Unseen* was a book that depicted the life of a teenager who was involved in a street gang that terrorized the city. It had an undertone of same sex themes based on the conflict the teenager had with his growing sexual attraction to the gang leader; an attraction that was later satisfied. It *was* for a class assignment and Ms. Sawyer left it up to us to choose the book and subject. I chose that book because I wanted to report on inner-city violence. However, though I would never tell Mama this, I wanted to satisfy my curiosity about my own attraction to men, dating from my discovery and lost virginity with my cousin, Jaamal. The report was solely on the violence topic and I got an "A" plus. But though it was for a report, Mama wouldn't have understood that. She would have done everything she could to get Ms. Sawyer canned. I liked Ms. Sawyer. I couldn't let that happen.

"Mama, wait!"

She stopped at the door.

"It's not for any assignment. I saw it at the library and checked it out."

Her eyes were lethal as she turned around. She lifted her hand and swung a hard, stinging blow that made my ears ring.

"That's for lying!"

Before I could recover my composure, she backhanded me across the other cheek.

"That's for reading this garbage in the first place," she hissed. She snatched up the book and began ripping the pages out of it.

"That is a library book, Mama! I have to take it back tomorrow!"

"You shouldn't have brought it into this house to begin with. That Bible is what you ought to be reading. But you'd rather read about faggots!" She said as she proceeded in tearing the pages out. I rushed to get the book from her hands. That was when her coarse hand cracked viciously across my face; and the force causes me to reel and fall to the floor. I could feel her whipping me. I could hear her screaming with fury.

Then again, I couldn't. It was like a part of me transported from my body and watched as she whipped me mercilessly.

After the beating was over, Mama went to the living room, grabbed her purse, and headed to the school. I moved from the floor to the bed, laid down, and just stared at the ceiling. I felt a burning orb of anger singe my heart, surrounded by a thin aura of hurt and humiliation. The questions I kept asking in my head were, *"Why? Why have children if all you can do is beat on them? Why didn't she give us up for adoption? We would have been much better off than we are now."* I heard a shrieking voice in my head, screaming out a word I forced myself never to utter for fear of being struck down dead.

"BITCH!"

After a few minutes, A.D. walked by my room. He glanced in and stopped short. As he viewed my bruised, welted, and wounded body, his face frowned in melancholy, yet the veins in his forehead pulsated with quiet, potent rage. Without a word, he went into the bathroom, got the first aid kit and antiseptic, and came into my room to carefully clean and bandage the wounds from the switch. It was one of those rare times that A.D. showed how sensitive he was. As he cleaned my wounds, I just looked at him. He had water in his eyes that he was forcing not to fall. The reflection in those tear-covered eyes silently cried out to me, "Yes, I know your pain. I've been there before."

As he left the room to grab the witch-hazel, I looked down at my legs. They were raked with long red welts and some of them were bleeding…

I couldn't help it…

I started crying…

A.D. came in and saw me and his face hardened. He sat down on my bed and told me these words. *"Don' evuh let 'er see yuh cry, yuh hear? Cry all yuh want now, but when yuh see 'er, don't let one tear fall."*

As I reflect on that memory, my anger brims. Mama may have cooked for us, clothed us, and housed us, but I don't think she ever loved us. That beating I received was typical of others aimed mostly at me and at A.D. It was ironic that they always happened when Dad was away. When he was around, she would put on this huge facade of being the loving, caring parent or the suffering martyr who was scarcely provided for by Dad and was constantly disobeyed by her children.

Hypocritical bitch! Hateful shrew!

My anger is boiling over. OK, I need to control this. I'm thinking this even as I am sitting in my living room. *Where are my pills? I need the one hundred milligrams.* I go upstairs to my bedroom and look in my nightstand... They are not here! I rapidly search the drawers. *I've got to find those pills... I need to sleep...*

Oh God, where are they? I can't sleep without them. Wait a minute... Last time I took them was last night and it was a full bottle. OK think, Lionel... Where were you?

The bathroom!

I race down the hall to the bathroom. *OK, I remember being at the sink.* I open the medicine cabinet. The twenty-five milligram pills are there, but those are not strong enough! I race back to my bedroom, frantically searching the nightstand drawer again. My senses are heightening by the second! I look under the bed and there are the pills. I hungrily rip the cap off the bottle, grab a pill, and I pop it in my mouth.

Sighing in relief, I go to the bathroom and pour a cup of water to wash it down. Then I amble back to my room and lay across the bed, fully clothed. I lay staring at the ceiling. My eyes become drowsy as I hear the sweet melody that the pills are playing.

Lullaby and good night.

I see my eyes lowering like curtains. The melody is becoming louder and louder and my surroundings begin to retreat. A huge tidal wave of drowsiness engulfs me and carries me to the merciful throes of slumbering oblivion.

Chapter Five
THE HOUSE OF GOD

Our mother's funeral. We all knew that this day had to come. The air outside is extremely hot and humid. It is two weeks after her death, and we are sitting in Mama's rose and eggshell colored living room on the plastic covered furniture. None of us are feeling too talkative. Even Corey is silent. He and Jojo are sitting on either side of me, rubbing my arms. Peep and Jimmy are sitting opposite A.D., whose head was downcast, and his face morose.

When I got the call that she passed, I felt dry of tears. I still am. This is my own mother and I can't cry for her. How does one mourn someone who has shown him the evils of pain since adolescence? I have no idea. I look over at Dean. He is just sitting there; draped and slouched in the armchair like an old cloth, rivers of tears flowing down his face, but his expression is blank. Brenda is in the kitchen, having coffee with Roland and her husband, Mercer.

I have always liked Mercer. We were cool from the day my sister brought him home from college. He reminded me a lot of a big boned version of Dad; very soft spoken, introspective, and encouraging. He is the first person close to the family that I told about my sexuality. The conversation came up one Easter when I came home for break from graduate school. Mama went hard on me about my being single and not bringing any women home. She told me, *"I'm starting to think that you are funny."* I went outside to cool off and Mercer came and found me. When I voiced my truth in a frustrated tone, Mercer told me, *"I wouldn't worry about it. How old are you?"*

"Twenty-seven."

"Well, you are at a time where you have to be comfortable with owning what is right for YOU. And whatever that might be has nothing to do with the opinions of others…not even your mother."

I received a call from Garrett, telling me that he was sorry he couldn't be here to support A.D. and me, but he, Mike Jr, Rachel, and Eunetta were praying for us. Rhonda couldn't be here, either. No doubt Windsor Correctional Facility would have released her to attend, but she opted not to come. *So, Mama's favorite is yet again a no-show,* I think bitterly to myself. *All those years of Mama letting her get away with murder, and she can't even come to the services to pay her respects. Lord knows, I've had my rounds with Mama, and I debated repeatedly whether or not I should come. But I showed up.*

My thoughts travel to the cause of my mother's demise. Her cancer came back with a vengeance. Just like her anger and bitterness, it spread throughout her body. And from what Brenda told me, she was impossible to deal with, until the day her doctor told her to start preparing her final arrangements because she only had a month left. Brenda told me that she spent Thanksgiving in the hospital giving the nurses hell. She would just go into hysterics, swearing a blue streak and snapping at the staff, Brenda, and anyone else who came over to help her. Worse yet, and as I predicted, she wouldn't go to any of her chemo appointments or take her medicines. She just opted to waste away. Without a doubt, I believe she died with curses on her tongue, violence in her mind, and hate in her heart.

The doorbell rings and Jojo rises to answer it. A tall, lanky man with thinning hair and gaunt face stands at the door. He introduces himself as the funeral director and, after a few preliminaries concerning funeral protocol, he tells us that the limousines are outside and prepared for our processional to the church. We all rise to collect ourselves and exit the house. My siblings, Mercer, and I climb into the sleek and black limousines and as I sink back into the comfortable black leather seat, I watch as Corey, Peep, Jojo, and Jimmy get into the rental car. After the police escorts station themselves fore and aft to conduct the vehicle chain, we begin the processional to Saint Jude Missionary Baptist Church

Corey's philosophy of life and lifestyle barrels into my memory. Ever since he gave that nugget of insight, I have been looking at my own life and that of those around me. That lesson between friends brings something my Dad said to my memory. *Lionel, I believe life can be full as well as empty. Regardless of the pain, it could either be fraught with realized purpose or full of excuses with goals barely reached and opportunities seldom taken. It could be filled with lessons learned or chained with ignorance and bitterness. You get out of life whatever you put into it, and if all you can contribute is misery, what right have you to expect anything but a miserable life?*

*****

As we enter Saint Jude, I scan the large church. St. Jude was always known in Yeti for its spacious and gothic sanctuary. On either side, there are five huge arched windows made of blue stained glass. Each has a red cross in the middle. The walls of the church are painted eggshell white and the carpet is periwinkle blue, as are the worn cushioned pews of white wood and oak trimming. The choir stand has five oak pews of without cushions. A white, custom painted Hammond C3 organ is on the right side and a white baby grand piano and drums occupy the left. There is a wraparound balcony lining the rear and side walls.

Dear God! The sight of that balcony takes me back to my childhood. We, the Davis children, sat beside each other in the front row of the right balcony. We were forbidden to move, talk, or even breathe wrong. Our mother was an usher stationed at the door to the left of the choir stand. So, she had a clear view of us, clear enough to give us the age-old eagle eye glare if we even whispered. If one of us kids got out of line (usually A.D.), she would put up her 'Baptist finger', march up the back stairs, grab the offender, and take him to the choir room for a whipping with a long strap she kept in her purse. Then she would order him to shut up, plop him back in his seat, and reclaim her position at the door. The worse thing about it was that the whipping at the church was just the beginning. The offender was punished worse when we all got home.

As I look around, I notice that there are only about forty people seated in this vast church. Pastor Jeremiah Lawson is perched in his chair like he owns the place and everybody in it. Looking at him now, with his yellowish white hair, beady intense eyes, lips that look like puffs of pink cotton candy and skin that resembles an ashy rubber tire, I have the urge to commence puking. He came to Yeti from St Louis and became the pastor when I was eleven years old. Ever since that time, he managed to run off members, associate pastors, musicians, and ministers of music. He is the type that will preach against gays; but is not above getting his dick sucked in the baptismal pool or fucking trade in the church bathroom.

Before he came, Saint Jude was a thriving church. I remember the days when this sanctuary was packed like sardines in a can. The choir stand was stuffed with choir members. Sixty members deep, they sang down home gospel and the contemporary music of the early nineties. The Right Reverend Dr. Jonathan Grissom served as pastor then. He was a young pastor, and a pretty damned good one. He was there for ten years, and the church grew exponentially under his care, so much so that the church had to add an eight o'clock service. He spearheaded the programs that increased funds to pay off the mortgage and, at the height of the AIDS epidemic, he took meals out to the hospitals to feed the stricken patients. Almost the entire church loved him. But you know there is always a small fraction of people that manage to fuck up a good thing. Deacon Charles Lattimore, Mama, and other church folk disliked him because he didn't dance to their tune. He followed his heart and put the needs of the people and the church first. But "the Amen Corner" nagged, pushed, prodded, threatened, and needled him until he could take no more. Tearfully, he stepped down on the day of the mortgage burning. He took a pastoral position at a church on the east side of Yeti, and most of the church went with him. Saint Jude never recovered from that.

I look at the choir stand. There are only nine people seated, and an older lady at the piano playing the hymn "Abide with Me". Oh my God! How depressing! As I continue my gaze, I notice that almost every one of the people in the sanctuary are Deacon Lattimore's cronies. I knew them from childhood, and they have the same snotty, self-righteous looks on their faces that they had back then. They look at Jojo and me and turn their noses up, wrinkling them with revulsion. Obviously, Mama told them about my sexuality and marrying Jojo, and judging from the look on their faces, her words were not exactly Christian.

In this sanctuary, I encounter gossips, character assassins, liars, thieves, cheats, and closet cases. *This is going to be one long service.* I feel a pang of despair, which leaves the moment my eyes rest on a wrinkled, elderly lady with a pleasant face. Ms. Nadine Frazier! Lord, she's still living! I remember her because she was my Sunday School teacher. She always had a sweet smile and a huge, brown paper bag filled with candies she bought just for me, which I would share with Jojo, A.D., and Dean. She would always caution me to keep them out of sight so Mama wouldn't take them. She was one of the few good people that stayed when Dr. Grissom quit. I remember when someone asked her why and she replied, "I was born in this church and I'll die in this church. My roots are planted right here... no matter what fool is carryin' on in the pulpit." She looks at me and Jojo, smiles her sweet smile, and waves her gnarled hand. Jojo and I smile and wave back at her as we take our seats in the front pew.

Pastor Lawson stands up and goes to the pulpit, intoning, "Now we will give the family a chance to render their farewell to our sister Lynetta."

One by one, Dean, Roland, Brenda, and I go up to the casket to pay our last tributes. A.D. kept his seat, saying that he saw enough of her during her embalmment. The floral arrangements were all in her favorite colors: yellow and gray. The casket was pearl gray with gold edging. Thank God we found out about the insurance she paid on. Otherwise, she'd be in a pine box. As I look at the choir and the ushers, I notice that the ladies are dressed in yellow blouses and black skirts. The gentlemen are dressed in black suits, white shirts, and gray ties.

When my turn comes, I approach the casket and look at Mama. The caramel skin on her pinched face is lined with wrinkles. She has a wig of dark brown hair covering her bald head. In looking at her, my body shudders. I can distinctly hear those long cherry switches, thick extension cords, and that ragged old paddle as they battered and tore my skin. I can hear the slaps as they rained on my face from her hardened hands, and the sensation felt like stinging bees. I feel my face harden as I pivot on my heel to take my seat. *She's dead. Good,* I irreverently thought to myself.

The service is dragging on, with hymns the "choir" sung flatter than my Aunt Mavis's ass. Of course, Corey couldn't refrain from complaining about the lack of pitch and clarity, in addition to the deadness of the choir's musical delivery. Then came the remarks (or reflections). I wonder why people cannot just comply to the standard request that they stay within the two-minute limit. We had to sit through sermonettes, diatribes, and loaded remarks aimed at Jojo and me. Remarks like this:

> *She was a holy woman, even living among wayward souls.* **That** one came from Miss Anniebelle Haynie, the Yeti Switchboard. If I had a dollar for every time she gossiped, I'd be rich enough to buy the

whole state of Alabama.

She lived for God and God alone. She did not try to please the flesh like some people I know. That's rich coming from Mrs. Gertrude Johnson, Yeti's resident whore and regular at the STD clinic. Seventy-eight years old and still trying to get her punanny long stroked. And get this: her husband is rotting in his coffin bearing the misbegotten assurance that he's the only one who stroked it!

I'm so glad we praise God in a real church and got a real preacher who doesn't sugarcoat the Bible. One that preaches the uncompromising Word of God. There ain't no doubt where she is right now. It behooves these young'uns to take heed and quit following the devil. He peers over his glasses at me. Uh-huh, Deacon Lattimore, the biggest brownnose in the church. He has his head so far up the pastor's ass, I can't tell where he ends, and the ass begins.

On and on, they went.

"I swear if I have to listen to another one of these 'ain'ts' testa-lying, I am gonna puke," Corey spits out.

"Shush, Corey. That old bat across the way is staring at you," Peep hisses, gesturing at Miss Anniebelle.

"I don't care. Let her look."

"Corey, act like you got some damn sense and hush."

"Don't tell me to hush." Corey hisses back. "Tell Ol' Man River up there. You know he done gone way past his allotted two minutes. We didn't come here to listen to him slobber." A.D. cracks up, struggling to contain his laughter.

Somehow, we got through the talking and another flat song from the choir. Then Pastor Lawson gets up to eulogize… and proselytize.

"My brothers and sisters, we are gathered here today to celebrate the life of a true soldier of God, Lynetta Wilkerson-Davis. She fought a battle with cancer for some time. And finally, God saw fit to remove the burden of life from her shoulders and let her cross that age-old river between life and death… She will be missed, by her family and this church."

I am trying to pay attention to his sermon, but my mind goes back to the bottle of oil poured on my head and the pastor's repulsive voice as he called me a fallen sinner.

"Lynetta was ready to go. She had her armor on and her Bible in her hand. She heard the voice of the Lord call her to His bosom."

"I am so sick and tired of these pastors preaching foul-acting folk into heaven. This whole sermon is a crock of shit!" Peep says before catching himself.

"Feli, watch your mouth! You know better than to be cursing in church," Jimmy says.

"Jimmy, you know I'm telling the truth. Mark my words. Next thing you know, he's gonna preach against us gays... and them deacons are gonna drool over every word. I don't know why, especially when it's the same slobber they use as lube whenever they want to fuck a fat ass." Brenda, Mercer, Roland, and Dean start sniggering, while Corey shoves Peep in the shoulder.

"Peep, quit yo' cussin'!" A.D. says, trying to keep a straight face. I'm having a hard time keeping one myself. Leave it to my friends to pick my mother's funeral to start cutting up.

"Peep, you just told me to act like I got sense, and here you are having a conniption," Corey admonishes, chuckling.

Jojo turns around. "Can ya'll please keep it down? We can talk about this later."

"She found the Lord at an early age and answered his call to salvation. That's why I can stand here and say that she is blissfully present with the Lord... But, I wanna ask you good people a question. Are you ready to meet the Lord? If He was to call you home right now, would your calling and election be sure?" He pauses, glaring in our direction. We hear the collective voice of the parishioners, saying "Amen" and "That's right."

"This world is not getting any better. There are wars, rumors of wars, crooked governments, violence even in the House of God... Oh, my brothers and sisters, this world is not the world I knew in my youth! Oh, my heart aches and bleeds over the state the world has fallen to."

My face is getting hotter and hotter by the second. If I could, I would go up there and ram my fist in his mouth before he says another word. Like Peep, I know what's coming. I've heard this shit many times before. I feel Jojo starting to squirm. I put my arm around him to let him know that I understand.

"I came here today to warn you to wake up. We are living in the last days. Even the ones God chose to do great works in His name are being deceived! Falling for every wind of doctrine, just like the Bible says." He pauses again, looking at me. A smirk distorts his face as he continues.

"Satan comes in seductive forms, and one of them is through the media we watch. We have false teachers pushing destructive agendas to corrupt our children. And what are these agendas?"

"Tell it, Pastor," Miss Anniebelle yells out.

"Make it plain, preacher," Deacon follows, his cold eyes boring into me and Jojo like a drill.

"I'm gonna tell it, church. The agenda is lasciviousness, adultery, debauchery, worshipping the body rather than the Creator. The media has fixed it so you can't even name God's name on TV. Remember the days when certain words were edited out of TV programs due to censorship? Well, those days are over. I turn on my TV, even to the local broadcasting channels, and I hear the very words that shouldn't be uttered. Remember the days when certain images were left unseen. Well, now we have sexual situations that our children are witnessing!"

"That's right," Ms. Gertrude gushes.

"Oh yes, there is an agenda! They are even trying to refute the law of God and do away with the family unit by promoting same sex marriage!"

I knew it! His hypocritical ass! I see red. In the midst of the rage, memories of him pulling his long, dirty dick out for me to suck began to lash at me. My face feels like a five-alarm fire and my hands are sweaty. My heart is racing, but not out of fear... but of anger. I reach for my keys to unscrew my metal pill fob and retrieve a small pill. I pop it in my mouth and pray for the effects to kick in quickly. From the corner of my eye, I see Jojo looking at me with saddened concern.

"Women sleeping with women. Men sleeping with men. Even marrying each other! Disgusting acts that violate the laws of God and of nature. Now I know we have people yet among us today who hold with those sick ideas. But I'm here to tell you that the Bible is right, and you are living your life in sin! You have a stench that offends the very nostrils of God. Repent, sinners! Fall down to your knees and pray hard to God for forgiveness!"

PRAY HARDER! PRAY HARDER! Those words force me into memories of my childhood trauma, stemming from him and Mama trying to "pray the gay away". From the muttering heard among my family and friends, I wasn't the only one bothered.

"Oh no, this fool didn't!" I hear Corey reply derisively. I turn to see pure ire on Peep's face as he stands and prepares to read the pastor the riot act.

"Now, you wait just a minute, you self-righteous hypocrite!" Peep yells out. He cannot finish. Jimmy admonishes him to sit down between clenched teeth, pulling him down to his seat and drawing self-satisfied looks from the parishioners.

"Jimmy, please. Go 'head and turn Peep loose! You heard what this two-faced closet case said!" Corey hisses fiercely.

"Yes!" Jimmy whispers back, agitated. "But not everything deserves a response. We are not here to cut the fool in this woman's funeral. Please ya'll, out of respect for the family, let's just get through this and then get the hell outta here."

Suddenly, I feel a movement in my legs and my vision adjusts as I find myself in standing position. Amid the silence, I turn and walk up the aisle to the double exit doors.

"Wait up, Lionel," I hear Jojo say. I turn around and I watch as one by one, all my family and my friends stand up and stride down the aisle to join me. I feel a head-spinning sensation of love. Love I knew would last for always. As we turn to exit the church, I hear the murmurs of the congregation uttering the words:

"Shameful!"

"What a disgrace!"

"Such disrespect in the Lord's house!"

I then hear the pastor say, "It's alright. You know that the Bible says that there will come a day when they will not endure sound doctrine. But the Bible is a two-edged sword, and if they take offense to what I've said, they take offense with God Himself."

Crimson with rage, A.D.'s voice bellows out loud and clear as he makes his way up to the base of the pulpit, "Yuh know wut, Rev'n? It's not God or de Bible we got beef wit. It's stupi' biggits like you an' ova haf de people settin' in dis chu'ch!" Scattered phrases echo throughout the sanctuary, sounding angry and disturbed.

A.D. went on, his strong voice overpowering that of the people, stunning them into silence, "Now, I dunno 'bout yo' God, but my God's a god uh luv, and His luv ain't got no respect of peeps! You oughta think about dat befo' yuh cherry pick shit in de Bible to beat people up an' send'em ta hell, den turn 'round an' call a trick tuh come give yuh some ass in de chu'ch basement."

The church takes a collective gasp. All gazes are directed at the pastor. There is absolute silence. I step forward to join A.D. and I see tears pouring down his face. I touch him on his shoulder.

"A.D., let's go."

A.D. looks around the church. At length, he says, "I don' mean tuh disrespec' anybody up in 'ere. An' I'm sorry fuh muh choice uh words. But rememba' dis'. If gay people cain' come tuh church fuh healin' from a world dat is already beatin' 'em down… If dey cain' sit in 'ere and feel luv in whatcha preach… If dey are picked on an' made tuh leave fuh bein' who dey are, den I'm sorry. But I cain' call dis de house uh God."

The tension is thick in the church. A pin could drop in the choir stand and you'd be able to hear it in the back pew. I look at my brother as he wipes his tears with the back of his hand. Suddenly, I see Ms. Frazier gather her things and silently push her walker towards my brother, then take his hand. Her croaky, emotional voice says comfortingly, "Baby, I want to tell you somethin'. The house of God ain't just in a building. It starts in the hearts of those who are open enough to be taught how to love people without being messy and mean. Look around this church. All the hateful faces you see are masks of those who hurt every day. They are just wounded people, honey. They are speaking from their own prejudice, not from God or the Bible. Even the pastor is wounded, and they didn't start out that way. They became that way. When people like that bump into you, remember that and show them the love they won't show you." She pulls A.D. down to her, plants a huge kiss on his forehead, and chucks him under his chin, causing a child-like smile to pass his face. She then reaches in her purse and pulls out a bag of candy. "Here you go, baby," she comforts, placing it in my hands. She pulls me down to her and gives me a big hug and kiss. After giving the same gesture to Jojo, she pushes her walker laboriously down the aisle. My friends and family part to make a path for her as she exits the church.

For a minute, we just stand there. Then, A.D. and I pay our final respects to Mama and we turn to follow Ms. Frazier and our friends out of the church. When we step onto the parking lot, memories begin to replay in my mind. The Christmas holidays. The family vacations. The dinners spent with Mama when she was in her decent moods. These memories overwhelm me and as they do, something in me breaks as I feel uncontrollable sobs and cries racking my body. I collapse on the way to the limo, with Jojo, my family, and my friends supporting me. I cry in the normal loss a son feels when he has lost his mother. But I mourn greatly thinking about the type of mother she could have been, as well as the rancorous woman that life had evidently turned her into.

A whole life lived and gone… with a lesson learned too late.

Chapter Six
CAGED BIRDS

Spring is finally here. The flowers are blooming riotously, and emerald green grass is springing up from the soil. Normally, I would enjoy all this new life because I am a bonafide nature boy and, as I've said, spring is my favorite season. But this spring brings a heavy heart and a wounded soul. It's almost as if wintery cold is withering the spring flowers in my heart. It has been four weeks since we buried Mama, and questions swirl chaotically in my brain. I'm still filled with anger at Mama and it's not only because of life with her. I'm now additionally angry because she left us without any closure. I find that I have two old friends to turn to on times like this, my trusty vodka and scotch. And since the funeral, I have found a new friend: Good old honey whiskey. I still take the Alprolozine, but I only take them when I know I need them, and I am certain that I am not going to be drinking.

After work, I decided to drive to Lake Montebello. I needed the time to stroll and meditate. I like Lake Montebello because it is only visited by joggers, lovers of any age, and others who need to get away from the hustle and bustle of Baltimore City. The Inner Harbor is cool, but it's full of people and conversation. This place is serene and quiet, especially during sunrise and sunset. This evening, the west setting sun paints the heavens a deep sky-blue color, with white clouds outlined in gray, yellow, and darkened amber.

As I promenade, I ponder the funeral we had for Mama. It was exhausting on various levels. We can start with the planning. We thought we would have to pool our money together to pay for it because we weren't sure if Mama had burial insurance. We had to consider all the expenses of the service like the casket, the flowers, the burial site, the musician (who couldn't play worth a damn), the limousines, and the list went on. Fortunately, at the ninth hour, a neighbor told us that she remembered going with Mama to Stewart's Funeral Home to plan her services. We went there and the mortuary officials informed us that she had full coverage, so everything was taken care of.

Shortly after the funeral, we met with the attorney to witness the reading of the will. My plan was to head back to Baltimore after the services. Why stick around for the reading of a will that she undoubtedly disinherited me from? But I stayed because my siblings insisted. Rhonda, who didn't even think to come to her own mother's funeral, conveniently got a pass from Windsor Correctional to show up to the will reading wearing all black and crying her trademark crocodile tears. Mother's wealth was quite generous, and, to my shock, she didn't cut me out like I thought she would. She had over three hundred thousand dollars in the bank, four hundred thousand in Daddy's pension, and her life insurance company paid out an additional two hundred and fifty grand. We took some of that money and paid off the hospital bills that the health insurance didn't cover. The rest of the money was split between the six of us. Another surprise was that she left us not only the family home, but also Grandma's house which was willed to her. We were going to discuss the houses while in the lawyer's office, but upon reflection agreed that time to regroup was necessary. After all, the houses weren't going anywhere.

My mind wonders what Mama would have been like if she was the flip side of the woman she became. Would it have made a difference if she was the type of mother that we see on reruns of *The Cosby Show*, *Good Times*, or even *What's Happening?* The mother in the third sitcom would beat your ass until you had to get an inflatable cushion to sit down, but Mabel loved her children no matter how hairbrained Roger's schemes were or how smart Dee's mouth got. Another barrage of questions confronts me. Would she have been accepting of me and my life? Would there have been hugs and kisses, instead of kicks and bruises? Would Dad still be alive? Then my brain screamed out, with such a terrifying force that made me shudder, *Yes! That would have made a big fucking difference!*

I believe that whatever shit Mama went through as a child ate at her until it consumed her insides and killed her. Modern science will give you their theoretical logic of how cancer develops in a person. But I believe their logic is still only a hypothesis. I have my own theories and one of them is that if you hold on to things long enough, they will eventually manifest into inner born illnesses that corrode and destroy a person from the inside out. And the illnesses do not just target the spiteful. They also sprint toward those burdened with guilt, grief, anxiety, and depression.

A paralyzing thought causes me to halt my pace along the lake's trail. Three of those items are attached to me. Plus, I'm afraid that Mama might've passed that debilitating anger onto me. That makes four. You see, this is what Corey, Peep, and Jojo don't realize when I tell them how important it is to have the particular medication I have; to put to rest at least the depression, anxiety, and hopefully the anger so that I won't meet that same fate of cancer. But realistically speaking, even medication to lull the agents of ire do not prevent the certainty of cancer. My God in Heaven! That was a thought to grip my mind severely. Is it my destiny to develop cancer as well? Is it hereditary? Would I have to go through operation after operation, then be hooked to a machine and fed chemotherapy that promises to cure me but leaves a ghostly pallor on my face?

Just then, I catch sight of a robin gliding in the sky. It alights onto the ground and skips its body to face my direction. With its head cocked to the side, it seems to look at me with peculiar curiosity. For a brief second, it just sits there. Then, suddenly, it opens its beak and chirps sweetly to me, as if to convey a message, then flies off.

Though I'm not sure why, the sight of that robin makes me smile. It makes my heart light. There is a long-standing fact that robins are fearful of humans. To get one to interact with mankind is almost like trying to catch a star. Humans have always indulged in the appalling practice of trapping fowl. Birds hate being restricted to the cage because they cannot sing as freely. They sing, but I seem to hear the most mournful tunes that can make some of the most brutal murderers weep stinging tears of sympathy.

William Blake, one of my favorite poets third to Maya Angelou and Edgar Allan Poe, summed it up well when he wrote, *A robin redbreast in a cage puts all Heaven in a rage.* I believe it parallels with the title of Maya Angelou's first book. I would have varied Blake's quote slightly because, in my mind, ALL caged birds possess the innate ability to make heaven rage. They sing a song that only the angels can grant, a song begging to be freed from their bonds. I exhale as I look at my own life as well as the life of others. In some ways, all of us are like caged birds bound by grief, despair, angst, past trauma, and hatred. There are many days when I feel so caged that I can't breathe, think, or function. My childhood abuse was my cage, but did I ever sing?

I jerk my mind from the thoughts of gloom and doom to focus on the song of the robin. Maybe its presence was to tell me that I'm thinking too much. Garrett told me that I tended to overanalyze things. I believe we all do at any rate, so I'm in good company.

A sweet, melodic voice speaks my name, interrupting my thoughts. I turn to see Jojo striding toward me with a grin. He is wearing a white buttoned short sleeved shirt with an open collar, revealing the gleaming thin gold chain I gave him for Christmas. It lies on beautifully moistened dark skin with a small view of his appetizing chest. His legs are clad in khakis that revealed the definition in his heavy thighs and calves. His hands, attached to thick chocolate forearms, reach out to me and pull me into warm embrace as I respond to his greeting. As I inhale, I catch his naturally clean scent mixed with his favorite scented oil, Patchouli. It makes me hold him closer... and longer.

Releasing him, I ask, "What are you doing here?"

"I had a feeling you would be here," Jojo replies, looking towards the multicolored horizon that paints his face a deep amber hue.

"I swear. Sometimes, I think you may be clairvoyant." I laugh out, prompting him to smile brightly.

"No, not clairvoyant. I just feel vibrations. I can't read minds."

"Sometimes, I think you do. You just don't realize it."

Jojo takes a step back and thinks it over. He then says thoughtfully, "Mmm... no, I really can't. I have a strong connection to you, Corey, and Peep. But I guess I feel the strongest connection to you because we've known each other so long; long enough for you to believe that I can read YOUR mind."

"I guess you're right," I say as I resume my stroll, with Jojo walking beside me.

"Besides, with Lynetta's death still being fresh for you, I figured that maybe you'd want to be around a quiet waterhole somewhere. I know how you like being around water."

"How insightful of you, Mr. Thompson."

"Why thank you, Mr. Davis."

A few minutes go by. Then Jojo says, "Anything you want to talk about?"

I exhale and think for a few seconds. Then I say, glancing at him, "I'm just thinking about Mama and how things were at the funeral."

Jojo rolls his eyes toward the sky, "Oh God, can you believe that shit?"

"Yes, I can. And it shouldn't surprise you at all. You knew what we had to put up with in that church. I'm surprised that we aren't *all* seeking professional help after the shit us kids heard."

"Especially from the pastor."

My anger flares up, remembering the hateful sermons he preached. "That hypocrite Lawson shouldn't be pastoring at anybody's church. Saint Jude went down ever since Dr. Grissom quit."

"We both know that, but as long as that church has people who think like Lawson, it will continue to go down."

"The church would be in a much better position if Dr. Grissom would have stayed. Mama and those bigots in the church ran him off and forced almost all the good people to go with him," I say.

"Hmmm... Why are you so worried about the church? When we were kids, you hated going even when Grissom was there."

I stop walking. "I hated going because Mama always dragged us out of bed and made us go. But when we got to the church, I enjoyed the singing and got a lot from the things Grissom said."

"But you do know he preached on gays too."

"Yeah, but at least when Grissom did it, you felt that he was coming from a place of compassion, which pissed Mama and her cronies off. Besides, I've never heard him say that gays were going to hell. He just quoted that God made male and female and said that he wouldn't wish being gay on anybody because of the hard life he saw us lead. But he always said that EVERYBODY had a welcome place in God's house, especially those who are seeking to believe."

Jojo thinks a minute. "Ya know, philosopher that I am, I've often wondered where the Creator got the female image from."

"What do you mean?"

"I mean we have been taught in church and from the Bible that we were created in God's own image. Would it be too much to assume that God saw the model and decided at the last minute to invent breasts and a vagina? Did God have both organs?"

I laugh. "I never thought of it like that."

Jojo chuckles with me. "I thought that might get a laugh out of you. You know, I believe that God holds a never-ending scale of what is considered beautiful from a celestial point of view, whether oddly shaped or ideally pleasing, man or woman, masculine or feminine. And in Heaven's eyes, all of us walking on this earth fit in that scale of beauty. The only rankings come in the affairs of the heart and actions of the hands."

"What do you mean?"

"Well, someone can be drop-dead gorgeous, but have fucked up values and do hateful shit. On the other hand, we can have somebody that the world sees as uglier than a mud swamp, but their hearts and motives are pure, and it shows in everything they do, you feel me?"

I look out at the lake, thinking about Jojo's words. "Hmmm... Good point. But you know, I wonder why we always pigeon-hole God with being a male."

Jojo laughs. "Oh, that's an easy answer. Men were the ones who wrote the Bible and women were way down on the totem pole in those days. Men were the inventors, the innovators, the farmers, and the shepherds. So, since the Creator was called these things in different eras of history, they went with the idea that God was male."

"Makes sense."

"Besides, the Creator is not just male or just female, but a spirit that knows about and lives in everything we connect with through the senses we were given."

"If God is a spirit that knows and lives in everything, why did that spirit stick me with Mother while knowing how it would be?"

Jojo places his hands lovingly on my chest and looks at me with a concerned expression on his face. "That's something you are going to have to find your peace with. But baby, you have to let go of this bitterness against Lynetta and forgive her for what she did to you. Because right now... it's pulling you down."

I suddenly exclaim, "Why does everybody keep saying I'm bitter? I'm not bitter! I'm just angry because I don't understand how this all-knowing, all-powerful God can allow homophobic hypocrites like her and those Lawson ass kissers at Saint Jude to continue hurting people with their double standards and vicious cuts against us."

"Lionel, calm down."

I say in frustration, "I'm sorry. But it just pisses me off that we have people like that."

"But like Peep alluded to when Corey was attacked, and it took a while for me to get the message, there will always be people like that when there is hatred still in the world. And if you let it, their hatred will eat at you."

"I know that."

"Then, why this anger?"

"I don't know. There are times when I just feel angry. Angry at Mama. Angry at life. Angry at you guys."

Jojo looks at me, surprised. "Why are you angry at us?"

The lapping of the water is the only sound we hear for an uncomfortable

The Cost

time. Afterwards, I ask, "Are you sure you want to know?"

"Please tell me."

"Because ya'll keep harping on the medication I take as well as my choice of doctors."

Jojo rolls his eyes and says, "Lionel, the only reason why we harp on it is because we happen to see a pattern developing that you can't right now." He grabs my hand and holds it. "Baby, you are not the same person you were before you started seeing Dr. Williams."

I turn away from Jojo slowly, saying, "I don't want to talk about this."

Jojo retorts in irritation, "'I don't want to talk about this.' Do you even hear yourself? It's like it's your mantra. You always say that whenever someone is trying to pull your coattail on something that forces you to look in your mirror. And it's getting old. Besides, you are the one who brought it up. I'm just answering to what you said."

I can't answer. We resume walking. After a few minutes, Jojo says tentatively, "Lionel, can I ask you a question?"

I look at him sideways. "What is it?"

After a minute of thought, Jojo says, "Please don't be mad, but did you research the pros and cons of that medicine before you started taking it?"

Lying, I exclaim hotly, "Of course I did."

"So, you know the side effects?"

"Yes!"

"You know about the mood swings, the headaches, the face swelling, the loss of appetite… and I have sources that tell me they've been known to heighten dependence as well as offer little to no combat against depression. They may even escalate the depression."

"Jojo," I state in a sour tone. "I am fine. I got this. Can we please move from this subject?"

Jojo replies bluntly with a resolute expression, "Yes, but after I say what I gotta say. I will not compete with pills to try to retain your attention. I cannot spend our partnership worrying about something that threatens to do you in. To give you the straight dope, I will call off this engagement in a hot Alabama minute before I get stuck in a marriage where those pills are ruling you, and you are stuck in a loop you can't get out of. Do you see where I'm going with this? I will remain your friend, but while you are in this state, marriage is out of the question." Jojo turns to walk back to his car. I grab his hand.

"Jojo, don't go off like this. I'm sorry."

Jojo looks at me sadly, "I mean it, Lionel. When you take these pills, you get into these awful mood swings, and those mood swings are capable of moving to physical violence. I'm being honest with you. We are not in a good place right now. We've been fighting a lot lately, and the look that comes across your face when you get pissed worries me. It almost reminds me of… Mike."

An electric shudder jolts me. Mike was Ms. Thompson's ex-boyfriend who beat her and Jojo, then raped Jojo when he was nine. *May God kill me before I end up being like that man!* I think about this carefully. I need the meds, but not as much as I need Jojo and his need to feel safe around me. I nod in assent and say, "Ok, I'll try to lay light on the pills. But how do I deal with my mental?"

"Go back to Dr. Banneker… or go to this Dr. Williams and tell him you need something else. But you gotta stop taking them. This is not to please your family, Corey, Peep, or me. This is to look out for you," Jojo says gently, pointing at my chest

I take Jojo's hands in mine. "Jojo, the last thing I would want to do is hurt you. You mean the world to me. This is hard for me, and I'm trying to find my way through all this."

Jojo hugs me and I hear his muffled voice, "Lionel, I understand how hard things have been on you lately. But your being in this deep dark place is hurting all of us."

I breathe in silence for a moment, then I pull back and say, "I'm sorry, Jojo. I don't know how I can get off these pills, but I will try. I want to make this work. I love you and I don't want you to go."

Jojo kisses me, then says, "I know."

We just stand there staring at each other, our hands clasped. Then we walk back to our cars.

"So, have you eaten?" Jojo asks.

"Not yet."

"Come on over to my place. I'll cook you something."

"We're not even married yet, and you're talking about cooking for your man."

"Just letting you know what you are in for, baby. I'm gonna spoil your ass rotten!"

*****

This Saturday evening finds me in my dining room playing UNO with Garrett and my two brothers. Dean is in Baltimore for the weekend and he is staying with me. We, the Davis brothers, try to do something every other weekend so we can update each other on our busy lives. It's usually A.D., Dean, and me but, every now and then, Roland tries to make it up here to join the fun. I believe this is good. I've often spent time with just The Fellas. But with three of us living so close to each other now, we are working on our communication as brothers.

"Draw two, A.D.!" I yell out, throwing a yellow draw two down.

"O' hell nah! I ain't drawin' shit! Draw fo', Dean!" A.D. throws down a red draw.

"Now A.D., you know you can't stack when we are playing straight UNO," Dean chides.

"Why not? Dat's wat makes it fun, dude! Besides, we always play wit' house rules. Da ol' way ain't no fun!" A.D. bellows.

"Why have official rules if we are not going to follow them?"

"You jes' don' wanna eat 'dem damn cards! Tell de troof."

"Whatever," Dean says, throwing another yellow draw down. "Draw six, Garrett!"

"Unh-UNH! Not the kid! Draw eight, Lion!" He throws a green one.

I look in my hand. No more draw twos! BUT... I do have a draw four in my hand. Against the house rules, I play it. Maybe I could slide through! "Draw twelve, A.D.!"

"Nah! You know good n' damn well you ain't s'pose tuh put no draw fo' on a draw two. Eat duh cards, Li'nel!"

"Shit, man! That's a crappy rule!"

"Duh cards, dude!" A.D. barks, laughing and pointing at the stack.

"Forget ya'll, man," I say, as I draw eight cards. "I'm gonna get you for that, Garrett."

"You started it!" Garrett retorts, chuckling.

We play a few more hands. Afterwards, I decide to bring up my conversation with my intended.

"So, listen up ya'll. I had a conversation with Jojo."

"Ah, lovebird convos. This should be interesting," Garrett says.

"Well, it sure as hell wasn't hearts and roses. Jojo brought up some things that have me a bit on edge."

"Dis ain't got nuttin' tuh do wit' ya'll callin' quits on duh hitchin', I hope," A.D. jokes. "I a'ready got duh cruise half payed fuh."

"And I'm seventy-five percent paid," Garrett quips.

A look on my face betrays my feelings. Dean sees this and says, "What's going on?"

A.D. and Garrett join Dean in his gaze at me. Almost simultaneously, we put the cards face down. I look at the paperweights my Dad left me. For some reason, they encourage me to speak. "He told me that he might call off the engagement because of the medicine I've been taking. He says he doesn't want to compete with them and that when I get mad, I remind him of his mother's boyfriend, Mike."

Total silence bombards the table. A.D. looks down at his nails. Dean has his lips twisted in a brooding way. Garrett just looks concerned. *Uh oh, Not good at all.* "Why are ya'll looking at me like that?" I press.

Still silence. "Don't tell me ya'll agree with Jojo."

Dean says, measuring his words like jewels, "Lionel, do you remember what Mama used to say when she asked us about something rotten we did."

A.D. breaks in, laughing, "An' it ran us crazy win she knew we was lyin'."

I know what she said but I try to sidestep it. "Who cares what she said?"

"Lionel," Dean says. "Mama said that our faces betray everything our mouths deny."

"So, what are you saying?"

"Wut're our faces betrayin' tuh yuh now?"

I look at all of their faces and a feeling of discontent covers me. And I hate it! They're taking Jojo's side!

"I can't believe this shit. Not ya'll too," I exhaust.

"What do you mean, 'Not ya'll too?'" Dean asks.

"First, The Fellas tell me that I'm slipping… and now you."

"Well, dat oughta tell yuh somethin'. How many mo' times yuh gotta hea' it befo' yuh listen?"

I push my cards to the middle of the table and fold my arms.

"Lionel, listen," Dean begins. "I didn't want to mention it, but I watched you when we were planning the funeral and at the church. You couldn't stop yourself from popping a pill in your mouth."

"And there are times that I saw you do it on Thanksgiving," Garrett says almost inaudibly.

I jump up. Slamming my hands on the table and glaring at all three in turn, I hiss, "Well, if ya'll were that concerned about me, why didn't you say something then? *'Brothers?' 'Friend'*?" Oooh! I felt venom when I spoke that last word and the venom now covers Garrett's rich ebony face as he looks at me in shock. He's never seen me like this.

"Hol' on now, lil' bruh," A.D. jumps up in like fashion, staring me down. "Don' turn dis aroun' on us. Rememba' dat night at Thanksgivin', I was tryin' tuh talk tuh yuh den. Garrett tol' me 'e saw yuh poppin' em dat night. He didn' know how tuh talk tuh yuh cause he didn' know yuh dat well yet. I said I'd say somethin', but I only got as far as yuh bein' pissed all duh time befo' yuh started shuttin' out wut I had tuh say!"

Dean speaks up quietly, "Lionel, you do have a bad habit of cutting people's hands off when they reach out, and that's the reason I didn't say anything."

I turn to my fireplace. Garrett comes up behind me and puts his hand on my shoulder. "Lionel, I'm sorry."

"Whatcha apologizing' tuh 'im fuh? YOU ain't dun nuthin," I hear A.D.'s voice ring out.

"A.D., this isn't helping," Dean says.

"An' bein' quiet while he keep doin' dis fuckery ain't helpin' neitha. Lionel's gotta quit dis shit. I'm jes' sorry I didn' say it dat night!"

I turn around, flaring, "You see, this is the part of Mama you got that I hate! You both write tickets on other people's lives, and you don't know jack shit about the things bothering them. You always think you are right about every goddamned thing, to the point where you think you can tell everybody else what to do. Like you're the father and we're the kids."

"An' YOU got a part a Mama dat I ain't too crazy 'bout eitha'. Makin' e'erbody else pay fuh yo' bullshit! An' if I *wuz* Daddy, yo' ass wood git smacked in ten fuckin' places at one time!" A.D. bellows.

"I think ya'll need to go."

Silence. Then A.D. says, grabbing his jean jacket, "Fine, I'm out. Cage yuhself up. Keep takin' dem damn pills. Win e'erthang said an' done, you go'n hurt a lot of folk, but not more'n you hurt yo' own fuckin' self." With that, he slams out of the door, leaving all three of us to gaze blankly at each other.

Dean breaks the silence by uttering firmly as he moves to the staircase, "I'm… gonna cut this weekend short. I've got a lot of work to catch up on before Monday anyway."

"You want me to run you to Penn Station?" Garrett asks.

"Yes, please. Thank you,"

I start to feel that old guilt surging in my stomach. "Dean, you don't have to go."

"Yes, I do. Because if I don't, I'll say something that we will both be sorry for. I'm going up to get my stuff," he says, before climbing the steps.

Garrett just stares at me. I wince under his scrutiny. "Why are you looking at me like that?"

Garrett replies sadly, "I'm wondering what going on with you. This is not like you at all."

I don't say anything. I can't. Not even when Dean comes down with his overnight bag and says to me, "Lionel, do yourself and everyone who loves you a favor. Get some help. Resolve your issues. Leaving them to fester will only make things worse."

Garrett and Dean stroll out of my door and I sink into the chair I had abandoned. I stare vacantly at the wall and finally a word issues from between clenched teeth and tight jaws.

"FUCK."

Chapter Seven
TROUBLE

It is Tuesday evening, two weeks before Corey is scheduled to leave for the tour with Darrell Alston. It was my idea to do a game night before he leaves, so Jojo and I are at my house preparing for a night of cards and conversation with Corey, Garrett, and Eunetta. Garrett has a big surprise to reveal to us all. I wonder why he insisted for Eunetta to come. It would usually be Corey, Peep, Garrett, Jojo, Jimmy, and me. Both Jimmy and Peep had to work.

I get the feeling that Garrett is about to ask Corey to marry him. He hinted at it when I called to apologize for this past Saturday. But I cannot pinpoint why Eunetta's presence tonight of all nights is bothersome to me. Maybe it's because Mother's Day is coming up. *Ok, I'm starting to feel incredibly jumpy. My stomach is tied up in knots. I need a pill.* But Jojo is standing right next to me and I remember the promise I made. Of course, promises are hard to keep. I took one this morning while I was cooking my breakfast. My eyes slink toward the utility drawer where I had placed the bottle of twenty-five milligram pills before going to work. *Maybe I could pass it off as Tylenol.* I think to myself. After meditating, I dismiss the idea. *No. Because after the medicine has me sailing, Jojo will know I took it.*

Well, if I can't take a pill, I can tie one on. Jittery, I hurriedly go into my cabinet for my shot glass and a bottle of Jack Daniels. After pouring a shot, I knock it back and wait for my stomach to register the effects. I readily pour another shot and prepare to drink it. But I hesitate because, in my peripheral vision, I sense that Jojo is watching me while he is prepping the snacks. "Lionel..." Jojo starts. I turn to him and I see his brown eyes misting over. His knitted brows are creased with worry.

"Yeah?"

"Are you alright?"

"Yeah. Why are you asking me that for?"

"Maybe because of the shot you just drank... and the one you were about to drink."

"Look, you already asked that I give up the pills. Let me have the whiskey at least. I'm trying to settle my nerves."

Jojo gently takes the shot glass from my fingers. After placing it on the counter, he grasps my hands and holds them for a minute. Looking into my eyes, he tells me carefully. "Lionel, I realize that you have been going through a lot lately with the job, your mother passing, and your own depression. But I believe you are strong enough to make it without a deceptive crutch. And right now, you are trading in one for another."

I pull my hands back roughly. "Jojo, you are a fine one to talk. Are you going to stand there and tell me that *you* don't knock back a few shots?"

Jojo's face appears plum colored as he makes apparent effort to keep his demeanor calm. He says with great control, "Yes, I do drink. But I try not to do it excessively. And that is what you are doing. Hats off to you for ditching the pills, but this is the next thing to go. Lionel, you used to drink responsibly, but, between that medicine and that whiskey, your filter seems to have vanished along with your good common sense."

The doorbell rings, saving me from a response. "I'll get it," Jojo offers dryly. He strides out of the kitchen. I mull over what Jojo just said. *I don't have a problem. I don't drink any more than any of the other fellas.* I look at the full shot glass, knock it back, and let out a loud, comfortable belch.

"Hey baby cakes! What's shaking?" I hear Eunetta greet Jojo. He laughs and greets her back. I stride out to the living area to see Eunetta and Garrett hugging Jojo. Eunetta, beaming an exuberant grin, has a covered pie plate in her hand and Garrett is holding four of them. He spots me and smiles warmly, but for some reason, the smile fades and deep concern furrows his brow. Despite this, he gives me a huge hug. Then, as we pull apart, he searches my face and says, "How are you holding up? Are you alright?"

Nervously, I laugh, saying, "I don't know why everybody has to keep asking me that? I am fine." Eunetta turns and looks at me. I am hearing my own voice slur as the room becomes hazy.

"Baby, you don't look fine. You look like you are as unsteady as a sailor on payday." She comes over to me and puts her hand on my forehead. "You don't feel feverish."

"Ms. E, I'm alright." My breath hits Ms. Eunetta's face and she recoils.

"Whew, baby! Anchors aweigh!" She guides me to my chair. "You just set yourself right there. Mama's gonna brew you some coffee."

"I'm fine, Ms. E."

"Hush ya mouth, now. I know this is yo house but my 'Mama sense' done kicked in. Garrett, come into this kitchen with me and help me cut these pies while I brew the Joe."

"Ms. Eunetta, I…"

"I said hush, now. Come on, Garrett."

Even in my tipsy state, I know better than to argue with a tone like that.

As I watch her and Garrett trek into the kitchen and close the door, I grumble. "I don't know why everybody's tripping. I just had two shots of whiskey."

"It's called caring, but you are too wrapped up in your own shit to see it," Jojo says with a hard edge in his voice. I look at him and I see an expression of rare irritation and sorrow in his face.

The doorbell rings again. I unsteadily attempt to rise but Jojo stops me, telling me to stay seated. He strides to the door and opens it. In walks Corey with a plastic bag of snacks. *OK, put a lid on it. I don't need him adding to the trio of worriers.* He hugs Jojo. "Hey, my loves. Has my baby and his mama got here?"

"They are in the kitchen." Jojo says in a harried tone.

"What's wrong with you?" Corey says. Jojo is silent as Corey picks up on the source of Jojo's trouble. He looks at me as a look of understanding crosses his face. Mercifully, he makes a gesture stating, *I get it…but we WILL discuss this later.* That's what I love about Corey. He won't make a big deal out of what's going on… right now.

"I brought over some Bar-B-Q Chips," Corey says as he holds up the bag. That comment causes both Jojo and I to laugh. Just what we need to liven the moment.

"You and these damn chips," Jojo says, still laughing. "You lucky Peep ain't here."

"Why, am I s'pose to be worried? I ain't scared a Peep!" He laughs good-naturedly. "Speaking of him, where is he?"

"He and Jimmy had to work." Jojo says. A few minutes later, both Eunetta and Garrett come out. Garrett goes right to Corey and gives him a luscious kiss. Eunetta comes to me and puts the piping hot cup of coffee to my lips. "Here, sip this for Mama."

I want to protest, but as loving as Ms. Eunetta is, I can tell that she has a little of *LY*netta in her. She doesn't play. After blowing on the coffee, I sip it. It is delicious!

"Mmmmm… That's good, Ms. E.!"

"See? I knew you'd like it. And Mama's got a nice piece of blueberry pie for you... complete with vanilla ice cream."

Blueberry pie... Blueberry Pie... Oh My God! The Diarrhea Pie! I look at her suspiciously. "What are you looking at me like that for?" She looks at Garrett. "You told him, didn't you?"

"About you and the neighbor that dumped Sloppy Joe sauce down your dress, and you got her back with the blueberry Ex-Lax pie? Yeah."

"Why did you have to tell him that?" she admonishes, trying to suppress a laugh.

"Ask your daughter why she called me 'Blueberry' in front of him," Garrett laughs out, pointing at me with wide eyes. "She knew he was gonna ask, and he did. So, I told him."

Eunetta chuckles and turns to me. "Well baby, in this pie, I mixed the Ex-Lax in real nice." She bends down and says in jest, "Come on now. Don't worry. You won't shit as much as he did when he ate it."

"Ma!"

Corey and Jojo burst out laughing. "Baby, you didn't even tell me that?"

"I was trying to mask it so I wouldn't have to."

"Uh... I don't think I want any pie. Thanks, though."

"Don't worry, it's safe," Garrett assures. "I ate some last night and I survived it."

"You said that even regular blueberry pies made you sick now."

"Mama tricked me into eating one. This is NOT the doodoo pie."

"Chile, I was just kidding before. There ain't nothin' in this one but sugar, blueberries, butter, cornstarch, and a little bit of salt. I only made the Ex-Lax Pie that one time. Come on. Try it. I promise you. You go'n like it," she persuades.

Haltingly, I comply. *Mmmmm! It is good as FUCK! It makes me want to dig my own mother up from the grave and slap her silly!*

"Damn!" I let out, catching myself. "Oops, I'm sorry. But that pie is scrumptious!"

"I told you. And it's even better with coffee."

"Ms E., did you bring anymore?" Corey asks.

"What do you think those foil covered-plates are? Get on in that kitchen and help yourself. I don't serve grown ass menfolk. I just brought him some because he's special." She turns to me and gives me a sly wink.

*****

The coffee and blueberry pie lessened my slight drunkenness. I'm still buzzed, but at more ease. This is the first time since Irene Hartfield that I spent time with an older lady who obviously has a high comfort level and boundless love for us gay folk. I remember one day when I asked her why, and she said this, "Chile, I was a fag-hag since I was in my dad's bag!" Eunetta's playful sense of humor was like a gust of flowers and summer breezes. I feel a plethora of contrasting emotions. Initially, I feel happy to be in her company and listen to uproarious anecdotes of Rachel and Garrett. I think to myself. *Her coming was a good idea, after all. This lady is a pistol!* But then as the night progresses, I feel sadness from seeing the interaction between Garrett and Eunetta. *This is the type of relationship I longed to have with Mama, but time and her personal demons robbed me of that need.* Slowly, I feel the sadness turn to jealousy, and then segue into disappointment and rage. *I need a pill. I need a drink. I need this feeling to leave me alone. But no! Not now! I just need to hold on until they leave, then I can "take care" of this feeling… Right now, I can smile. Yes. That's it. Smile. Ask the one doling out the cards to deal me into the game. I have to keep it together.*

"Ms. E, this pie is delicious." Jojo says, as we are playing cards.

"Thank you, sugah-baby!" Eunetta beams.

"And that coffee was just as good. What kind is it?" Corey asks.

"My great-great grandmama's Cinnamon Pumpkin Crème Coffee."

"How do you prepare it?" Jojo asks.

"If I told you, I'd have to kill you. It's an old family recipe."

"Seems kinda easy to figure it out: coffee, cinnamon, milk, allspice, and sugar with whipped cream," Garrett says.

Eunetta muses quietly. Then she says, "Some of it. Do you know what the most important ingredient is, Mr. Know It All?"

"Uh…"

"Exactly! Sometimes you're too smart for your own good! Mama always got one up on you. Remember that! Ha-HA!" Eunetta exclaims, laughing. Garrett keeps pressing her to give up the 411 on the secret ingredient. But she won't give an inch, so he gives up. After five minutes of conversation, she says, "So, what is this news ya'll gotta tell me? And it best be good! I'm missing my game shows."

Garrett clears his throat. He turns to gaze at Corey, with love in his eyes. Clasping his hand, he says, "Well Mama, as you and The Fellas know, Corey and I have been friends for years, ever since we were seven years old. Slowly, it grew into romance." He stops there. It is obvious that he is revisiting the past with Corey in that orphanage because tears stream down his face. Corey clasps Garrett's large hand and squeezes, showing him that he understands. Garrett swallows hard and continues. "I won't go into the gory details of what went on at the orphanage. But I will say that our stay there ended when loving families adopted us both. I had to move with the family to North Carolina, then Texas, because Dad was in the Air Force. We lost touch, but a couple of years ago, we found each other again… and the passion never left. My love grew stronger for Corey every passing day… and now it is too enormous to ignore."

He then stands Corey to his feet. Taking a ring box from his pocket, he kneels in front of Corey. He looks into his eyes and says, "You have always been first class to me. I intend to love you in a first-class way." He opens the box to reveal a twenty-four-carat diamond set in a gleaming gold ring. Corey's eyes double and he gasps in shock. Garrett takes the ring from the box and puts it on Corey's finger.

"Cordell James Kennedy… my Simon… my sweet love… Will you marry me?"

Corey's surprised face begins to morph into that of clear joy. He yells out, "What took you so long to ask me?! Hell Yeah, I'll marry you!" Garrett stands up and grabs Corey, picking him up and twirling around the room. "Boy, put me down! I'm getting dizzy!"

"I knew it!" Eunetta blurts out with joy and happiness all over her face. She comes around the table and hugs Garrett as well as Corey. "I am so happy for you both!"

Her happiness heightens my misery, because all I can remember is my own mother's sterile and silent contempt in that hospital room when I told her I was marrying Jojo. I hear her make a toast to Corey and Garrett. Then again, I don't… I hear my mother's voice.

You wanna be a faggot? Then stay your ass away from us and don't you ever come back!

"Excuse me," I say in a nasty tone as I stalk into the kitchen. My anger causes me to slam the door without my being conscious of it. I place my palms on the counter, getting angrier by the second. *All I ever wanted that woman to do was love me! To give me hugs and kisses and tell me that I was worth something! All she gave me was hell!*

I pour myself another shot to chase away the ghosts of the past which plague my thoughts. I gulp it down and wait for the effects of the alcohol to kick in. It doesn't work. I still feel hostile and ugly! I reach in the utility drawer and pull out the sweet relief enclosed in the orange plastic cylinder with a childproof cap. I remember the promise I made to Jojo, but I need this. *I am just going to take one pill so I can make it through tonight.*

I hear a voice behind me. I turn and there is Jojo. Startled, I close my hands around the pill bottle and hide it behind me.

"What are you doing?"

"Nothing."

Jojo looks suspicious. He cranes his head to look behind me.

"What is that in your hand?"

"It's nothing." I swallow nervously.

Suddenly, he rushes and tries to reach behind me. Amidst an attempt to hide them, the bottle slips from my fingers and falls to the floor. He seizes the bottle before I can intercept it. I stand at the sink, biting my lips in distress. He looks at the pills, then looks at me. I see that sympathetic look that I have come to hate.

"Don't."

"Don't what?"

"Just don't look at me like that."

"Lionel, you said that you were done with these pills…"

"I know what I said! Look Jojo, I'm going through a lot of shit right now. I got drama going on at work. I just buried my mother who was a mean rotten harpy to me while she was living. I don't know how to sort out my feelings like a normal person would, so forgive me if I need medication to get me through this shit."

"Baby, we talked about this. I know you been through hell. Look who you're talking to. It's me, the person whom you've known all your life and you know the crap I went through. But I deal with it. I cope the best way I can, and I don't look for a magic way out. Lionel, you are hooked on these pills."

"I am NOT hooked!"

"If you can't stop taking them on your own, I'd call that hooked. I think we need to get you some help. Maybe a treatment program. And nobody has to know. We can do it discreetly."

"That is the last thing I need. I don't want other folks in my business."

"Well, we need to do something because these little white pellets are taking you to a place that you are not prepared to go."

"Well, at least I won't be hurting when I get there."

"Goddamn it, Lionel! We all have our fuckery that we deal with. But this is not the way to deal with it!"

"Then how do *you* suggest I deal with it?" I ask nastily.

"Go back to Dr. Banneker."

"I don't need Dr. Banneker," I reply with emphasis.

"Then you need to do something before you end up losing your grip on reality."

"I don't need a fucking lecture from you about how to handle the shit in my own life!"

Jojo spins on his heel and walks towards the kitchen sink.

"What are you doing?"

He turns on the garbage disposal. *He's getting ready to trash my medication!* I rush forward to snatch the pills from his hand, but he held on to them. We start to struggle, with Jojo having the upper hand. I try to pry the bottle from his hand and in my struggle, my hand went up and I backhand Jojo across the face, weakening his grip on the bottle. He staggers backwards and falls to the floor. There is absolute stillness. He looks at me, horrified. *Oh my God, what have I done?* Seconds pass arduously by. Then Jojo stands to his feet, his face unwavering and his character filled with potent fury. His hands are clenched into fists as he strains to keep them at his sides.

He speaks, his voice colder than I've ever heard it, "The only thing that's keeping me from mopping the fucking floor with your face is the fact that we grew up together. I went through being abused by my mother's no-count boyfriend. I am not gonna spend the rest of my life dodging blows… The engagement is off. We're through."

He starts to walk out, then he turns to face me. He steps directly in front of me. Suddenly, his left hook crashes into my right jaw. Both the pain and force make me reel back towards the counter, where I stop and look at Jojo in shock.

"Eye for an eye, asshole."

Then, angrily yanking the kitchen door open, he pivots, treads out of the kitchen, and passes through my front door, slamming it shut while Corey, Eunetta, and Garrett look on in concern and confusion. I put the pills in my pocket and cross the floor to my counter as if I'm walking across glass. I grab the tumbler and the bottle of Jack, only to discover warily that it's empty. *Dammit! There's gotta be some whiskey in this kitchen somewhere. I need a shot.* I go back into my cabinet and pull out a bottle of Blanton's Whiskey. Miserably, I uncork it and sit at my kitchen table. *Fuck the shot. I need a fucking double.* With beads of sweat popping and running down my forehead, I pour and gulp it down. After pouring another, I pull the pill bottle from my pocket and stare at the pills inside as if transfixed. I need some relief…

I need a lullaby…

I need an end to the hurt… An end… A quick painless end…

I could empty the bottle into my hand and swallow them all… and just end it… because I just made the worst mistake of my life. But all I can do is fling the pill bottle violently across the room where it ricochets off the wall and opens, pills flying everywhere before they fall, like my self-respect, to the floor.

Chapter Eight
YOU SEE... BUT DO YOU KNOW

I hear the voices in the next room as Corey bids goodbye to Eunetta and Garrett, assuring them that things will be fine. I hear the uneasiness in their tone, and I want to go out there to talk with them, but the anguish of the moment, the haziness from the liquor, and the guilt stemming from my fit immobilizes me and nails my ass to the chair. After a few minutes, Corey comes in the kitchen and looks at the pills on the floor.

"Alright, Lionel. Do you want to tell me what that shit was all about?"

"It's nothing, Corey. Just go home," I say before inhaling my second tumbler.

"Hey, hey, hey! Take it easy!" he says, taking the tumbler from my hand. Then he stands back and looks at me before continuing, "You are gulping this shit down like it's Kool-Aid. What is wrong with you?"

"I told you... Nothing," I say as I gaze at him stupidly.

"You storm out during the time that Eunetta announced her happiness at our engagement, pretending that we didn't hear you when this kitchen door slammed. And then you get into a fight with Jojo, only for him to stomp out of here. I wouldn't call that nothing."

I am starting to feel the effects of the liquor... but the deceptive liquid promise of escape from my troubles is nowhere to be found and Corey's probing is not helping. I rise and walk shakily towards the kitchen sink to hide my tears.

"Look Corey, I am fine. Please, just leave me alone."

Corey comes beside me and put his hand on my shoulder. After a beat, he speaks with his voice thick with emotion, "I can't go anywhere knowing that you are in trouble."

"But I'm not in trouble."

"You are… and what just happened is proving it. Lionel, you've been my shoulder to cry on. Let me be yours. Please tell me what is going on."

I heave a deep sigh as I look out the window. I drunkenly begin to speak my heart. "Do you ever have a time where you can't look at yourself in the mirror?"

"I used to."

"What would be your reason?"

"Hearing all the shit I was subject to when I was lost in the system. All the names I was called. Remembering the rape and the times when I was messed with. Losing people who really cared. Not knowing my real parents before they died. Compound that on top of the constant bouts with my self-esteem."

I look at him and encounter tranquility in his eyes. I recall when Jojo and I first met him. As beautiful as he was, his eyes looked troubled. And when I read his entry into my journal last year, I saw the reason and it broke me to tears. When we were in college, he was defensive, self-depreciating, and afraid to let anyone get close to him. I understood that all too well. I know Jojo did too. Maybe that's why we became tight from the start. But looking at him now, I see a huge difference. Why is he, Peep, and Jojo at peace with their pasts while I feel like a fish in a hot frying pan?

"I have a hard time shaving… brushing my teeth… washing my face nowadays… because every time I do, I see my mother's face."

"But what does that have to do with Eunetta? Why did you storm out?"

I pour another glass and I prepare to knock it back, but Corey stops me. "No more, Lionel. You're going to make yourself sick."

Angrily, I shout, "Who are you to come into MY house and tell me…"

"I'm your friend and if you value our friendship as much as you always say you do; you will put the bottle down and talk to me!" Corey interrupts firmly.

I pour the whiskey into the sink, saying, "There! It's gone! Are you happy?"

"No, I'm not. There is something eating at you and before I leave here tonight, I want to know what it is. Now, I'm going to ask you again. Why were you so angry?"

I exhale and resume my wary gaze out the window. Then I lament, "I saw the pride in Eunetta's eyes when she looked at you and Garrett, how happy she was that ya'll were getting married… I've always wanted my mother to see something in me that made her proud. One of the few times that I ever got an acknowledgement from her was when I got in a fight with somebody who was picking on Brenda. I sent him home with two black eyes, a broken jaw, and a cut lip. She had this tight little smile that said, 'my son ain't no punk', but all I could think about was what I did to him. I knew in my heart that I couldn't go around beating people up to make her happy. I never fought like that again, but sometimes, I would try too hard... overachieve... over rationalize, just so I could see that look on her face for something good I was doing, but all she gave me was contempt for doing 'sissy shit'." I pause to catch my breath. I stumble back to my seat and Corey joins me as I continue to talk through my stupor.

"Do you know that I joined the wrestling team in high school? Yep. I did. I thought that if I was involved in a sport, she would see me as a man. She said that wrestling was not a real sport. 'Two men rolling around on the floor looks gay to me...' I just can't understand how some mothers and families can accept someone being gay, but others can't... Sometimes, I get so angry with life and God because of the shit that swirls around in mine. Because I feel things differently than everyone else to the point where I feel like a fucking freak. Because I need these pills to get through the day. Because life made me have to put up with that evil, conniving bitch of a mother." I catch myself. Oh my God... That was the first time I ever audibly called my mother a bitch. I've said it in my mind, but never out loud. I am expecting for Corey to give me a spiel about how grateful I should be to have a mother; as well as lay me out about how wrong I was to call her a name reserved for female dogs. As churched as he is, I'd expect him to remind me of the fifth commandment, "Honor thy father and thy mother." Lord knows, as drunk as I am, I still fear that God will send a bolt of lightning to strike me dead. But he simply says, "Maybe it was to show you how important it is to know how to survive anything."

"Mama wasn't needed to show me that!"

"How do you know that?"

I can't answer.

"Lionel, we are not given the types of parents, families, or childhoods we want. We are given what we're dealt to make the best out of different situations. Some more challenging than others. The good thing is that when you get to a certain age, you get to choose your own makeshift type of family: one that validates you."

Silence dominates the room, with only the refrigerator engine humming.

"Lionel, I hear you talking about everything your mother did to you, and I agree. That shit was evil. But have you taken the time to know her story and what made her the way she was?"

"Why would I? Her life was not for me to analyze. She should have got that shit correct before she left here. I hope her ass is somewhere roasting where nothing but the memory of the shit she did to me in life will keep her company."

"You know, you are starting to sound a lot like her."

"I am nothing like that evil old bat!"

"Maybe not. But you should listen to yourself sometimes. Your voice is so full of anger. The same anger you told me she had. I've never met her, but I have met people like her in my childhood. And I've seen enough of their shit to know that this path is going to lead to a bad end for you… Maybe even worse than hers. Now I'm going to repeat my question. Do you know her story?"

My anger is beginning to rise. "Look, don't be sitting here trying to analyze me."

Corey's voice becomes firm, yet unnervingly calm. "I'm not trying to analyze you. I'm just asking a question that you have yet to answer. Do you know her story?"

Frustrated, I reach down to pull up my pants leg, revealing the scar from my mother's paddle. "Do you see this? This is my mother's story! Her killing my dad is her story! Whatever fucked up shit she dealt with, she passed down to her children!

"That scar is something you can see. Your dad getting killed is something you can feel. But do you know the motivation behind what you sense? Have you ever taken the time to read between the lines?"

I jump to my feet. "What the fuck are you getting at, Corey? I just told you." Corey rises to his feet, standing toe to toe with me, but as calm as a puddle.

"No, you told me what you see and feel."

"Get out of my face, Corey!"

"Or what, you gonna hit me like you did Jojo?" He is still very calm. *Where is the Corey who is mercurial and excitable?* His collected demeanor for some reason is pissing me off royal. I want him just as pissed as I am so he can feel the heartbreak I'm feeling! But all I can see is a slow tear moving down his face.

"Get out."

"I'm not going anywhere until I'm sure you are alright."

"Get the fuck out of my house! Go! Get out!" I scream over and over until tears run down my face. Suddenly Corey's arms encircle my body and holds me fast where all I can do is scream… then whimper… then sob uncontrollably. I still struggle to get free, but Corey does not release his grip. I feel myself fall to the floor and Corey falls with me… and it is then that I hear the words, "It's ok. I got you… Let it out… You've been holding it in for too long… Let it go…"

All the fight I had dissolves from me. How can you fight against someone who matches every blow with serenity, truth, and love? On that kitchen floor, I see the facet of Corey that I've wished he would show more, but I can't savor it because I feel so guilty about my own petulance. He holds me for a few minutes more.

"It's OK, Lion… I know this feeling… You against the world… and it's a fucked-up way to feel. Here, lean into me so I can help you up. Let's get you upstairs."

I didn't resist when he hoisted me to my feet and upstairs to my room, where he laid me down on my bed, laid next to me, and just held me. From my open window, I can hear the sounds of the city, the animated conversations of my neighbors, and winds rustling the branches laden with newly formed leaves. Above all this, I hear the beat of my heart and the words of my best friend:

"I got you."

Soothed with these sounds, I fall into a mercifully deep slumber.

*****

"I admit I don't know my mother's story," I say on the next morning. I am sitting up in my bed and Corey is perched in the recliner. "Dr. Banneker asked me a question to that effect when I was going to him."

"And that question was?"

"He asked me if she was treated that way as a child?"

"What was your response?"

"I told him that I knew a little of the animosity between her and Granny. I saw it once when she and Mama got into it on a Thanksgiving at her house."

"But you are not privy to the full extent, correct?"

"No."

Corey scrunches his face and takes a deep breath. Then he speaks carefully, "Well Lionel, I gotta tell you this as a friend. Not knowing where her mind went when she was abusing you is affecting your whole life, making it so you can't do without those pills and you shutting us out for telling you to get off them. And it's not stopping with you. Your brothers and sisters are affected too… even Rhonda in her own way."

I cannot answer. I know he's right. But, even now, I need a pill to wash over my troubled thoughts. Corey went on, "The reason why I asked you if you know her story was to get you to *admit* that you don't know. You kept telling me what you saw and felt, which gave way to your emotions.

But I have read somewhere that although seeing and feeling is a gateway to learning a story, the ability to feel is far different than the ability to know."

"I don't understand."

"Well, you were basing your feelings of anger off your senses, and those senses only let you see your mother's cruelty and her hatred towards gay people. But what helps is knowing why she was so cruel to you and your sibs."

I exhale calmly, processing Corey's words. Then I say, "To be honest Corey, I am not really interested in whatever her sordid tale is. As far as I'm concerned, it did not give her the right to ride down on us… the very ones she gave birth to."

"And I agree with you. But for some people, the only logical way to alleviate pain is to make others hurt the way they were hurting. In their mind, that serves as their therapy. Twisted, but true."

"You think so?"

"How else would you explain what happened between you and Jojo… then you and me?"

I think a minute. I was angry last night. And that anger made me lash out at the ones who tried to understand. "How did you know that I hit Jojo?" I ask mournfully.

"He texted me the minute after he left, see?" He pulled out his phone. I read the words.

> **Lionel hit me. The engagement is off. I don't know about the relationship or even the friendship. But I do know that I'm not standing around to watch him throw his life away over some fucking pills! And I'm not going to be his punching bag.**

These are words to sear through my heart like poison. Almost forty years, down the fucking drain. I feel like I'm in a bottomless pit and I am falling…

Falling!

I absently pass the phone back to Corey, half-aware of the creases of worry that distort my face. Corey sees this and says, "Jojo loves you. Lord knows, he spent a whole lifetime proving it." He stops. After a breath, his face and voice become firm. "But he's tired of this shit. I'm tired of it, to say nothing of Peep, A.D., Garrett, and the rest of us who love you. Your anger and dependence on these capsules are steadily killing you and, as much as we love you, we can't help you get past either one. It's like you are dying onscreen and we can only watch the horror and do nothing."

"How in the fuck do you think I feel? If I could stop, I would."

Corey gets up and faces me decisively, shocking me with his angry expression and preceding words. "Well, maybe this will help you along. We are close to washing our hands with you. The only thing that is holding us together is the length of our friendship. But this shit is threatening to destroy even that. When you are ready to move past this, we will be right here to help you every step of the way. But until you make the first step…" He pauses, trying to hold back his tears. I can tell that his next words are killing him to utter. "We can't do anything… but watch you die."

He bends down and kisses me on the forehead. Holding his kiss there, I feel his lips become tight from restraining his tears. He then turns and rushes from my bedroom. I sit unmovable, plagued by his words, and lost in my own thoughts.

They say that you can get back up when you fall… But for the first time since taking this shit, I'm wondering: *How far had I fallen?*

The phone rings. I look at the screen as it displays the name, Floyd Alexander. I look at the clock on my nightstand. It says eight-fifteen. I'm not late for work… so why is he calling? I answer wearily, "Hello, Floyd. What's wrong?"

"Hey, Lionel. I'm calling because I want to bring something to your attention before you come in today."

"What is going on?"

"Well, I have been noticing that you have been dragging since the Va-Voom campaign. I am glancing over your marketing reports and I'm seeing a few discrepancies."

"Discrepancies?" I hear my voice squeak out.

"Yes. I need you to stay late today. I'm going to stay as well so we can correct them. We don't have enough time during the day because we have another campaign to work on."

Damn. "OK," I say with a sigh.

"Oh, come on. Take the 'woe is me' out of your voice. The discrepancies aren't that bad, but we do need to fix them. I am taking into consideration the death you had in your family. I know you must have a whole lot of emotions tied to that. I don't know if this will make you feel better, but it's not just you who's struggling. Other members on the staff are beginning to falter as well. And to be honest, I'm beginning to see double myself."

I sigh again. "Well, I can't speak for the rest of the staff, but I'm sorry for my part in not checking the reports."

"No apology necessary," Floyd consoles. "Listen, do you remember when I brought up the annual company getaway Mr. Robertson organizes?"

"How could I forget?"

Floyd ignores the sarcasm evident in my voice as he goes on, "Well, I know you said you were not interested in going, but I think you ought to reconsider and come with us."

"'Us'? Who's 'us'?"

"Marianne Dewitt from the Art Department, Ben Longwood from Accounting, and your co-worker Shawn Tolbert to name a few. About twenty-eight other employees are coming as well."

"I don't know, Floyd."

"Well, I do. We all need this. I think this might strengthen our resolve for the accounts we got coming, Besides, it might take your mind off everything you got going on."

I consider his offer. I really do need new scenery because things are looking bleak around here. I exhale heavily and relent, "OK, I'll go…"

"Great," I hear Floyd's voice ring out in excitement. "We have a four o'clock flight to Myrtle Beach on Sunday afternoon. Pack light but include business casual attire."

"Fine…"

"Lionel, this could be good for your career. Trust me. I'll see you at the office."

"OK."

I hang up the phone and toss it to the other side of the bed. I sit up, putting my elbows on my knees and my head in my hands. I don't feel like going anywhere. I want to stay in this bed and just go back to sleep while the rest of my life crashes around me. I feel utterly washed up.

My work is slacking off.

My friendships are floundering.

My engagement with Jojo is over.

And my self-worth is in the goddamned toilet.

I sold them all for some tiny white pills given by a shitty shrink... and now I can't stop myself from taking them.

I need help...

Chapter Nine
*D*RUNKEN *D*ESIRE

On this balmy Sunday evening, Marianne Dewitt, Ben Longwood, and I are seated in the courtesy airport shuttle headed to the Mandarin Paradise Resort. Our plane just landed an hour ago. I am listening to Marianne and Ben's conversation, but I remain quiet and rather sullen. *I don't want to be here at all*, I think to myself. I had to talk myself into packing my bag after church today.

Speaking of church, I saw Jojo at Unity and Love and his expression was colder than the North Pole when he glanced over at me. After that, he avoided me like the plague. The guilt in my heart is weighing on my head like an anvil. I really need to talk to him. I called him every night since the fight, but he will neither answer nor return my calls. There is so much that I want to share with him... like how sorry I am about how things went down. I'm sure he wants to unload some shit off his chest too. But for some reason, we are like two icebergs that float past each other without collision.

These past few days were awful. They almost became impossible because when I walked down to the kitchen to clean up the pills (and take one), I saw that the kitchen was cleaned but the pills were gone. I knew Corey probably threw them away and I'm almost out of the hundred milligram meds. I felt like cursing. But I remembered that I had a reserve bottle in one of my shoes in the closet and it had seventeen pills in it.

I try to banish these thoughts of gloom from my head to focus on the conversation of my excited co-workers. Marianne Dewitt comes from Muskegon, Michigan. A summa cum laude graduate of Hampton University and a Delta Gamma Epsilon soror, she has been the Director of the Art Department at Robertson and Moore for six years, and she is as zany as a bedbug. I think it's the cannabis she partakes in that makes her so off-the-wall. She knows about nearly every strain there is, so she can tell the difference between "loud" and "reggie".

I liked her from the day I first met her. She is bright, imaginative, funny, and self-assured. It is because of her that this company has enjoyed the reputation of rendering bold and award-winning artistic expressions for clients. When I come up with an ad concept, I take it to Marianne and her department, and they work magic! Also, I have always found it easy to talk to her because of her open, friendly, and confidential demeanor. On days when I am completely frustrated, I would go to her office and we would be seated in her comfortable crimson sitting area, drinking hot cinnamon apple tea, and having a good old-fashioned bitch-session. She, Floyd, and Ben are the only ones that know about my engagement with Jojo. But all three have stayed silent.

I would call her a unique jewel in God's ring, with a style all her own. How she is dressed even now proves that. Her nappy, blond dreadlocks with shells are pulled up in a blue, green, and beige headwrap she made by braiding three of her husband's worn oversized ties. Huge gold hoops dangle on her ears with an emerald swinging by a catch in the center of each hoop. Her wrists are adorned with thick golden bangle bracelets and her neck sports a puka shell necklace. Her five-eight, bronze, ballet-trained body is clad in a brown leotard with short sleeves and a flowing maxi skirt of blue, green, and beige floral print. Brown "Julia" high heels with gold studs grace her feet. She is the type that lives life without caring about what others think of her. I have had the pleasure of meeting her husband and children, and they are just as open and zany as she is.

Benjamin J. Longwood hails from a small town called Goldsboro, North Carolina. He is a huge enigma. He came to the firm through Shawn Tolbert's recommendation, a graduate from Howard University with a degree in Accounting. He is the Head Bookkeeper of the firm and works very closely with Floyd and the other VPs. I like Ben a lot. With pecan tan skin and average build, he stands at six-five and looks as though he weighs well over two hundred pounds. He is wearing a short beige, walking suit and on the feet of well-shaped legs are beige mesh loafers. His balding hair is hidden by a straw braided porkpie hat.

Normally, Ben is noticeably quiet, except when we are in the boardroom or around Shawn, his best friend. The latter occurrence surprises me because those two are as different as night and day. I've often believed that he lacked confidence in himself and his abilities. The things he can do outside the office has everyone in complete awe! I remember being out with The Fellas at a jazz club and, unbelievably, it was him on the platform with the band, fingers flying over the keys. Even Corey was in awe. He is incredibly intelligent and good at his job. However, when looking into his huge bespectacled eyes sometimes, I sense something deep and peculiar. On the sly, I've noticed him walking around the office with melancholy draped on his face that he puts away with a smile that says, "Please don't judge me."

"So, Lionel," Marianne's thin, clear voice interrupts my thoughts. I turn my startled attention towards her. "You finally decided to join us this year, yes?"

"Yeah. Floyd jumped on my back telling me that I needed this."

"Baby, we ALL needed it."

"I second that," Ben chimes in.

Marianne peers closely into my eyes. After a few seconds, she asks, "Are you alright?"

"Yeah, I'm fine. Why do you ask?"

"Well, you just seem 'out there', like something's troubling you," she says in concern. Ben looks at me, his big eyes soft and caring.

"I'm fine. I'm just not feeling this trip. I'd rather be at home."

She looks at me shrewdly. "OK. What's up? What done happened?"

I glance at her and Ben, saying, "I don't want to go into it right now."

She raises her hands as if to say, *I respect that.* Ben moves his eyes to the window, gazing absently at the passing buildings. She says, "Well, we are on a getaway to do just that- get away from the stress. Let's just look at this trip as a way to really unwind. And just in case you can't get into the groove, Little Mama's gonna keep some brownies in her purse!" she laughs out, patting her bag. Apparently, those were exactly the magic words to make Ben turn toward Marianne with a grin.

"You remembered! Thank God!" Ben enthuses.

"Brownies?" I ask.

She leans towards me. Lowering her voice so the driver won't hear, she says sneakily, "You know... brownies with a little sum-sum in 'em!"

"Oh!" I exclaim.

"You got my drift. Good! For a second, I thought I was hanging with a square."

"Trust me," I joke. "I know a little sum' about that!"

I remember kidding about Dr. Banneker doing the puff-puff, but it's true that I keep a little Mary Jane. Every now and then, The Fellas and I have a little ganja-ganja session, courtesy of a choreographer friend of Corey's named Quentin. Sometimes, Garrett's cousin Melba hooks us up with a little bit of indica strain to roll and smoke. We usually get lit on holidays, like Thanksgiving or birthdays. Most times, though, I prefer to do the edibles that Quentin cooks up, like gummies and homemade cookies, because the odor of the bud gets in your clothes and on your breath when you smoke it. I also prefer the edibles because they open my senses a little better than when I roll a tree. As quiet as it's kept, I find it easier to focus on new concepts when I partake in "the medicine of the earth". Hmmm... This might be right on the money. I hadn't had a good ganja buzz since seeing Dr. Williams.

"How many did you bring?"

"Oh Lionel, baby, I didn't bring any. I got a good-GOOD girlfriend named Carol who lives thirty minutes away from the resort. She is an awesome chef and she bakes them for me whenever the getaway is at Myrtle Beach. I give her the money. She buys the oil and mixes it into the brownie batter. When they are done, she brings them to the resort."

"Is it THC?" I query.

"Yes and no. I get two kinds of brownies. I call them heavies and lights. The lights just have a specific type of CBD, which will just relax you and improve activity in the brain. They won't make you high, but they will help you to think better." A mischievous smile and an impish expression pass her face as she says, "But the heavies got a Fruity Pebbles strain of THC that will get you right and keep you laughing. But being that we are also here on pseudo-business, we'd better go with the lights, my darlings!"

After thirty minutes, the van pulls up to the Mandarin Paradise Resort. We climb out of the van to stretch our legs, walk into the spacious atrium, and look around. I've got to hand it to Mr. Robertson; he definitely does not half-step when it comes to organizing a retreat. The sprawling resort is beautiful! There are two five-floor stucco cylindric towers painted a salmon pink color. They are joined by an enormous glass atrium of equal height. Beside the left tower is a huge tempered glass and stucco structure called The Haven. It houses a fitness center, a spacious lounge, an indoor pool, conference rooms, and an internet cafe. The top of that structure is used for stargazing and rooftop shindigs. Beyond the right side is a golf course, tennis courts, and a pool designed to surround the parameter of the right tower. In the brochure, I learned that the right side housed the penthouse apartment, occupied by Mr. Robertson himself. As I look out of the windows and behind the hotel, I see a beautiful sunset gracing the waters of the ocean with a breathtaking golden shimmer.

After checking in, the concierge hands me my key, instructing me to go on up to my room and leave my bags for the bellhop to bring up. The moment I step into the room, I close the door and lean my back against it, asking, "What in the hell am I doing here?"

*****

Mr. Robertson planned a meet and greet tonight at the Haven's lounge. So, after a short nap, I take a shower, change into a fitted white shirt, beige slacks, and tan loafers, and head to the Haven with a small notepad and a pen in my pocket. I always try to keep these items handy for when I have spontaneous advertisement ideas.

I step out of the elevator to encounter a large room full of different and colorful people. Many are employees like me, but there are also those who are obviously well-heeled, judging from the clothes they wear. I am a little nervous. I want to take a pill to settle my jumping stomach, but amazingly, I resist. I catch sight of Ben and Marianne who see me and stroll over.

"Hey Lionel. Are you rested up?" Marianne asks.

"Yeah, I'm good. Didn't get enough though. Could've used more."

"I hear you. I'm kinda tired myself," Ben says.

"Listen, did your friend give you the brownies?" I ask Marianne.

She discreetly shows me her bag, saying, "You know it! I decided to go ahead and ask for both while we are here." She motions for Ben and me to join her in an unoccupied space. When she is sure that no one is watching, she reaches in her oversized handbag and pulls out two large bags of small brownie bites. I notice that one batch has a lighter brown shade than the other. She says, "I suggest doing the lights for now. We don't need to be high and giggling while discussing concepts. We just need a boost to get us going. We'll save the heavies for when the muckity-mucks aren't around, and we can let our hair down."

"Good idea," Ben agrees.

"We won't get in trouble for this, will we?" I ask.

"Please, child! Floyd is the one that asked me to bring them."

"Then why are we whispering in this corner?"

"Because I don't want everybody to know I got them. Everybody and their mamas are gonna want a taste! Only a select few know what Little Mama is packin'!"

"You got that right," I hear Floyd's deep voice. I turn to encounter him standing there with his beefy frame tastefully draped in a flowered shirt and flowing white silk shorts, displaying his plum black, defined legs with calves that look like bowling balls! He steps to Marianne to give her air kisses, as well as greet Ben and myself with backpats. When his body touched mine, I thought, *Hmmm... his rock-hard pecs got my prick harder than petrified wood. Thank God I got on a jock.* I kill the thought by remembering that he is my boss.

With a grin, Floyd says, "I see you have them both this year. Give me one of those lights, will you? I'll get a heavy later on." He bestows a conspirator's wink at her.

"Sure," Marianne says with a lively, wicked smile. She opens the plastic bag and motions for us to take some. I grab one, pop it in my mouth, and wait for the effects to register. They taste rather good, but I don't feel anything.

Heading back to the party, Floyd beams brightly at me, patting me on the shoulder. He says, "I'm glad you decided to come. I have a sneaky feeling that this will benefit you a lot more than you think."

"I hope so. I'm not sure what I'm doing here."

Floyd laughs, "Well, go and grab yourself a drink and meet me back at my table in five minutes." He then disappears.

Ben offers, "I'll get the drink. I need one myself. What do you want?"

"Um… A cosmo?" He nods and disappears.

Just then, I see the athletic, honey-colored, smirking form of Shawn Tolbert walking towards me. He is wearing a see-through silk shirt that shows off his cut definition and shamelessly brief shorts that ride up past his thigh. His ass reminds me of two huge melons held up by legs made by the Roman god Vulcan. He is a sculptor's vision. I'll admit that. But the sneaky look on his face causes me to tense up.

"Well, well, well… if it isn't Lionel Davis."

OK Lionel, keep a lid on it. "Shawn… how are you?" I barely spit out, trying my damnedest to keep a pleasant look on my face.

"I'm making it. Mr. Dennis told me that you might be coming," he said, alluding to the Junior VP of the firm.

Um-hmm. Probably after you got through giving him the ass all fucking night, I thought. "Well, he was right."

"Well, it is nice to see you. Uh, tell me. How have you been? I've heard about your mother. So sorry that she passed," He says in a syrupy voice and a saccharine expression on his face. At least, I think it's syrupy. Who could tell with Shawn? Under his sweet tone, there could be a nasty cut. That's how he operates, which is one of the reasons I don't like him. *I want to take a cantaloupe with slimy seeds and smear it in his face. Shawn had better not say a thing off-filter to me or I'm reading this bitch for filth.*

"Thank you. I'm handling it."

"I'm sure you are," Shawn smiles with a simpering insincerity that I can feel on my skin. *Where is Ben with that fucking drink? And how long will it be before this brownie kicks in? If this doesn't work, I'm going to my room to get a pill.* "So, tell me. It hasn't been affecting your work, has it? I have been noticing that you've been dragging a little. And with those bags under your eyes, it seems that you aren't getting enough rest."

You smug, shady motherfucker! I state calmly, "Why don't you ask Floyd? He IS our superior, you know. Although with you being an employee like me, he would tell you that my job performance is strictly a managerial concern, and not any concern of yours."

"Why are you getting hot under the collar?" Shawn asks with his eyebrows up in sincere shock. "I was only aski…"

Out of nowhere, Ben interrupts, holding the drink, "I'm sorry, Shawn. I have to steal Lionel away. But hold tight, and I'll be right back so we can talk, you and I." Ben put a stern emphasis on "you and I", with his eyes peering over his glasses, saying, *You are being a real bitch*.

"Fine with me," Shawn says in offense.

"Lionel, Floyd is expecting you at his table. Here's your cosmo. Let's head over there," I smile at him gratefully and take it from his hand.

"Thank you, Ben. Well Shawn, we have to talk some other time," I say as Ben and I begin walking toward Floyd's table.

"Oh, we will," Shawn says with a derisive tone.

When we are out of earshot, I mumble to myself, "You shade-throwing, apple bobbing, opportunistic bitch!" Ben lets out a short, restrained laugh.

When we approach Floyd's table, Ben excuses himself to talk with Shawn. Floyd sees me and says while gesturing to the spot next to him, "Lionel, come sit here." When I have done so, Floyd's voice becomes more confidential as he leans toward me. "Thank you for taking this invitation to come. I know it has been rather hard for you to function with everything that has been going on. But I've asked you to attend for two reasons. One, because as I told you, it was needed. We all had to have a break from the normal office humdrum. And two, this is another grooming that I'm giving you."

"Gotcha," I say, feeling abruptly lighter, yet alert. The brownie must be kicking in. *Hmm. I like THIS feeling!*

"OK. Now, as with everything else in this company, this getaway is an investment. It's not just to give the employees a week in the sun. Of course, it won't always be stuff-shirt business. But it is extremely important that you understand this. Everything that Manford Robertson does has a profit margin attached, so you really have to be on your P's and Q's, you got me?"

"With my catcher's mitt." I say, with a smile of confidence.

"I knew that you could," Floyd grins. He gets up with his drink, instructing me to pick mine up and walk with him. He circles his arm around my shoulders and surveys the enormous room as we saunter. "Now, I want you to take a long look at everyone in this room. What do you see?"

"A bunch of people with nothing but time on their hands."

Floyd stops and looks at me. "I haven't taught you anything, have I? That might be true, but I'm talking about other than the obvious. Aside from the firm's employees, almost every invited guest in this room is filthy, stinking rich with ideas and inventions that made them such."

I grow quiet and think about the lesson Floyd laid out for me. He says heartily, "Come on. Buck up. You were right, they have a lot of time on their hands, but what I'm trying to teach you to do is look beyond what you can see. Remember, behind every invention... behind every idea... there is always a story."

"I understand."

"Good, Now listen up. These men and women all have potential to be multi-million-dollar clients, but you must use your eyes and your ears to determine which one would be the RIGHT client for the firm. In events like this, it is important for you to circulate. Talk to people to find out what their product is. Ask them, in so many words, what necessity their product contributes and what inspired them to invent it. If you feel a tugging to talk to them more, see where their heads are at. You must find out what their style is. Sometimes, you may even be pressed to discover their color of choice. All these things matter in a client's campaign. Remember what I told you when I first bought you on. In these types of settings, your mind must become like a computer, dictating the given info so that the next time you talk to the person, you can regurgitate what you observed or talked about the night or two before. They are impressed by that. It shows that you listened. Are you following what I'm saying?"

"Like a driver follows GPS," I say, taking a sip.

"Floyd, honey-bunch," a cultured, Southern belle-type voice croons. We turn to see a tall, slender, brown-skinned lady dressed in an asymmetrical flowing short-sleeved dress with multi-colored tropical flowers against a white background. I think to myself, *Good God, she is at least two inches taller than me!* Yet, I quickly remember Floyd's cautionary words to look beyond physical appearance and I shrug it off. Her dark hair is pinned up into a wide-brimmed white hat and her face is beat. As I survey her feet, I take note of the uniquely made white stilettos with straps around her ankles. She has a blue clutch bag in her strong, slender hand. In looking at this lovely lady, she reminds me of a young Ja'net Dubois, especially when her lips curved into an easy, endearing smile.

Floyd air kisses her in greeting. "Katherine, how wonderful to see you again. Tell me, where is Vander?"

"Oh, he is in the room, nursing a headache from the flight. I don't know how many times I've told him, drinking scotch on a plane is not good for him. But all I can say is he is as stubborn as an old mule. And my oldest boy is just like him." She releases a laugh that is down home and pleasant, as well as startling and loud. I find her personality to be very engaging.

"How is your son? Um… Gerard, right?"

"Yes. He's well. About to walk across the stage to get his medical degree. I can't tell you how proud I am."

"That is great, and he is a smart young man. I envy the patients who will call him doctor."

"That's my boy!" The beautiful lady beams with pride.

Floyd then looks at me, puts his hand on my shoulder, and says, "Well, Katherine, I would like to introduce you to Lionel Davis, one of our finest marketing executives."

Her eyes light up, "Ah yes. Robertson & Moore's secret treasure! Floyd has been talking our ears off about you over the past five years."

"Has he?" I say, looking at him and beaming.

"Yes, he has told me how brilliant you are with artistic concepts and marketing strategies."

"Well, thank you, Floyd," I say, patting Floyd on the shoulder. "And you are?"

"Oh, I am sorry. I am Katherine Nesbitt," she says, as she extends her hand.

Katherine Nesbitt. Oh my God. The founder of Nesbitt Women's Clothing! I am astounded. I take her hand and shake it gently. "Ms. Nesbitt, it is a complete honor to meet you. I have an aunt who swore by your dresses. She told my mother once that dresses from other manufacturers could not fit her because of her height." I look at Floyd, who stands there with a pleasantly surprised look on his face.

"How tall is your aunt."

"Six-one."

Her face illumines with clarity and newfound confirmation. Turning to Floyd, she gushes, "You see, this is why my late sister and I founded the company. You have fashion corporations that make dresses for petites, full-figured, and regular sized women. But they forget that tall women want to look sexy and catch the eyes too!" She vivaciously finishes the last statement while looking at me, obviously pleased.

"I couldn't agree more. Everyone can't be 'Tiny Tina'."

A look of interest and admiration passes her face. She laces her arm through mine and steers me to the sitting area. "Come with me. Let's chit-chat."

"You do that. I see A.J. McKendrick from Jones' Woodworks has arrived. I must greet him. Excuse me," Floyd says. He winks at me, then disappears into the crowd.

*****

Several minutes into the conversation, Ms. Nesbitt and I began talking business. She told me that she's trying to expand her marketing base. Whether it is the brownie or my own imagination working overdrive, ideas started bombarding into my brain even as I listened to her.

Tall Women in dresses like the one she has on… Could work! Hmmm… The scenes would change… Different frames… Transitions that slide between each… Arrows… yes! First frame- Cover girl… That's good! White and Black Formal Dresses… Supermodel type…Tall, confident women striding into a ballroom as suitors look on… Could work… Use Colors for the second frame… Fun… Beach… Park… Yes! Pull three of the brightest colors. They have to be bold… Daring… Sexy… Hmm… Red, Orange, and Yellow. Then again, use the whole spectrum! After all, there are different personalities… One might want more serene colors… Hmm… Third frame… Slow motion… Darker colors with dresses flowing… when she's feeling sexy… A pair of long legs… Camera pans up to reveal a bathing suit and a face with lips smooching at the camera? Yes! Nice! Now, what about the fourth frame? Let's see… Ah! City scene! Sophisticated corporate wear when she's on the job… walking the sidewalks wearing power suits… More earthy tones… We can have a few bold tones too… But only a few… Simple… yet… sexy… … Yes! Each frame seven seconds long… Paper roll up to reveal the company insignia… Could work!

Using my newfound knowledge and the ideas that swirl in my mind, I took out my notepad and pen and began to draft a rough sketch that rolled her over. She was so impressed that she called Floyd over and told him to expect a call from her once the getaway was over and that she wanted me to handle her campaign. I am completely ecstatic! Working with Katherine

Nesbitt is a big deal and I get the feeling that her marketing requirements will be a hell of a lot easier than Vivian Harrington's. Strengthened by this accomplishment, I circulated and talked with more people, and they were a colorful bunch with even more colorful inventions. I did see Shawn across the room. He is talking with Ben and the conversation looked a bit strained. I simply tipped my glass which contained the second cosmo of the evening and shrugged my shoulders as I continue to work the room.

Feeling a bit lightheaded, I told Floyd that I wanted to leave the party early. I am somewhat of a social introvert. I can handle crowds pretty well. But after two hours, I believe recharging is necessary.

Now I am sitting in a comfortable chair on the rooftop of The Haven, gazing out into the ocean and sipping my drink. I am happy about the success with Ms. Nesbitt, but I'm still worried about my relationship with Jojo, as well as my friendship with The Fellas. Is this really the end? Will we ever patch things up? I thought about Corey's words throughout the plane ride. Am I really killing myself with these pills? The statement he made about watching me die scared the shit out of me. I was so afraid that I had a dream about it. I was repeatedly stabbing myself in my heart and backing into a gigantic open jet-black coffin where my mother was pulling me. I saw my father, my friends, my family, and even Mike Junior moaning and crying as they consoled each other.

Should I go ahead and chuck the tablets? And would it be so bad if I did break it off with Dr. Williams and go back to Dr. Banneker? I admit that I felt cared for when I went to see him. Plus, if I did, perhaps Jojo would come back and we can put all this behind us.

But I remember the tranquility I feel after taking a capsule. The need for my peace of mind must be addressed and this medicine is doing that. There is no way that Dr. Banneker would give me that prescription if he was weaning me from the Doxepin, which had half of the same number of components as the Alprolozine. I shrug my shoulders, thinking, *I need that medication and if Jojo and The Fellas can't see that, then maybe this is the end of the road for us. Friends ought to want you to be well and happy. They wouldn't ask you to ditch something that keeps you steady.* But the thought of my life without the friends I've known for so long makes me miserable and causes me to question whether or not continuing with these pills is really worth the risk. I finish my drink with one big gulp and ask the server to bring another so I can chase those questions away.

I look over to my left to see Ben leaning over the railing, holding a glass of burgundy wine, and looking up at the moon in rapture. Something about the way he's standing there in profile is extremely sensual. He changed from the black polo and sand-colored slacks that he wore at the party. Now he is dressed in a white linen short set and has a white fitted newsboy cap on his head. He has his left foot up on the railing for him to rest his left elbow on and a gold chain surrounds his ankle. The heavy linen cannot hide the muscular contours of his ass. *Mmm... sexy as hell. I've never seen this side of Ben.*

As if something is beckoning, he turns his head to look my way and smile sweetly. I jerk my head, signaling him to come keep me company. He saunters over and sits down next to me.

"What are you doing over there by yourself."

"What are *you* doing over *here* by *your*self."

"I asked you first," I laugh out. Ben joins me.

After inhaling the ocean air for a few seconds, he responds, "When I'm in a setting like this. I like to limit my time with other people."

"Same answer," I follow.

He looks at me with tenderness. Then he gazes upward. "I'm not really good at mixers. I'm a bit shy."

"I've figured that out already," I say, tipping my glass in his direction.

"Besides, look at how beautiful this is," he says, gesturing at the sea and sky. "I'm willing to bet that as rich as some people are, they don't take the time to see the beauty around them."

I chuckle. "So, I take it that you are an old soul and nature boy."

"I am, yes," he says in a deep, elegant voice. "I love nature. Everything about it inspires me."

"I'm a nature boy myself, so I understand. What's your favorite season?"

"I like summer. What about you?"

"I'm more of a spring kind of fella."

He smiles at me, then looks back toward the sky.

"By the way, thanks for rescuing me from Shawn."

"Don't mention it. He's my good friend, but he can be an asshole at times. I know how he likes to needle people. And he wonders why many folks don't take to him. Still, there is another side to him… a better side. I've known him for twenty years so I can attest to this. That side is really beautiful, and it cares about people. It only reveals itself when people are sharp enough to spot it." I could have sworn I heard his voice change. He has a dreamy look on his face. Oh my God! He likes Shawn! *I hope he isn't fool enough to jump in the bed with him, or he may be taking a trip to the clinic real soon.*

"Ben, I don't know you very well. But you seem to be the type that sees the good in everybody you meet. I have yet to find that in Shawn Tolbert, so I'll just take your word for it."

*****

A few hours later, we are enjoying lively conversation. Ben is actually great company. I like this side of him. In his unique way, he is very alluring.

"So, Ben, tell me. Where did you learn to play the keys so well?"

"How did you know that I played?"

"My friends and I were hanging at Harry's Jazz Club and we caught your band's set."

"Wow, I didn't know you were there," Ben says, amused.

"Yeah, we were… and you were awesome."

"You think so?"

"I know so. Believe me. Whenever you can shut Corey Kennedy up where all he can do is stare, the word awesome fits the occasion."

"Corey Kennedy was there?! I have heard about him and I went to his concert last year. He is one of the coldest pianists and organists in Baltimore!"

"Yeah, and he's one of my best friends."

"Well, damn. I feel like I should lay prostrate! I am humbled and honored that he liked it. And to answer your question, my mother made me take piano lessons from ages five to eighteen. I learned jazz and gospel by listening to CDs and watching the musicians at the church I grew up in."

"Oh… so you are a church boy."

"I was." His open and cheerful mood changed when he said that.

Melancholic and pensive.

"What's wrong?" I ask him.

He looks out into the ocean as if he's searching for an answer to pluck from the waters. He says after a beat, "I sorta fell out with the church"

"No kidding. Why?"

"Well, I was in this particular Baptist church pretty much all my life. As a teenager, I played for the choirs along with the hired musicians. I even went back to serve as the church bookkeeper when I got my accounting degree. I enjoyed the daily work, but I started to hate attending and playing for regular Sunday services because it was like a contest on who was more 'saved' and 'sanctified', even among the children."

I look out at the ocean for a minute, then I direct my eyes back to him and point to myself, saying, "Different church. Same problem."

"Sad, isn't it? I clung to the church because I felt like being there could give me answers as to why the world is in the screwed-up state it's in and why I felt things differently than others. But after a while, I started noticing things within the church walls that weren't right."

"Like what?"

"Like the pastor barking at people about being sinners every Sunday, guilting them to give and give more. It didn't matter that some of the givers were a paycheck from being evicted. He would ask, 'Do you trust God?' If he felt that the tithes were down, he would start in with the 'will a man rob God' speech."

"Hmmm. The pastor at the church I grew up in pulled that shit."

"I think it is like an unspoken rule for pastors to do it," he says as he looks down.

"Well, what straw broke the camel's back?"

Ben looks at the stars and lets out a long sigh before saying, "I was fired."

"Fired?"

"Yeah. The pastor replaced the assistant bookkeeper. Between my keeping track of the money and her eagle eye on the expenses, we kept things on the level. But in his mind, she had too many reasons why he wasn't able to use his position to just take money out, so he fired her. He hired his son as assistant, and that fool started cooking the books when I wasn't in the office. The hired musicians, office workers, and custodians started coming to me saying that their checks were coming up short. I began investigating and keeping track of expenses of the church as well as the salaries of the pastor and his son, only to discover that large sums of money were going into both their pockets. Cash was placed in an envelope that one of the deacons found in the shelf inside the pulpit and brought it to me. The amount in it matched the week's amount docked from the staff's pay, as well as a third of that Sunday's offering. The deacon and I brought this to the pastor's attention, with the receipts and books in hand. I told him that when people give their money, they are also contributing their trust and to pocket the money is breaking that trust. I was fired on the spot."

"That is low."

"Yeah. That was shortly before I was hired to work for the firm."

"I'm sorry that happened."

"Oh, don't be. I'm not. Feel sorry for the pastor. I hear that he and his son are in deep shit now."

As the night wears on, we are becoming more comfortable with sharing each other's stories, especially with the flow of liquor between us. I tell him about Yeti, and he tells me about Goldsboro. Boy, I thought Yeti was country! His mystery makes me want to know more about how he sees things.

"A while back, you said you were shy. Why is that?" I ask, with my voice slurring.

He looks at me again, his huge eyes warily staring at me. He says, "Can you keep a secret?"

"If you tell me to."

He looks down at the floor. Then he giggles, saying, "Being around people makes me incredibly nervous."

"Really?"

"Yeah, they do."

"Why?"

He exhales as he looks out at the watery horizon. "I don't know what their intentions are. When I am in a room filled with people, I feel insecure. Even when I was a kid, I hated birthday parties and family holidays because that would mean I'd have to be around people, worrying about what shit might be said about me."

"But that makes no sense. You seem to be an extremely attractive and intelligent man. People would kill for your height alone."

He then points his finger at me, laughing. "A lot of people say that, but it's not the blessing you think it is. Being the tallest guy in the room is unsettling. It feels like everyone is staring at you."

I smirk at him. Then I say, "Stand up for me."

"Why?"

"Just stand up."

When he tipsily complies, I tell him, "I see a tall, good looking guy. You got power in your height and you are talented as fuck. You just need confidence." I attempt to stand, but I feel woozy. Whoa! Too many cosmos!

As I am unsteady on my feet, Ben grabs me gently, laughing and saying, "Wow, looks like we both have had too much to drink. Let's lean on each other to get back to our rooms."

"If we can make it to our rooms."

We look at each other and burst out laughing, as we drunkenly make our way to the door.

Somehow, we make it back to our floor. After using my key to gain entrance, we crash through the door.

"Ya know what?"

"What?"

"Why don't ya stay here tonight so ya won't have to walk all the way down the hall? I got the other bed."

"Oh, I'll be alright."

We stumble to one of the beds where I, fully intoxicated, fall on my back, laughing hysterically. Ben hovers over me, giggling and saying, "Are *you* alright?"

In my inebriated haze, I see him standing over me. His lips look so inviting and enticing. His eyes hypnotize me with their softness and passion. I pull him down to me and kiss him full on the lips. Oh, they are as soft as a cushion! Ben pulls back.

"Lionel…" He utters, as if seeing me for the first time.

I kiss him again, suddenly feeling the fire in my loins. Behind my closed eyes, I hear Ben moan with reluctant pleasure. But he pulls back again as I open my eyes.

"Lionel, I don't think we should be doing this."

I pull him to me once more, this time kissing him with a fire that singes the pelvis and pulsates hot blood to the phallic shaft. I feel Ben's strong hands slowly cup the back of my head as I feel the heat of his breath blowing air into my mouth and his tongue jostling with mine. He rips off his shirt as he kisses me and stumbles out of his pants and underwear. When I sit back to take a breath, I gape at the vision standing in front of me.

To have Ben's naked body in front of me is heart stopping. His tall, pecan-tan frame is thick with sleek and hard flesh. His arms are long and sinewy, and his hairy stomach is flat and firm. His black carpeted massive chest displays big erect nipples. His thighs and calves are stoutly built as if Michelangelo sculpted them himself. And the dick... oh this huge dick... is curved upward and bears the color of a velvety Snickers bar, sporting a dark brown head.

Blistering sexual fire blazes from his deep-set brown eyes. He approaches me, cagey like a tiger. I seductively take off my shirt and remove my pants and boxers. Apparently, his eyes marvel at the sight that meets them because he breathes out, "Damn!" He stands me up and spans my waist with his huge soft hands and he kisses me once again with a fervor that is frightening, precarious, and exhilarating at the same time. He trails wet kisses down my heated body. I feel his warm mouth engorging my shaft! I throw my head back in ecstasy as I grab his shoulders and thrust forward... backward... forward...

Oh, the bliss of this man's tongue is driving me mad. Yet... through my hazy euphoria, an arrow of clarity pierces my mind, and with it comes Jojo's hurt face when I hit him. In this flash, I see thirty-eight years evaporate before my eyes. Thirty-eight years built on Jojo's hope that I would be his one and only love. Thirty-six of those years were wasted by my quest to find the right love that never measured up to his.

Oh my God, what in the fuck am I doing? I already hurt Jojo once by hitting him. But if I do this, our relationship AND our friendship may disappear forever and, deep down, I don't want that to happen.

If I ever had a moment that sobered me through all the liquor I drunk, this is it. I push Ben back and run out on the terrace. *I can't believe what I just did! I am the lowest of the low!*

I hear the terrace door open. I turn to look into Ben's huge eyes filled with concern.

"Uh, Ben..."

"What's wrong?" Ben asks, with concern in his voice.

"I'm so sorry. You are right... We shouldn't do this."

Ben doesn't say one word more. He just nods in understanding, goes back into the room, and begins to put his clothes on. I follow him inside, swaying unsteadily.

"Ben..."

He turns and looks at me with a blank expression on his face.

"I'm sorry... I'm just in a crazy space right now."

"I know. No need to explain," Ben says. "We are cool. But before we tempt ourselves more, I think I'd better head to my room."

"Ben, you don't have to do that."

"It's ok."

"No, it's not."

Ben comes to me and sits me down on the bed. He then grips my shoulders gently while looking at me with tenderness. "Lionel, I've been in this space before. You just lost your mother. You're going through craziness at the firm, and I don't know what else may be going on, but I'll bet that things seem like they are falling apart. Right now, you don't know what you want. You are all over the place... and all the drinks we both had are not helping any. That's why I said we shouldn't. If I remember correctly, you are engaged to marry Joseph Thompson, right?"

"Not anymore."

"Why not?"

I look down at the carpet and say, after letting a few seconds pass. "I fucked things up. He broke up with me." I begin crying. Slowly, I feel Ben's hand massage my shoulder with compassion, as we hear the waves crashing. He releases me and I can scarcely meet his eyes.

"Lionel, look at me."

I raise my eyes to meet his as he says, "Do you love Joseph?"

Slowly, I say, "Yes, I do..."

"You said that you fucked things up, but do you think you can fix it?"

What a question? If it was a small fight, I would say yes without hesitating. But I hit Jojo. I chose the pills over our relationship. Knowing that, I'm not so sure that I can.

"I don't know," I say tearfully.

"Well, I do," Ben says. "If you love Joseph, then being hugged up with me or anybody else is not an option." He puts his hand on my knee. "Talk to him. Work it out." He pats and massages me reassuringly on my thigh, then finishes dressing and walks to the exit.

"Ben...I'm sorry."

"No harm done. We will talk more tomorrow. Get some sleep," he says, before walking out and closing the door.

As I sit on the edge of the bed, my loneliness and despair are now amplified. My guilt is now doubled by the fact that I found pleasure in the arms of another man. Whether I stopped it or not is irrelevant. It shouldn't have happened in the first place. I started kissing *him*, not him kissing me. I made the first move. Where did it come from? Was it because I was lonely or was it sheer desperation?

Oh God, I am so confused! Confused and Ashamed! I don't deserve Jojo! I don't even deserve to have happiness because I would just fuck it up every time it's promised.

I stumble to my suitcase to unzip the side pocket and retrieve my medicine from the bottle. With a sadness I can barely contain, I pop the pill in my mouth, place my naked body between the hotel sheets, pull them over my head, and sink into troubled, drunken sleep.

Chapter Ten
I GOT THIS!

"Ya'll didn't have to come with me, you know," Corey whines as we lug his bags into Thurgood Marshall.

"How else were we gonna get your shit down to the airport?" Peep huffs, gasping for air.

"What? Is Mr. Health, the fitness trainer, out of breath? You're telling your age, my brother. You are telling your age!" Corey finishes with comic emphasis.

"My age ain't got shit to do with it. It is having to carry this heavy ass keyboard across the damned parking garage."

"Peep, it is not just a keyboard; it is a workstation."

"Workstation, keyboard…Whatever you want to call it, the shit is heavy."

"I don't know why you have to carry this thing all around the world anyway," Jojo says. "I'm sure that whatever venue you're playing will have a piano."

"Oh, come on, Jojo," I interject. "You know that Corey has had this keyboard…"

"Workstation."

"What he said… for eighteen years. Besides his piano at home, he needs this to keep cranking out the hits. It's his inspiration." I attempt to sidle up to Jojo, but he steps away from me. It has been two weeks after the fight and Jojo is still not speaking to me. He is obviously still pissed. When we all met at Corey's house to pick him up and take him to the airport, Jojo was like ice. He wouldn't even look at me. *Boy, you really fucked up this time!*

"Thank you, Lionel," Corey says with a grateful nod in my direction. "How wonderful it is to be understood."

"I understand *these* things... But I'm still at a loss as to how I can understand *your* changeable ass as a whole!" I joke.

"Changeable! Hmm, improving our vocabulary, are we?" Corey quips.

"Love, my vocabulary is fab and fine. I'm just expanding it."

"Alright, Mr. Professor."

Corey goes to the kiosk to retrieve his boarding pass. While we are carrying on conversation, I look at Peep as he steals anxious glances at Corey.

"Peep, is there a reason why you are looking at Corey like you are worried?" Jojo asks.

After a pause, he returns, "I just have a funny feeling."

"And that is?" I say as I scan the terminal.

"I guess I'm just worried about this trip overseas. Corey has never been this far away from the States by himself."

"Oh, I'm sure he will be fine," Jojo assures.

"Guys, I had a crazy dream last night," Peep whispers.

"What was it?" Jojo asks as we lean in to listen.

"I dreamed that I was in this house, and I saw a portrait of someone that looked like Corey. He had a look of fear on his face. I went up to the painting to check it out, but there was a knife slash that suddenly sliced out of nowhere and it was across his neck."

A piercing headache throbs my temples. I've been getting them a lot lately and sometimes they make me dizzy. Thankfully, it's a short one. When the pain subsides, I consider what Peep is saying and I feel a chill that involuntarily shakes me. The night of my drunken close call with Ben, I had a dream about a shadowy figure holding a bloody hunter's knife in one hand and a gun in the other. The shadow was at the foot of my bed and I couldn't make out the features of his eyes or nose. But what I did see was a blinding white smile, then black blood seeping out of the gums. The dream had me shaken for days, but I keep quiet because I don't want to alarm them. Plus, it was the first time I took medicine with liquor in my system. I won't be doing that anymore.

"Oh Peep, that's just superstitious nonsense."

"Superstitious, my ass. Listen, I know what I dreamed, and that shit seemed real as fuck."

"Look, you are stressing over nothing. Ain't shit gonna happen to Corey. He'll be fine."

I catch sight of Corey waving us over to bring the bags for checking.

"I'm surprised that Garrett isn't here to see you off," Jojo says.

"He had to work. Besides, we said our farewells last night."

"Inquiring minds want to know the nature of your 'farewells'," I taunt.

"You know what? Y'all are some nosy bitches."

An uneasy quietness settled on us all as the sounds of other passengers are intensified. Corey then says, "Well, I guess this is it. I'm going international." He stares in the direction of the security checkpoint. I see a nervous look on his face.

"You look scared. Are you alright?" I ask.

"I'm shitting bricks, y'all."

"Why?"

"This is a different ball game. It's not the university choir where we were doing music by other composers. Darrell and I are doing my music. People never heard this shit before." Corey starts hyperventilating. Then he looks frantic as he gushes, "Oh my God! What if they don't like it? What if they can't connect to it?"

"A better question would be this: why are you letting this stress you out so much? Just go over there and do what you do, and it will be fine."

"I- I- I can't do this!" Corey exclaims. He heads back to the ticketing counter.

"What are you doing?" Jojo asks.

"I'm going to turn in my ticket and get my bags back. I'm going home."

"And what about Darrell? What are you going to tell him?"

"I'll call him on the way."

"Like hell you will!" Peep shouts authoritatively, causing people to glance our way. He goes behind Corey and forcibly turns him around. I look at Peep in shock.

"Now you listen to me. Do you think Darrell Alston would have recorded your song if he thought it was trash?"

"Of course not."

"Would your ass be going on this tour with him if he thought that way?"

"No, Peep."

"I don't have to remind you of the response you got from that concert. Corey, your destiny is not to be found in your house writing songs that nobody can hear. Look where I'm pointing." Peep emphatically points towards the security checkpoint.

"It lies OUT THERE. And you are getting on that plane if I have to go up there with you to strap you into your seat. Now, you best get to marching! You got a dream to catch." Peep finishes. Then he smiles a bright smile and gives Corey an encouraging wink.

Corey just stands there with tears in his eyes.

"You can do this," Jojo affirms.

After a long pause, Corey shakes Peep's hand, then pulls him in for a tight loving hug. He hugs me and Jojo tightly as well.

"Knock 'em dead, Corey," I encourage.

Corey pulls away from us, then walks toward the checkpoint. He turns around with a radiant smile on his face and a pure light in his eyes. "I'll text you when I get there. Thanks, fellas."

We watch as Corey makes his way to the line for the scanners. Then, obscured by the abundance of people, he disappears from our view.

*****

Two weeks after Corey's departure, Peep suggested that he and I meet at City Café for an early dinner. I am sitting here now with him. Honestly, I am a bit antsy. One reason is that I ran out of both my medications last night and my refills won't be available until tomorrow. I had a proverbial fit this morning in the pharmacy when the clerk told me this. At least, this white wine is calming me down a bit. Another reason why I am nervous is because whenever Peep calls for a dinner with any one of us, it means he has something serious to discuss. I hope this isn't going to be too heavy.

"OK, Peep. What is going on? The only time you suggest dinner is when something is bothering you."

Peep sighs deeply, then continues, "I have two things that are bothering me."

"OK. What's the first one?"

Looking blankly over my shoulder, Peep says, "I think Jimmy is hiding something from me."

"Such as?"

"I don't know. He has been working pretty late these past few months. And when he gets home, all he wants to do is sleep."

"So?"

Peep looks at me in disbelief. "So?! Lionel, he hasn't touched me in two months. He gets up hours before I do and gets home long after I've gone to sleep. We rarely even see each other."

"What about his days off?"

"On his days off, *I'm* the one always working. There was one day when we were both off, but he just slept the whole day." Peep cast his eyes downward. "Lion," he says in a small voice.

"Yeah?"

After a pause, he asks, "Do you think… that Jimmy might be cheating on me?"

"Oh no! He would never do that!"

"How can you be so sure?"

"Felipe Alexander Walker-Hartfield!"

"Oh God! My whole government name?"

"Have you looked in the mirror lately? I mean, let's list the qualities. Good looking, Tight ass body, smart, and got style! You are an entire deluxe package! Why would Jimmy be looking for a K-Fried Strawberry Shortcake when he has rich Crème Brûlée at home?"

"Yeah, Crème Brûlée with a gut just beginning to show."

"Oh, Peep. Set it to music, will you?"

"Really, Lion. I just turned forty and things are starting to slide."

"Again… Such as?"

"I'm seeing lines in my face that I didn't see before, my hair is getting gray and I'm spending more time trying to color it away, and the workouts that I used to be able to do with ease are straining me when I do them now."

"Oh shit, Peep. You may as well start singing 'Ol' Man River' because you are giving me the blues!"

"I'm serious, Lion."

"Well, when did you start noticing these changes?"

"About three weeks ago."

I take a deep breath, then I say, "Well, I can't say much about the gray hairs because all of us fellas are getting them. That's something we can't avoid… But we still look damned good! In fact, I say we look a hell of a lot better than some men half our age."

"I guess…"

"You guess, but I know!" I state emphatically. "Now about the wrinkles and workouts, have you stopped to think that you are stressing about Jimmy so much that you can't focus on the things you need to do to stay healthy?"

"I suppose."

"Well, there ya go! Look, how long have you and Jimmy been married?"

"Fifteen years."

"Has he ever given you a reason not to trust him before?"

"No."

"And you two are well past the seven-year-itch."

"Oh, trust!" Peep brightens a little, showing a bit more of his kick-ass personality. "We both had the itch!"

"What did you do to scratch it?"

"We talked about it… then we went to an orgy."

"Shut up!"

"I'm as serious as a heart attack. It was hot and we enjoyed it. But after we got back home and discussed it, we discovered that everything done in that orgy was nothing we hadn't done in the bedroom by ourselves. It felt meaningless, just something to do to pass the time with guys we didn't know. Truthfully, we felt kind of cheap. It was like these dudes were saying, 'Boom Boom. Good. NEXT?"

"Ya'll were safe, right?"

"Trust, we were. I have utmost respect for you, Corey, Jojo, and others who medicate daily due to something they have to live with, but I want to stay negative and so does Jimmy."

"Smart choice."

"Well, what do you think I ought to do?"

"What you just said you two have been doing. TALK."

"How is that possible with both of us working these crazy hours?"

"If you both love each other, you will make time."

"I suppose."

We then take a long sip of the coffee. Afterwards, I ask, "Now, what is the other problem?"

Peep looks down, playing with the flakes on his croissant. There is an unbearable silence. *Why do I have this feeling in the pit of my stomach.*

"Feel free to tell me anytime today," I half-joke sarcastically.

Peep exhales and says, "I'm thinking about the best way to bring this one up."

"Why not just come right out and say it?"

"Because it concerns… *you.*"

"Me? What about me?"

Peep suddenly sits up, making a ramrod of his spine and looking at me with concern. There's a sternness in his eyes that unsettles me as he says,

"Lionel, I care about you, and it's *because* I care that I'm bringing this up."

"What is it?" I say impatiently.

"I had a talk with Dr. Camden about you this morning."

"Why would she be talking to you about me?"

"Because she happened to be at the Chase Brexton pharmacy, and she said that you went on a severe tirade about your medication."

I am stunned to silence. An annoyed look must have passed my face because Peep says, "Before you get in your feelings, I want to point out that she was just concerned about you. She was calling for Jimmy to relay the message to me. But Jimmy was busy, so he texted me her number. I called her and she told me what went down.

"Look, it's not that big a deal."

"Your screaming at the top of your lungs and reducing the technician to tears seem like a pretty big deal to me. Not to mention that fight with Jojo."

"Peep, I don't need you reading too much into this shit. I was just angry because I couldn't get my pills."

"Maybe it's good that you didn't get them."

I growl, "Peep, spell it out plain and simple. What are you trying to say?"

"I'm not *trying* to say anything. Trying means that the words haven't come out of my mouth yet. I've been *saying* it... Jojo and Corey... A.D.... All of us have been *saying* it for months. You are spiraling out of control. It's that Alprolozine, isn't it?"

I don't answer.

"Look Lionel," Peep begins. "I have been reading up on that particular drug, and, from what I've read, it can be addictive. I know you get them through this Dr. Williams fool, but do you know what doctors write that shit up for? Schizophrenia and bipolar disorder... and unless you know something I don't, you don't have either one. You need to get off that shit."

"Oh Jesus, Peep! Give it a fucking rest already! I already heard this shit from ya'll more times than I care to remember. Why do I have to hear it over and over again!"

"Ok, let's list the reasons, shall we?" Peep says in a hard tone. "I see muscles twitching around your eyes and mouth. Your face is swollen, and it's not because you are eating too much. Even now, you can't keep your left leg still. Plus, your attitude has been fucked up lately. For the past week, you've been complaining constantly about headaches. And you ought to think about this. With you having a pre-existing condition, there is a chance that they might be fucking up your system and you don't even know it."

I breathe out, but my breath feels like it's coming out in a shudder. "Peep, I am fine!"

"No, you are not. I know you believe that these pills are helping you to sleep and keeping you level, but you can't see that they are also taking you through some weird shit. We are all worried that you are going to do some major damage to yourself."

"For the last time, I know what I'm doing! And I'm done talking about this! DONE!" At that moment, I look around and I notice people staring at me... *Oh shit... I have got to calm down... See, if I had my pills, I wouldn't be sitting here looking like a circus sideshow! This is that pharmacy's fault!* As moments pass and the other customers drift back into their separate conversations, I look into my friend's eyes as he stares at me like I'm a different person.

"Fine, Lionel..." Peep sits back and stares at his croissant. I feel the emotions of worry and disappointment radiating off of him. The next few minutes trudge by as we finish our food in silence. Peep stands and says in a terse tone, "I have to get home." He grabs his briefcase and starts to leave.

"Peep?" I call out and he turns around slowly.

"I got this. Don't worry about me. I'm alright."

Peep responds with a dejected expression on his face. "I hope you are right. For all our sakes, I sincerely hope you are right."

*****

I am entranced in deep thought as I stroll out of Chase Brexton to walk to the parking garage on Cathedral. After Peep left, I called to check my messages at home and the pharmacist said they had my medication ready for pickup tonight instead of tomorrow. Since it was forty-five minutes before they closed, I went in to get them, but the feeling of relief I usually have when they are in my hands is absent. As I pop the pill of the lower dosage in my mouth and stand at the water fountain to sip and wash it down, I thought about the afternoon with Peep and the look on his face during my outburst. There was an expression of pure hurt. I thought about the conversation I had with Corey a few months back as well as the fight with Jojo.

I exit the Chase Brexton building and pace the sidewalk with my head down. I wouldn't admit this to any of The Fellas, but everything Peep listed was true. *I know I have been going through a few changes. And yes, I had that fight with Jojo. But...*

My thoughts are halted as I bump into a medium sized body. I look up and my initial emotion is disgust. Before me stands a five-eight, freckle faced, light skinned guy in full drag. If I was to guesstimate his age, I would say he was about twenty-one. He sports a wig of reddish hair swept up in a bun with a few strands of hair hanging near his defined, made up cheeks. He is clad in a pale green short-sleeve shirt of and white fashionable weathered jeans. Slung over his narrow shoulder is a JanSport Bag. On his feet are white patent leather heels. He has a beat face, but I notice traces of discoloration around his left eye.

When I regain my composure, I say, "Excuse me." I hear my own voice. *Why do I sound so cold?*

"No problem, love," he answers with a light, friendly tone. I start to veer past him when I hear him call out, "Hey mister."

"Yes." I feel my face harden. *What does this queen want from me?*

"Would you happen to have any spare change?"

Oh Lord! I am always leery about giving money to homeless people, especially in this city! You heard about that woman who gave a panhandler some money and got killed two years ago. It turned out to be her husband and daughter. Sometimes I push past the fear of giving it, but most times I just say no and keep walking.

Then, there are times when I ask what they need it for. This is one of those times. When I ask him this, he looks me straight in my eye and says, "I'm trying to get something to eat and get enough to get by in DC. I got family down there."

"How did you end up in Baltimore?"

"I was born and raised here."

"Then why are you trying to get to DC? And why can't you ask family for the money?"

He exhales and rolls his eyes in frustration. *Oh, he is definitely not getting anything from me now!* "Look, mister. Do you have any change or not?"

"Not for you to blow on worthless shit after telling me that sob story."

"Wow!" he exclaims, laughing sardonically and glancing toward the opposite side of the street.

"Do your folks know that you are walking the streets in drag and begging hard working people for money to do God knows what?"

He then looks at me, his eyes snapping fire. "You see? You are just like so many others who condemn people before knowing what their story is.

I bet you think I'm just telling a pack of lies."

"How could I know? I don't even know you. How old are you, anyways?"

"Seventeen." *Goddamn! What in the hell is a seventeen-year-old kid doing out here?* Just that quick, my emotions go from disgust to concern.

"What happened? Why aren't you at home?"

"My dad beat me up and kicked me out of the house."

I cannot speak. Here before me stands a kid who is living and breathing the craziness that I was afraid to face at his age: getting kicked out for being gay.

"If you don't believe me, take out your phone and dial this number. 202-811-6459. Ask for Miss Zena. Tell her Orchid is coming."

I pull out my phone to dial the number. After two rings, an androgynous voice with an edge answers the phone. "Hello?"

"Uh… yeah… Is this Miss Zena?"

"In the flesh, baby."

"I'm… uh… calling for someone named Orchid."

Suddenly her voice switches to concern. "My God! What in the hell is taking her so long to get here? Tell her to hurry up and get down to the bus station. Her ticket is already paid for. She can call Greyhound to verify." *She? OK…*

Shocked and befuddled, I answer, "I-I'll tell him… uh… her."

"Ok, honey. Bye."

Why do I have the bitter taste of crow in my mouth? I think to myself. I glance at **her** as she stands with an expectant look on her face. When I relay the message to her, she laughs with relief.

"That's Mama Zena for you. Sweeter than a homemade German chocolate cake."

"I'm sorry I didn't believe you."

She shrugs her shoulders. I immediately feel guilty, and sudden trust for someone I don't even know. *I must be crazy.*

"Here. Walk with me to the parking garage. I'll take you to Burger King to grab something to eat. Then, I'll run you to the bus station. You cool with that?"

She nods and grants me a beaming smile.

Chapter Eleven
BURGERS… WITH BULLETS ON THE SIDE

We are sitting at the table and eating our burgers at Burger King on North Avenue and Gold Street. I'm noticing that people are staring at us and it's making me uncomfortable. Orchid is wolfing the burger like it is her last meal.

"So, what is your real name? I know it can't be Orchid."

"It can if I want it to be, but it is not. My given name is Shane Thornton. But I like Orchid, so let's stick with that."

"How long have you been out in these streets?"

"Two days."

There is an uncomfortable silence. Then Orchid looks at me.

"You're embarrassed, aren't you?"

"Oh no, not at all."

She looks at me pointedly, with an expression that spells, *Be honest.*

"OK. A little, but it's not because you're gay. I'm gay too and got plenty of gay friends."

"But you don't really mix it up with us trans girls, do you?"

"No," I assent admittedly.

"I thought not because, if you did, you would know that trans girl and gay are two different things."

"From where I'm sitting, it's kind of hard to distinguish between the two."

"Not if you try. Trust!"

"How so?"

"Well, you have men who like men and are as masculine as all get out. Then you have those who are fem that prefer men, but they still consider themselves men. Those fall under the category of gay."

"I knew that," I encourage, intrigued by this bright young person.

"Now those of us who are trans, the doctors and parents identify us as boy or girl, depending on what equipment they see on the ultrasound. But there is just something deep down in us that tells us otherwise. We 'boys' go through childhood being forced to play with Tonka and action figures when we would rather fiddle around with Barbie."

At that moment, I thought about my own childhood and how it was natural for me to want to play with trucks and to roughhouse. But we had one cousin around my age named Joshua. He was dubbed as the "family embarrassment", at least until I came along. When he was growing up, his features were very delicate and his mannerisms dainty. He didn't like roughhousing or shooting the breeze with the boys. He was content with playing with Brenda or messing with Rhonda's doll house when she wasn't around. Try as my relatives might, they just couldn't "toughen him up". He was picked on worse than Jojo ever was, by both family and schoolmates. I remember a time when Uncle Timothy, a pastor at a church in Birmingham, tried to make him fight this boy named Donald from around the neighborhood when Joshua was sixteen. He was known for being a first-class bully, but Joshua wouldn't fight him. The boy pounded on him, but he just laid there and took every blow and kick. After the fight (or beatdown) was over, Uncle Timothy beat him worse than Donald did. His mother, Gail, couldn't help him because she was just as timid and soft-spoken. I believe she drank to dull the pain of watching Joshua get treated so badly. And as quiet as it's kept, I believe Uncle Timothy was beating on her too. Joshua left Alabama that very night and moved to Houston to live with a distant relative. When I told my mother about me and she flipped, Joshua got wind of it and tried to reach out to me. But I kept my distance because I didn't want to be associated with him. Two years ago, he went ahead and had the surgery to turn him into a woman. He now goes by the name of Jocelyn. But although I applauded his courage, the idea always disgusted me.

"Hello, sir?"

"Huh, what?"

"Are you alright?"

"Yeah, I'm fine. Uh... when did you start... uh...," I hesitate.

"Dressing up?"

"Yeah."

"I started at fifteen. I would lie to my parents about going to my friend's house for the weekend, when I was really going up to DC to participate in the balls. That's how I met Mother Zena. She taught me everything there is to know."

"I'm kind of curious to see what you look like as a boy."

"OK, I'll show you." She reached in the purse and pulled out a picture. It depicted a light skinned boy with a strong yet curvaceous frame. He had naturally full lips that most women achieve by injecting silicone. His facial bone structure was sharp with a definite feminine jawline. Now I see why "the boy" dressed all the way up. He looked feminine enough to be a lady.

She looks at the picture wistfully. Shortly, she says, "Yep, that's my parents' idea of what they want me to be, but I'm saving up my money to pay for the operation so that I can be what I need to be. It's my inner born truth."

"I understand."

"But I'll have you to know that although I dress up and do the balls, I am keeping up my grades. I just have to transfer schools and Mother Zena is helping me with that. I still want to graduate next year. I want to go to UCLA."

"Why UCLA?"

"Well, because DC and Baltimore are not the best places to live as a transgirl. There are more of us in Los Angeles, and I want to make a fresh start after I emerge from my 'boy' cocoon."

"Good for you. You know, you are pretty smart to be so young."

"I take after my parents, hateful though they may be." She stops and looks past me, her lips quivering and her eyes watering with tears.

"I never thought that they would actually do it. My father and I were always at odds, but I could at least lean on Mother. She was the buffer between us." She looks down at her burger for a minute. Then she continues. "Dad found panties on the floor that I dropped on the way to the laundry room. At first, he was patting me on the back and saying, 'That's my boy.' But after all the lies I told about going to my friend's house, I just couldn't lie anymore. I told Dad that the panties were mine. He threw a fit, punched me hard in my eye, and told me to get out. I looked toward Mother for support, but she just kept crying and going on about what an abomination I was." Orchid stops again, with tears rolling down her face. As if a hurt is billowing from her soul, she cries, "How can parents just cut their children off? Whether I dressed up or remained as they demanded, I never thought that they would just toss me away... Girl or boy... I never stopped being their child!" Upon hearing her words turn into loud sobs, I move to her side and hold her. She clings to me for dear life. There are people staring in disgust, but I continue to hold her as my heart weeps with her.

Abruptly, I catch a pair of booze-laden eyes attached to a tall, lanky brown skinned man with cornrows and a dark mark on his face. His whole aura is filled with inebriated poison. I can feel its overwhelming vibrations.

"Got a problem?" I demand as I continue to hold Orchid. I can feel her body tense up with fear.

"Yeah. Lookin' at you faggots is my problem," he spits out hatefully.

Though my good common sense tells me to keep my mouth shut and ignore this fool, my mother's bold and careless disposition rose up in me. *Fight him or I'll kick your ass when you get home.* My mother's words echo from my childhood to this moment. *If you let him get the best of you, you're a goddamned punk.* Foolishly, I say, "Take a look in the mirror, asshole."

A dangerous look crosses his face as he approaches. "I know you ain't talkin' to me, motherfucka," he says murderously.

"No, I'm talking to the picture behind you," I say as I stand and move my body to shield Orchid from this stupid Neanderthal. "Only the picture has better looks and bigger brains."

Suddenly, I feel a hard fist crash into my face. I reel back, stunned. But, quickly recovering with a move courtesy of my dad teaching me how to box, my left hook slams into his jaw, sending him to the floor.

"Hey, hey, hey!" A short, stoutly built lady with a bald head rushes from the back. She is carrying a Louisville Slugger baseball bat. "What the fuck is goin' on in here?" She positions herself between us and him.

"This guy just stepped over here and started hassling us," Orchid defends.

She turns slowly around to contemptuously glare at the bully. Giving him an "I'm tired of this shit" smile, she spits out, "Sonny Daniels, I know you are a stupid, simple motherfucka... but you can't be that hard a' hearing. I done told you twice not to come back here no more."

"Don't tell ME. Tell these faggots with their gay ass shit," Sonny says as he scrambles to his feet.

"You must have forgot that you are talkin' to a dyke right now. They ain't done shit to you, so you need to move out that door before I call the cops."

"Get out of my way, you ol' cunt eating bitch!" Sonny makes a move toward me, but the lady flicks out a long switchblade and aims it at his throat, stopping him dead in his tracks.

"Which one do you want, the bat or the blade? This ol' cunt eating bitch can lick the kitty and kick yo' trifling ass at the same goddamned time. Do you want me to prove it?" Sonny says nothing, but I can tell she's still getting angrier by the second.

"If you don't get off the premises, I'll cut you so deep you won't be able to piss or fuck no more. Now, get the fuck outta here."

Sonny squares his shoulders, and backs slowly toward the door, pointing ominously at Orchid and me. He spits out, "Watch ya back, faggit motherfuckas!" When he exits, the lady goes to the door to make sure he's gone. Then she approaches us, "Y'all a'ight?"

"Yeah, we're good. Thanks, Miss," Orchid says, still shaken up. "Thank God you were there."

"Aw fuck, I ain't done nothing. I know Sonny. He is just like his piss poor daddy. Ain't got no mother wit. The dames AND the dudes say he's a good fuck. But common decency ain't made it to his head yet," she says, looking out the glass door and shaking her head.

"That's sad to hear," I sigh.

"Yeah. Well, y'all better get on to where y'all gettin' to. It's closing time and good ol' Katie gots to close up so I can get home to put my feet up."

"Well, thanks again, Katie."

"No problem."

We pass through the door… Then we hear the words, "Bitch ass punks!" I see Sonny swing out from the restaurant's side where he was obviously lurking. A fear grips me as I see a gun in Sonny's hand. At that moment, I shove Orchid out of the path of fire. A sharp, searing pain tears through my side before I hear a heavy metal object clank on the pavement. My body hits the ground hard before I see everything slowly turning black.

Oh my God… I've been shot!

Lying on my back, I hear Orchid's voice yelling hysterically for help. I hear Katie curse Sonny and bellow for someone to call 911, then I feel her press a wet towel on my wound as she cradles my head, saying, "Stay with us, baby! You ain't going nowhere. Hold on. We gettin' you help!"

My vision blurs and darkens... *Oh Lord... I'm dying!*

What is this light I see? It is so bright... Someone is coming... I can't quite make out the shape... He is moving pretty fast... Oh my God! DAD!

Standing before me is my father. He is dressed in blinding, shimmering white. His skin is almost golden, and his handsome face is filled with urgency. He looks at me and shakes his head frantically.

Son... go back!

Dad, where are you coming from?

No time to explain! Go back!

He rapidly pushes his hands out as if to ward something off. Suddenly I hear a whistling wind. I feel a vacuum sucking my body into darkness. I land in a place of absolute stillness. I feel immobile, stiff as a board. I am unaware of my surroundings... Unsure of whether I am alive or dead... Then, faintly, I hear my father's deep haunting voice and a gentle wind with the fragrance of fresh rain chills me to the bone.

Let it go. It's killing you.

Although my mind feigns ignorance, my heart knows what he is talking about: the hatred towards my mother. The wind ceases blowing, and I feel my own mind probing the question, *I have, haven't I?*

I feel a coolness touch my forehead. Feels like a gentle hand. I feel the rain scented wind again and with it comes my father's voice, more clearly.

No, you haven't, son. You are still holding to your grudge like an addict gripping a needle. Your mother was a broken woman... broken by life... by abuse... by her own self-hatred, and her brokenness made her bitter.

I can't feel sympathy for her, Dad. What she went through doesn't excuse her from what she did to me. My mind says. Suddenly, the wind becomes sharp and biting as my father's voice grows stern.

You have love all around you, trying to tell you that you are walking a dangerous road, but you are abusing that love by not listening. Your anger is transforming you into her with each passing day. I'm coming to warn you. Don't make the same mistake she made. Break the cycle… and LIVE!

*****

The wind and the voice are gone. I suddenly feel an expanse of air filling my lungs. My senses are alert as I hear beeping machines.

"Lion?" I hear a voice say. I open my eyes to find that I am in a hospital room and the first face I see is Jojo's. His face lights up with relief and joy. He goes to the door and opens it, shouting, "Ya'll come on in here! Lionel's awake! Nurse! Get Dr. Camden and tell her to come in here!"

As they rush into the room and stand around the bed, my grateful eyes see the concerned faces of my three brothers, my sister Brenda, my friends Peep and Garrett, and my ex-fiancé, Jojo. Roland and Brenda's mates; Angela and Mercer, move to stand beside them in comfort mode. "What happened?" I manage in a croaky voice. I stir myself to try sitting up, but the pain in my side forces me to stay down.

"Don't move, baby," Jojo soothes. *Baby? Hmmm…*

"Thank God you are alive!" Brenda exhales as she kisses and touches my face tenderly, crying and laughing at the same time.

"We have been praying for you," Angela informs in a sanctimonious tone. I look at her, surveying her long and lean body, her sallow skin, and grayish green eyes looking at me with scathing pity. She is clad in a dreary black dress and has an unsightly black purse dangling from her arm. Angela has always been a strange bird to me. She is the type that will pinpoint the shortcomings of others while leaving out the fact that she has quite a few of her own. Ever since Roland told her of my coming out, she comes at me with this "Give your life to the Lord and be delivered from that wicked lifestyle" tip. To be honest, I am surprised that she came at all. I could never be around her without feeling an inward shudder. Roland just met and got engaged to her, which is odd because he usually has good taste in women.

I wearily try to raise my hand from my side, but I can't move it. It feels like an anvil is weighting it down. "How long have I been out?"

"Almost a week. You weren't responding when they got to you. Then when you did respond, they put you under so they could perform the surgery," Mercer says. His tall, portly, redbone frame shadows Brenda protectively. His handsome face looks relieved.

Just then, Dr. Camden walks in and sees me. She smiles. "So, how is my patient?"

"In pain."

"I can imagine. You know, over a year ago, you were in this hospital for Mr. Kennedy. Now, here YOU are! You gave us quite a scare!"

"You can say that shit again," Peep follows.

"Well, it ain't no July fourth picnic for me either," I retort, hoarsely.

"Still, we are just glad you are alive and well," Brenda says, rubbing my arm like a mother would. I feel a little bit of strength returning so I try to move when a sharp pain causes me to yelp in response.

"See," Jojo says. "I told you not to move."

"Well, dat's Li'nel fuh yuh, hard-headed as fuck," A.D. returns shakily.

"What else is new?" Roland jumps in, smirking.

I sit there for a few seconds, then I say, "So you gonna tell me?"

"Well, Mr. Davis," Dr Camden begins carefully. "You had a severe wound to your left abdomen, and you lost an alarming amount of blood. It was a good thing you were near someone who knew what to do. Otherwise, we wouldn't be having this conversation. The person who was with you held a towel to your wound until the paramedics got there."

"Wait a minute." I think for a few seconds, then gaze wildly around. "What happened with Orchid? Katie?"

"Calm down, Lion. They are fine. We met them that night. Katie is at work and Orchid is in DC. Katie had to make her go," Peep says.

"Thank God," I say with relief.

"We stopped the bleeding and did the surgery. We are going to monitor you for a couple of weeks, maybe three. But your body needs time to heal. Once it has, you will be fine."

"How long will it take for him to heal completely?" Mercer asks.

"Well, it could be anywhere from three to six months. But the bullet missed all your vital organs. That is the good news."

"What's the bad news?" Dean asks.

"Well, it's not really bad news, but you should know that because the bullet went considerably deep into your abdomen, we had to leave it in."

"What the fuck?" I rage weakly. "You mean I have to live with a foreign object in my body for the rest of my fuckin' life?"

"Mr. Davis, I am going to be very frank with you. If we take it out, it will do more long-term damage, the type that a simple operation would not fix. You may even die while we attempt it."

A.D. thumps me on the head, "It ain't nothin', bruh. I got wun in muh back wen I got shot at twinny-three."

"I don't care. I don't want this shit in me!"

"Mr. Davis, do you know how many gunshot victims I have patched up? The number is almost as high as my grandmother's age. Look, almost every victim that came through my doors got a bullet still in them and they are doing fine. After you heal, it won't make one difference in your daily routine."

"If you say so," I mutter darkly.

"Ok, I'm going to let your folks linger for a few more minutes and then you have to get your rest. One of them can stay if you feel that it will benefit you."

"I'll stay," Jojo assures. *Hmm… maybe this ain't gonna be too bad after all,* I think to myself.

"OK, then. I will look in on you later," Dr. Camden says with a reassuring smile as she grasps the door handle and exits the room.

"Uh, Lion? You have a caller long distance that wants to talk to you, but we need to keep it short, so we won't tire you out," Garrett says, holding out the phone with a teasing look. I attempt to reach for the phone, but the pain in my side starts screaming bloody murder. Garrett tells me to rest and presses speaker phone.

"Hello?" I croak.

Corey's voice hollers, drawing a girlish giggle from Brenda, "Lion, what the fuck done happened to you?! Not even two weeks since I flew out the States. and you get yourself shot! My God, what…."

"Calm down, Corey. I'm fine. I got pain but I'll live."

"What happened?"

"Some drunk shitwit started static with me and some young'un I met. He shot me when we were leaving Burger King on North."

"Lionel, you know that Burger King is on a dangerous corner. No one oughta be in that area after dark. But skip that. Right now, I'm worried about you getting out of that hospital and back to your old self. I'm gonna ask Darrell to get my auxiliary musician to carry out the rest of this tour. Corey's coming home."

"No, Corey. I will be fine."

"I'm not trying to hear that shit right now. I gotta lay eyes on you. I knew I shouldn't have left," I hear tears in his voice.

With difficulty, I attempt to assuage Corey, "Please don't come back now. Your staring in my face ain't gonna do anything but irritate me and stop you from doing what you gotta do. *Finish your tour.* Trust me, I'll be fine... I'll be here when you get back in *two months.* Not before, and I mean that."

"But Lion..."

Garrett rescues me by taking the phone so that he and Corey can talk privately. "Look, Simon," I hear Garrett say, calling Corey by his birth name. "The Fellas and I got him. His family is up here, and we are going to do whatever it takes to make sure he's alright."

Jimmy enters the room, "Lionel, you are out of the woods. Thank God! I won't ask how you are feeling because I know your side is catching hell."

"Duh!" I grumble listlessly.

"Well, given time, you will be fine. You're lucky that the bullet came from one of those 32's and not a semi-automatic, considering the distance Katie said was between you and the gun."

"Yeah, whooptee do," I mutter in sarcasm.

"I know... This really sucks. But you're in good hands."

"Thanks..."

"OK. Frances told me that Jojo is sticking around for tonight, but it's time for me to kick the rest of y'all out so Lion can rest."

"Ok, baby," Peep says, pecking Jimmy on the lips. "I'll see you at home." I see a look of love shared between the two of them. *Hmmm... maybe Peep and Jimmy talked. That is good news.*

Jimmy injects a sedative into my I.V. tube. I sense tears coming as I feel the lips of my sister on my forehead, as well as that of all departing the room, except Angela. Brenda thumps me on the head. "Get some rest," she tells me, emphasizing each word firmly.

"Yes, 'little Mama'," I kid. She smirks as she heads out the door.

"Try not to worry," Mercer says, punching me lightly on the arm and grinning before he follows Brenda out.

When they leave, I am engulfed in a deluge of sadness. Then I am reminded of the question that Jojo asked two years ago when Corey was in this very hospital. "Why do they hate us?" The pain and anguish of that question overtakes me as it must have overtaken Corey. I begin to cry, weeping rivers of tears at the knowledge that there will never be a time

where we as gay people of any color will quit paying in blood for being
who we are. But then, I feel Jojo's soft and nurturing hands wiping my
tears as they fall. I look at him and, seeing tears pooling into eyes looking
with love into mine, I am overcome with shame.

"I am so sorry, Jojo. I didn't mean to hurt you."
"Shhh... don't..."
"I was so wrong..."
"I know. We'll talk about it when you are better. Right now, I want you
to rest."

I feel his lips press on my closed eyelids and his hands caressing my
face. As the sedative begins to immerse me in its shimmering cloak, I float
seamlessly into the dark and peaceful abode of slumber, where questions
of the world's hatred are banished and forgotten... if only for a while.

*****

I am sitting up in my hospital bed, playing cards with Jojo... and
stealing looks at him. He looks even more beautiful than before. I feel a
mixture of emotions. I feel happy that he is here with me, yet I feel guilty
about my hitting him, as well as my aborted sexual escapade with Ben. He
looks up from his hand and catches me staring.

"What?" he asks.
"I'm just looking at you."
"Why are you looking at me for?"
"Thinking of how blessed I am to have you in my life."
Jojo lets out a weak laugh. "That's nice. Draw or play?"
Whew... I felt an arctic chill from the coldness in his voice. There is
obviously an elephant in the room, and we need to deal with it. "OK, fuck
the cards for a minute. We need to talk about what happened."
"I told you, I forgive you."
"You might have told me, but just like you said that I can't tell a straight
lie to you, the reverse is also true. You can't tell one to me either."
There is an uncomfortable silence. Then Jojo speaks with anger
trembling his voice, "Lionel, you hit me! That shit hurt me to my heart! I
thought of Mike and how he railed on Mama and me almost every fucking
day. I thought about how much my mother had to love him to stay tied to

that shit. Maybe it was because she felt like she didn't deserve better. Maybe she was afraid. I don't know. But I do know that Mama and I are two different people. I have been through too much hell to allow you to take me through more."

I cannot speak as I recount the events of the night in question. Is this really a forecast of things to come? Would I be so out of control that I would lash out physically at the very one who served as comfort and peace throughout my life?

"It's those pills… and your own fucked up anger issues, Lionel. You can't have them and me too."

"Those pills…"

Jojo interrupts, "Those pills were prescribed by a shrink who was probably informed of you getting shot but has yet to call and check on you or schedule an appointment to discuss the trauma tied to this."

"Jojo…"

"Listen, I'm not trying to tell you what to do or how to cope. Neither is anyone else. We are just trying to get you to see where you're at right now. I didn't like the Doxepin, but I eventually dealt with it because you didn't have all these changes when you were on them. The residue from that Alprolozine is probably wreaking havoc in your body right now. I already know that you are taking it more than you are supposed to."

I weigh the gram of truth in Jojo's words as I look into his eyes. Eyes that are filled with worry and distress. I look closely at them and I see small lines forming at the corners. Oh my God, am I the cause of those lines? The guilt washes over me like a shower as I feel Jojo take my hand and stroke it gently, even as he speaks his next words.

"Lionel, I need you to seriously consider what you stand to lose. And it's not going to be just me. It's going to be a domino effect where you lose a whole lot more. Your family, your friends, and most of all… yourself."

I look out of the window and meditate. I think of the sessions with Dr. Williams and the apathy I sometimes face when discussing my confusing life. I think of my tight bond with Corey, Peep, and Jojo, as well as the others I have come to love, and how I drifted away from them in pursuit of the brief euphoria the pills gave me. Through my distance, I isolated myself from people who cared. Abruptly, I glimpse a vision of my Dad and recall my out-of-body experience. It is sad that it took a near death experience to tell me what a mess I'm making of my life. Something broken must have shown on my face because I feel Jojo's arms encircle me, and though I feel pain in my side, I feel comfort in the arms of my love.

Jojo holds me for a few more minutes before releasing me. He puts his hands on my cheeks, using his thumbs to wipe my eyes lovingly. As I look into his eyes, I see his love for me, bordered in pain. *How can I remove that hurt?* He says, "I'm going to go grab some food. You want anything?"

"No, I'm not really hungry. I need to think. You go ahead. We'll talk when you get back."

Jojo nods, gives me a sweet smile, and prepares to exit. I call out Jojo's name.

"Yeah?"

"What about the engagement?"

Jojo breathes out a reflective sigh. "I told you that I wouldn't marry you and those pills too… But that doesn't mean that things can't be reversed. It just depends on you, Mr. Davis, to show yourself to be stronger than your crutch. If you feel like your existence on this earth and our lifelong partnership is worth fighting for, prove it by getting your life together." He winks at me, smiles, then leaves.

I lay my back and head against the abundant pillows and fold my arms, thinking about the best way to mend things between myself and everyone I caused pain to. *Get my life together, huh? Maybe I can. The question is,* "How?"

PART II:

KEEP IT MOVIN'

Chapter Twelve
BACK TO LIFE

Three months later, I am sitting in my chair and writing furiously. Dr. Camden tells me that I am mending very well, but I will have to walk with a cane for a few months. I don't know who I'm madder at. It's a three-sided block toss amid that homo-hating asshole with his gun, this hunk of metal in my body, or having to walk like I got the fucking gout.

Countless vases of wilting flowers occupy almost every space in my living room. You know, I often wonder why people send floral arrangements when a person is either injured, sick, or dead. They just serve as a reminder that no matter how beautiful you are, eventually you die, rot, and blacken into dust. *OK, I should quit complaining. Shit, I'd be bummed if I didn't get anything at all.*

When I was in the hospital for my three-week stay, not a day went by where I didn't have visitors. Katie came by, sneaking in my favorite cherries' jubilee ice cream from After's Cafe. When I asked her how she knew it was my favorite, she told me that Jojo told her. I tried to get her to bring me some Whoppers, and she sidled up to my bed saying in a sneaky undertone, "Baby, I ain't trying to have yo' fine ass nurse pissed at me. She been givin' me the eye. I'm feelin' her feelin' me! I'm still trying to get her number! You gotta do it her way for a while because I'm working on my rap!" She sat with me and kept my sides splitting from her boisterous sense of humor and unique views on life. I began feeling a strong sense of comfort and trust with her. So, I told her about my situation with Jojo and the pills, lamenting the engagement being called off. She told me, "Well, Cap'n. You know what you got to do. If you are serious about being with Jojo, you gotta man up and fix some thangs, boy! And, from what I see, that thickie-juicy ass is definitely worth fighting for." I was touched that a lady I didn't even know (and in times past wouldn't grant the time of day, given her type) cared enough to be there for me, encouraging me to do what needed to be done. She reminded me of Irene and Eunetta. Maybe good friends are not just limited to the male perspective in this life we call Gay.

Orchid came down from DC to visit a few times. She felt guilty about what happened and kept saying that if I wasn't trying to give her food and a listening ear, I wouldn't have gotten shot. Of course, she is young and doesn't understand that sometimes shit happens and we can't always foresee it. But I tried to reassure her as best I could. She also told me that she was trying to acquire a scholarship to go to UCLA, and I told her that I was proud of her.

You know what's funny? Katie and Orchid come from the LGBTQ spectrum that I shied away from. I didn't mix with trans or lesbians. But seeing them by my side with care and love on their faces, I realize that they are just another part of the bright rainbow family. It would be crazy to ask the world to accept me if I am not man enough to correct my own prejudices and belief in stereotypes concerning not only transpeople, but also lesbians, feminine gay men, and those who may be gender-fluid. I also have to include those who are big or skinny in body and are deemed by status quo to be lacking in stature. We are all in this fight together... A fight to be at least understood and respected, if not wholly accepted. I was so inspired that I hunted down Jocelyn's number and called her. Turned out to be the best thing I could have done, because through talking long into the night, she helped me to disperse a great deal of my own transphobia. Since then, we have been contacting each other frequently. I'm still a bit nervous around trans, but I have a better understanding and hopefully my knowledge will expand.

My siblings stuck around to check on me all through the first week of my homecoming. Afterwards, I made them get their asses on a plane back to their families and jobs, assuring them that I would be fine. I couldn't get rid of A.D. that easily though. I mean, how could I? He lives in this city. Even when I was at the hospital, with Jojo and Peep there every spare minute, A.D. stood nearby with his arms folded and his eyes narrowed, making sure the nurses did their jobs... and there was hell to pay if they didn't.

I learned later that A.D. went on a vigilante mission to find Sonny. He hooked up with both of Garrett's crazy assed cousins- Craig and Melba- and they tracked Sonny down. They kicked his ass until he could barely breathe and waited until he *could* breathe so they could fuck him up more.

When I heard about it, I talked to A.D. to let him know that I was both grateful and pissed. I told him, "You could have gotten yourself killed." To which he replied, "'E had it comin', messin' wit' muh bruva." I was concerned about Sonny retaliating until Garrett calmed me down, saying, "A.D. is safe. He hangs with Melba and Craig; those two are the type NOBODY wants to fuck with. Do damage to any friend of theirs and you'll be praying to die by the time they finish kicking your ass."

Corey came back home a month early … and he is as nutzo as he always was! Four days before his return, the FedEx man delivered the painting he promised. I was shocked at how big it was when Peep and Jojo hung it up for me. It practically dominates my bathroom wall. But it is beautiful. Anyway, he called Peep for a ride from the airport. Of course, we ALL piled in Peep's car. When we scooped him up and got to his house, he took his keyboard (workstation) and two of his suitcases inside. He then came out and locked his front door, popped the trunk of his car to put the remaining suitcase in there, and prepared to jump in. When I stopped him to ask what he was doing, he told me that he was coming to spend a few days with me.

I gagged, "What do you mean?"

"Did you hear me stutter?"

"Don't you think he should have a say in that?" Peep asks.

"Yeah, but if I let him have his say, you know he would sit in that house not doing shit… except jacking off to some eighties porn with guys sporting those greasy handlebar mustaches, looking like Sonny Bono." He turns to me and jabs his finger into my chest twice, jokingly saying, "And you know this, my dear brother!"

I laugh, "OK, Maestro, but for one week."

Corey retorts playfully as he gets in his car, "Please, like I ain't got a life. I ain't go'n be your Siamese twin, you know. Oh, and your painting is coming in the mail."

"I just got it. It's up on my bathroom wall."

"Why didn't you just bring it with you?" Jojo asks.

"To be at the mercy of airline luggage handlers? No thank you! An original piece needs to be shipped with care."

The few days turned into a month. Somehow, having Corey stay with me has strengthened my resolve to recover and kept me rolling, especially when Garrett came by to visit. I needed strength and laughter if I was fated to use that god-awful regulation metal cane for four months. Damn. As if

I didn't already have these gray hairs to remind me of how old I'm getting! Thank God I only got one month to go.

A funny thing happened though. A month out of the hospital, I was bitching to Garrett, Corey, Jojo, and Peep about having to walk with a cane. Those four nuts went to four different stores and brought me a walking stick from each one. Corey's was a gag cane with a green glow-in-the-dark dragon handle that groaned when you walked with it, Jojo's was a red and white striped cane made of real candy, Garrett's was a silver rapper's cane with a chrome top (he even demonstrated by pimp-walking around my living room), and Peep's was a tall staff with a glowing orb. Neat. I get to walk around casting spells like the Death Fairy! After seeing these canes, I laughed for two minutes straight! I kept them all, but Garrett's cane is what I use most. I ate Jojo's within a week.

Shortly thereafter, Dr. Camden asked me to come to her office so she could express a few concerns. I was shocked to discover that since starting the Alprolozine, my kidneys started to decline. I jumped when she told me this, relaxing only after she assured me that the kidney damage was minimal and able to be contained. But, as I had been told ad nauseum, I had to get off that medication. She told me that the pharmaceutical companies were recalling it due to adverse effects on various patients worldwide. She checked my heart and liver and was happy to report that both were functioning well. I decided, at her and Jojo's insistence, to go into detox, then get into an outpatient program where I would have to report a few times a week.

I look at the huge arrangement of red and white roses Floyd sent me from the company along with a note saying to get well and not worry about work. I also got a lot of cards from my co-workers, including Ben Longwood. When I came across his note, I couldn't help but remember the sexual encounter we almost followed through with. So far, the only ones that know about it are Ben, Peep, and me. I told Peep during one of his visits and he told me that as dumb as that move was, I redeemed myself by stopping it before it went further. Ben and I talked it out and made the decision to keep our dealings professional and our friendship platonic. Maybe I should tell Jojo. I remember what Garrett said about keeping things honest. But my fear is that this info will send him packing... again.

Floyd gave me a six-month paid leave of absence after I explained to him about my Alprolozine dependence. He told me that he was going to sit down to talk with me anyway. I was doing well up until after the signing of the VaVoom contract. That was when my work started to slip. My marketing reports were incomplete, my numbers were falling off, and my professional appearance even began to suffer. He considered the passing of my mother very carefully, as well as my roping Katherine Nesbitt as a client, and decided to wait until an appropriate time to discuss the paid leave with me. Armed with the time off, I could have done an inpatient program, but I decided that I didn't want to be staring at four walls and other addicts *all* the time.

The group sessions and individual therapy are enough for now, in addition to spending time with Jojo. Until recently, he and I have seen each other non-stop, getting to know each other again since leaving the hospital. I'm a little concerned now though because I haven't seen him in almost three weeks. We talk on the phone, but he seems incredibly distant. I am beginning to assume the worst. Have I lost him for good or am I just jumping to conclusions? Oh boy, do I need a professional to talk to… and quick! Dr. Williams is woefully disqualified. So, who should I get?

I am looking down at my phone to scroll to a name that I put off calling for months… because of my pride. Hmmm… Well, in my encounter with Dad, he did tell me to break the cycle and live. What better way to get back to life and find a new perspective than going to a professional I know who *is* qualified and knows what he is doing? It beats imagining negative scenarios that may not even exist, except in my own mind.

I take a deep breath and thumb the green phone icon beside the name I scrolled to. When a female voice answers, I clear my throat and say, "Uh… Yes, this is Lionel Davis. I would like to schedule an appointment, please. Do you have Dr. Banneker's calendar?"

*****

It is Monday afternoon and I am now walking into Dr. Banneker's office. The air is familiar and comforting, and it is great to see his calm, reassuring smile and understanding eyes as he comes from behind his desk to shake my hand. This is a welcome change from that sick fuck, Dr. Williams. Speaking of him, his Ass-Holiness didn't even call to check and see how I was doing since the shooting. In fact, the only correspondence I got from his office was from his secretary *two weeks* after the fact, talking about an appointment I missed and the balance I owed thereby for a no-show fee. I tactfully read her the riot act, telling her that I couldn't come because I was shot. I went on to tell her how pissed I was that Dr. Williams didn't check his service for messages from Dr. Camden about my hospitalization. It was the hospital's policy to inform other members of a patient's medical team about severe emergencies, so I know his ass got the message. I'm thinking about asking Peep to find his friend, as well as other patients, so we can go to the medical board and demand his dismissal.

Walking into this familiar space, I can see that Doc has changed the dynamic of the office. The bulletin board with the long color swatches is still there. The multi-colored drapes still adorn the two windows facing Madison Avenue, but, instead of its usual placement in between, the big mahogany desk is positioned diagonally in the right corner of the large office. Now, the sickly green armchair with poppies is positioned in front of one of the windows, facing toward the office door. In front of the second window is an armchair of equal size. It is obviously new, and it has every color of the spectrum on it. It directly faces the window with closed drapes. *This is odd*, I think to myself. *Why is one chair facing the window, but the other has its back to it?* I shrug off the question. This is Dr. Banneker we are talking about. Everything in his office is a teachable tool. There is a concept behind the eccentric nature of this setup.

I choose the familiar chair and sink back into the comfort of the cushions as Dr. Banneker takes the colorful one. We talk about the events since the shrink switch.

"So... where shall we start?"

"Wherever you like."

"A lot has happened since I was here last."

"Let's talk about that. When you were here before, you requested your regular dosage of Doxepin. Why?"

"I needed it to go to sleep and the lowered dosages were not helping."

Dr. Banneker looks down at my file, saying, "My notes state that you were staying up late due to your mind being full of the demands at your office."

"Correct."

"Are the anxiety and lack of sleep the only reasons you requested the regular dosage of Doxepin?"

"Why wouldn't it be?"

Dr. Banneker looks at me for a second. He then writes in his legal pad and asks, "Let's talk about your mother."

"What about her?"

"Do you still think about her and the presence she had in your childhood?"

"From time to time."

"What feelings surface when you think about her?"

"Most times, I feel angry with her. And it's crazy because I thought I put it behind me. I mean, what was that long ass rant at the hospital all about? And I feel even more anger now… because she died without giving any of us closure."

"If she had given you that closure, would you still feel that anger?"

I lean forward, putting my elbows on my knees. I feel Dr. Banneker's eyes on me as I continue, "Honestly, I don't know. I believe I would move through life a lot better than I am right now."

"In what way?"

"My friendships wouldn't be suffering. My engagement to Jojo wouldn't be over, and I wouldn't have needed those goddamned pills to get through the day."

"According to your file, you were taking the new drug, Alprolozine, after you began care with Dr. Williams."

"Correct."

"And you recently had to go to a facility to detoxify them from your system."

"Correct."

"Do you see a link between you requesting the regular dosage of Doxepin and your need for the Alprolozine, as well as the alcohol?"

"No…"

Dr. Banneker writes in his pad.

"Is there a possibility that these agents serve as a defense against your past as well as your feelings tied to it?"

I look down at the yellow carpet, pondering his question. But I say nothing. After a few moments pass, I rationalize, "I needed something to level me out."

"Do you still have nightmares about your mother?"

Another long silence. Then I break it. "Yes."

"Did you have them before you requested the regular dosage of Doxepin?"

"Yes."

"So, that brings me back to my first question. Why did you need the regular dosage?"

Caught! Well, I might as well say it. "With the regular dosage, I was able to sleep through the nightmares and function the next morning. With the lower dosages, I kept waking up in a cold sweat after the nightmares."

Dr. Banneker writes in his pad and asks, "Is there a reason you did not mention this in our previous sessions?"

"Yes."

"And that would be?"

"Well, I'm going to therapy, and I thought I would have been past all this by now, especially after unleashing my resentment to Mama. I was embarrassed to admit that I still had unresolved issues."

Dr. Banneker looks at me squarely and says, "Well, healing is an ongoing process, and while initially confronting the catalysts of earlier pain is a good first step, it is, in fact, just one step. When we do not continually acknowledge our feelings of hurt and anger, they can become hard to handle. That's when we use seemingly therapeutic defense agents to *keep from* handling them. The term is avoidance."

"Avoidance?"

"Yes. Now this is not to say that you yourself may be operating from avoidance. That is for you to determine. But it is important to remember that no one magically obliterates their grief or pain. It is a process that takes time."

"I know that."

"How have you been dealing with your nightmares?"

"Well, I'm not taking the Alprolozine or the Doxepin, and I've been three months clean as far as drinking. But I still have them, and they unsettle me. Do you have something that can counter the nightmares?"

"Unfortunately, the chemists of modern medicine have not invented remedies that specialize effectively in dream suppression. In your case, with all the regular thoughts about your mother and the hustle on your job, it is not insomnia. It is your anxiety and it has been proven that our anxieties can manifest into dreams and nightmares. Doxepin is no longer a viable option because it has had damning reports lately, and the reports are tied to long term problems for the patients who continually take them. I should have just written you a prescription for another medication. But I got such a huge resistance from you when I first told you about the Doxepin that I attempted to shave off the meds little by little. My notes say that you first got on the Doxepin when your former partner and you separated, and the therapist that prescribed them was Dr. Logan Reynolds, correct?"

"Correct."

"And you had to discontinue care with him in May of 2018 because he moved his practice to another state, thus explaining your first lapse with the Doxepin prescriptions."

"Correct."

He writes in his pad again. "Are you still journaling?"

"Yes. It's the one thing that has kept me somewhat sane."

He sits back and muses, "That's good. My suggestion is for you to continue doing that but add other activities that cause you to find your center. Like exercise, meditation, and… Wait. Are you going on that cruise this year?"

"I paid to go, but it's been up in the air because of the shooting."

"Well, that may be an activity to push toward attending. It would be a positive and much needed distraction."

Dr. Banneker gets up from his chair and motions for me to come over to the desk and be seated in the adjacent chair. He sits behind his desk and pulls out a prescription pad to write on.

"Ordinarily after a case like yours, I would not write you a prescription unless I'm sure you have the Alprozoline out of your system, but Dr. Camden told me you had been without medication other than pain meds and you seemed to be doing fine. Plus, proof of your rehabilitation from the clinic causes me to relax a bit. I'm going to put you on a low dosage of Monodycizan. These are highly recommended because they have a chemical known as Hydribital which promotes proper kidney function as well as lessen anxiety. You are to take them when you wake up in the mornings. Now, I caution you. Common side effects are dizziness, headaches, nausea, and slight loss of appetite, but your system must adjust to them. Then you can function as normal."

"Thank you, Doc."

Dr. Banneker peers over his horn-rimmed glasses. "Now, I want to be very frank with you. Chemical medicines are not the end all solution for anxiety and depression. They are meant for the purposes of coping for a short time. The goal for having specific types of meds for depression and anxiety is to arrive at a place where you don't need them. And if you do need them, you won't need to take them as much. Once we settle our anxieties, we are able to find our periods of serenity."

*****

My truck becomes my haven of reflection as I mull over the session in Dr. Banneker's office. He raised some valid points concerning my need for the pills and ultimately the alcohol. Avoidance…. Hmmm… I've used work as my avoidance even before I got on the Doxepin.

The Cost

I drum my fingers rhythmically on the steering wheel while endeavoring to collect my thoughts. Ever since the episode with Mama in the hospital, I have been able to function without revisiting the evils of my childhood. Apart from a brief remembrance felt at Corey's concert, I was able to purge my mother's cruelty from me as well as retain and magnify the few decent times we shared. As abrasive and harsh as she was, she had some endearing qualities that made me hopeful for a closer relationship.

My Christmas at nine years old vividly comes to mind. I recollect the plush living room sporting the colors of rose, eggshell, and silver. Dad bought an eight-foot tree and we decorated it and the living room with beautiful ruby red and emerald green trimmings. This room was generally off limits to us kids, which was fine with us because we had the den. We all hated being in Mama's living room because we were always afraid that we would break something, thereby incurring her wrath. In the den, we could yell, watch TV, play the Atari Console (yes, the Atari!), and have fun. Dad had just secured a job as a public relations representative with a prestigious investment firm in Atlanta. It came at the right time too because Mama was holding down a job working the jewelry counter at the mall. It was difficult because Dad was going on one interview after another and every day that he went without a job was a day he heard Mama complaining. With him having the job, he was able to provide a lot more for us.

Anyway, what I wanted for Christmas was a Nintendo; and I mean the original Nintendo with the orange and gray gun and dual game cartridge, Super Mario Bros and Duck Hunt. A boy I knew had one that his parents had given him for his birthday. When they invited me to his birthday party, he let his "friends" play with it. When I asked him if I could play it, he said, "You are not one of my friends. You're just here because my mother made me invite you." My answer to that was a punch in his nose. His mother came and saw his nose bleeding. She asked who hit him and all the kids' fingers pointed at me. She told me to go home and she would be calling my mother. That night, Mama whipped the daylights out of me. Not because I hit him, but because of how embarrassed she was to get the call. It was worth it! The boy was a snob and so were his siddity assed parents.

A few weeks later when things had calmed down, I began begging my parents for one as a Christmas present. However, because I got two "Ds" in Science and Social Studies, Mama remarked that the Nintendo was out of the question and that I needed to get my grades up before thinking about video games. Dad said nothing, but he seemed to be in complete agreement with her. Still, a boy can hope, right? I woke up on Christmas morning thinking that my parents might have reconsidered. My siblings and I dashed to the living room and went straight for the tree, while Mama and Dad dragged sleepily down the stairs. In a matter of minutes, the rose carpet was littered with wrapping paper and ribbons. I opened every present under the tree that had my name on it, but there was no Nintendo in sight; just clothes and shoes. I, of course, was totally bummed and it must have shown on my face because Mama came over to where I was, and asked me:

"What's the matter with you, boy?"
"Nothing."
"Your face don't look like it's 'Nothing'?
I shrugged my shoulders as I looked at her. She met my look with amusement.
"I know what it is. You didn't see your precious Nintendo under the tree. Right?"
I shrugged my shoulders again.
"When I speak to you, answer me back. We talked about you shrugging your shoulders."
"Yes."
"Yes, what?"
"Yes, Mama."
"That's better. So, tell me something. After those 'Ds' you brought in here, should you expect to get anything other than stuff you need from day to day?"
"No, Ma'am."
"Right. So, are your grades going to stay low?"
"No, Ma'am."
"Nothing less than a 'B' in this house, right?"
"No, Mama."

"Good, because your Daddy got something for you." With a secret smile, she looked toward the living room closet where Dad was holding the console in his hands! You never saw anybody happier than I was at that moment. Before he gave it to me, he made me promise to keep it in the den for my siblings to play with it too. I was permitted to play it all that day, but on the next day, Mama dropped the bomb that I couldn't play it until the summer because I needed to focus on my studies. It was torture watching my brothers and sisters playing it, while I had to study all through the semester. But from then to my high school graduation, if there was anything lower than a B, it wasn't any of MY grades.

The Cost

The abuse started when Dad's job began to take him out of Yeti. He started traveling two weeks out of the month… and that was when Mama started changing. Her voice, wherever it was in the house, began to strike fear in all of us. She began beating on A.D. and me for the slightest things, and when she did, the others went outside so they wouldn't get caught in the crossfire. She also began drinking heavy booze and the more she drank, the meaner she got. I remember how happy all us kids got when she quit drinking. She was still mean, but she was better to deal with than when she was drunk.

Suddenly, it hit me. The destructive paths that Mama and I took weren't all that different. We both used tools of avoidance to put off dealing with our issues. Whatever her dysfunction was, she had the booze as well as mistrust and cruelty to mask it. I had the pills, bitterness, and the excess booze came later when I couldn't get the pills. The unifying factor between us was that our negative behaviors were causing our loved ones to jump ship and love us from a distance because they just couldn't stand to see what we were doing to ourselves. A.D. was right. I am Lynetta Davis' child, bitter and angry to the point where I unload it on friends and supportive family members.

My cell phone rings. It is Peep. "Hey, you."

"Hey, what's going on? I tried calling you."

"I'm sorry. I was in the appointment with my shrink."

"That's right. You told me you were going back to Dr. Banneker. Thank God! So, what did he say about what's been going on?"

"Well, he told me that I couldn't take the Doxepin anymore because of the crazy long-term shit it was doing to people. I felt mighty stupid hearing that because he tried to tell me before. He put me on a new medicine, low dosage."

"Did he explain everything concerning the medicine?"

"Yes, and he also told me that I needed to get into some activity that will help boost my positive standpoint."

"I couldn't agree more."

"Yeah. So, what's up?"

"I'm calling because we need to discuss whether we should postpone the cruise until next year. I spoke with Corey earlier today and he said that he is not sure as to whether he can go or not."

"Didn't he pay for it already?"

"Yeah, but he got a call from Darrell. Apparently, there's another tour being negotiated that he needs Corey for. This one is three weeks long and the first week of the tour is the week of the cruise."

"Wow… Thank God we all sprung for the insurance. Where are they touring now?"

"I'm not sure, but I think he said Stockholm, Madrid, Brazil, and Sydney."

Wow. The world is really clamoring for his music. He told me that the places they went were going crazy over "Love Makes Me Beautiful", as well as another song on the album, "Can You Love You?"

"This is awesome!"

"Yeah. I've gotta admit it. Even with all our nicking and nagging over the years, I'm really proud of him."

"Me too. So, what do you want to do?"

"Well, I feel like we should still go because we all need it. I need to reconnect with my man. And you and Jojo could use the time to get back to where you were."

"But it won't be the same without Corey."

"Remember, I said that the tour is in negotiation phase… and you know Corey. He'll find a way to go and drag Garrett with him."

I smile to myself as I scan the street. "Let's hope so."

"Is Corey still staying with you?"

"Yep."

"Then he will probably tell you more."

"Maybe. I'm heading inside now," I say as I spot Corey's red Mustang. "I see his car so he must be in the house."

"Oh ok, chit-chat later. Kiss-kiss."

"Kiss."

As I open my front door, I see Corey sitting on the chaise reading a stack of papers. He looks up and grins at me. I grin back.

"So, your music is hitting Stockholm? Madrid?"

"Big-mouth told you, didn't he?"

"Yep."

"Darrell is not even sure if he wants to go because it starts on the week of the cruise. But this is a lot of money, if the figures on this contract are legit," he says while waving the papers in the air, then throwing them on the table.

I sit beside him on the chaise. "Ok, but how do *you* feel about it?" I see him heave a huge sigh.

"I don't know. I had forgotten how exhausting touring can be. When I was younger and traveling with the high school and university choir, it was no problem because I had a lot of energy. But now, my old tired bones are telling my age."

I scoff, "Oh come on, you are talking as if you are seventy-five years old. You are just thirty-eight."

"Thirty-eight and tired as fuck."

"Ok, ok... but aside from all that, how does it feel to have other nations loving your music," I say with an encouraging smile as I rest my arm on the chaise's back edge and prop my head on my fist.

A dazzling smile lights up his face as he says excitedly, "It is amazing! I mean, this is something I've dreamed of for years and now it's actually happening! Darrell is so easy to work with. He's the one headlining the tour, but he shines the spotlight on those around him. It's awesome to just sit and talk with him about how he feels about his music. A light comes on, especially when he is creating, and it is amazing to watch."

I laugh and say, "Now you see how we feel whenever we watch you create or perform. It's like you are in a totally different world."

"You notice that?"

"Yes. It's one of the times that we like you most. When Jojo and I met you, we were amazed at how much emotion you put into your playing. And let an idea barrel into your head. This bright look crosses your face like someone gave you a one-way ticket to Heaven. Sometimes when we're out, you will even ditch us to get to your piano and hammer it out."

Corey chuckles. "Well, it's good to know that you are enamored of me."

"I said we liked you. I didn't say we were in love!" I laugh.

"Whatever. Did you go to your session with Dr. Banneker?"

"Yes."

"How was it?"

"It wasn't bad. I'm on a new medicine, but it's low dosage and he read up on it to make sure it was safe."

Corey gives me an 'I rest my case' look. "Now, you see how good it is to have a professional that knows his shit and puts his patients first?"

"Yes."

"And maybe he can give you some insight on how to strengthen your relationship with Jojo."

I suddenly gaze ahead. "I'm not so sure," I hear my voice sigh with sorrow. Corey just stares at me. I look blankly at my hands and I feel heartache coming. When I look up at Corey, my voice chokes out, "I really fucked everything up."

"Oh, Lionel. Don't beat yourself up."

"No, really. I was so stupid. I couldn't even see past those fucking pills and the booze to acknowledge the baggage I was unloading on him... on all of you." I droop my head down in shame. After a moment, I state mournfully, "Corey... I think I've lost Jojo."

"Oh, no. We are gonna kill this right now. First of all, you had a lot of shit happening. If it wasn't the job, it was your mother's death. And we have to factor in the anxiety. Second, other than that text before you got shot, did Jojo confirm that he was breaking up with you?"

"No. I haven't seen him though, Corey. We do manage to talk on the phone, but he seems so distant. It's been like this for three weeks."

"Well, it so happens that the Oakley Law Firm is going through a severe audit next week. I'm only telling you this because you need to know what the deal is. They have been agitated about it for months and Jojo is concerned about whether this will affect his job."

I am shocked, as well as remorseful. Here I am, going on about my own sordid life and bullshit. It didn't even cross my mind that Jojo might have had his own problems. "I didn't know," I say shamefacedly.

"How could you know? Jojo didn't want to tell you because he felt you had enough to deal with."

"But he could've come to me."

"And you would have added this on to all the other bullshit weighing you down. How would that benefit you or him?" He pauses, as if waiting for an answer. Assured that none is forthcoming, he answers for me, "It wouldn't. Not at all. And as to your concern, Jojo is not talking about breaking up with you, especially after you went into detox and then back to Dr. Banneker. In fact, during that same conversation I had with him, he told me that he was proud of you for moving forward and getting your shit in order." Corey pauses, then gives me a sarcastic smirk as he goes on. "Here you are again, overthinking things. Stop it, please. Jojo's love ain't never, has never, and will never go anywhere. It's gonna stick around for as long as my dick and ass stay black," Corey says, wagging his head in a mocking way. Then he gives me a teasing smile and playfully pinches my cheeks.

"Why you always gotta touch my face?" I say, laughing and shoving him.

"I can't help it, it's just sooooooo cute!!!" Corey says, swatting me on the shoulder. Then he rises, picks up the papers, and heads to the stairs, saying, "Well, today is when I make my way back to my own house."

"So, you're leaving?"

"Yeah, baby," Corey says, stopping at the foot of the stairs to turn and look at me. "Corey has gone without his man's dick and ass for three months. I love ya but I need some fulfillment from my Black Lightning."

Chapter Thirteen
RENEWAL

My brothers, sister, and I decided to finally clean up Granny's house and sort through all the stuff we intend to keep. Whatever we don't keep is going to the church mission program. They are taking a week off work so we all can fly back to Birmingham where we booked rooms at the Embassy Suites. I don't have to worry about taking off because I'm still on my paid leave.

I have been thinking a lot about Mama, and my mind lugs a painful weight of truth. We funeralized and buried a woman who never really knew what life was. She was tough to deal with for many of the years I've known her as my mother. But I remember Corey asking me if I knew what her story was and, for the first time, I wonder where all the hatred came from. These thoughts cause me to pity her. Something must have happened to her that made her the way she was. No one just becomes mean and nasty to people without reason. I think back to my grandmother, whom we buried several months before we buried Mama. Those two had a troubled relationship. The way they carried on suggested that they blamed each other for some things that happened long before any of us kids were born.

The flight to Birmingham is in two weeks. It was decided that I pick up A.D. from his place, then we stop at Mount Washington Station to park the car and take the Light Rail. It beats parking at the airport and paying ridiculous fees.

Oh… speaking of ridiculous… Good God! It's been months since Mama's burial and the reading of the will, and courtesy of dear sweet sister, Rhonda, we had nothing but drama. She emerged from prison four months ago and was staying at Mama's house, per the conditions of her release. The only time she could leave the house was when she was looking for a job. Roland, A.D., Brenda, and I wanted to discuss the house while she was on lockdown, but Dean said that it wasn't right to continue without Rhonda. So, we agreed to wait until she returned home.

We had a conference call last night to discuss what to do with both houses. A.D. and I were at my house on speakerphone, and the others called from different places. We started the call with Brenda telling us that we had a buyer who offered us top dollar for Granny's house. That went over easily, especially after she told us that we were getting five hundred grand for it. But when we came to the subject of Mama's house, Rhonda started running her mouth. She fed us all this bullshit about it being the only tie we have with Mama and Daddy as if she cared for either one of them! Without missing a beat, A.D. said, rolling his eyes, "Yep, an' dat's the main reason we needta get rid of it. We needta jes' cut de cord an' move on."

"The clause in the will said that ALL of us have to agree on selling Mama's house, and I ain't agreeing."

"What else is new?" Roland mumbled.

"The only reason you don't want to sell the house is because *YOU* are the only one who wants to stay there. I would think that it's a perfect opportunity for you to hock whatever isn't nailed down," Brenda says in a curt tone.

"Well... My, my, MY! Who knew that my darling BABY sister could turn into such a siddity, shade-throwing bitch!"

"Well, you came before me, so I learned from the best."

"I wish you would learn to shut your goddamned mouth for once!" Rhonda shrieked.

"Why? Am I hitting a nerve? You don't care about this family, Mama, or that house, Rhonda. All you care about is yourself."

"Like *your* ass won't profit by selling it!"

"KNOCK IT OFF!" Dean shouted. All got quiet. Then he cleared his throat and said, "Alright, let's just sleep on it and we will talk about this tomorrow."

"There ain't nothing to talk about. You are NOT selling the house and that's that!" Rhonda snapped. Then we heard a click. She hung up.

After a few moments of silence, Brenda said sarcastically, "That's YA'LL'S sister."

"No, that's **YOUR** sister!" Roland countered jokingly.

"Ain't no needta pass the fuckin' buck. We ALL stuck wit' er dumb ass!" A.D. retorted.

"What are we gonna do?" Roland asked.

"I don't know," Dean said, his voice filled with dismay.

"Lionel, you got any ideas?" Brenda queried.

I kept quiet throughout the time Rhonda was ranting and raving. I weighed the pros and cons of selling Mama's house, then said, "I for one want to sell it. It represents a lot of pain for all of us and I'm thinking that maybe another family could turn the energy around for the better."

"That's wut I'm sayin'," A.D. agreed.

"On the other hand, Rhonda is not going to give on this. So, maybe we need to cut our losses and… just let her win this one."

"What?! Oh, Hell No!" Roland and Brenda chorused in disbelief. A.D. at first looked at me like I was smoking crack. But then he switches his look to a more meditative one.

"Are you sure about that?" Dean asked.

"Yeah, it might end up better for us in the end."

"I'd like to know how," Roland said. I look at A.D. and a perverse, delicious smile creeps across his face.

"Wait… Yuh know, Li'nel's got a point," A.D. said in his slow, deep way. *Uh oh!* I thought to myself. *I know that voice and face from way back! He has a scheme in his head!* A.D. thought a minute, then he continued, "Let Rhonda have 'er way… but with a catch."

"Uh oh. Something tells me you got something up your sleeve," I said. A.D. smirked as he chuckled and nodded.

"An' you'd be right. Dis way. We kin ALL git fat pockets… an' teach our dea' sweet sista' a lesson at de same time. Yuh know dat game we usedta play, 'Tug-o-war'?"

"Yeah?" Brenda replied.

"E'er now an' den, when you wanna prove a point tuh de peeps on de otha' end of de rope, whuduya do?"

Roland caught his meaning, "Let go of the rope and let them win. But the win comes with a fall."

"Exackly, and dat's wut we go'n do. She kin have de house… an' err'thang dat goes wit it. She kin deal with de mayt'nance. She kin pay de house bills. She kin pay de taxes, de utilities, an' fuh all de repairs. Now… y'all know as well as me dat Rhonda's a dummy with money an' she ain't gonna be able tuh handle it. Her ass'll be beggin' tuh sell dat house."

Brilliant! I gave A.D. some skin. "Damn, you're good, brother!"

"Welp, what kin I say!" A.D. bragged.

"Ooooh, big bro! You are sneaky! I like that idea," Brenda laughed over the phone.

"I don't know about this," Dean said skeptically.

"Wha..?" A.D. let out.

"This could play out dirty when Rhonda realizes what we are up to."

"So? I ain't wurr'd 'bout dat. Duh way I see it, she been bookin' fuh a schoolin' fuh years. Well, she got one comin'."

"Right. We still love her, but this lesson is long overdue. She's always used to getting her way, but this will teach her that there are some victories you have to pay for, especially if they weren't achieved the right way." After Brenda said this, Dean agreed.

"Well, you know me. I like a good gag." Roland assented.

"An' think 'bout dis, the five hunnit stacks we getting' fuh Granny's house ain't nothin' to sneeze at," A.D. said matter-of-factly.

"Right." I followed. "We are all going to profit from that, but if I know Rhonda, she's gonna blow through her share in two months… and that's when she's going to start banging down our doors for help."

"Which we won't give until she agrees to sell the house," Roland finished, catching my drift.

"So, we are agreed then that we won't lend Rhonda any money for upkeep of the house. Let her have ALL of what she is fussing for."

"Agreed," My brothers and sister said.

*****

"So, what are your feelings about the man who shot you?" Dr. Banneker says. We are in the same set up, with him facing the window and me facing the door.

"What *should* I feel about him?" I say sardonically.

"You sound cynical. Why?"

"Which subject should I address first? My cynicism or my feelings? Seems to me that how I feel is obvious."

"Not necessarily."

I shrug my shoulders, evoking the memory of my old habit. "I guess I'm cynical because I know that nothing is going to happen to the guy that shot me, as far as the law is concerned."

"What makes you say that?"

"Well, I don't know if I told you about my friend, Corey, getting stabbed."

"You alluded to it, but never went into detail."

I take a huge breath, then I continue, "He was attacked by the Penn Avenue Counts. They had been terrorizing residents in our neighborhood for years, especially the gay ones. The leader of the gang, Pervis Bateman, stabbed Corey five times in the side. He got off for that due to a technicality. But he got sent up for murdering a cop eight months ago. He is doing life at North Branch Correctional. I guess the Black or gay lives don't matter, but White and cops' lives do."

"That sounds pretty general."

"No. That sounds pretty real," I snap, angrily.

"And that angers you."

"Hell yeah. And on both accounts,"

"And why?"

"Why ask me why? Isn't it obvious?"

"Well, different people have different reasons. Now, although you can go with a broad generalization, it helps to understand why it bothers you as an individual."

I chew on that for a few seconds, concluding that his statement makes perfect sense. I begin to explain. "From a racial standpoint, it bothers me that my degrees, my accomplishments, and my accolades aren't worth shit if I happen to be detained by a white racist police officer. They only see one thing: my skin color. The way things are now, I consider myself lucky if I'm pulled over by a Black officer or I can turn on my car and go home after having dogs in my car, sniffing for drugs that aren't there. That happened to me once. I was leaving the gym one night and my lights were not on. A white police officer stopped me and told me what the deal was. I thought that was the only thing. But he had me place my hands on the steering wheel as he let his police dogs roam my car. When it was over, he gave me the old 'you fit the description' line and told me to keep my lights on from now on." I sit back to catch my breath. "I had to count as high as I could until that shit was over, just so I could keep my cool. I started thinking about Eric Garner, Sandra Bland, Freddie Gray, and Philando Castile and praying to God I wouldn't meet that same fate."

Dr. Banneker nods his head in understanding. I wonder if he can truly comprehend where I'm coming from, though. He is white and many Caucasians are not privy to the injustices we constantly face as a race. However, I remind myself not to judge by perception.

"What about the other standpoint?" He asks, his inquisitive eyes looking at me.

I shift my position in my chair, preparing my answer. "On the gay standpoint, it bothers me that homophobes can maim, torture, and murder us, no matter what wrapping we come in."

"Wrapping?" Dr. Banneker asks, giving me a quizzical look.

"You know. Lesbian, transgender, cisgender. The whole gambit of LGBTQ."

"Ah, I see."

"Like I said, they can kill us off and the police won't do shit, because they have their own fucking biases. I think about the ones who were killed last year alone. Eighteen trans - that we know of. Now I admit, I have my prejudices. Aside from that though, I believe they have it a helluva lot harder than those of us who identify as gay or bisexual. I remember hearing something from a TV show I got hooked on recently while in the hospital. A new young friend of mine named Orchid told me that I just had to watch it."

"Who is Orchid?"

"She's a young transgirl. Real smart. Only seventeen but already seems to know what she wants. Anyway, this character summed up the reason why transphobes kill their victims. Because they hate what their desire requires. They struggle with their insecurities and they make transgenders pay for it all the time. On a separate degree, we gays go through that in different parts of the world. Uganda just passed a bill to put gays to death. Jamaican homo-haters are still killing us and dumping us in ditches, then have the raw gall to call the practice "their duty". So, would anybody blame me for being angry and a bit vengeful at the person who put this bullet in me?"

By the end of this impassioned speech, I am totally out of breath and exhausted from my own wrath. Dr. Banneker just looks at me with a blank, detached look. He says to me, "Lionel, do you remember that bulletin board exercise we did two years ago?"

"Yeah?"

"Remember what you said then, relating to the association of the colors?"

"Not really."

"Well, with your time being up, let's talk about that next week."

"Fine."

The Cost

As I walk out of the building, thoughts begin to take flight. The session with Dr. Banneker is giving me a lot to digest. I wonder why he asked the question about what I said regarding the bulletin board exercise. Who remembers what was said two years ago, aside from my spoken decision to go back to Alabama and root out the truth about my father's death, as well as his bisexuality? Oh wait. Now I remember. I said that I oversaw whatever feelings I have and could decide how to navigate through each emotion. Well, the emotion I feel now is fury.

I'm outraged about this bullet in me and the maniac who put it there. But perhaps the question I should ask myself is this: am I spending too much of my energy being angry? Maybe I am. I recall how drained I felt after venting my feelings to Dr. Banneker. Of course, I'm looking at other factors triggering my anger. One of them is that the cops were given the gun dropped on the scene as well as the description Katie gave them, but they aren't doing jack shit. I think I have too much time on my hands to think about what happened.

To be completely honest, I am ready to go back to work. To sit around the house doing nothing is driving me crazy. My walks along water are helping, but I need to be around people. All the Fellas are busy working, especially Jojo. I do get to talk to Corey, Garrett, and Peep on the phone in the evenings, but it's not enough. I called Floyd this morning and told him that if he needed me to come back, I would do it after I got back from Birmingham. He told me that I didn't need to rush back and that I could work from home. I let him know that I appreciated it, but I needed to get back to the office before I drove myself crazy with boredom. He assented but told me that he expected me to pace myself.

*****

It is two days after my appointment, and I am walking into Teresa's with Jojo. He called me and let me know how sorry he was that he was so distant. As Corey stated, the audit took up his time and he had to stay late in the office to sort through years of receipts and ensure that the books were in order. There were many nights during this last month where he came home too tired to lift his hand. The upshot of it was that he still had his job.

We sit down at the table and we see Katie sauntering over in a waitress outfit. "Well, if it ain't my new road dawgs, Lionel and Joseph. What's hap'nin', cap'ns?"

"Hey Katie," Jojo says as she hugs him, then hugs me.

"Hey love. You work here, too?"

"Hell to the yeah! B.K. ain't compensatin' worth shit and I'm tryin' to snatch them damn benjamins so I can save towards the down payment on this rowhouse on McCulloh."

"I can't believe you would want to remain in that area. I mean, the Counts are still terrorizing those blocks. And look at what happened to me."

Katie puts her hand on her hip and gives me a determined look. "Baby, I was born on McCulloh and Presstman. No amount of gang shit is forcing me from my home. Besides, I might be able to help that area. Ain't nobody gonna try shit with THIS dyke, honey! I got a blade, a bat, and a foot to put up their ass!" She chuckles, then continues, "Enough about me, though. How are you healing up, baby? I see you are walking without your cane."

"Yeah, it was making me look old as hell."

"That ain't the point, chile. How are you *feeling*?"

"I'm alright. I still have a little pain; but it's nothing I don't have in check."

"That's what the cane is for, boy! Quit trippin'. You need to let yourself heal."

"See," Jojo agrees, half-joking. "That's what I told you. Maybe now you'll listen."

I smile. "Ok, Katie."

"So, whatcha'll want to drink?"

"Miss Teresa's Tea," I reply.

"And you, sweetness?" Katie asks Jojo.

"Well, Corey told me that you had this drink called Green Splash."

"Oh, you'll like it. It's Lemon Lime Kool-Aid with Sprite and green cherries."

"Ooh, that sounds good," I say. "Forget the tea and give me that!"

"Me too."

"Ok, I'll be right back." Katie says, then strolls toward the kitchen.

We look around the restaurant. The place is medium sized with wooden tables and high-backed modern chairs, decorated modestly with pink tablecloths and black cloth napkins rolled into sterling silver napkin holders. The black marble tiled floors are buffed to a brilliant shine. The walls are painted a salmon pink color and there are black framed newspaper clippings hanging on them, displaying the accolades of Baltimore's best. The opulence of the eating area blows most first-time patrons because the outside looks like a run-down, faded blue tenement.

Teresa's is a soul food spot that was opened in the late sixties by Teresa Nash. Her food was said to be among the best in Baltimore. She began in 1963 by fixing lunches for the numerous Baltimoreans who were going to DC to attend the March on Washington. Legend had it that she didn't just do sandwiches. Oh no! This lady cooked fried chicken, yams, collard greens, and cornbread, as well as other dishes from her great grandmother's recipe book. She also provided six large drink coolers of sweet tea that nobody could make but her. After the raves she got for the lunches, she decided to enlist the help of a close architect friend who renovated the inside of her grandmother's house on Belair Road and converted the bottom part into a restaurant. She hired young teenagers who hung around the block slinging dope and taught them almost all her recipes. That act of kindness began their turnaround. She always said that was her greatest accomplishment because it gave them purpose in life. Most of those teenagers grew to become doctors, lawyers, city officials, and government workers. She was pressed to create a chain, but she refused saying that she wanted to keep it small as well as safeguard the familiar atmosphere that held the spot in good stead for years. Upon her death, her daughter, Devetra Nash, took the helm and her catering is just as good as her mother's.

"This is a nice place. How did you find it?" Jojo says, as we turn the attention to our menus.

"By just driving around the east side. A.D. and I were trying to find a soul food restaurant like the one we had in Yeti."

"Gertrude's… Right!"

"She had some good food, didn't she?"

"Yeah. She might have been a sanctified homo-hating 'ho, but old girl could cook."

"Does she still have that restaurant?"

"Yep, barely. A friend of mine told me that she almost lost her license last year for unsanitary conditions."

Katie reappears with a smile, and our drinks. She says, "Here you are. Do you know what you want to eat, or do you need more time?"

"Naw, I think I know what I want," I say.

"Me too."

"Ok. Well, fire away," she says, looking at Jojo.

"Cool. Let me have the two entrées. Fried chicken and smothered pork chops."

"Ok. You get three sides and a bread."

"Well, give me cabbage, sweet potato casserole, rice pilaf, and cornbread."

"And you?"

"Well, let me have the same, minus the pork chops. Give me oxtails with hot sauce instead." I glance briefly at Jojo, who has a distasteful, yet playful grimace on his face.

"Coming right up."

Jojo shakes his head, smiling. "What?" I say, wide-eyed.

"You and them damn oxtails."

"I like them," I tell him with a laugh.

"I can't see why. You are eating a part of an ox's ass."

"A *tasty* part of the ox's ass," I corrected.

Jojo chuckles. Then he says, "Well, I guess I'm going to have to learn how to cook them if we are getting married."

"That would be good," I say, without thinking. Then, it hits me. He said *if we are getting married.*

"Did you say what I think you said?"

"Well, you didn't hear me stutter, did you?" Jojo says, laughing with love in his eyes. That love makes me feel somewhat guilty. The image of Ben and I in the hotel room comes to mind.

"Do you think we are ready?"

Jojo looks down at the tablecloth. He looks like he's measuring his words. Finally, he says, "Maybe… maybe not… Who knows? But how you have handled your situation in these past months told me that you care about me, yourself, and everybody who loves you. You went into detox and stayed with the program. You swallowed your pride and made the call to Dr. Banneker. You admitted what made you lash out at me and others. That takes balls for days, baby. It shows how strong you are… and I would be happy to be your partner in life… your husband."

The audacity of those words and the guilt of my failures cause me to break down. The water from my eyes stains the tablecloth. Jojo sees this and touches my hand.

"What's wrong, baby?"

"I don't understand how you could love someone like me."

"What do you mean?"

Well, here goes. "Jojo… I have to tell you something."

"What?" Jojo says, recoiling back in his chair with a skeptical look on his face. I take a deep breath to prepare myself for the worse.

"Remember the trip I took to Myrtle Beach with the company after we had that fight and broke up?"

"Yeah?"

"I… almost… got involved with one of my co-workers."

Jojo looks at me, with a blank expression. I explain further, "I'm not saying this to excuse myself, but we were both drunk… We went back to the room. We kissed… got naked… and he went down on me."

Jojo takes a deep breath and looks around the restaurant.

"I am sorry, Jojo."

"What else happened?" Jojo asks, his jaw jumping.

"What do you mean?"

"I'm not happy about this, for all the obvious reasons. But I need to know if anything else happened. You said you *almost* got involved with him. What does that even mean? Either you did or you didn't."

I let the sound of silverware and plates fill the hush in the air. Then I look in Jojo's eyes and I say, "Nothing else… I started thinking about how I hurt you… and all the years we had been close. I thought about how I felt when Nate cheated on me. I thought about how I might still have a chance to patch things up. So, I said no… but even the little bit we *did* do ate me up."

Jojo scoots forward in his seat and clasps his hands together, saying, "What does the co-worker have to say about this?"

"We talked it out. I had a working friendship with him when he first started at the company. Nothing ever happened until we went on that getaway."

Jojo gazes down, looking meditative. "Are you sexually attracted to him."

"No. I was though, but only because he reminded me of your personality, and I couldn't have you at that time, because of my own bullshit."

Jojo lets a small smile cross his face. "That's a good answer. I don't like the circumstance the answer stemmed from. But the redemption is the word 'almost'. At some point, you cared enough to stop it before it went further. Plus, it would have been a lot worse if you hadn't told me on your own. Honestly, the confession endears you to me even more, because I can sense the sincerity and the reprimands you gave your own self before telling me."

"I feel a 'but' coming on, though."

"No 'buts'… though I'm wondering whether you or I will turn to others for satisfaction when things aren't right between us. When we marry, we have to remember the connection we've always had where we could talk to each other about anything. And if we can't talk to each other, then maybe we can bring in a counselor that specializes in gay unions."

I look at him, with the love still in his eyes. "So… you still want to get hitched?"

"Are you surprised?"

"I thought for sure you wouldn't."

"You'd be right if you said you actually did it. But you didn't. I do have a question though, Mr. Lionel Davis," Jojo smiles.

"And what question might that be, Mr. Joseph Thompson?"

"Will you love me, cherish me, keep me only to you, forsaking all others?"

I smile back at him, bursting with endless love. "With all my heart." I hold out my hand, prompting him to place his in it. His damp hand is warm and full of romantic energy. "Same question."

Jojo takes his other hand and caresses the back of mine. He pulls my hand to his lips. He kisses my knuckles, letting one kiss linger as he licks the skin. With eyelids lowered seductively and sexy dreamy eyes piercing my soul, he says lovingly, "More than either of our hearts can contain."

The heat from hearing the sudden change in his voice makes me snatch my glass of Green Splash and gulp the contents to cool off.

His voice… so deep.

So sexy.

So bodacious; and all I can do is sit in puzzlement and whisper breathlessly…

"Damn."

Chapter Fourteen
TEARS OF BLOOD

The song in my heart is loud, strong, and full of promise! It has been four days since my date with Jojo and the renewal of our engagement, and I have been on a cloud higher than any of the pills could match. I am at Dr. Banneker's office, rhapsodizing on and on.

"I can't believe that we are actually back on again."

"Was there any doubt that you would be?"

"A little. I was scared that Jojo would break it off with me after I told him what happened with Ben Longwood, but he appears to be even more in love with me as I am with him. We have been talking nonstop for the past few days about the plans for the wedding. Well, Us, Peep, and Corey. Corey is handling the music for the wedding and Peep is handling the clothes and decorations."

"I see, and this will be on the cruise you mentioned. Yes?"

"Correct. We have to postpone it though, because of something that happened with the particular cruise ship we were to sail on."

"What happened?"

"Two days ago, a representative from the travel agency sent us an email containing a letter from the cruise line. According to their corporate official, the boat was due for a complete renovation at the time when we were supposed to go. They offered us another boat for the cruise, but Rainbow Pride specifically wanted the Regality vessel. So, they offered us a cruise for the last week in February."

"A slight hiccup. But you seem excited."

"Duh!" I say playfully. "I am out of this world! I mean, how many people can say that they are going to marry someone they've known all their lives, literally since they were born?"

"Not many."

"Exactly."

"So, things are working well with your friends and your now fiancé. How are things with your family?"

I shrug, "OK, I guess. I'm going back to Alabama next Monday morning. We are cleaning out Grandma's house so it will be ready for the new homeowner."

"So, you are not selling your mother's house?"

"No. Rhonda raised a big stink about it, so we are letting her have what she wanted; to keep the house. But thanks to A.D., our sister is going to learn a hard lesson called 'Everything That Goes with It.'"

"I don't think I follow."

"You see, Rhonda has always been the one to grab what she feels she is entitled to without owning up to the consequences. We tried to tell Rhonda that it was in the best interest for all of us to sell the house, but she is digging her heels in protest. So, we decided to let her have it, with a catch. She has to pay all the bills on the house. And knowing that she is not financially astute, it will be a matter of time before she starts begging us for money to pay bills."

"I understand."

I sit back in the chair, folding my arms. "I wonder sometimes if Rhonda will ever know the joy that life holds."

"Do *you* know?"

"Sometimes I think I do. I mean, when I'm around the Fellas, we really live it up. I know I feel it when I'm in Jojo's company." I stop… thinking about Mama, as well as my injury.

Dr. Banneker notices. "You seem pensive. Why?"

I glance at him. "I was thinking about the things that contribute to my failure in knowing that joy."

"Those things being?"

"My past… My hurts… My mother… This fucking bullet in me. When I think about these things, it makes me feel a whole gambit of destructive emotions."

Dr. Banneker shifts in his chair. After adjusting his glasses, he asks, "Have you given any thought to the question I asked you on our last session?"

I nod, "Yes, I have."

"And where do your thoughts take you?"

I focus on the bulletin board with the color swatches. "I know that I have autonomy over my feelings. But sometimes, they become so overwhelming that I doubt whether I can control them."

Dr. Banneker nods. He gets up and goes to sit behind his desk. Retrieving a blank sheet of paper, he gestures for me to sit in the adjacent chair. When I comply, he hands it to me, as well as a pen. He says, "I want you to write down four negative feelings you have that can potentially cause you to lose control, and next to it, write the reason behind that feeling."

For the first few seconds, I stare at the paper. Then I write:

Anger: *My mother beat me, treated me like shit because I'm gay.*

Rage: *Sonny Daniels shot me and left a mark of his hate in my body.*

Sadness: *I don't know if a day will come when I will be accepted, regardless of who I sleep with or what color my skin is.*

Fear: *I'm afraid that my getting shot may happen again. I'm also afraid that my friends might get attacked as well. I'm afraid that those who are pledged to be our protectors won't do anything to punish the perpetrators.*

I sit up after I have completed my task, giving the paper to Dr. Banneker. He peruses it and hands it back, asking, "You wrote both anger and rage. Why?"

"Because I believe there is a difference."

"Care to explain?"

"Well, I can physically do nothing about the anger I have towards Mama, even if she was here. I believe that there is a line between mother and child that you just don't cross. With her being my mother, I owe her that respect even though I'm angry with her. But the anger would turn against me and manifest into other things, like it did Mama. I once felt rage with her, but it has since softened. Rage, on the other hand, would make me want to kill or at least inflict long standing pain on Sonny Daniels if he were in the same room with me. I know that would negatively affect him and me eventually. Him dead or laid up in intensive care and me in prison. Maybe even a psychiatric ward."

Dr. Banneker nods before saying, "I want you to take this paper home. When you get there, write down everything else that may be troubling to you. Do you have a fireplace?"

"Yes."

"Good, get a fire going and nuke what you wrote. When you come back for your next appointment, we will talk about your feelings concerning the exercise."

"OK, doc."

*****

The flames. The beautiful golden flames. They warm my face as I sit in front of the fire, writing in this journal.

I took Dr. Banneker's advice. After the appointment, I went home, sat in my chair, and wrote every negative feeling and thought I had at that point, and it shocked me how numerous they turned out to be. I had to get three more sheets of paper! Looking at the list, it is no wonder why I feel overwhelmed and out of control of my feelings sometimes. That list was way too much negativity for any human brain to contain. I had to stop myself from writing more before I wound up in a dark place.

After opening the damper, I grabbed some firewood from the back deck, as well as old newspapers and documents, and placed the wood in the fireplace. Before laying the extra debris on the logs, I suddenly remembered how my dad taught me to build a fire: using the log cabin method so that the flame would burn longer. I took everything out and placed the logs and the debris the way my Dad taught me. Then I lit the match and watch the flames lick the wood. After stoking the fire, I took a deep breath and added the last element to it: the sheets of paper representing my past hurts, grievances, thoughts, and fears.

The walls of my living room flashed with the flickering of the flames as I watched the pages disintegrate into ashes. Sparks flew upward with the sweet-smelling smoke. Gradually, I felt relief. This exercise proved to be therapeutic because in watching the smoke rise, I am reminded that I am in control. I master the emotions and the emotions do not master me. I decide what emotions I keep whole, as well as what emotions I consume. I caught a glimpse into what it meant to overpower my negativity. And it felt good…

*****

It is Sunday evening, the day before my Alabama trip. As I am packing my bags, the phone rings. It is Corey.

"Hello?"

"Hey, Lion." Corey answers in a weird tone.

"Corey, what's going on? Getting ready for the tour? You leave next Sunday, right?"

"Yeah, I just got back from shopping for it." His voice trails off. I take note of how troubled it sounded from the start of the call.

After a few seconds, I ask, "Are you alright?"

"Huh?" Corey says, obviously dazed.

"OK, what's going on?"

"I'm sorry. You know, I'm thinking about moving to another part of Baltimore."

"Why?"

"Well," Corey says with difficulty. I detect worry in his speech.

"Well, what?"

"Do you remember when we were in the gym back in March and I told you someone was watching me leave the house?"

"Yeah?"

"The same dude was watching me when I was taking my shit out of the car a few minutes ago. This is the third time he's done it."

"What?"

"Yeah. I shrugged it off then, but now it's starting to creep me out. I feel a dangerous vibe coming from him," Corey breathes out, his voice filled with terror.

"Ok, take it easy... Let's think back. Does he look like anybody you know?"

Corey takes a breath, then continues unsteadily, "I think I recognize him from the night that I got stabbed. He looks like one of the gang members."

"Can you describe him?"

"Tall, skinny, brown skinned, hair in cornrows, and a dark birthmark on his right cheek."

I shudder. Why does he sound familiar to me too? I say with nervous laughter, "You do know that you just described over thirty percent of the guys in Baltimore."

"This isn't funny, Lionel. I'm really scared," Corey sobs out in pure dread.

"OK, Calm down. Where's Garrett? Maybe you ought to stay with him tonight."

"He and his family flew to Puerta Vallarta for vacation yesterday. They won't be back until Saturday."

"Well, have you called Jojo? Peep?"

"Peep is working late; and I don't want to bother Jojo. He's been dealing with all the work after the audit and it's wearing him out."

"Listen, sit tight. I'm calling Southwest to cancel my flight. I'll just tell A.D. to go without me."

Silence is felt through the line. It is a silence that scares me.

"Corey?"

"I'm here. No, you need to go. I'll be fine. I'll just lock and deadbolt the doors."

"But Corey..."

"I'll be fine. I'm sorry for making you worry. It just shook me up. I started remembering when I got stabbed. But I'll be alright."

"Corey, I'm not trying to hear that. I don't like how your voice is sounding."

"Lionel, I'm fine. I just got a little spooked."

"Well, if you won't let me stay. At least call Peep or Jojo and have them come over and sit with you."

Silence again. "Yeah, maybe."

"I'll be home as soon as I can."

"Promise me you won't worry. I don't need that."

"You call me talking about some stalker, and you expect me not to worry?"

"I just got shook up. That doesn't mean I need y'all over here belly aching."

"Are you sure?"

"Positive."

Something is telling me to disregard Corey's protestations and keep my ass in Baltimore so I can be near him in case some shit pops off. But I know Corey. If I do, he'll be even more pissed off because of my worrying. I compromise with my beating heart and my nagging conscience by saying, "OK, Corey. But the minute I get to Alabama, I'm calling you, and I'm going to check on you every time you run across my mind."

"Ok. But you don't have to call every ten minutes... Every thirty minutes will do," Corey says, with a little of his sense of humor shining through.

Breathing easier, I say laughing, "I'll try to restrain myself, Maestro."

"Ok, well. You'd better get off the phone. You got a plane to catch tomorrow."

"Ok, love."

"Lionel," I hear Corey call, with rare heartfelt affection in his voice.

"Yes?"

"I love you. I know I don't say it often enough, like I should. But I do."

I feel a tear squeeze through my eye. I swipe it away as I say with strong emotion, "Friends as tight as we are don't always have to say it. You've already proven that you love me. I can only hope that I've proven it on my end… because I love you too. All of us love you. But what prompted you to say that now?"

Corey, with tears of his own in his voice, replies, "I just felt like saying it. Can't a guy get emotional every now and then?"

"I believe that is allowed."

"Damned straight it is. And you have proven it, Lionel. Trust me. You ALL have. Call me later. Kiss Kiss."

"Kiss."

I hang up the phone with a sinking feeling. I know I need to make this trip back home, but why do I get the feeling that my friend's very life, one that I hold as dear as my own, is in tangible danger?

*****

My brothers, sister, and I are exhausted!

Amazing how one can accumulate so much! It took four days of hard work, but we got the house cleaned out and carted off everything except the unsealed boxes in the attic, a huge mirror in a gilded frame, the living and dining room sets, and the wine in Granny's wine cellar. The buyer said that he wanted the latter two as part of the package.

The trip back to Alabama didn't go as smoothly as I had planned. I mistakenly left my phone back in Baltimore. When I packed my small bag to carry on the plane, I remember packing my tablet and my phone the night before. I woke up to my house phone ringing late the next day, two hours before the flight. It was A.D. calling me to ask where the hell I was. I bounded out of bed and threw on my clothes without even showering. I prepared myself to walk out the door, but I didn't have my keys. I emptied out my bag, and there they were. I grabbed them and hurriedly threw my stuff back in the bag, rushed out, and locked my door. I jumped in the truck to pick A.D. up from Hamilton Springs in Cedonia, then headed to the airport. My blunder shot holes in the plan to avoid the parking costs and I hate that I had to pay them.

It wasn't until we got past security and to the gate that I realized my phone was missing. I was a bit frantic, but A.D. called Jojo, who went to my house, unlocked it with his key, and confirmed that I left it on my coffee table when I emptied my bag. Geez, I wonder if I'm going through mid-life crisis! I'm forgetting stuff now? I already saw gray hair and had to walk with a cane. What next? Glasses? Clothes that smell like mothballs and Brut cologne? Sensible shoes? Oh, hell no! I've got to get it together! I'm way too young to be forgetting shit all the time or losing the ability to do what I enjoy, like sexing Jojo every chance I get when we finally get married. I hope that my dick will still stand at attention when Jojo needs it, instead of lying there wrinkled and limp. I want to be able to fuck until the day I die without the benefit of Viagra, Cialis, or that Blue Chew shit. Thank God for my Sour Diesel strain!

Through A.D., I am in constant contact with Corey. Sometimes, he's in good spirits. Other times, he is jumpy. Just this morning, he told me that he saw the guy again. I tried to calm him down, but I am a little jumpy and scared myself. We do not need a repeat of what already happened... to both of us. I thought about the dream of the shadowy figure with the gun and the bloody knife. Could it be an omen... or could it be my overreactive imagination?

I hope it is just my imagination...

*****

"A.D., we didn't really talk about what happened at the funeral. What you said was pretty decent. You almost sounded like a preacher," I remark, as we are taping the last few boxes.

"I jes' felt like I needed tuh say it," A.D. informs me. "Yuh know, Gays an' street folk ain't dat different."

"Really?"

"Yeah. Yuh oughta see de looks I git from deez church mothas, even afta I cleaned up. Dey see me or anybody from de streets comin', and dey grip de purses like a wino grips a fuckin' bottle."

"In other words, they treat you like some straight folk treat us."

"Yeah. An' lemme say dis. All street folk don't steal. We got sum good folk who jes know de streets. Dey know de places where yuh go an' don' go. A lot of 'em are workin' regular jobs. It ain't no Secetary a State, but dey gettin' de money honest. Now, keepin' it one-hunnit, some of 'em are drug dealas, street pharmacis', an' regula' big bollas' who call de shots. Dey are de street's ansuh to a legit nurse, a docta', or a businessmay'n. De only difference is dat dey on de wron' side uh de law."

"Maybe those mothers and suspicious folk see what street folks could be."

"Whatcha mean?"

"Well, you just said it. You can be a doctor just like you can be a street pharmacist. It's all in the direction you go in."

"True dat. And lookin' at all de bullshit I see hap'nin out dere now… kinda makes me glad I ain't in dem streets no more."

"Are ya'll gonna keep yapping or get busy? I want us to finish before it gets dark," Brenda snaps, putting her hands on her ample hips. Looking at her narrow, light brown face, her full figure, and her expression, I can't get over how much she looks uncannily like Mama. But there is a playfulness under her stern expression, as well as a bright smile that Mama rarely showed.

"Are we scared of the dark, Brenda Faye?" Dean teases.

"I ain't scared of anything. I just don't like being in a musty, dusty old attic when it's dark."

"Look, there's a rat!" Roland suddenly yells.

Brenda shrieks and climbs up on the folding chair, hollering, "Shit, kill it!"

"Gotcha!" Roland shouts, laughing.

Brenda scrambles down from the chair. "That's funny, huh?" She grabs a newspaper, and playfully hits Roland on the shoulder. "Here! Laugh at that, wise ass!"

I smile to myself. It is times like these that I really love being around my family. I had forgotten how much the playful squabbles between Roland and Brenda, A.D.'s streetwise point of view, Dean's orderly way of doing things, and my way of thinking creatively were needed to build a unit of loving individuals. As I ponder, I mutter a prayer of thanks to God that Mama's bitterness didn't prevent the closeness we now have. It's a shame that Rhonda cannot relate, but maybe it's not too late.

I pick up one of the heavy boxes and I spot a large, bulging, terribly faded pink journal with a green leaf pattern lying in a darkened alcove. I put the box down and crawl to fetch it. The covers are curved due to age and it stinks of decay. I open the journal. On the inside cover is the name Lynetta Wilkerson. As I thumb through the yellowed, weathered pages, I notice a pair of faded yellow panties stained in dried blood, hanging by a staple on the inside back cover.

A sadness grips me. I hope this doesn't mean what I think it does. I slowly leaf through the earlier pages of the journal and I was disheartened at what I read. The bitter words written by my mother leapt from the pages and bore into my mind. She wrote about how much she hated her mother, her father, and her youngest uncle. She even wrote ways of how she wanted to see them die. Then at the beginning of the journal, I read something that nearly broke my heart.

All I can see is red. Red blood mixed with spunk gushing from my ass and pussy as Daddy and Uncle Larry took turns fucking me. I heard the mattress squeaking as my back and their knees pressed upon it. I closed my eyes to keep back the tears and shut out the images I saw, but the pain forced me to open them. I saw my father at the foot of my bed getting ready to fuck me. His own goddamned blood daughter! I saw the darkness of my uncle's ugly black dick and balls and the smell made me sick. Uncle Larry called me a bitch while ramming my mouth. And the tears wouldn't stop falling.

I kept thinking, "It will all be over soon. Just a few more minutes. Hold out for a few more minutes. It can't last too long. Sooner or later, they will both get off and leave my room so I can go to sleep. I may cry, but at least I'll be able to sleep away the pain."

As my eyes were fixed on the ceiling, I felt my father pull out of me and the mattress squeak with the sudden heavy weight on either side of me. I saw my father's ass and legs with his dick swinging over me. I then saw the sickening vision of my father's younger brother breathing hard and getting ready to suck Daddy's dick. I saw his throat bulging. As my uncle's slobber and their sweat dripped down on my face, I heard Bobby Blue Bland's "Stormy Monday" coming from the radio. My mother was in the next room, watching "Make Room for Daddy". I swear I could hear it turned up louder.

I Hate Them! I hate them so much that my head is hurting worse than my ass and twat. The whole thing makes me sick. I hate having to see my faggot father and uncle making out with each other while fucking me bloody every chance they get... My mother knows what they're doing. Why is she letting them? Money... Dad is well off and

The Cost

she traded me for a kept life. How could a father and uncle rape a thirteen-year-old, and the mother let them without saying a fucking word?

I WISH THEY WOULD ALL DIE!

"Lionel?" Brenda's voice calls out. I turn around, startled.

"Yeah," I say shakily.

"What's wrong? Why are you crying?"

A.D., Dean, and Roland stop their sorting to look at me. I can't get the words out to express my feelings about what I just read. Brenda comes close to me and looks at the book. "Let me see?" she asks carefully.

I hand her the book, and she begins to read aloud the contents of what I perused. Suddenly, her voice withers away at the words, "fucking me", and she becomes stone silent as her face grows blank. She passes it blindly to Roland and he picks up where she left off. After he finishes, the attic became still. Through my tear blinded eyes, I look at Dean and Roland, complete horror on their faces. A.D. is straining to keep his explosive rage under control.

Finally, Roland says, "I'm floored... I mean... Why didn't she say something?"

A.D. booms, "Oh right... Who de fuck wud she tell? Them sick ass bastids prol'ly said they'd do worse to 'er if she did. Besides, wud you want folks tuh know you got raped?"

I wipe my eyes and look at Brenda and the blank expression is still on her face. "Brenda..." No answer. I snap my fingers in front of her face. She blinks and looks at me, then scans the room as if something is lost.

"Brenda Faye, what's wrong with you?"

She looks straight ahead and after a beat, she says in a monotone, "Mama wasn't the last one."

Shock number two. We listen in stunned silence as she continues in a trance, "It was Mother's Day... I was eight years old... Uncle Larry... He lured me to the back shed. It was dark and he had music playing... It was Bobby Blue Bland's 'St James Infirmary'... He told me that he had something I would really like. He gave me some candy. That was nothing new because he knew I liked Now and Laters and Red Hots. But while eating the candy, he said, 'your uncle gave you some candy. Can your uncle have a little kiss?' I tried to kiss him on the cheek, but he made me kiss him on the mouth. I pulled away from his grip and opened the door.

I almost made it out, but he snatched me by the back of my dress, ripped it off me, pulled down my panties, unzipped his pants, and forced it in me. I screamed, but nobody came because the music was playing. He pressed his body on me so I couldn't move. He turned the music up with one hand and he had his other hand over my mouth. After he finished, he pulled up his pants... and wrapped his hand around my throat. He told me that if I told... he'd kill me."

"Dat sick sonuva fuckin' bitch!" A.D. yells as he grabs a silver paperweight and slings it with deadly force at the large mirror, shattering it into tiny pieces. He darts down the stairs and I trail him, with pain throbbing my side. He tries to get in the rental car, but I stop him by positioning my body between him and the door.

"A.D., where are you going?"

"Move out muh way, Li'nel," he intones in a fatal voice.

"Listen, I know how you are feeling, but..."

"Ye ain't gat no clue ha' I'm feelin'. I sed move out muh way now."

"A.D., I'm just as mad as you are. But leave Uncle Larry alone. Don't do something you are going to be sorry for later."

"Move out muh fuckin' way!"

When A.D. gets in this state, only one thing will calm him down. Stand toe to toe with him. "You are going to have to knock me down. But you are NOT getting in this car!"

A.D. explodes with tears flying, "Why you stickin' up fuh dat sick assho'?! You done heard wut he did!"

"Think about what you're about to do... about those older residents at the home, and how scared they'll be if you go over there halfcocked, causing a row. A.D., Uncle Larry is in a rest home with dementia. He's had two heart attacks and a stroke. Time is punishing him already."

For the second time in my life, I see a mix of brokenness, anger, helplessness, and hurt in my brother's eyes. It was the same look he had when he tended my wounds after Mama savagely whipped me. His face crumbles as he says brokenly, "Move, Li'nel. I needta go."

I can't refuse him in that voice, so I step aside. "Ok, go on." He reaches for the door handle, but my voice stops him. "Which one do you want? Ten years? Twenty years? Life?" His head bows. "Forget about your job at the airport. Forget about your Criminal Justice degree. Forget about all the work you put in to prove that you are better than the monster the world and Mama tried to make you. Forget about Rachel and Mike Jr and the fact that they love you. Forget about us... This is it. You know the system is rigged against us Black folk. They will lock your ass away for life. And if that doesn't happen, driving off in a fit might land you in an accident you can't walk out of."

A.D. turns around. His eyes are bloodshot, his face worn. I put my arm around his shoulders. "Come on. Let's walk to the backyard. We don't have to talk but the air might calm us down."

*****

There is a huge irrigation ditch behind the property line that belongs to Granny's next-door neighbor. A.D., Dean, and I used to throw stones in that ditch and really talk about the things plaguing this crazy family. A.D. came back here quite a lot, particularly after a run in with either Granny or Mama. This was the place he chose to think about things. We are sitting at the edge of the ditch, talking just like we did as children.

"I'm guessin dat I'm mad cuz… all'dem years Mama beat on us, she wuz makin'us pay fuh'shit we didn' even do to'er. An' duh ones who did de deed… one uhvum dead… de other so fucked up in de head dat 'e cain' even rememba' de shit 'e did."

"Yeah, I feel that way too."

"I'm 'bout like Roland now. Mebbe she shoulda talked tuh somebody like a counsla."

"You already know Mama wouldn't have gone for that. She was always private about her shit."

"But she took it out on *us*! Dat shit wudn' right!"

"I know."

We are quiet for a minute. Then I say, "I keep remembering what Dad always said. 'Things always happen for a reason.'"

"Wha' reason cud dere be, Li'nel? Two chil'hoods got swiped becuz two grawn-ass men couldn't keep dere dick in dere fuckin' pants. Dey hadta rape girls who cudn't fight fuh dey self. An' damn betcha, dey did dat shit to sum boyz 'n da family too! I keep thinkin' 'bout cuz'n Josh. Mebbe dey did dat shit ta him too. It pro'bly made 'im duh way he wuz. Dey did sum coward sick ass bullshit. Ain't no reasonin' fuh dat!"

"Some reasons have to do with things they haven't resolved from their childhood. It doesn't excuse it… A.D., listen… I want to do the same thing that you feel like doing… I felt the same way last year when I found out that Mama killed Dad."

"Wha…?!" A.D. suddenly swivels his head. *Oh shit! I told!*

Letting a few moments pass, I say slowly, "Mama was the one who shot Daddy."

"And you din' tell me?"

"No. Because that would've been more shit the family would have had to deal with. Plus, the man who took the rap told me not to."

A.D. looks straight ahead. "I need fuh you tuh go insi' righ' now. I needta think about sum thangs. Don' worry, I ain't go'n do nothin' crazy, but I jes' needta be by muhself."

"Ok..." I get up, dust the grass and dirt off the seat of my pants, and trek back to the house. Walking in the backdoor and going to the counter to lean on it, I try to piece it all together. I can't lie. This is some sick shit like A.D. said. I feel like beating the brakes off Uncle Larry for what he did, then turning around and digging Gramps out of the grave just for the satisfaction of kicking his corpse until the dust billows from his bones.

Suddenly, I hear squealing tires in the driveway. I run out to the front porch to see A.D. in the driver's seat pulling out onto the street, pure murder on his face! I stumble down the steps. "ANDREW MARTIN DAVIS! Get back here!" He bestows on me a freezing look of anger and hurt, then speeds down Lindcross Boulevard and disappears beyond the bend in the road.

Chapter Fifteen
BURN, BABY! BURN!

Three hours later, Dean, Roland, Brenda, and I are sitting in the living room, worrying about A.D. I keep glancing at my watch. It is now two minutes to nine. *Where in the hell is he?*

"I feel like this is my fault," Brenda sobbed, her tears streaming down.

"Why? You couldn't have known that A.D. would go off like he did," Dean comforts, patting her on the shoulder.

"But we saw how mad he got about Mama. What I said might have made him fly off and cause more trouble than we already got."

"Oh, come off it, Brenda Faye. Nobody can make A.D. do what A.D. volunteers to do. He has always been a hothead and you know this," Roland reminds.

"I think it might be my fault," I said. "I told him something that may have set him off."

"What did you say?"

"Dean, you know."

Dean looks at me with puzzlement. Then understanding fills his eyes, and he breathes out, putting his fingers wearily on the bridge of his nose, "Oh, Lionel. Please tell me that you didn't tell him."

"Tell him what?" Roland asks. I wish I were in any place other than where I am right now. "What is going on?" he persists.

I take a deep breath. "Are you sure you want to hear this?"

"I asked, didn't I?"

I go to the window to look out. I count the rails on the porch banister. On count twenty, I say, "Mama was the one who killed Daddy."

Again, a long silence stretches for several moments. Then, after the grandfather clock in the upstairs hallway chimes nine times, Brenda says, "What?"

"She caught Dad cheating and shot both of them." For some reason, I stop there. Something tells me that telling them the identity and gender of the cheater was just asking for trouble.

"Wait a minute, now. This is crazy. Mama said a mugger killed him." Roland says.

"She lied."

"I can't believe that. It just doesn't make sense!" Brenda states.

"OK, well the next time we go to Mama's house, let's go to her box of keepsakes. There is a letter explaining the whole thing from the man she shot when she caught him and Daddy fucking," Dean tells her. *Oooh shit!*

"Well, goddamn! Do we have any more fucking shocks today? If we do, you'd better tell me now."

"Look, we got A.D. to worry about. We'll talk about this shit later."

"No, I think we need to talk about it now! It's not every day that you find out that your mother's a killer or that your dad was a punk..." Roland says before stopping his words. Before I know it, my hand shoots out and socks him in his jaw. Without warning, Roland rebounds and charges at my midsection, knocking my wind out as we both collapse to the floor. He pounds my sides with his fists as I pound his back with mine. Somehow, Dean and Brenda manage to separate us.

"Look at you two!" Brenda snaps. "Y'all are brothers and you are fighting each other."

"Well, he hit me!"

"Well, you called Dad a punk!"

"That's what he is!"

I lunge at him, but Dean holds me back. Brenda steps to Roland, threatening through clenched teeth, "Say that shit again, and, so help me God, I'll slug you my damn self!"

Roland calms down. "If that was how he was, then what the fuck can I say about it? But his cheating destroyed our family. And you..." he says, pointing at me and Dean. "You both knew about this and you didn't say a damn thing?"

"Well, excuse us for trying to keep down the family bullshit... Lord knows, like we don't have enough already!" I snap.

"WILL YOU BOTH PLEASE JUST SHUT UP!" Dean yells with sorrow in his voice. Assured of the silence, he sits down and puts his head in his hands. After a few minutes, Brenda sits down beside Dean and says, "Arguing is not helping. We are forgetting what is most important right now and that's A.D. Now, I called the home ten minutes ago and they said he didn't show up there and that Uncle Larry was in his room."

"Thank God for small favors," I reply.

Dean looks down for a minute, then gazes at me and Roland. "You both got something to say to each other," he says firmly. "I can't speak for Mama, but you know Dad wouldn't have stood for us clawing at each other's throats."

Just then, the door opens and A.D. strolls in with red rimmed eyes. "A.D., where..." I begin, but the look on his face stops me. He sits down and throws the keys on the coffee table.

"I tole' ye I wudn' go'n do nothin'," he says. "I jes' neededta git somewhere an' think."

"Where did you go?"

"To de rest home... I sat out on dat parkin' lot thinkin' 'bout wut to do bout dat coward... but his sick ass ain't worth go'n tuh jail ova." He sits back and sighs. "Wut you tole' me, Li'nel... 'bout Mama killin' Pop... made me even mo' mad. Pop wuz de only one dat understood me an' she took 'im from us... like she always took wha' we loved de best. I know she wuz mad'n all, but dat shit wudn' right." He looks at me reproachfully and says, "I undastan' yuh had yuh reasons fuh not tellin', but I jes' wish I'd known wut happened. Mebbe I coulda dealt wit' it betta."

After a few moments of meditation, Dean says, "Y'all, let's pack it in for today."

"I second that," Roland agrees. He then looks at me, thinks a minute, then extends his hand, "Lionel... I'm sorry."

I take his hand in mine. "I know... I'm sorry I hit you."

"Whatcha hit 'im fuh?" A.D. asks.

"Just over some shit that rose up after telling him what I told you."

"Why do I got duh feelin' dat dere's more tuh the story of Mama's icin' out Pop?"

"You didn't tell him the whole thing?" Dean asks.

"No."

"Is SOMEBODY go'n tell me?" A.D. exclaims.

"Well..."

"Oh Jesus, I'll say it," Roland shouts impatiently. "Mama eighty-sixed Daddy because she caught Daddy fucking another dude."

A.D. looks from me to Dean, then he looks at the floor. He takes a deep breath. "Dean, Gramma still gat dat liquor in de basement?"

"Yeah," Dean answers.

"Do yuh know if she got any Scotch down dere?"

"How would I know that? I don't drink that much."

"I needta make a trip down dere. I needs me a double... Matta fact... fuck dat shit," A.D. says as he stands up and heads to the front door.

"Where are you going now?" Brenda asks.

"I'm goin' in muh bag and getting' muh bud so's I kin roll me a gotdamn tree, cuz dis is sum fucked up, insane shit!"

*****

A.D. went to the back yard to "calm down" and Dean and Roland went back to the hotel. It's amazing how none of us wanted to stay in either of the houses we fell heir to. I went up to the attic to get the last of the boxes and put them in the trunk. Before the final descent into the kitchen, I laid Mama's journal on the seat of the folding chair. As I wash my hands at the sink, I thought about her. I felt a pang of despair thinking about the girl she'd been. How alone and scared she must have felt. Amazingly, all the anger I had for her drains from me, leaving a strong residue of personal hurt.

What she went through is the ultimate reason she was so mean and hateful to most of the men in the family, but treated Rhonda like she was royalty, no matter how many times she fucked up. Rhonda looked and acted just like her. When Rhonda needed money for bail or some other reason, Mama was her supplier. It still amazes and horrifies me to this day when I think about what she did with the money I gave her for that second mortgage that she supposedly took out to pay for A.D.'s bond. Roland recently gave me the straight on that. There was no second mortgage and she didn't bail A.D. out: she used it to purchase a car for herself and to pay the three month's back rent that Rhonda owed. As for A.D., she said, "Serves his ass right."

She pretty much ignored Roland and Brenda. Maybe it was because they always made it a point to stay out of her way. They looked at A.D., Dean, and me, and saw us as an advisory on what not to do... You know, it occurs to me that Mama never knew the jewels she had. Not just us older ones, but Roland and Brenda too. Aided with academic scholarships, they both graduated from Shaw University. Brenda got her bachelors' and masters' in social work and Roland got both his degrees in child development. Brenda has a beautiful family and, even though I'm not a fan of Angela's, Roland seems to be in love with her. I chuckle to myself at the logic I'm able to glean from this. They both saw how fucked up we were as kids and determined between themselves that they would prevent and stop the same shit in other's homes… as well as heal their own hurts.

Things always happen for a reason.

I walk out to the front porch and I see Brenda leaning out on the banister. The night air is filled with the scent of roses and freshly cut grass. I stand beside and lean on the railing with her.

"Brenda, you ok?"

She glances at me, grants a small smile, and looks at the darkened sky.

"Yeah… I'll be alright… You know, when working in the social work field and trying to fix everybody else's problems, you numb yourself from thinking about the problems you have to own."

I take a deep breath and offer, "That can happen."

She continues gazing quietly, watching the stars twinkle in their places. Then she says, "I told Mama about what Uncle Larry did to me."

"You did?"

She nods her head solemnly.

"What did she say?"

"She told me that I was lying and quoted the Bible saying, 'A liar will not tarry in His sight'. She threatened that I'd better not let her hear that shit again. She said if I repeated it to anyone, somebody would come and take me away and that I'd never see my family again."

I bit my lower lip. *Oh Mama, you did the same thing to her that Granny did to you. Granny closed her eyes to you, you closed your ears to Brenda, and you made Brenda close her mouth and say nothing. See no evil. Hear no evil. Speak no evil.*

Silence hangs in the air for an eternity. I break it with a question. "Did it happen more than…"

"No," She said, reading my mind. "It was only once."

"That would explain why you always had one of us boys around you when he was in the room."

"And why I kept my kids away on major holidays. I asked Mercer to take them to be with his family. After a while, I started going with them, because as much as I love you all, I couldn't stand hearing Mama's mouth or seeing that pervert's sick face."

As I listen to her pour her heart out, I think of the journal I wrote, chronicling my mother's rejection of me, the things she did, and the break-up with Nate. I thought about Dr. Banneker's suggestion of writing things down and burning them. Maybe I should unlock my time capsule and burn it. It's full of hardship, hurt, and regrets.

But then, I think about all the magical moments I wrote about.

My capers with The Fellas.

The cruise.

The sessions with Dr. B.

The start of my romantic relationship with Jojo.

And on... And on... And on...

I recall a scripture Rev. Washington preached from recently.

Finally, brothers and sisters, whatever is true, whatever is noble, whatever is right, whatever is pure, whatever is lovely, whatever is admirable--if anything is excellent or praiseworthy--think about such things.

I believe that passage is a good lesson in positive thinking. It is common to focus on the evils of this world, but we rarely concentrate on the things that prove virtuous. That journal is filled with all of that and then some. And like Dad said, things happen for a reason. What that reason may be, I don't know. But I have to believe there is a purpose behind the process. So, hell naw! I ain't burning that. There is too much healing in those pages. Who knows? I might even use a pseudonym and publish it, but I would have to dig it up and beg The Fellas to let me tell their stories under assumed names. It might stop some of the hurt because... Well, let's face it, the things we suffered as children are still plaguing our youth today. It might be a source of help for those who struggle with their sexuality, their depression, the gay bashing, and their inability to see the good they have to offer. Hmm... I like that idea. It may not make bestseller, but at least it may stop someone from committing suicide or even impress upon them the importance of seeking decent professional help.

Before I placed the notebook in the time capsule, I remember writing the words, I CHOOSE PAIN, on the cover. Why did I write that? Why? I struggle to find the reasoning. But then I think about the words of my father and I tie them to my relationship with Jojo, as well as my own life.

Son, if you have someone that you really love, as I love your mother, what hurts them will hurt you too. But you will bear the pain, because you chose to love them for better or for worse. That is the type of pain we choose gladly.

My own view of choice is somewhat different from Dad's. I am gay. I knew people would be disgusted by that, but I chose to live my life in honesty and to tell the truth to those I felt would receive it and love me anyway. I knew about the trouble that came with that choice, but I felt that the pain of not being accepted by Mother would be temporary. I'm seeing the proof of that now through my friends, my family, and Dr. Banneker.

I also know that there is a pain that many choose without knowing: the pain of hiding who they are because of how people would think, feel, and react if they told them the truth. To me, that's living a lie. And the pain attached to that can end up haunting them until they die.

I think about Mama's journal… The bitterness was like a cloud of foul-smelling dust rising and stinking up the air. When Brenda finishes talking, I say, "Brenda, listen. You know I've been going to a shrink, right?"

Brenda laughs and says, "Yes, and before you say anything about me going to one, I'll have you know that my shrink is Dr. Mercer C. Odom. And I love going to him!"

"Why wouldn't you? You are married to the man. I wonder when you go to your 'sessions' if he fraternizes with the patient."

"Fringe benefits, dearest brother. Fringe benefits."

We both laugh. Then I say, "I have an exercise that my shrink gave me. I write down whatever negative feelings I have at that point, and then burn them."

"Good exercise."

"I think we ought to do that with Mama's journal."

Brenda thinks a minute, then says, "Well, it's not doing Mama any good wherever she is. And it sure as hell ain't helping us, other than dropping clues as to why she became so mean. We could use it to make sure Uncle Larry pays in prison for what he did to us both, but iron bars cannot do what time alone has dumped on him. So, if everybody else agrees, I say 'Burn, Baby! Burn!'"

We laugh and resume stargazing. A few minutes roll by.

"Brenda Faye?"

"What?" She says in her sweet, teasing voice.

"You know, we never talked about how you feel about my marrying Jojo."

"We haven't talked about a lot of things, including your attraction to men in general."

"True," I say, looking at Granny's azalea bushes and then at the freshly manicured lawn that A.D. mowed this afternoon. I remember how immaculate her yard always was. Not a shrub out of place. "So, what do you think?"

Brenda takes a deep breath and scans the pavement of Lindcross Boulevard with her beautiful doe eyes. I can tell that she is really pondering her next words. Then she says, "I'm more concerned about your life than anything else. I would imagine that it's hard enough being both black and gay. But in marrying Jojo, you are making a public official statement that you love and want to be with a man. And many parts of society are still not willing to accept that."

"I know."

"If you are going to do this, you need to be prepared for the fact that it's going to piss people off for any number of reasons. Then again, you didn't ask me what the world thinks."

"No, I didn't."

There is a silence hovering over the atmosphere of this whitewashed porch. She then says, "In response to your question, I'm going to ask you a couple."

"In the words of Roland, 'What else is new?'"

She playfully bumps my side with her body, smirking with her full lips, "Will you shut up please?"

"OK, ask your question."

"Do you love Jojo?"

I feel a bright smile creeping across my face as I envision him in my mind. After a few seconds, I say, "I love him double-triple."

"If the whole world were against your being with him, would you still love him?"

"Yes, I would."

"So, that answers your question as far as I'm concerned. I don't give two fucks about your being gay or loving Jojo. I love my gay, smart-ass brother and that ain't never gonna change. Now I'm as straight as an arrow and I am not inclined to cross to the other side. But I've been around long enough to know that we only got a few chances at true love, regardless of what gender it comes in. It just boils down to owning your choices."

"Owning my choices?"

"Yeah. I mean, you didn't choose to be gay, but you did choose to love him and be truthful on what completes you as a person. So, honey, if ya'll love each other that much, I say have the biggest wedding on this side of the Mason-Dixon Line!"

I grab her and hug her short, robust frame tightly, both of us laughing.

Stepping back and playfully swatting me on the shoulder, she asks, "So, when is the wedding? I mean now that the cruise ya'll were going to do it on changed their dates to the last week in February."

"Yeah. We are still doing it on that particular cruise ship. The new date is February twenty-third."

"Ok, then. I need to make my last payment."

"You're going?"

"You're surprised? You know that's around the time that Mercer and I celebrate our eleven-year anniversary."

"The twenty-sixth, right?"

"That's right!"

"Our friend, Corey's birthday is on the twenty-fifth," I stop then, wondering if he is alright. I have to get A.D. to call him so I can hear his voice.

"I really like him! He is a hoot and Felipe is a sweetheart"

"He is. I'm lucky to have friends like them.

She looks at me, shrewdly. "You know what? Honestly, I am not surprised about you and Jojo getting hitched."

"You're not?"

"Nope! You and Jojo were like peanut butter and jelly as kids. It's only natural for y'all to end up linking together. Besides, only starstruck lovers would go to college together, live in the same city after college, and keep a friendship going for years and years. It doesn't matter how long it took for you to see the connection. The point is that you are there now."

"Right."

"But your little sister has some advice to give you," she teases coyly.

"And that would be?"

"Well," she begins, looking humorously at her nails. "I don't know how spicy your sex life has been, but keep your eyes peeled and your mind open because, looking at my future brother in law, something tells me that you are getting ready to marry a bona fide, straight-up FREAK!!!!"

"What do you know about freaks?"

The Cost

"Please, big bro! I married Dr. Mercer Odom! And the things THAT man does in the bedroom… Whew!!!"

"What?"

"Let's just say that porno stars wouldn't be able to touch it without blushing!"

*****

It is Saturday evening, and A.D. and I are prepared to go back to Baltimore. But surprise! We have a four-hour delay. Roland and Dean decided to go back tomorrow afternoon. We were going to burn Mama's painful keepsakes this morning, but we all had stuff going on. So, after learning of the delay, we all decided to gather in Granny's backyard to burn them an hour before A.D. and I leave for the airport. When I shared Dr. Banneker's suggestion of jotting down our hurts and burning them, they heartily agreed. I am anxious to get this going so I can get back to Baltimore to see about Corey. I talked with him yesterday morning. His voice sounded strange and I could tell he was still worried. I let him know that we would be home soon and to hang tight.

A.D. pulls out a small grill that Granddad had, and we put a box containing Mama's journal and blood-stained panties on it, along with our written hurts. I snuck Troy's letter to Mama from the box and put it in my pocket. I intend to mail it to Troy when I get the chance. After all, he was the one who wrote it. Maybe it will give him some peace. I might share the burning exercise with him if he thinks keeping it is fruitless.

Brenda lights the match and throws it in. The lighter fluid catches the small flame, transforming it into a blazing fire. We watch as the bright and hungry inferno licks across the faded pink and green journal, the blood speckled panties, the papers, and the box. Watching it burn, I suddenly remember a day when I was eight years old. I was washing the dishes after getting my ass whipped for not doing them before, and I felt Mama just come up behind me and put her arms around me. *"I'm hard on you 'cause Mama has to be. I'm trying to teach you responsibility. But your Mama loves you. Don't you ever forget that."* I heard her rough voice say. She then kissed me on the top of my head and walked back into the living room.

That was one of the few times that I remember her showing me any type of affection, but I can't forget how it made me feel. I felt protected and loved by her at that moment. The memory of that stretches across my mind, blocking out all resentment and anger. While feeling the warmth of the flames on my face, I feel my heart utter the words… *I love you too, Mama.*

Chapter Sixteen
SWAN SONG

On this plane ride back to Baltimore, A.D. and I engage in a long and interesting conversation. We talk about things that we kept quiet about as kids as well as young adults. There are times where his voice vibrates with pain and anger, but he is trying to hold it together. It surprises me how open and evolved he is. There *is* one question that he asks me, and I almost spit out my Bloody Mary mix when I hear it.

"Li'nel, why you gay?"

After I swallow and regain my composure, I ask him humorously, "A.D., what the blue fuck is wrong with you? You can't ask me a question like that when you know I got food or liquid in my mouth. You're lucky I didn't do a spit take and your shirt is still dry."

A.D. grins at me, saying, "Im guessin' dat question di' come outta lef' fiel'? What I wuz meanin' tuh ask is dis." He hesitates, then says, "Whatcha find appealin' 'bout… bein' wit a may'n?"

I turn my face to the window, trying to hide my twitching lips that threaten to reveal my humorous reaction to his question. When I look at him, I ask, "Are you sure you wanna know this?"

"Why would I ast if I din' wanna know?"

I take a deep breath, trying to find the words to answer him. Then I tell him, "I can't really explain it."

"Try."

"Why do you really want to know?"

"Jes' curious. You ain't gotta ansuh'. I undastan' if ya chicken!" A.D. jokes.

I shove him on the shoulder, playfully. "Who you calling 'chicken'?"

"I'on see nobody else settin' ere beside me!" A.D. laughs. I join him.

"Ok. Well, remember... you asked for it. Let's see..." I gulp down the rest of my drink... then I meditate. When my answer is focused, I explain to him, with my beloved fiancé in mind, "I guess it is the resilience of a man."

"Resilience?"

"Yeah. You know what that is, right?"

"Yeh. Bein' able tuh bounce back from shit." *Alright, A.D.!*

"Exactly... Hmmm... I like the power that a man possesses where he overcomes almost anything. I am fascinated with how a man looks when he sweats. The veins popping out of his arms and even sometimes the muscular thickness. The ability to be hard and yet soft when he's in the bedroom with me. I like the aggressiveness; yet I like the sensitivity. I like the hardness of his muscle yet the softness of his cheek. I like the swag when he walks down the street or when he is sexing me down... and yet... I like the vulnerability when he trusts his body to me. There is a lot of things I like about men that women would never be able to duplicate. If I could put it simply, I would say that... it's just right for me."

A.D. nods his head and replies, "I gotchu."

"My turn to ask a question."

"Shoot."

"Have you ever been with a man?"

A.D. breathes out a heavy sigh and says, "Yeh."

Turkey shit and corn grease! I think to myself. *A.D. actually did a dude!* I'm glad I drunk all my beverage because that definitely would've been the spit take of the night.

"Are you shitting me?"

"Nope, I dun been wit a dude befo'."

Questions fly like butterflies in my brain. Who could he have done it with? What was it like? Was it serious?

"I been wit' two dudes in muh life. An' it wuz one time each. Duh second one wuz dis dude I wuz in de cell wit'. He wuz a kinda tall, dawk skin dude. Real diesel, built like a Ford truck."

"Please tell me he did not rape you."

A.D. sucks his teeth and gives me a cocky look before answering, "Naw, he wudn' crazy. Three yea's in de jownt, I dun already had a rep fuh fuckin' up dudes wontin' tuh try me. Anyways, I wuz jes curious. I'd always wonted tuh know wut it wuz like. Wut took it to duh bridge wuz dat I done heard all duh talk 'bout dudes hookin' up wit other dudes when dey git on lockdown. I knew 'e did it off an' on, so I ast 'im pretty much de same thang I ast you. He say tuh me, 'I show yuh betta' than I kin tell yuh.' I wudn' doin' shit dat day so I wuz like… whateva."

Intrigued, I ask, "What did he do?"

A.D. grins like a cat that ate the canary. He sat back, folded his brawny arms, and sucked on his gold tooth. "Sucked muh dick and tol' me tuh fuck 'im up de ass."

"Shut up!"

"'E did."

"So, I assume you fucked him."

"Yeh, I did." He still has that shit eating grin on his face.

"And how did it feel?"

"Well, it wuz tighta' than a lotta kitties I dun been in. An' I gotta tell ye," A.D. pauses, then lowers his head and peers at me. "Dat shit felt good too."

Damn, I feel just like the time when we were kids at the dinner table, and he whispered to me that he farted! "Oh my God, I cannot believe you did that!"

"I di'. Ain't been wit a dude since den. It wuz fun, but de dames do sum'n fuh me dat de dudes caint."

"And what is that?"

"Well, I like the screnf of a dame. Duh resilience. How dey kin make babies an' still come up swangin'. How dey kin hol' down two 'r three jobs to support de family when deez sorry ass men who gave 'em the babies caint. I like da curve of a woman, I like da boobies, I like da folds of a pussy. I like when dey git wet when I make love to 'em. And I luv it win dey cry an' tell me dat I'm lovin' em right when we's in de bed."

"And you feel that way about Rachel?"

"Yeh. Dere's just sum'n 'bout dat girl an' lil Mike dat make me happy. Thangs ain't always roses, but we luv each udda."

I turn my face back to the window, thinking about my brother's words. *Wait a minute! He said he did it with two guys.* I stare at him.

"So, who was the other one?"

"Da otha' one?"

"The other guy you fucked."

"Hol' on. I ain't fuck him. I jes' kissed'm an 'e sucked muh dick. I wuz fitteen an' 'e wuz 'bout 'fote'teen."

"What brought it on?"

"Welp, ya know how dat freak of a passuh wuz preachin' aginst gays all de time?"

"Yeah."

"I wuz nosy e'en back den. An' yuh know da bad boy I am. Ev'rythang 'dem hypacrites like Lawson sed wuz wron' made me wanna do it. So, I met wit lil' dude an' had a lil' smoocheroo an' a dick suck in da boyz bafroom afta school."

"Who was it?"

"You sho' ya wanna know?"

"Why would I have asked?"

A.D. breathes out a long sigh. *Why do I feel like I have to brace myself?*

"It was Jamall."

Good grief! I laugh to myself. Jamall was an all-around ho'! I thought he just had heat for me and Jojo. Now we can add my seemingly straight brother to the list. I wonder. Who *else* has my dear departed cousin either fucked or kissed in my brother, cousin, or childhood friend rolodex?

"Whatcha laughin' fo'?"

"You wouldn't believe it if I told you."

"Try me."

I feel a wicked smile stretch across my face that resembles The Grinch's as I say, "Jamall was my first fuck."

A.D. jumps in his seat, turning around to gaze at me with his mouth wide open.

"A.D., close your mouth before your tongue falls out."

Suddenly, A.D. lets out a huge laugh that made other passengers stare at us. "Oh muh Gawd!"

"Put a cork in it, will you? I don't want everybody in my business!"

A.D. points at me, snickering and whispering, "I knew it! I knew ya'll wuz fuckin'!"

"How is that?"

"I rememba' when you an' Jamall cudn' stan' each otha! Alluva sudden, you wuz always goin' tuh his house! An' yo' skin wus clearin' up an' it wudn' cuz a no damn Clearasil! Now yuh gat me wonderin' how it happened."

"Now A.D., there are some things a brother got to keep to himself. But I do have a question."

"Shoot."

"Well, you told me that you had relations with men twice in your life. How do you know that there won't be a third, fourth, or fifth time?"

A.D. looks dead ahead for a few moments. Then he says, "To be hones', I don' know. But if it gits tuh dat place, den I guess it's s'pose tuh happen, an' I'd have tuh change muh moxie to straight attracted or bi."

"Would you tell Rachel?"

It's my brother's turn to give me the Grinch grin. "Wud ye believe I tol' her a'ready!"

"I know you're lying through your teeth!" I chuckle out.

"Hand tuh de Bible, bro! She ast me dat question too, so I tol' er. Fuh sum reason, it got 'er turnt on. Bro, dere's a side tuh dat girl yuh don't know!"

"And what side is that?"

"To steal yo' words, 'Now Li'nel, dere's sum thangs a bruva gots tuh keep to hisself!' But I'll say dis! Don' give dat girl no fake ding-a-ling or lube, 'cause she know jes where tuh put it… an' she ain't jes' using it on 'erself," he finishes with a sly wink.

"Uh, TMI!"

"Yo' words agin. You ast fo' it!"

*****

It is 12:34am and I enter my home with the relief of a weary marathon runner. I drop my bags to the floor and toss my keys on the coffee table. Then I sit in my chair and muse.

This week was a crazy week, with us cleaning the house and making sure that all the furniture and knickknacks Grandma had were either sold or donated to goodwill. But oddly enough, the trip home turned out to be therapeutic in many ways. I can't explain how but discovering and burning Mama's diary helped me to release the anger I had for her. I still feel a little pain and the revelations about my mother's childhood rape unsettled me, but it also strengthened what love I had left for her. I had to surmise that Mama and I could've had a much better relationship if the circumstances of her past were different.

I look over to my end table where I left my phone. It's out of juice. *I should have told Jojo to charge it then turn it off.* I plug it up and walk upstairs to take a shower. As the hot water hits my skin, I think about the free and flowing conversation I had with A.D.

Color me shocked as hell. A.D. stuck his hands-free finger in a cannoli-cream and all! The thought of it makes me laugh and what he said about Rachel was icing on the cake. No wonder she is so embracing of us gay folk. I'm even more shocked that he told me, and we were able to discuss it. When was the last time we talked like that? When we were kids? When we were in the hospital after Mama's operation? I don't know. Maybe Mama's death opened the door of communication and sensitivity that my gruff and tough oldest brother kept locked tight. A.D. was always the indifferent one. He rarely showed emotion and when he did, it always took me by surprise.

During the time I was home, I got reacquainted with Roland and Brenda better. Brenda told me that she's going back to school to get her Ph.D. She felt that the additional education could help the clients more and probably give her insight on adult behavior stemming from childhood trauma. I wished her success. As far as Roland, he told me that life was good on his end and that he broke off the engagement with Angela. I asked him why and he told me that Angela kept going in about how the life my friends, Jojo, and I were living was disgusting and that I got what I deserved for willfully practicing it. Apparently, he saw a parallel between Angela and Mama's disdain, and thought about what lot his own children would've fallen into. He was concerned about how Angela would have reacted if one of them ended up gay. Being convinced that she wouldn't have the motherly instinct to love instead of judge, he told her to hit the road. *Thank God!* I applauded his decision and told him that he could find someone better. Like I did with Brenda, we talked about my being gay and marrying Jojo. Roland admitted to me that he didn't understand how two men could have sex with each other. The idea frankly grossed him out but, in his words, he said, "My brother and father are going to stay my brother and father. I may not like it, but my love won't leave just because I don't understand what makes your boat float." Well, I have to accept the fact that the magic of "The Life we call Gay" will go over the heads of even the ones who love you.

I go downstairs to check my phone. There are six messages from Jojo that began four hours ago. *Hmm… that's odd.* Each of them told me to call him immediately. It hits me that I forgot to tell A.D. to call him about the delay. I wonder if he is still up. I scroll down to his name and touch it to ring his phone. He picks up after the second ring.

"Hello," he says, as if transfixed.

"Hey baby. I am so sorry. A.D. and I forgot to call and let ya'll know we got delayed. What's going on?"

"Uh, Lionel," he begins in a mournful, disturbed voice that he struggles to control.

"Yeah, in the flesh, love," I joke. "What's going on?"

"When did you get in?" *Hmm…* No change in his voice.

"About forty-five minutes ago. I got all your messages telling me to call you. What's wrong?" I ask, starting to grow suspicious. "Why do you sound so strange?"

"Lion, I- I need you to get over to my house."

"Why?"

"Just come to my house."

"Can you just tell me over the phone?"

"No. We need you over here."

"We? Who's we?"

"Peep, Jimmy, Garrett, and Eunetta."

"What are they doing over there? Why can't you just tell me what's going on?"

Suddenly it hit me. He didn't mention Corey. A sickening, cold feeling drapes on me, followed by an oppressive gray cloud that feels like it's sitting on my shoulders.

"What happened? Is Corey over there?"

There is a long, frightening hush over the line, but I can hear faint sobs and Eunetta's consoling voice edged with sorrow.

"Lionel, I can't tell you over the phone. All I can say is that you need to come over here. Now."

I am frustrated and confused. I want him to hurry up and tell me what the hell is wrong. I feel a shudder move through my body that causes me to jolt uncontrollably.

"Fine, I'll be right over."

Before I can say anything else, Jojo ends the call. What else can I do but grab my keys and dash out the door? As I lock it and run to my truck, I still feel this dread feeling cloaking me with an unshakable force and unyielding heaviness. Why do I get the awful feeling that if I go to Jojo's house, I'm not coming back to my house tonight because this news is going to shake the very ground that I walk on? For a few minutes, I sit motionless in my seat, and I grip the steering wheel as a mountain climber holds a breaking rope, plummeting him into a bottomless pit of anguish.

As soon as I prepare to start the truck, my phone rings. "Hello?"

"Li'nel?"

"A.D.?"

"Wha's wron' wit' yuh voice?"

The words are trapped in my throat as I hear A.D. call my name. When I can speak, I croak out, "A.D., I think something is wrong with Corey."

"Whuduya mean?"

"I just got off the phone with Jojo. He told me to come over to his house. Peep, Jimmy, Garrett and Eunetta are over there. I thought I heard Garrett crying. Jojo didn't say whether Corey was with them."

"Shit, I betta git ova dere!" A.D. exclaims in panic.

"Over where?"

"Corey's. I'ma holla atcha to letcha know wha's hap'nin."

"OK."

*****

The moment Jojo opens the door, I see his blood shot eyes as well as his struggle to keep whatever trauma he faced at bay. Following him inside and scanning the room, I see Peep standing at the kitchen door holding onto the door frame weakly for support. Obviously, he is severely inebriated. That's a bad sign because Peep does not drink to excess unless he's hurt about something. He sees me, and he rushes drunkenly over to me to grab me and hug me. I can smell the alcohol on his breath.

"What is going on? Why are y'all acting crazy?" Peep's response to my questions is a tighter embrace and I feel his tears on my shoulder. I force him to both let me go and lie down on the sofa. His head lolls across the arm like that of a limp ragdoll. I look over at Garrett who is just sitting in the armchair, despondent and traumatized. Eunetta is sitting on the arm, cradling Garrett's head in the crook of her arm and wiping his tears as they fall.

"OK, y'all are scaring me. Why is everybody so quiet? Why is Peep more smashed than a wino on Penn Avenue? *And where in the hell is Corey?!"* I shout the last question in fear and frustration while looking around the living room aimlessly. Jojo wears a look of panic mixed with sadness.

"Baby", Jojo says with a choking voice as he comes over to put his hands on my shoulders. "I don't know how to tell you this."

"Just tell me."

Jojo stutters, "You'd better sit down."

The tears in his voice begin to foreshadow the news. Something awful has happened to Corey! I try to process whatever I'm getting ready to hear. For some reason, I feel that sitting down would make me more vulnerable to the news than I am already. I mutter with suspicion as I back away from Jojo and stand in front of the fireplace, "No, I'm fine. I want to know what the problem is… and right now! What is going on?"

A tearful Peep sits up unsteadily. He points at me and speaks, with his voice guttural and his eyes blearily meeting mine, "I think you're gonna need a drink."

I say while trying to maintain my control, "I don't want a drink."

"You're gonna wish you had one after you hear this shit."

"Will someone cut the bullshit and just tell me what happened?!" I shout at the top of my lungs. There is an uncomfortable silence, which is broken by Garrett's uncontrollable sobs of pain and grief.

Then I hear Jojo's plaintive voice as if it is coming from far away. "Lionel… baby… Corey is gone."

"Gone? What do you mean he's gone?"

Jojo bites his lips to keep the tears from falling. With a shaken and horrified delivery, he laments, "Corey was killed last night."

I feel a subzero chill spread throughout my body, numbing me to the bone.

"I don't believe you. I just talked to him… on A.D.'s phone… yesterday morning."

I try to convince myself that this is all a cruel joke. But the looks on their faces scream the truth. That guy following him had a plan to kill him and he succeeded. My legs give way under me, but Jojo catches me. I hold to the mantle of his fireplace to keep from falling. In a voice similar to a wounded animal's, I bray out, "What happened?"

"Garrett went over to his house to check on him. He said Corey called him worried about some guy stalking him, but Garrett was in Puerta Vallarta with Eunetta, Rachel, and Mike Jr. They came back to Bmore early this morning and Garrett rushed over to Corey's house to check and see if everything was alright... He saw that Corey's door was wide open. He went in and found the place trashed. He went upstairs and found Corey lying in the hallway with his... his pants and underwear bunched down and his ass bleeding... When he looked closer, he saw more blood pooling on the floor near his neck... His throat was slashed."

A violent shudder rocks me and I blindly stagger across the room to reach for the back of Jojo's Queen Anne chair for support. I try to talk but I can't. I try moving my lips in hopes that the tones from my throat would issue past them. Doesn't work. I try to breathe but all I can manage are short heaving gasps. The room seems to be spinning out of control. I feel a painful pull at my heart as my energy drops drastically. It's almost as if a part of my soul is leaving my body.

Slowly, my voice returns as I hear myself utter in a voice so frail, "It can't be true. I can't believe it. Corey..." My voice trails off. My breath returns as I feel a hot sphere of fire flame my aching heart. I suddenly feel angry as I shout. *"He's not dead! After all the shit he went through to get to his success?! I won't believe he's dead! HELL NO!"* I rush outside to jump in my car, but Eunetta overtakes me.

"Chile, where are you going?"

"I'm going over to Corey's house!"

Eunetta places her hands on my chest, looking up at me with her watery dark brown eyes. "Honey, what good is rushing over there going to do you? You don't need to view that scene. That's not going to do anything but widen the wound and make it worse for you."

"I'm going, Ms. Eunetta... I gotta see for myself..."

"Then one of us is going to drive you over there. You are in a state right now. I don't think you should be behind the wheel," Jimmy says with a voice shaken by tears.

"I'll drive," Jojo says, jumping in his car.

"Baby, I think you oughta let me drive. I'd feel better knowing that neither of you are driving," Eunetta cautions, motioning Jojo to get in her car.

"Hang on. I'm coming too," Peep slurs from the doorway. "I want to track down that low-life motherfucker that killed my brother!"

"No," Eunetta shouts authoritatively. "What YOU are going to do is lay your ass on that couch and try to sleep that booze off. Jimmy, you stay here with him and my boy. Tell Garrett that Mama's coming right back. Jojo, what are you still sitting in your car for? You two hurry up and get in mine! Come on!"

*****

The moment we turn down Linden Avenue, I feel a sense of horror. There is an unmistakable stench of death in the air. We see A.D. standing in front of the house, and he looks as if he's seen a ghost. So many of the things I am seeing now will forever be etched in my memory.

The yellow police tape...
A.D.'s angry and shocked expression...

I hear windchimes clinking loudly as the breeze blows, but I say nothing...

As we move through Corey's unlocked front door, we are devastated at the sights we see, as well as the overpowering scent of blood. Eunetta pulls out her handkerchief and masks her face to block out the scent. As I look listlessly toward Jojo, I see a haggard expression on his face as a river flows down his cheeks. His body violently quakes, accompanied by loud sobs of fear and grief. My hands want to comfort him. My heart aches to hold him and tell him that everything will be ok. But my mind and my eyes are consumed with red hot rage. I look around the living room and more agents of wreckage seem to threaten my eyes as well as my sleep for years to come.

Corey's expensive figurine of the preacher playing the organ lying
broken in pieces on the ground...
The room in total shambles...
Corey's handwritten sheet music scattered all over the floor and on
his baby grand piano.

I still say nothing...

As a sobbing Eunetta comforts Jojo, I charge up the stairs to Corey's upper hallway, and, stopping short, I see the ultimate display of horror, one that shakes my faith and causes me to fear, yet rage against the heavens for all of us... trans, lesbian, gay, and bisexuals alike.

A streetlight beaming through the window at the end of the hall.

Three haunting doors on each side of the hallway, half obscured by shadows.

The chalk outline that seems to glow.

The sickening vision of blackened blood seeping through the glinting, blond hardwood floors.

The green spray paint on the wall, spelling out the word, "FAGGOT."

But still, I say nothing…

I back away to amble blindly down the stairs, totally numbed and dazed. I move past Jojo and Eunetta and stagger back outside like a lumbering giant. I look at the neighbors that wonder who we are. I look at A.D., sitting on the curb with his head bowed and staring trancelike at the pavement below.

My times with Corey flash before my eyes, and along with those times, I feel a sharp wind blowing. I hear the turbulent, haunting piano solo from his symphony, accompanied by the horror of discordant loud windchimes rapidly clanging. They echo in my mind… as visions swirl around me…

The concert where Jojo and I first met him.

The manic moments in college when we all would go to the McDonald's at the now ghosted Northwood Plaza.

The pizza and movie nights on Fridays at the Student Center.

The nights at the Link where we danced with abandon.

The long conversations over the phone.

The embraces we gave each other.

The visit at the hospital when he was attacked.

The advice…

The laughs…

The tears…

And on… and on… and on…

I remember the dream about the shadowy figure with the gun and the bloody knife. It *was* an omen. The gun was for me and the knife was for Corey. One survived… One died. But when I hear the words that he uttered to me while holding me fast on my kitchen floor, "I got you," somehow I find a loud, rage-ridden voice to scream… to bawl… to rain curses down on the killer's head. I found enough movement in my hands to pummel and scrape at the pavement where I find myself now. I had collapsed. Even with Jojo, Eunetta, and A.D. holding me tightly, I claw the air with scraped and bloody fingertips and cut flesh as I begin to shriek and howl with the madness of a beast devoid of reason.

I scream Corey's name repeatedly. Upon every utterance, I hear a maddening echo that seems to climb to oblivion without promise of an audible response. I believe it, yet I don't believe it. I scream, yet I'm silent. I'm full of hurt, yet I'm hollow with grief.

My gifted, beautiful, and brilliant friend… my brother… Cordell Rodgerick James Kennedy, is dead.

I want Blood. I want Corey's death to be avenged.

I want his murderer's skin to be eaten away…
I want his lineage cut short…
I want his family to grieve worse than I am grieving right now…
I want his heart to shrivel up and disappear…

I WANT HIM TO DIE.

But under all the anger, hatred, and grief waxes a question, posed with the hurt and anguish of a cruelly chastised child…

Why? Why did you kill my brother?

Chapter Seventeen
TO LOSE… TO LAMENT…
TO LOVE…

Four walls. All I see are these four walls. It is now almost a month after Corey was killed and the gray cloud of misery still hovers over this house. The days flew by in haunting hues of gray and brown. Because he had no relatives living in Baltimore, we had to contact his aunt, Freida Andrews, who flew up to identify him. She wanted to fly him back to Miami to bury him in his birthplace, but she conceded after learning that Corey took precautions and acquired burial insurance. He added a notarized request to be buried in Baltimore one week after his death.

We had the funeral on October seventeenth and Corey planned everything, even down to the tiniest flower. That surprised all of us because Corey was impulsive and preferred not to plan anything. He always said that too much planning can hamper spontaneity. He gave his wishes for the homegoing to Peep, as well as the numbers to call upon his demise and details regarding his last will and testament to be read on December sixteenth. I don't know how Peep was able to do it and keep his sanity.

The homegoing was beautiful, yet heartbreaking. The church was so packed that the ushers had to open the fellowship hall to accommodate the overflow so they could watch the service through TV monitors. Shawn Tolbert, Ben Longwood, Marianne DeWitt, and my boss came to the funeral for moral support. Floyd told me that he extended my leave of absence, saying afterward, "You can't be one hundred percent at your job, when grief is constantly hawking you."

The Cost

The altar in the large sanctuary of Unity and Love Community Church was covered with countless red roses and Corey's pearly casket graced the front of the pulpit. In the casket is Corey, dressed in a black suit with red pinstripes and a white shirt with a red, black, and white tie. Lovely even in death, Corey looked as if he was sleeping and enjoying a pleasant dream. When I went up to say my farewell, I looked at him with my heart in my eyes. I spoke his name mournfully, expecting him to open his eyes, smirk, and sling a barb about my face looking like a torn wet-t-shirt bunched up and discarded on the porch after a slip-n-slide. Still, he laid there without a move or a word.

It was Corey's wish that the service would remain uplifting and devoid of excessive grief, especially concerning the music. At the request of Elijah Pearson, Corey's second in command and the new director of music, the worship arts ministry invited the voices of Baltimore's finest choirs to combine with theirs, including the choral ensembles from Morgan, Towson, and Howard Universities. The blended effort proved effective in exceeding his expectation. Dressed in Corey's favorite colors of black and red, two hundred and fifty-seven singers sang upbeat, contemporary gospel music, including a song he wrote called "Fight". They also sang the timeless gospel song "Stand" and a small, slim guy named Eric Greenfield led it.

I remembered Eric. He was a bartender for The Sportsman Bar before it was condemned. The Fellas and I would trek to that bar on Tuesday nights for karaoke and he would always sing that song. Corey told him on countless occasions that when he died, he wanted Eric to sing it and Eric would always laugh and say, "Baby, you ain't going nowhere." When the choir got to the drive of the song, Jojo, Garrett, and I broke. Jimmy and A.D. just sat straight up with tears rolling down. Peep looked straight ahead, as if entranced. Many a Sunday, we would sit in these same pews and listen to Corey belt out this song while playing the piano. Though Eric did an amazing job, the fact that Corey was not there to lead the song was painfully evident.

Rev. John Kelvin Washington, tall and dignified, got up to deliver a moving eulogy. Though I was grief stricken, I managed to catch his sermon. Even as I lay in my bedroom repeatedly watching the recorded live stream of the service on my Smart TV, I believe that no truer words were spoken.

"When a light is extinguished, the darkness can be tangibly felt. When a note is no longer heard, the silence can cut into your soul. Cordell

Kennedy was that light... that spark... He was that note that made the whole symphony worth listening to. The only ones that didn't share this view of him are those who lack light... who lack music. They would rather wallow in the bleakness of hate than to know how beautiful it is to really love somebody. His murder reminds us of the work that we can no longer pretend to carry out. We have to fully take on the daily assignment to affirm and bolster our community; all our lives depend on it. The days for us demanding to be seen as human beings and not freaks are full of more trouble than ever before. But we must keep fighting, and not with our fists or weapons of war. We have to fight by using the strengths that we are blessed to have. I know that we may have people in the congregation who believe in various higher powers. My belief is built on God and His Son, Jesus. But regardless of what power you hold in high esteem, we can all agree that we have access to a power that strikes down darkness and injustice. Some. like our dearly departed, are endowed with music. Some are good with figures. Some can paint pictures that depict reality. Some can write the truth in hopes that one may read it and have hope. Some can speak and through their words, lives begin to change. And the list goes on. These are our weapons and we must employ them to help keep our community safe and alive.

I don't know who raped and killed Brother Kennedy, nor do I know the motivation behind his acts other than hate. But I do know that the man has more to deal with than just the police. He has to contend with his own conscience, his own guilt, and his own inner turmoil. He is now a fugitive, and to run from justice is to live a tormented life every day until he surrenders. As angry as I am over the hatred and bigotry that he possessed in order to do these heinous acts, I pray for him because he needs it as a human being. As for us, we must pray or call upon our higher self for strength to continue fighting for justice. And we can't just contend for the rights we need as a community. We must also fight for and with those who may not understand what we go through... those who would sooner spit on us before holding our hands... those who would rather send us to hell than walk with us on earth and to heaven.... those who hate what we are. Yes, family. We must battle even for them, because that is the way that true children of love show goodness as a community and, ultimately, as a people."

Immediately after Corey's funeral, I took to my bed. The only time I got up was to take a piss, a shower, or a shit, and the only things I ate were fried eggs and cereal. When the containers were empty, I trashed them but after the trashcan overflowed, I left them on the counter. The kitchen now stinks of decomposing food that I took out of the fridge to eat but left on the counter after one bite. I just didn't feel like cleaning anything other than my body. I showered often just so I could hear the soothing sounds of the rushing waters hitting my body and the tiles. Now, lying in this dark bedroom, with the phone playing constant music, I long for a message of hope... a clue that Corey is still with me. My depression was so strong that I spent my thirty-ninth birthday in bed crying.

I hear my landline ring, and after the beep, I hear Nate's deep voice. "Lionel, it's me Nate. I'm calling to check on you... Called your landline because I knew there was a chance that you'd be home. Tried your cell but you didn't pick up. I left town for a while and I just got back this morning. I heard that Corey was killed... (Sigh) I know this is hurting you. He was your best friend... and I ... God... I must sound so stupid... Listen.... I just wanted to let you know that I am here if you need me... Call me anytime... Much Love..."

Add him to the list of callers. My brothers and sister, as well as Peep, Jojo, Eunetta, Rachel, Katie, Orchid, and Jimmy, called constantly to check on me, but I just didn't feel like talking to anybody. I had an appointment with Dr. Banneker two weeks ago, but I didn't go. I knew that if I did, I would have to tell more than I was prepared to relate about Corey's murder.

I tried not to drink or take anything except the pills Dr. Banneker prescribed. The pills help me to sleep without major side effects, but those pills cannot cure grief or the visions at Corey's house that haunt my dreams at night. So, right next to me, I have an empty bottle of ninety proof vodka that I finished off just this morning. The pills are back in the drawer. I still have full bottles of Alprolozine in the truck. I put them in the glove compartment on the night I got shot.

I hear a window crashing from a distance. It's probably one of my neighbors. I want to go to my open window and check to see what's going on, but my hangover and exhaustion keeps me in my bed. I know that, at some point, I'm going to have to face everybody. Get on with my life. That's what Corey would want me to do. But right now, I'd rather just be miserable. I'm too full of questions. Full of anger.

I look at a framed picture of me and The Fellas, hanging on the wall, and an involuntary shudder ripples through me, accompanied with a loud, tormented sob. Corey wore his trademark megawatt grin that melted the resolve of many men before he reacquainted with Garrett.

Garrett! I wonder how he's doing. How torturing it must be to get engaged to marry your childhood love, only to have life and bigotry fling them into a sinkhole with countless others who were killed just for being who they are.

"Lionel." I hear a fatigued voice say. I look towards the doorway and there stands Jojo, out of breath.

"How did you get in here?" I demand in a weakened voice. "I had all the deadbolts and chains on the doors."

"But your windows don't have bars on them... yet."

"You came in through the window? Are you crazy?"

"Well, what else am I supposed to do? All of us have been calling, worried sick about you, and all we get is silence. You ought to know by now that this shit ain't going to fly, not when you have people that care about you like we do."

I sit back, unable to find the words to counter that.

"And don't worry," Jojo assures wryly. "I made sure that nobody saw me breaking and entering."

I issue a small laugh... yet, I feel like crying. Breaking and climbing through windows to see what's going on with me... That is exactly what Corey would do.

I glance over at the vodka bottle. "You ain't gonna say anything about me drinking myself under the table?"

"No," Jojo says.

I gesture weakly towards my armchair. Jojo walks slowly over and sits down to catch his breath. I resume my blank gaze toward the wall. Minutes fly rapidly by. All I can hear are the sounds of Baltimore City and the chirping of neighbors' conversations on this warm autumn evening.

I break the silence. "So, you just gonna sit there and say nothing?"

"What is there to say?"

"Well for starters, maybe to reason how we could lose our best friend. We lost somebody that really mattered... because of hate."

"Well, what are you gonna do about that hate? It doesn't look like you're doing that much right now other than sitting in this bed. You've been in this house for almost four straight weeks..."

"Feeling sorry for myself, right? That's what you were about to say."

"Lionel, I didn't come over here to fight with you. I came over because..." Jojo stops and looks away. After a few seconds, he cries out in pain, "You're not the only one that's hurting! I'm hurting too, OK?!... Lionel, I met Corey the same time you did. I fell in love with his flightiness, his zest for life, and his ability to go after what he wanted in life, something I was never able to do. I never needed to hear him play to know that he had music in him that was not just restricted to what was on the keys. I am just as angry and feel just as displaced as you do. We both lost Corey... we both are hurt... All of us who loved him are hurting, but there is no sense in you being hurt over here and me being hurt at my place. We might as well hurt together. And then maybe we can help the members of OUR family and remember Corey for what he was, not for how he died."

He turns away from me then, facing the window. He holds onto the beams for support while his inner cries are quaking his body.

Inebriated though I am, I come up behind him slowly and turn him gently around. Jojo looks down to the ground, his tears dripping to the floor. When he raises his head, I hear his pleading voice breathe out, "Lionel... please hold me." The pain in his voice and the iridescent tears glistening in his eyes moves me. I gently wrap my arms around him, draw him closer to me, and squeeze him tightly. I feel his arms squeeze me and hear his muffled sobs as I hold him tighter. I hold him as a mother holds a son when his father is not around to do it. I hold him as a friend holds another when that friend is going through pain. I hold him as a lover holds his love while he remembers the vows for better and for worse. I hold him for all the gay children crying and dying every day to be embraced. To be heard. To be loved. I hold him for all of us.

Instinctively, his lips find mine. I take my hands and I cup his face as we kiss. I suddenly have a huge need to have him in my arms... to feel his body next to mine.

Just then, the stream on my phone plays a beautiful love song called "This Woman's Work" by Maxwell. As the opening harp strings begin to play and Maxwell's sexy voice croons, he trails his hands up to twine around my neck. We sway, lost in the music with love in our thoughts. He unbuttons my pajama top as if he is handling jewels, then eases the shirt down my arms. He then gently pulls my bottoms and underwear down. Taking in my nakedness, His fingers trail feather-like up my sides, causing my senses to heighten and my breath to still. He gently places his hands on my waist and kisses my shoulder blade... then my neck... then my ear.... Breathlessly, I push him back to look deeply into his eyes... those beautiful soft eyes. I kiss him on his forehead... on his eyelids... on his nose... and on his full lips. His sweet minty tongue caresses mine as we softly French kiss.

I ease his shirt off as he kicks off his shoes and pulls off his socks. Kneeling, I pull his pants and underwear down to his ankles and I watch as he steps out of them. I look up at him and I am so aroused by what I see.

The deep muscled chest...
The veins popping out of his forearms...
The large and hard nipples...
The slightly protruding stomach...
The thick bushy carpet of hair covering his chest and stomach...
The heavy massive thighs and the granite calves built as if sculpted of marble...
And the sleek dark skin of onyx.

As I stand up, I look into his eyes again. They are filled with water. I caress his cheek and wipe away his tears. He looks at me with the expression of a reserved child as he says three words:

"Lionel... I'm hurt."

The pain Jojo has is not foreign to me. Through the water in my own eyes, I say, "I'm hurt too."

I gently embrace him, and we kiss tenderly, my tears mixing with his as we sink to the bed.

*****

It's nine in the evening, four hours later. We are looking into each other's eyes and talking as he caresses my face. The comfort I feel as I experience the warmth of his presence is ethereal and fraught with glittering euphoria.

"So, did everything go well with your brothers and sisters?"

"Correction: Sis*ter*. It was my brothers, Brenda, and me. Our dear sweet sister, Rhonda, ditched us on the clean-up."

"You can't be surprised."

"I'm not. But, you know, the hard truth is that people are going to be people. I know now what made Mama the way she was, and like Corey said..." I stopped short.

After a few seconds, Jojo urges, "Say it, Lionel. Let it out. What did Corey say?"

I blink back tears as I think and answer, "Well, he pretty much said... that we can't make assumptions about people without knowing their story, even those that are the hardest to deal with."

"But you knew that already, right?"

I look towards the windows, thinking before I say, "Sometimes I forget that."

Jojo thinks for a moment and he says, "So, what *was* Lynetta's story?"

I don't really want to go into the full detail because it would alarm him and cause him to revisit some things he saw in childhood. So, I ask him, "Would you be satisfied with an abridged version of the story?"

"Would I have a choice?"

"Well, let's just say that her hatred of gay and bisexual men is completely understood now, even beyond her killing Dad. It causes me not to hate her for what she did, but love her for who she was… my mother"

"I think you are catching the train, my love. Of course, that 'abridged version' isn't really telling me anything, but I respect your decision to not rehash it."

I kiss him. "I will tell you at some point. But right now, we got too much to deal with. How's Peep handling things?"

"Day by day. I'm a bit worried about him. Planning the homegoing really took a lot of his energy. He's also planning our ceremony, which is draining him more. Plus, he's dealing with some legal stuff concerning Corey's estate and conversing with his lawyer as he was Corey's financial advisor. Hopefully, this will be the last thing he has to do because he is whipped. I can also tell that this is hurting him even though he is fronting. He's dressing a little bit drab. I'm talking NO color or vibrancy at all."

"Oh boy, that worries me," I say in concern.

"Me too! I went by his office to check on him. His face looked pale and he looked like he hadn't slept in days. Whenever I try to talk to him, he just clams up. When I talked to Jimmy, he told me that all he does is work and go to the gym, but he won't say a thing about Corey or how he's feeling."

This is heavy! I think to myself. *But then, he is grieving like all of us, and grief wears many faces,*

"What about Garrett and his family?"

"Eunetta is ok. So are Rachel and Mike Junior. But Garrett, I don't know. He was pretty torn up at the funeral. I do know that he took a few weeks and went down south. He told A.D. that he had to get out of Baltimore for a while."

"I need to call him… and A.D."

"Yes, you do. He was at my house yesterday and he was torn up about Corey AND you. That's why I said I would come over to check things out. We ALL were worried about you. You shut us out, Lionel."

"I know... but Jojo. this is hard for me. Corey wasn't even forty years old yet. He was cut down before he had a chance to really live life."

Jojo ruminates, "Oh, Corey lived life. It just wasn't in the way you thought he did."

"I know, but for somebody to just rape and kill him. It seems so random. It has me questioning as to why God took him from us," I say despondently.

"Honestly, it's hard to disagree with you. God and I have had it out about it since that night. But there's one thing I know for sure."

"What's that?"

"God did not take Corey. Hate did that through that crazed man. Hate raped him for sport. Hate sliced open his throat."

"But God allowed it, Jojo!"

He falls silent, wondering how to answer that rock-hard fact. But then, he replies, "Well, Lionel, I can't give you a reason why Corey's life was cut short or why it was allowed. But I can tell you how sad it is that the one who did it fell on his own sword of hate."

"What do you mean?"

"I saw it on the news last week. The guy who raped and killed him was the same guy who shot you, Sonny Daniels."

"What! Oh my God! The same one?"

"Yeah... But now, he's dead too. He jumped out of an eight-story window trying to evade the police that came to arrest him. When he hit the sidewalk, the impact killed him instantly"

I think it over. "Wait a minute. How do you know it was him that did it?"

"When they searched the room that he rented after taking his body away, they found the knife with his fingerprints on it. Those prints matched both the prints on Corey's body and on the gun that he dropped on the scene where you got shot. Plus, he was part of the gang that was responsible for Corey's stabbing two years ago."

"Penn Avenue Counts?"

"Yeah."

Divine justice, I think to myself. My mind goes back to the old saying; *What goes around comes around.* Sonny's retribution came quickly. "I'm sorry he's dead; but look at the lives he thought belonged in the crapper, enough to kill them off because of his own insecure shit. People like him are the reason we are minus a close friend, along with numerous others. They don't think about the fact that every life is precious; and even if they did, it doesn't matter to them until it lands on their doorstep."

"Then we have to make it matter. I've been thinking a lot about the eulogy Rev. Washington gave and he's right. I am scared as fuck, but I am not going to stop fighting for my right to live in this world. The way I see it, we can either spend the rest of our lives mourning Corey and so many others, or we can take that grief and turn it into something that can help heal our community, maybe even heal ourselves."

I look at our picture, pondering over what Jojo says. Then, looking back at him, I ask, "Do you really think so?"

"I know so. Listen babe, I believe that healing is not just found in a shrink's office. It can start there but real healing happens through getting involved and trying to make a difference on behalf of those who need it. And there are different ways to do that. Some picket. Others boycott. The rich write checks. The poor shout in council meetings and give the higher-ups hell until they listen and do something about it."

I smile at him. The first smile I've had in a while. "I see your point."

"I can tell you this, though. You might get rest, but you won't find healing being stuck in this damn room."

"I know."

Jojo nudges me playfully. "So, come on. Let's get out of this house for a bit. We didn't even get a chance to reflect on us turning thirty-nine."

I really don't want to leave just yet. I say, "Jojo?"

"Yes?"

"I'm not really ready yet. I'll come out but just give me a little more time," I say gently.

Jojo looks at me apologetically. "Oh... Lionel. I'm sorry for trying to push too soon. Sometimes I forget that it takes time to deal with grief. When Mama died, I just kept going because the work and being out of the house gave me comfort. But that doesn't mean it works for everybody. We handle grief on our own strengths and there can be strength in saying, 'Let me pull back and get myself together.' I respect that. You need that time."

I kiss him saying, "Thank you, baby."

He repositions his body so that I can lie on his chest as he embraces me. "Don't mention it, gorgeous. But I do have two promises I need you to make me."

"What are they?"

"One, that you will at least make an appointment to go see Dr. Banneker."

I pull in my breath sharply, preparing to refuse. But in thinking about it, maybe I really need to unload my feelings. "Ok... I'll call him to set something up. What's the other?"

"The second is to remember that you have friends and family for a reason... We understand now that you need space to grieve... but just let us in every now and then."

A slow smile crosses my face. "Deal," I say. I feel Jojo squeeze me tightly. "Good."

I craned my head around to kiss him on his full lips. Then we just lay there for a few seconds before a horrifying thought strikes a loud chord of fear in me. *Oh my God! I feel like I played a part in Corey getting killed. Sonny couldn't get me, so he goes after one of my friends. And plus, that gang is still out there. Peep and Jojo could be next.* I start listing all the LGBT people I know that they can target. A violent shudder goes through me. Jojo feels it and asks, "What's wrong, baby?"

"I feel like some of this is my fault."

"Why?"

"Because Sonny tried to kill ME first. He only succeeded in putting a bullet in me that I can't remove, so he turned around and killed Corey. Sonny's dead, but so what? He belonged to a gang that terrorizes all of us just for kicks... and they are STILL out there, Jojo."

"Those gangs are always going to be out there, hating, humiliating, and killing anyone with a mindset and life that disagrees with them."

"Baby, I'm scared that maybe you and others I love might get killed too. God, I can't believe I am saying this! But, even though he stole Nate from me and is the biggest slut I know, I'm even worried about Shawn Tolbert. He flirts like there's no tomorrow, and one day he might flirt with the wrong one. And let's not even get started on what could happen to *me*. They could come back and try to finish the job on me, you know."

"Oh, come on, babyboy. You worry too much. Listen, life cannot be lived well if we live it in fear. If you do that, you might as well stay in this room and never come out. And you know as well as I do... that is no way to live."

"Maybe..."

"Remember, Lion. Corey said that this is life and shit is going to happen. But, in his own words," he says as he moves from under me, stands, and wags his head, much like Corey. "'We're gonna get our gorgeous asses in gear and keep it moving.' Find our cray-cray to dance our nae-nae!"

As I hear those words coming out of Jojo, I feel a huge avalanche of boisterous laughter begin to build up in me. I open my mouth and release sound and the laughter, joined by Jojo's hearty guffaws, bounces zanily around the room.

Jojo says between laughs, "That's what I'm talking about!" He smiles a smile of absolute sweetness. I smile back at him, but I feel my smile collapse as the energy in the room changes to embody the color of scarlet with enchanting sparkles, chasing the gray clouds from the room. His smile falls as he looks at me. His facial expression morphs from humorous to overwhelmingly seductive; his eyes from wide to hooded and shadowy. He advances to the open window and shuts it; then he steals toward me slowly, climbing onto the bed and straddling my body. He takes my hand and kisses my palm sweetly. He then kisses each of my fingertips and trails his kisses on my arm... back up to my neck... then my lips.

After a moment of kissing passionately, my lips and tongue find their way to Jojo's erect right nipple while Jojo adjusts his straddle to my sides. I start by sucking it, then I swirl my tongue around his areola. Jojo moans in unbridled ecstasy as I flick my tongue rapidly at his nipple before gently biting it. Jojo cries out in passionate bliss. He adjusts his straddle again to where he is now sitting on my chest and his cucumber phallus is on my lips. In a deep, sexy, bass booming voice unlike his usual light sweet tone, he commands, "Suck it." *Hell yeah!*

Oh my God! Who knew that Jojo could switch his voice from a tenor to that of a basso profundo? I open my orifice and I feel his phallic wonder widen my throat to accommodate it. I feel him thrust his pelvis forward and I am thoroughly aroused at the sight of nothing but his ebony torso catching the light from the window... advancing and retreating as he feeds me.

Once more, he turns to adjust his straddle to where his ankles are parallel to my shoulders and he's sitting on my face. I sniff the scent of sweet sexual aroma and lick my tongue lightly to tease his sphincter for a few minutes. Then, as I thrust it into the hole, Jojo yells, "Holy shit!" and reaches backward to grab the back of my head and gyrate his ass on my face. *Oh fuck! Brenda was right! My baby is a fucking freak!*

After receiving my tongue in his ass, he stands up, his thick, muscular, ebony body eclipsing the light from the window. With his new sexy deep voice and a hungry look, he says, "Lay on your stomach." *What is he getting ready to do?* I think to myself. I oblige his request and I feel him take absolute charge as he wraps his hands around my ankles to jerk me abruptly toward him. Yet afterwards, I feel his large fingertips touch the back of my thighs ever so softly.

I feel them finger my hole.

I feel his lips kiss the flesh of my glutes.

I feel his hands part the cheeks of my ass.

I feel his lips kiss my twitching hole.

I feel his tongue lapping lightly at my sphincter.

I feel his licks grow stronger, mounting in intensity until I cry out in delight. I feel a huge pleasurable tornado turning in my ass and the wetness of his saliva lubricating me.

I feel his hand slapping my ass... making it tingle and provoking sensual moans to pour from the very center of my being.

"Jojo..."

"Yeah, baby," he moans deeply, his voice sensual and sultry.

"Oh... Jojo."

"That's my name, baby." Who knew that he could sound so deep... so bass booming... so authoritative and... hard core! My mind goes back to when he hit me back. I was shocked... but secretly, I was painfully aroused! Not at him hitting me back, but at his flipping the situation to where I could only look at him and respect the masculinity that told me, "I give just as good as I get."

In a breathless and sexually exhausted voice, I gush, "Love me..."

"I already love you, baby."

"You do?"

"Yes."

I am weary from my desire, "Take me..."

"You sure, baby?"

"Yes! Yes! Yes! Take me!" I feel a sexual demand coming from my center, screaming to be satisfied.

I feel Jojo gently turn me around. Looking into my eyes, he says seductively, "I want to see your face as we make love." I position my legs around his hips as he lowers his sweaty ebony body to mine. His body is made darker by the dimness of the room. He begins his entrance into me, very gently. I feel the pain as he approaches... but I grit my teeth and bear it. When he gets halfway in, I am driven wild! Then he thrusts his body powerfully into me, and I feel my eyes widen in blissful shock! Oh my God! Is THIS beautiful, forceful, gentle, yet firm specimen of manhood the same shy boy I grew up next to? I wonder what other fantasies and fetishes he hides... and how many more I can explore!

Over and over again, he thrusts his large zucchini into me, gyrating his hips in fluid and wide circular motion, making me abundantly wet. I scream in ecstasy, "Oh, Jojo, fuck me! Fuck me senseless!" His thrusts get harder with the repeated force of a freight train! I have never been loved and fucked like this! Not even by Nate! I look in his face to see a look I've never seen before. It was a look of adoration mixed with erotic passion and fervent furnace heat. I throw my ass back on him.

"Oh yeah, baby. That's right! Give Daddy that ass!"

Hours pass, and by now, I am riding Jojo's dick like a fucking cowboy. Then he tells me to turn my body around… and to stay on his dick. I comply and, as I turn, I gasp wildly with passion. It's like his jimmie is a key unlocking my innermost passions. He grabs my body and lays it down as he spoons me, with one sexy, vascular arm around me and the other hand clutching my phallus and jerking it.

"Oh babe! I'm about to cum…."

"I'm cummin' too, baby. Gimme that nut!"

"I got you…"

I don't know what happened, but those words, "I got you", cause my passions to erupt and spray a thick, sexual substance on my satin sheets as I feel Jojo pull out and erupt, painting my thigh with his love juices. The words that reminded me of my anguish of loss also provided total recall of the love abounding with their utterance. My watery eyes shed tears that join my sexual glue in turning the rose red color of my fitted satin sheet to deep wet crimson.

After lying there, he turns me around to face him and as we gaze at each other, I see moisture in his shimmering eyes as he smiles sweetly at me. Jojo pulls me to him and tells me, "I love you, Lionel."

'I love you too, Joseph."

Silence blankets the room, then I say, "Jojo?"

"Yeah."

"I'm sorry… you know… for everything."

"I know. I told you, we're cool. Let's just move on with the love we have. Life's too short."

If there was ever a reminder of that statement, it happened upon the death of our friend and brother, Corey.

The events of this autumn night are myriad.

We lament… We caress… We talk… We hold… WE LOVE.

Chapter Eighteen
"I SHOULD HAVE DONE SOMETHING"

True to my promise to Jojo, I made the call to Dr. Banneker. A week later, on a cold Monday afternoon, I'm back in his office, seated in the same chair Dr. Banneker first directed me to upon my initial return. It took everything in me to walk out of the house. Now I see what Corey went through when he was attacked. My home became my cocoon, my protection from the outside world. But last week, I began to painfully realize something through Corey's murder. Even our homes are not the safety nets we think they are, especially for us as gay family. But as Jojo said, the worse thing in life is to live in fear. That fact was enough to propel me into opening my door and proceeding to join the living.

My emotions are as varied as a rainbow. I resumed taking the medication Dr. Banneker gave me and laid off the vodka. Though I grieve greatly over my friend's life and I awaken from the visions of that night occasionally plaguing my dreams, I can get at least seven hours sleep each night. However, I still experience anger and fear in my waking hours, I still have questions as to why things happened, and I still have the Alprolozine in the glove compartment. It keeps slipping my mind to dump the pills. Maybe I'm subconsciously holding on to them due to my fear of releasing completely, especially after everything that has happened. It has crossed my mind to take them once or twice. But then, I remember Jojo and the Fellas. I remember my family and my career, as well as how taking those pills almost cost me everything that I hold dear. Knowing this, those pills are right where they need to be, until I dump them for good.

It amazes me how much love I have around me that I shut out... again. I spent one day in my living room calling everyone in my circle and letting them know that I was ok. They were very understanding considering how hard I took Corey's death. I also called work to check in with Floyd, Ben, and Marianne. Floyd told me that Ms. Nesbitt has been asking about me and that she would hold on moving forward until I became able enough to handle the workload.

Oh, you will never believe this. Shawn Tolbert came by to see how I was! Amazingly, we exchanged a remarkably interesting and pleasant conversation, during which he gave me a beat-around-the-bush apology for what he did with Nate, as well as how he sometimes behaves. I also learned that he took a similar position at a large marketing agency in DC, so he's leaving the firm. I asked him why and he said, "You are R&M's hot commodity right now. Va-Voom Perfumes are really selling. You roped in some good leads at the getaway. Let's be honest, Lionel. When you come back to work, there ain't gonna be enough room for both of us." After I offered my congratulations and he offered his concerning my upcoming marriage to Jojo, I asked him why the sudden concern about me. He had an unusual sad look on his face when he told me that after hearing about Corey's murder and my getting shot, he thought about how short life was and how it pays to have and give peace while you're still living. "It doesn't pay to be a perpetual bitch. And, believe it or not, I was raised right," he told me. It sounded so unlike him. Usually he's very flippant and flighty, but I am seeing that Ben was right. There *is* a side of him that I could really like. Of course, I pause on the idea of us becoming friends... for now. Time always has a way of revealing the sincerity of a person. At least, we were able to clear the air on some things. In the same conversation, I learned that Shawn and Ben moved past friendship and began seeing each other romantically a month after I got shot. I suppose that opposites do attract.

Beginning my meeting with Dr. Banneker, I apologized for missing my prior appointment and he told me that I had extenuating circumstances and needed to retreat a while.

"It seems like I just leapt over one hurdle, dealing with my mother, and someone put another hurdle in front of me... Corey getting killed. And that hurdle I don't know if I will ever hop over. Corey was like a close blood brother to me."

"Let's talk about the initial 'hurdle' first. How did you manage to leap over that?"

I focus on the heavy mahogany door. "Well, my siblings and I found a diary she kept, detailing abuse from her father and uncle. Both sexual and physical. One entry even talked about Granddad and Uncle Larry fucking each other while raping her."

Dr. Banneker shifts in his seat. I can't tell whether it is due to discomfort concerning the news or the way he is seated in his chair.

"Anyway, now I see why she became the way she was. I'm not excusing her because what she did had lasting negative effects on all of us. But knowing that she had that type of trauma causes me to feel sorry for her… enough to begin forgiving her."

"So, the trip home proved fruitful?"

"In more ways than one."

"How is that?"

"Well, my brothers, sister, and I really had conversations that gave me hope for our future. It made me realize that, although I love The Fellas dearly, I missed the connections I could have had with my own family because I was so blinded by my drama with Mother. Maybe it's not too late to start mending bridges and putting old hurts aside."

Dr. Banneker takes off his glasses and placing the ear hook on his lips. This is known as his "a-ha" sign.

"So, what about the second hurdle."

I grow silent as sadness and anger builds up in my heart. "I can't forget the night I went to his house after Jojo told me he was dead. Whenever I didn't take the vodka or the medication you gave, those images kept me awake most nights."

"What images?"

I feel a tear squeeze from my eye as I say, "For starters, the green tag on the wall."

"Green tag?"

"Yeah. The killer spray-painted the word "faggot" on the wall."

Dr. Banneker puts his glasses on and looks at me. "When you think about that tag, what goes through your mind?"

I think for a few seconds before I respond, "I think about all the many years I fought to be seen as a person and not judged as a thing that sleeps with the same sex. That tag reminded me that we are no closer to people understanding who we are than we ever were. I remember what my boss Floyd told me about things changing but not by much."

"What would be your idea of change?"

"My idea would involve a world where everyone is seen as humanity and not as objects. Where no one is abused or killed for how they express themselves. Where kids and teenagers can retain their childhood and grow up to be well-rounded adults without some pedophile or abusive parent riding down on them. Where everyone can coexist without hatred or bias."

Dr. Banneker says, "Well Lionel, everyone living in this world struggles to be seen for the good they offer as a person. But have you ever thought that those who see people as objects have difficulty seeing their own worth individually? Maybe it's hard to see or identify with human connection if it is missing inside themselves."

Good one, doc! "That could explain why people kill. They may have lost touch with their own humanity."

"Hmmm..." Dr. Banneker reflects.

"But that does not give anyone the right to steal a life that wasn't theirs to give or take in the first place," I say, my anger returning.

"Did you know the man who killed Corey?"

"Yes."

"How?"

"He was the same guy that shot me, but I didn't know he was the one who killed Corey until Jojo told me."

"Hmmm..." Dr. Banneker hums as he writes in his pad. He then raises his eyes to look at me asking the question, "Where do your thoughts take you, knowing this fact?"

I jump up and pace the floor. "I don't know what to think... I'm angry because Corey's gone. I'm floored that his killer had to die twisting on his own hate. I wished him to die when I saw how he killed Corey. I'm glad that he can't hurt anybody else... but I'm scared of what people like him are capable of... He was in a gang that was known for killing and bashing gays... When the fear sets in, the first thing I think is, 'What's going to happen to my friends?' 'What's going to happen to *me*'?"

Dr. Banneker writes in his pad again. The next few seconds are a mass of confusion because I don't know what emotion I'm supposed to feel. "Lionel, is there any other feeling you may have that you are avoiding?"

"What other feeling should I have?"

"You alone can answer that."

"How can I answer for what I don't know?" I snap.

Dr. Banneker sits there quietly. I sit back down and begin to mutter to myself, "I should've known Sonny was going to do something. Corey pretty much handed me a description of him on a silver platter. Why didn't I tie it together? I even had a dream about a shadow with a bloody knife and a gun! Peep told me about a dream he had of a portrait of Corey with the neck slashed…. I…." I stop myself.

This silence prompts Dr. Banneker to say, "Lionel, the phrases you utter are 'I should've' or 'Why didn't I'. Are you certain you aren't feeling any other emotions?"

I look at him impatiently, "Ok. You want me to say it? I'll say it. I feel guilty, ok? I should've been here. My family shit in Birmingham could've waited. I could've told my family to go on without me. But I went to Birmingham and I let one of the best friends I ever had get killed."

"Could you have protected him?"

"I don't know."

"What would've been the case had you stayed?"

"Corey would have been pissed, but he'd be alive."

"And you know that for certain?" Dr. Banneker quizzed.

"I don't know, but the chances of him getting killed would have been lower."

"Meanwhile, how would that have helped you?"

I can't answer that question. Instead, I ask Doc, "Is my time up?"

"Yes, Lionel. Shall I pencil you in for next Monday?"

"Yes."

*****

After my appointment with Dr. Banneker, I decide to stop by Teresa's. I called ahead to get a "to go" plate and head on home because the restaurant closes at seven on Mondays. It's six fifty-one, too late for me to sit down and eat. Once I walk into the restaurant, I see Orchid wiping down tables and listening to music on her earbuds while swaying happily to the beat. She is wearing a pink T-shirt and black jeans with a black wig bearing pink highlights. As always, her face is beat to perfection. She sees me walk in and beams a smile, rushing over to give me a hug.

"Mr. Lionel, how are you?"

"I'm ok. How are you? What are you doing here in Baltimore?"

"Well, Ms. Katie snagged me a weekend job here at the restaurant. I missed school today so I'm going back to DC later tonight, so I won't miss tomorrow." She then looks at me with concern. "How are you doing? Me and Miss Katie have been calling you. Sorry about Mr. Corey. I heard the killer was the same guy that shot you. It's stupid that people can hate us enough to kill us off."

I nod my head sadly, saying, "Yeah, well. That's the way of the world. And you're right. It is stupid."

Sensing that I needed a change of subject, Orchid goes on in rapid-fire narrative, "Well, you look a whole lot better. I see you walking without a cane. Good. It wasn't doing you any favors on the hot guy scale."

"Excuse me?" I say with a huge grin on my face, my mood brightening.

"I mean, you *are* a hot guy. That cane was cramping your style. Now that you ditched the cane, your gorgeousness got turned way up," Orchid says, with a flirtatious wink as she goes back to the table she was wiping.

"Orchid, you quit that now," I say, suppressing a blush. "I'm old enough to be your daddy."

"And I'm old enough to keep it one-hunnit. Ha! It doesn't mean I wanna get with you. But I'm just giving you real talk. You are a real hottie… for somebody in their late twenties."

Whoa! That was the best remark I've heard all day. I can't wipe the grin off my face. "Thank you, Orchid! How are your studies going?"

"Pretty well. I got the scholarship to go to UCLA."

"Oh, you got it! That's good! What are you studying when you get there?"

"I want to study law, particularly the type that deals with our community," Orchid beams as she wipes another table.

"Law?" I say, surprised.

"Yeah, 'Law'!" she says, mimicking me. "I want to do what I can to legally help all of us."

"That's good. But why not stay on the east coast?"

"Because they hate us trans and gays here. At least in California, you are somewhat embraced."

"Well, you do know that hatred can show up anywhere."

"True, but it's nice to be able to go where there is a greater abundance of people like me. Plus, Baltimore and DC are changing, and not for the better."

"Lionel, you are out of the house!" I hear Eunetta's voice.

"Ms. E.! Hey," I say as we embrace. Katie comes from the back with a bag of food in hand. "I thought I heard ya'll's voices out here."

"Hey Katie, chile!"

"Hey, 'Netta. Devetra told me you would be by to pick up the four gallons of Teresa's tea. She got it in the cooler," Katie says as she hands me my food.

"Yeah, Garrett done got hooked on it, same as me. Devetra has GOT to come clean with the recipe."

"Oh, she ain't telling nobody shit!" Katie says, pursing her lips and waving her hand dismissively. "You know she is taking that recipe with her to the grave, just like her mama did. How's Garrett holding up?"

Eunetta says enthusiastically, "He's ok. He just got back three days ago. Needed time."

"You two know each other?" I ask, gesturing between them.

They both look at me humorously. Eunetta laughs, "Yeah, chile. I met her at the Burger King on North Avenue two weeks after I moved to Baltimore."

"Lawd, that had to have been six years ago."

"Yeah, and she's been my ace boon coon ever since."

"Yeah, ever since you complained about your Whopper not having no cheese!" They both laugh at that memory. Katie turns her attention to me.

"And you, Mister Man," she says, swatting me on the arm. "Up there scarin' us half to death. You dropped clean off the face of the earth."

"I'm hanging in there, Katie."

"That's what's up. Lord! Thank God ya'll are the last customers of the day. My poor feet can't take no more and I gotta get home to call my lady."

"So, I take it you got the nurse's number."

"Now I know you've been *way* under a rock. You're asking too late! I got her number two months ago." She surveys the restaurant. "Well Orchid, it looks right good out here. Devetra's got your pay. Go on back there and get it. Then get your stuff so I can drop you off at Penn Station."

"OK. Bye Mr. Lionel," Orchid says as she disappears behind the curtain.

Katie looks at me, saying, "It's good to see you out. How are you dealing with all this?"

Feeling pensive, I say, "I don't know, Katie."

Katie, catching the tone in my voice, gestures to a nearby table, "Come on. Let's cop a seat for a minute." Eunetta sits daintily in one chair and Katie takes another and straddles it backwards.

As I sit, I say, "I still feel like I'm lost."

Katie says, "I don't see why you wouldn't. Your best friend done got killed."

"And I feel like I'm responsible."

Katie scoffs, "You oughta go on with that bullshit. Sonny was the one

The Cost

that killed him, so why're you blaming yourself for?"

"Katie, Corey told me that Sonny was following him. I should've stayed here to make sure he was alright."

Eunetta says as she places her hand on mine, "Lionel, you know as well as I do that it would've happened even if you were here. Hate takes no holidays just because you decide to put your life on hold to fight it."

"Maybe, But I still think I could've helped Corey. Maybe I could've stopped it."

Katie looks thoughtful. Then she says, "Lionel, there's some things you can't stop from happenin'. I know. My son, Randy, is dead proof of that."

"Right. I remember when we lost him," Eunetta says, looking at Katie in concern. Katie's breath becomes short as I see her swipe a tear from her eye. After measuring her phrases, she begins to talk.

"His daddy and I tried to get Randy off the streets. It wasn't easy to co-parent because we had separated when he was six. To keep it real, we didn't set the best example for him with all the drugs and booze. But when we cleaned up, we tried to reel him in. By that time, it was too late. He got sucked into the street life and started hanging out with the Counts. He got killed in a drug deal gone bad."

I look down, thinking of her words. Although I feel the pain of her loss, I'm puzzled as to the connection between what she's going through and my own personal hell. She seems to sense my confusion.

"I know. You can't see what this old dyke is saying. Baby, the thing we both got in common is that we both lost someone we loved, blaming ourselves for them dying. Now, Randy's dying is something to take responsibility for, and for a long time, I felt like I helped to kill him by not raising him better." She stops, looking deep in thought, then continues, "I don't know, though. When you look at people like Sonny and the type of upbringing he had, it kinda makes you want to chuck that notion. I knew Sonny's mama, Lisa. We met at a group started by Irene Hartfield."

My eyes perk up. "Irene Hartfield?"

"Yeah. You knew her?" she asks quizzically.

"She was my friend Jimmy's mother."

"Oh yeah, I know Jimmy. His mama was a good woman. She would always tell us how proud she was of him."

"Small world. So, what was the name of the group?"

"It was called MOGM, Mothers of Gang Members. Anyway, I remember talking to Lisa and how tore up I was to hear her story. Made me remember my own mama and all the shit I did to her. Man! It hit my heart like a freight train. Lisa really did the best she could. She raised Sonny up in the church, had him in school, and she tried to keep him off the streets, 'specially the corner of Penn Avenue and Laurens Street 'cause that's where his daddy, Harold, was dealing. But when he turned fourteen, Harold, who was Mr. Incommunicado before then, popped back into Sonny's life. He started pulling on him by promising fast money. After a while, he started makin' Sonny deal dope for him, and even though his mama loved him, she had to kick him out at sixteen because she couldn't take it no more. He went to stay with Harold, and when Harold went to prison and got killed, Sonny joined up with the Counts."

"What happened to his mother?" I ask, engrossed.

"She died shortly after he turned seventeen. The doctors said it was a stroke. I partway believe that, but I think her heart got broke because Sonny chose the streets and she kept saying that she failed him."

I became sad. Sonny had a good mother. I would've killed to have her as mine. As I ponder, Katie continues, "But I'm getting away from the point. So, here it is. Your friend was killed, and you got shot for two reasons. One, because Sonny was angry. He always was an angry child and he grew even angrier as an adult. The second reason is that Sonny hated the "put-away" part of himself that ya'll represented out in the open: dudes who happen to like dudes. It was not because of anything ya'll did. You are runnin' yourself through a guilt wringer for no reason. And you oughta think about this too: If your friend was here, what would he say?"

I search my mind for what Corey would think about my agonizing over his death. I finally conclude to the two ladies, "Well, he would want me to get on with my life and to quit blaming myself."

Eunetta asks, "Well, look at yourself now. Are you doing that?"

I slump in my chair like a child, "No, but it's easier said than done."

Eunetta laughs and says, "Well, I'm gonna tell you like my Mama used to tell me. 'Easier done when practiced.'"

I feel a smile tugging my lips, "What does that mean?"

Eunetta sits up, saying matter-of-factly, "It means, the more you practice doing something, the easier things we think are hard can become."

After letting those words sink in, I sit back and nod, "Makes sense."

"It should. It's what makes life worth living. Baby, the way I see it, we can all choose things in life from poisonous to pure, but there is a cost attached to whatever you choose. And you choosing to wallow in guilt ain't doing anyone any favors, least of all you. No guilt is worth the cost of your peace. Am I right, Katie?"

"Ya ain't never lied, Netta!"

Chapter Nineteen
A TREE GROWS

Eunetta persuaded me to come over to her house and have dinner. I reminded her that I bought my food already, but she told me to save it for the next day. She also said that Garrett was at her house, watching Mike Junior, and Rachel was coming later. I said I would because I hadn't seen Garrett in a month and a half. He was despondent and distraught at the homegoing. I remember he kept yelling out Corey's birth name, Simon. Because of the size of the attendees, the church ran out of programs. So, some mourners had to borrow their neighbor's programs to confirm that they were attending the right funeral. When the designee read the obituary aloud and revealed his birth name of Simon Lee Bradley, they understood. I am wondering what state of mind Garrett is in now.

Eunetta's car stops in the driveway of a medium-sized, two-tiered Covington brick house. The small well-kept lawn is divided by a pristine cement walkway. Beyond the walkway are steps leading up to a spacious porch with a white steel glider and table on it. There are yellow and blue chrysanthemums planted along both sides of the steps. The left side of the yard displays a stone birdbath with a squirrel on top. In the middle of the right side is a small tree with red leaves that had obviously just been planted.

I pull my truck over to the curb in front of her house. By this time, she is already out of the car and at the trunk, removing the gallons of tea. I rush to assist her in bringing the jugs to the white and gold beveled glass door. When she has it open, we walk in and she instructs me to put the jugs on an ebony credenza. She takes my coat and puts it in the hall closet. "I'm gonna pour myself a glass of tea. Do you want some?"

"Yes, thank you."

As she goes into the kitchen, I look around the spacious living room. It is very contemporary with Afrocentric art of beige, pink, and black colors, beige leather living room set, black lacquered coffee and end tables, and a rose carpet. On the mantle of the fireplace are small African masks and wooden statues, and above it is a portrait of Garrett, Rachel, and herself standing around a light brown, corn-fed man with a big-hearted smile holding a baby whom I presume is Mike Jr. I deduce that he is her husband, and Garrett and Rachel's father.

She comes back in, holding a tray that bears three sweating glasses of tea and yelling, "Garrett? Junior? Where ya'll at?"

"On the back porch, Gramma!" I hear Junior's voice call out.

Eunetta reaches my side and hands me the glasses. Smiling, she says, "I'm going outside to give Corey his water, then get dinner on the stove. You just go right down that hallway and out the back door. Give Garrett this tea and make yourself at home. It's an enclosed porch and the heat is on, so you'll be nice and warm."

She turns on her heel and goes back into the kitchen. I know she must have seen me flinch. Did I just hear her say she was going to give Corey water? Puzzled, I trek to the back porch where I find Garrett and Mike Jr. sitting cross-legged on the floor, playing a game. Garrett sees me and beams a bright smile. *Good sign.* I think to myself. Mike Jr. follows his look, then cries out happily, "Mr. Lionel!" They both stand and Mike Jr. comes to me, sticks out his fist, saying, "Gimme some dap."

"How're you doing, young'un?" I hand Garrett his tea and put mine on a nearby table to greet Mike Jr. with a dap and a quick finger snap. He shines a big and bright smile on me.

"Fine. I'm beating Uncle Garrett in a Trouble game my Gramma gave me for my birthday. Are you staying for dinner?"

"Sure, Jitterbug."

"Good, then you can teach him how to play!"

I cover my lips to hide my laughter at this precocious kid. Garrett says warmly, "OK, Mr. Show-off. Your old uncle's gotta talk to Mr. Lionel. Take your tea in the kitchen and drink it. Then you can play some video games for a while. I brought the XBOX and set it up."

"That's what's up!" Mike Jr. yells happily jumping up and down.

"Do you know how to turn it on?" Garrett says with a smile.

"Of course! It does have a start button!" Mike Jr. says, giving him a playfully sarcastic look.

"Alright, Smart Guy, get on in there!" Garrett says, with a noogie on

Junior's head. After Junior leaves, Garrett smiles and moves to embrace me tightly. Afterwards, we pull back and I ask in concern while keeping my hands on his arms, "How've you been?"

Hearing this question, Garrett bites on his lips and looks away. I can tell that this is still hurting him. He gestures halfheartedly to one of the chairs, offering me a seat as he lowers himself to the vinyl sofa. I can feel a strong vibe of exhaustion radiating from him.

It takes a minute, but he finally begins to talk. "Funny how you leave to clear your head... to try to make sense of something that makes no sense at all... and you still feel lost when you come back." He reclines, focusing on an overflowing plant hanging from the corner of the porch. When he speaks again, his voice is touched with grief. "I'm trying to convince myself that there has to be a reason why these things happen, but I just keep coming back to the same conclusion. Corey did not deserve to die. He was just starting to live his dream, the same dream he had when we were kids. We were about to get hitched. Things were turning around for us... for him. That was needed after all the crap he went through in that shithole..." Garrett looks at me with a mix of sadness and anger in his eyes. "Why did this have to happen?"

I exhale and sit back in my chair, pondering over the question while looking out into the backyard beyond the screen. I let a few moments pass, then I look at him saying, "I wish I had an answer for you. But I don't, and I have a feeling that any answer I could attempt wouldn't remove the tears or fill the void that Corey left in all of us."

Garrett says, "That's why I left town after the homegoing. I had to get out of this fucking city. I couldn't shake the fact that I was not here to protect Corey from that asshole. And that guilt tore me up."

"Where did you go?"

"Back to Miami. I remembered how you said that going back to your hometown helped you. I guess I was hoping I might find some peace."

"Well, did you find it?"

Garrett leans forward to put his elbows on his knees. "A little. I visited the Yancey Home for Boys, only to find out that it had burned down. I sat on those brick steps that led to nowhere and meditated. I guess I was trying to conjure up memories of Corey when we were kids. After leaving there, I went to see my birth father who lives in Tallahassee."

"No shit!"

"Yeah, he had been emailing me for the past year, but I didn't answer back because I was so angry with him for abandoning me. Corey kept telling me to reach out, but I wouldn't. After losing him, I thought about what Corey said one time when we talked about it. 'I didn't even know my dad and I won't ever get to know him. But you got a chance to meet yours. I'd take it if I were you.' So, I finally answered him."

Garrett temples his hands under his clefted chin. A thoughtful look crosses his face as he stares blankly ahead. He says, "Corey is the only person I've ever told this, but my birth mother died while she was having me." Garrett purses his full lips and folds his arms before he continues. "My real father was nineteen at the time and fatherhood was not on his agenda. He split after Mama told him she was pregnant. Her family couldn't take me in for some reason, so I ended up being shifted to the first of two children's homes. The first one was cool. It was called the Open Hands Home for Displaced Children. The staff there really cared, especially one heavyset white guy who ran the place." A smile creeps across his face as he ruminates over his past. "His name was Mason Baxter and he always had a big smile and a strong bone-crushing handshake for each of us. I remember when I had a problem dealing with bullies, and it was Mr. Baxter that taught me how to fight, block, and box. He always said, 'You gotta keep your guard up, and not just with fighting a bully. You gotta do that in life, too.'"

I muse, "Hmm... Sounds like something my father would say."

"Yeah."

"So, how did you end up at Yancey?"

"The Open Hands home lost their funding and got shut down, forcing the administration to split and place all of us kids somewhere else. I was nine when they placed me in Yancey, and it was hell. Because of my dark skin, the other boys called me tar-baby, coal coon, or just plain old nigger. And if I wasn't going through that, I was being forced to suck Mr. Baker off."

"Oh Garrett... He didn't fuck you, did he?"

"No. I didn't go through what others went through. Baker's abuse of me was more psychological and physical, with molestation thrown in.

He stops. After a few seconds, he glances at me smiling shyly. He says, "But a good thing happened. A few days after I arrived and before all the other shit went down with Mr. Baker and the boys, I saw this golden brown, cute boy around my age with big eyes, curly hair, and dressed in a red polo shirt and black jeans. Simon Lee Bradley, known later as Cordell Rodgerick James Kennedy.

"He was sitting by himself in the school cafeteria, eating and marking on manuscript paper at the same time. Now, I didn't know shit about being intimate with someone. The closest I got was at five when I was in the school closet, kissing a girl I had a crush on. But when I first saw him, I felt drawn to him. He was so quiet and shy. Totally different from the Corey ya'll knew."

He laughs at the pleasant memory as he continues, "I remember going over to ask him what he was doing, and he told me that he was writing a song. I asked him if I could hear it and he said, 'OK, but we have to wait until free time, because that is when the counselors and other boys are going outside.' Later, we snuck into the attic and he sat at an old dusty upright piano, played, and sang it for me. The moment he opened his mouth and started singing this beautiful song about love, I fell in love with him. From that day on, we were close. He was the one that taught me what little bit I knew about playing the keys."

"He did?"

"Yep." Garrett said, brightening. "He was my one and only piano teacher. I remember how we had to steal moments to go up to the attic to practice and how much fun we had. But there was one time when we practiced and his hand grazed and lingered on mine. At that second, I felt something in the air as we looked up at each other, something both of us needed... Love." He looks down, bashfully smiling.

After a beat, I nudge him playfully, saying, "Well... what happened?"

Garrett looks up at me, grimacing and saying, "You are nosy as hell, you know that?"

"I already know you kissed. I just wanted to hear it. We don't hear about real romance nowadays so it's always fascinating how it happens, especially when we are talking about MY best friend," I say as I sip my tea.

He chuckled and rolled his eyes upward, saying, "Yes, we kissed."

"I knew it."

Garrett stands up and goes to the screens to look out. "After Ma and Dad adopted me, we lost touch. In one of the meetings we had before I went to live with them, they asked me how I felt about leaving Miami. I was initially happy to leave, but then I was sad because it meant that I had to leave the one who really showed me what love was... and I really loved him. But I remember what a friend of mine at Open Hands said. 'If we like each other, we'll find each other again.' I told Corey the same thing, only I used the word 'love'." He then breathes a long cleansing sigh.

He wonders aloud, "How could I possibly know that I would see him again? Talk to him again? After we reacquainted as Corey and Garrett, it was like the romance never left." He turned and looked at me. "You know what? To this day, I am grateful to God that Jojo called me and pressed me to go on that cruise with ya'll, because I never would have known that the same one that you called Corey was actually my Simon."

"What?" I say, shocked.

"Yeah," Garrett says, as he saunters back to his seat. After taking a sip of his tea, he continues, "Jojo called me after some meeting ya'll had about the cruise and practically begged me to go. He said that he felt a strong vibe between me and 'Corey', and he saw it as his duty to convince me to 'get my ass on the boat' so we could get to know each other."

My baby, the matchmaker, I think to myself, grinning as I remember an exchange between us both:

"We have to get these two officially boo'ed up."
"Since when do you have matchmaking skills?"
"Please, baby. You don't know all the skills I got. That's just one of them."

"What are you grinning about?" Garrett asks, bringing me back to earth.

"Huh? Oh, I was just thinking about the man I'm about to marry."

"He's full of surprises, isn't he?"

I grin uncontrollably as I remember the night when we made love. I smirk at Garrett and retort, "You don't know the half of it. I've known Jojo all my life, and he stills surprises and enlightens me." We laugh. Abruptly, I remember the tree with the red leaves on Eunetta's front lawn.

"Garrett?"

"Hmm?"

"Ms. E. said that she was going to water Corey. Is Corey that tree out on the front yard?"

"Yeah. It was actually Mike Jr's idea. He reminded me of what Rachel did when Mike Sr. died. So, before I skipped town, I went to a nursery. I saw this Japanese striped bark maple sapling. It looked so beautiful. Like the first day I met Corey, its red leaves grabbed my attention and drew me to it. So, I bought it and Mama, Rachel, Mike Jr., and I planted it."

"It caught my attention when I first drove up." I agree. I reflect for a minute, then I say, "That tree does remind me of Corey. Vibrant and unique."

"Yeah. After planting the tree, I thought about all the trees and how some of them might represent people. I remember when we moved to

Austin, and I would sit in awe as I looked at the tall trees that surrounded the house that we lived in. Thinking back on it now, I wonder how those same trees might have begun their growing process. How many of them represented someone who needed to be remembered, how many were just planted for the hell of it, and how many were around since the beginning of time."

Wow! What he is saying is strikingly profound. Silence stretches between us as I savor my "a-ha" moment. I then say, "So, given time and proper care, there's no telling how long this tree may live or how tall it's gonna grow. It could outlive all of us."

"Like Corey." He gives me a bright look of promise. "That fool might've thought he killed him. But he couldn't kill his music or what he meant to all of us."

"And he sure as hell couldn't kill his spirit!" I say as we stand up and exchange a strong handshake that ended in a hug.

"Hey 'dere," I hear A.D.'s voice yell out. I turn and there he is with Rachel standing next to him. She smiles and steps forward to give me a tight hug. "Oh Lionel," she lets out before releasing me. "We've been worried about you. How are you holding up?"

I look at Garrett and smile, then turn back to her, saying, "I'll be OK." I look at A.D. and he smirks at me.

"So yo' ass fine'ly got out'cha house."

I can say nothing. All I can do is just pull him to me and hug him.

I hear him laughing. He says, "Wut's dat fo'?"

Still hugging him, I sigh and breathe out, "Do I need a reason to hug my brother?"

I feel his arms around me. "Hell nah... I'm heah fuh ya, bruh."

*****

I am in my bathroom putting my smell-good on. I'm having dinner with Jojo and Peep at an Italian Restaurant called Carrabba's. Peep called both of us and said he wanted to meet to discuss the wedding. This would be the first of many meetings we would have as a trio, not a quartet. So, I am bracing myself because it might be a bit awkward and emotional for all three of us.

I'm quite proud of myself, I must say. Last Monday, before the Thanksgiving holiday, I finally went back to work. After talking with Garrett and Eunetta the week before, it seemed pointless to waste my days grieving and groaning. What a fuss the office staff made over me! I had to check and see if I came onto the right floor. I saw a big edible fruit arrangement in the middle of my desk, with a huge lollipop that said, "Welcome back." They also gave me a welcoming party in the break room with cake and punch, during which Floyd handed me a check for fifteen thousand dollars as a personal bonus from Miss Harrington for the work I did on the VaVoom campaign. *Will wonders never cease*! I was so glad to be back that I didn't even blink upon seeing the five accounts waiting for me, Katherine Nesbitt's being one of them. Who cared? I was only glad to be out of the house and doing something besides crying or lying in my bed watching sad movies on Netflix.

On Thanksgiving Eve, after drafting new ideas for Ms. Nesbitt's campaign, I left the office with my bags already in my trunk. I swung by the airport to grab A.D. from work, so we could drive to Atlanta. Jojo and I didn't celebrate Thanksgiving together. I wanted to, but Jojo told me that I needed to spend the time with my family and that Eunetta invited Peep, Jimmy, and him over to her house to eat. So, for the first time in three years, my brothers, Brenda, and I came back together for the extended weekend. Mercer and their kids went to Bismarck to spend the holidays with his mother and family. Brenda told him that she wanted to spend the holiday with us instead of going with them as usual, and Mercer wholeheartedly agreed.

We were all at Brenda's place, talking and prepping the food. None of us wanted to spend that day at Mama's house, where Rhonda was living now. By the way, A.D.'s plan worked like a charm. Rhonda went to every last one of my sibs to beg for money for the house's upkeep, and she went ape shit when they refused. She didn't call me until Thanksgiving Eve. Brenda and Dean were cooking and A.D., Roland, and I were playing cards and talking trash. We all were laughing it up and having a good old time when Rhonda called me. I answered, "Hello?"

"Lionel, I need you to help me," her distressed voice belted out.

"Well, hello and Happy Thanksgiving to you too," I said. I gestured to my phone and mouthed the words, "It's Rhonda!"

A.D. whispered, "Put 'er ass on speakaphone."

"Yeah, I want to hear this one," Dean said, sitting down.

"Lionel!" Rhonda's voice screeched.

Brenda came over to the table, wiping her hands clean of flour as I hit the speaker button.

"WHAT THE FUCK ARE YOU DOING?!" Rhonda asked, screaming.

I kept my voice extremely calm. "Rhonda, why are you yelling?"

"What is your problem, numbnuts? I ain't got time to be waiting on the phone. I told you I need you to help me."

"Why Rhonda, what's wrong?" I asked in mock concern.

"These fucking house bills are driving me crazy. Soon as I pay for one bill, here comes another. I need you to step up and help me."

I smiled as my other siblings tried to hold their laughter in. I said, "I'm sorry, Rhonda, but I can't help you."

"I can't handle these bills by myself!" she whined.

"Well, lest we forget, you *are* the only one that wanted to stay there when we wanted to sell the house. Besides, what happened to all the money you got from Mama's will and Grandma's house?"

"I had stuff to pay for. I spent it already."

I smirked at A.D., who mouthed to all of us, "Din' I tell ye?!"

"Jeez Rhonda, you blew through that money pretty quickly. You got almost two hundred and fifty grand. What could you possibly have spent it on?"

"Listen, are you gonna help me or not?"

"Afraid not. I got my money tied up in other things right now," I said, as I looked casually at my nails, then blew on them to buff them on my sweater while everyone else snickered.

"What other things can you have your money tied up with other than helping to pay the bills for the house Mama left ALL of us."

"Well Rhonda, like I said, not ALL of us have the same burning desire to keep the house that you do." I knew that the coolness of my voice was pissing her off royally. Her voice just got louder and more hysterical.

"Well, what the fuck am I supposed to do?"

"You do have a job, don't you?" I replied nonchalantly.

"OF COURSE, I GOT A GODDAMNED JOB!" She screamed at the top of her lungs, causing everyone to crack up.

"Well Rhonda, I thought this was what you wanted."

"I DIDN'T WANT IT LIKE THIS, YOU FAGGOT MOTHERFUCKER!"

"Oh please, call me that again. You know how it thrills me."

My brothers and Brenda couldn't hold their laughter in. First A.D. fell on the floor, laughing his ass off. Then Roland and Brenda started. Dean threw back his head and howled.

Rhonda heard, "WHO IS OVER THERE! ALL OF YA'LL ARE OVER THERE TOGETHER, AIN'T YOU? THIS IS A DIRTY TRICK YA'LL

COOKED UP, AIN'T IT?!"

"I don't know what you mean," I said mockingly.

"YOU NO GOOD MOTHERFUCKERS! FUCK YA'LL! I DON'T NEED YOUR HELP!"

I did feel a little twinge of heart for her, so I told the others to quiet down and said to her, "Rhonda, listen. We are doing this because we need to move on. We all love you, but the shit you've pulled over the years is foul as fuck. This is our way of saying that we are sick of it. If you want that house, you can have it. But keeping it means that you might not have enough money to live on after you finish paying the bills. On the other hand, if we sell the house, you can get yourself a nice condo with your share of the money or do a down payment on a smaller house with lower maintenance. And here's free advice, put some in a checking account and the rest of it in an interest-bearing savings account that comes with a penalty for taking money out. It will benefit you in the long run."

A.D. resumed his seat quietly. There was silence over the line. Then, Rhonda furiously mumbled to herself, "I can't believe this shit."

"So, is it a deal?"

"FINE. SELL THE FUCKING HOUSE!" Rhonda yelled before she hung up.

A.D. held out his hand for some skin, which I gave him. "Too smooth, my brother! Too smooth!"

"Not bad fo' a street bruva!" A.D. said as he grinned, sucking on his gold tooth.

I thought about it and that compassion for her was still there.

"What's wrong?" Roland asked, looking at my face.

"Look, ya'll," I said. "Maybe we still ought to invite her over for the holiday."

"Nah, dude," A.D. replied. "I came down 'ere to 'ave a good time. I ain't tryin' to be fussin' wit 'er."

"Me neither," Brenda agreed.

"No indeed," Roland followed.

Dean just sat there in deep thought. Afterwards, he said, "Ya'll, Lionel is right. Even though we had a good laugh, everybody at this table knows how sad it is that we had to trick her into doing something that is going to benefit all six of us. She was blind to that, as she was for years about so many other things. She might be as mean as a junkyard dog, but this is our sister we are talking about and we can't just leave her out."

I jump in, "And it's a bad feeling when you are at home knowing that your family is elsewhere for the holidays. You start thinking that they just don't care. I went through that when Mama disowned me. Besides," I heard myself rephrase my fiancé's words. "We have to do right by people, even when they treat us dead wrong. That especially includes family. You hear what I'm telling you?"

A.D. sat back, saying skeptically, "I don' know, Li'nel."

"A.D., come on. It goes back to what you were telling me about being bitter against Mama. Rhonda has her shit but that doesn't mean we have to feed into it. If we extend the olive branch, and she refuses it, then we can let her go knowing we've done our part by including her... but we'll never stop loving her."

After a few seconds, they all agreed. I then pulled my phone back out to text her.

Rhonda, if you want to come for Thanksgiving dinner tomorrow, we are at Brenda's house. We are still your family and we still love you.

That Thanksgiving was among the best we have ever shared together. Of course, Rhonda decided not to come, but we texted her greetings anyway. She answered back...

EAT SHIT!

When we read that, all we could do is shake our heads. When someone goes out of their way to be hateful, it is best to leave them be until they see the consequences of their actions, sister or not. We put our phones away, clinked our glasses, and let the good times roll once again.

*****

I'm thinking about this as I'm putting on the royal blue spandex shirt, white jeans, and Tims. Peep made me buy this two years ago, saying, "I'm gonna get you out of that corporate dress bullshit if it kills me. It's ok to wear it now and then. But you got to learn how to have a little pizazz." I survey myself in the mirror, and I am at awe of what I see: a good-looking, sexy, peanut-butter brown man with a cool body under the threads and eyes that are lively and full of sparkle. Even the gray hairs make me look distinguished and sophisticated, yet alluring and rugged. I think to myself, *Not bad for someone approaching forty. I'm holding my own. Maybe Orchid is right.*

I hear my doorbell ring. Tripping down the stairs and opening my door, I see a rail-thin, pale white guy in a UPS uniform.

"Mr. Davis? Mr. Lionel S. Davis?"

"Yes, that's me."

"I have a certified letter for you." He pulls out his electronic clipboard and instructs me to sign. When I have done so, he hands me the UPS envelope and says, "Have a good day, sir." Then, he turns to hop in the van and drive away.

I open the envelope and as I do, I get a whiff of familiar perfume. Wind Song! Strange. Inside the envelope is another pink envelope that says, "To Lionel". I recognize the girlish cursive handwriting. It is my mother's! I tear open the envelope and encounter a four-page handwritten letter, front AND back. Composing myself from the shock, I begin to read.

February 27, 2020

Dear Lionel,

I asked for my lawyer to mail this letter nine months after I pass on. This way, it will give you and your brothers and sisters time to settle everything legally.

I am sitting here hooked to my chemo machine and watching as the doctors run more tests. I hear the words, "You have one month to live," but I hear something stronger… something that says, "Make your peace." This is what I want to do, and I realize that it must start with the ones that I've hurt.

I want to start off by saying that even though I am not an affectionate woman, I truly do love you. I also loved your father and the rest of my children. I didn't realize how much until this very moment. But sometimes, you get so wrapped up in your resentments and the haunts of your past that you can't see the hurt you put on others in the present. With you, all I could see was you and that boy, Joseph, and how close you were. In my mind, you were getting too close and I tried to stop it because I wanted my son to grow into a well-functioned, successful, straight man. But when you told me that you were gay, I started thinking about your father, about some things that happened to me, and I snapped.

I didn't understand how two men could love each other more than they did the opposite sex, and part of the reason was that I have had my fights with gay men, and 98.9% of the time, those battles left me devastated, to say the least. I can't believe that I am feeling free enough to write this, but when I was a teenager, I was raped by two men who were supposed to be my protectors: my father and my uncle Lawrence. It was continual and went on between ages twelve and eighteen and the abuse planted a seed of hate in me that grew into a tree I couldn't cut down.

This was my position when I caught your father and Troy Matterson screwing. What started it was a yellow sticky note in your father's pants pocket. I found it when I was doing the laundry and it said, "Come see me tonight." It doesn't take a rocket scientist to figure out what that note meant, and when I read it, I was mad as hell. I didn't know who your father was screwing; I just knew it wasn't me and it should've been. From that day on, I began to watch him carefully, grilling him about where he went some nights and going crazy when he didn't give me any straight answers.

On June 16, 2008, I got my straight answer when I followed him to where I thought was some woman's house, learning that she lived just a few blocks away from us. After waiting five minutes, I walked up to the window and saw a sight that sent me into a tailspin: two naked male bodies hugging and kissing, and one of them belonged to my husband. I was so heartbroken and furious that it felt like I was in a dream. I drove back to our house, grabbed my dead father's shotgun, and came back. When I kicked open the door, I saw your father bent over and Troy fucking him. That was when I lost it completely. I cocked the gun, thumbed the hammer, and Kenneth started pleading for his life. As I initially squeezed the trigger, I thought of my father and uncle and how powerless I was when they raped me. But I swear to you that in the split second that followed, I thought of you kids being without a father if I carried through with this. But, before I could remove my finger from the trigger, I realized that it was pulled all the way back. The shot was fired, and your father fell dead at my feet. Troy was too stunned to move and I thought, "I killed my husband in front of this man and he'll tell the law if I don't silence him." Another shot was fired, and another body fell to the floor. I didn't stick around to see if he was alive. I just jumped in my car, sped home, and hid the shotgun. I told you kids that Kenneth died and didn't go into detail as to how.

The Cost

When I learned a month later that Troy was alive, I panicked, then became puzzled when the police didn't come after me. Finally, a year later, I learned why through that letter Troy wrote me from prison. He took the fall for me. But, as guilty as I felt, I stayed quiet, placed the letter in my keepsake box, and told you kids that a mugger killed your father. The letter remained unseen until someone saw it and sent it to you. I believe it was Dean who sent it because he went into the box to get my health insurance papers for the hospital.

If I could turn back the hands of time, I would have tried to understand your journey. I would have pushed my past so far behind me to the point where I saw nothing but love and kindness to give. I wouldn't have written that hateful letter denouncing you. I wouldn't have beat on you and treated you and Andre as I did. I was wrong. Your Sunday school teacher, Ms. Frazier, came to see me at the hospital and she helped me understand that. I wish I had done things differently, lived life, gotten help, and valued ALL my children more.

You were right in saying that I favored Rhonda. She reminded me of me at that age with my personality, my outspoken nature, and my big mouth. Until Brenda came along, she was my only girl: pretty, smart, and self-assured. But, over time, I began to see that as beautiful as Rhonda was, she was also selfish, cruel, and conniving. I understood that very well because that how I learned to become by watching my own mother. Still, I did the polar opposite of what Mother did with me; I spoiled Rhonda, put her on a pedestal, and gave her as much of the world as I was able. Kenneth told me on several occasions that Rhonda was not the perfect little girl I said she was and that spoiling her that much would lead to heartache for me, but I didn't listen. It hit home when you told me that everyone, but Rhonda, chipped in to pay for my operation. I was ashamed and heartbroken, but too proud to show it. Lately, I've been haunted by the fact that since Rhonda was born, I spent so much time catering to "my little girl" that I neglected the rest of my children, and the results damaged all of us.

I don't understand how you became gay. Lord knows, I don't. But I do know the look of love. I remembered that it was how Kenneth looked at me when he first met me while driving a cab, a job he took to put himself through college. Andre was almost one year old at the time. Andre's father, Bertram, was in the Army and was stationed in Fort McClellan. He courted me, we had sex, and I got pregnant. Amazing how men will promise you the moon and romance you up until the time when you say the words, "I'm pregnant." When I told him, he revealed that he was married and accused me of sleeping around. He split and Momma told me that I had to get an abortion because she didn't want an illegitimate grandchild. She took me to a back-alley abortionist that she knew from her church, but after seeing those tools, that dingy table, and the uncaring, vacant look on the woman's face, I couldn't go through with it. Momma and I had a big fight and she kicked me out of her home. I moved into an apartment in Yeti, had Andre, and got a job on the jewelry counter at Macy's.

When Kenneth met me, he called it love at first sight. I remember thinking at the time, "How could he love someone like me?" Oh, I was mean to him in that first cab ride. He took an alternate route to the store and I went ballistic because I thought he was trying to make the ride longer so he could charge more money. I laugh when I think about this now. When we got to the store, I found that the fare was two dollars cheaper than I would have paid. I felt so guilty that I went down to the cab company to apologize and give him a tip from what little money I had. That was when he told me, "I'd be even more forgiving if you gave me your number." I played hard to get for months. But during that time, your father baked me strawberry pound cakes and came to the jewelry counter every Monday to give them to me. Upon eating the last piece of each one, there was an oily piece of paper saying, "Stop playing and give me your number." Eventually, I gave it to him because Andre and I were getting fat from those pound cakes. We started seeing each other regularly and after a year, he proposed, telling me that he would take care of me and Andre. and love us like a father and husband should. We got married and had you and Dean Anthony, then Rhonda Denise, then Roland Morrice and Brenda Faye. The rest is history.

In spite of the fights, the separations, and his affair, I believe your father loved me. He spent thirty years proving it by providing for me and his family. He tried to reach out to me frequently during our marriage, but I shut him out. I saw that love in his eyes, but I couldn't let go of my past enough to embrace it. So, I pushed him, nagged him, picked fights, and made him so miserable that he resorted to traveling for work just to get some peace. I drove my husband away from me.

I can't shake the fact that if I had ditched the booze sooner and been the wife and mother I should've been, perhaps Kenneth wouldn't have sprinted into Troy's arms. Standing at the window that night, I saw that look of love in his eyes as he looked at Troy. I became insanely angry. That was the look I should've been getting. Certainly not another man. But last week, I decided to watch one of those movies involving two men in love. I forget the name of it, but when I saw the actions of true love… the real love between them, it reminded me of the love

Kenneth tried to give to me. I was too afraid to let him get too close to me. Too cowardly to fully love someone without having strings attached.

Even now, I'm a coward. I've wanted to pick up that phone so many times to call you and tell you this person to person, but my pride wouldn't let me and, before I knew it, time passed and I drifted further away from you each passing day. So, I decided to write this letter. Maybe this will give you some peace of mind and finality after I'm gone.

I promise you, Lionel, that I was trying to be the best mother I knew how to be. But it was hard. I didn't have any examples to follow, and my children didn't come with a manual. All I had to go on was the phrase, "Spare the Rod, Spoil the Child." In my mind, I thought that was the parents' way of showing love and providing discipline. I never learned that hugs, kisses, and positive guidance had to EQUAL the discipline, because they would keep you from going too far. It is a shame that it took standing at death's doorstep when I could have seen it all along. I had become so bitter at being hated and abused by my parents and uncle that I couldn't see I was doing the same thing to my own children. I didn't lock you in closets, make you drink loads of castor oil until you threw up, make you do housework for scraps of food, or touched you in an inappropriate way and traded you for a kept life as my parents did me, but my harsh words, mental abuse, cruel neglect, and relentless poundings are just as bad as if I had.

I hadn't meant to write so long a letter. I guess I had a lot to say and explain. But now, I'm running out of steam. So, I want to close in saying that you ARE my son. Though I may not understand who or what you are, it cannot change that fact. I tried to deny it, but a mother can't unbirth her own child. I know this letter cannot wipe away thirty-nine years of hurt, but I hope it counts as a good beginning for the years you have remaining.

My prayer is that you can forgive me for being a stubborn, bitter, and hateful old woman who learned how to love too late. And I do love you, Lionel. It may not look like it and I may not have shown it. But I do, and don't you ever forget it.

Sincerely, even when I'm not around, I will always be,

Your mother.

I am blinded by the tears in my eyes. This is the first time she ever broke down and told the truth about anything concerning her past. Even though we learned of it from her journal, it had to have been hard for her to relive that, enough to relay it. Us kids already knew of A.D.'s father from hearing her talk about him, describing him as a "piss-poor, womanizing deadbeat." I suspected that she hated him for ghosting on her and resented A.D. for resembling him, but I didn't know about what went on between those two in the time before A.D.'s birth. I shift the papers and another rectangular sheet falls to the floor. I pick it up and peruse it in surprise. It was a Cashier's check for five grand and in the memo was typed, "Second Mortgage Repayment."

In my hands is the closure I searched for. It's funny how a few pieces of paper can bring such relief. Such serenity. Such a light feeling that transports you into cloud nine with ease. Silently, I thank Mama for the closure as well as the admission of her tumultuous past. This was needed. Now I know I'm ready to move forward with a life of no damning secrets, few unresolved issues, and most importantly, no crippling bitterness.

The doorbell rings again. I answer it and there is Jojo standing outside, dressed in a yellow knitted turtleneck, tight eggshell-colored jeans, and some Tims. A thick gold chain is draped around his neck and a high-wattage, winning smile lights up his face. He looks like sunshine! Good to see that Nate is not the only one who can wear yellow. This is the color Jojo hates because he says it makes him look too dark, but he looks so sexy that I want to carry him up the stairs and enjoy a little "one-on-one."

"Baby," I let out with a grin. "What are you doing here? I thought we were meeting at Carrabba's."

"We were," he says, nodding his head. "But I figured you hadn't left yet so I decided to come get you. It'll save you gas from driving the truck."

"I could have come to you, you know."

"I know. But I wanted to come to you. Besides, it'll give me time, there and back, to be enfolded in the mystery known as Lionel Davis."

"Lord, what a mystery to unfold. You are a very brave soul," I kid as I grab my keys, then kiss him on his full lips. "Well, let's not waste a minute. And might I say, you look as delicious as a lemon meringue pie."

Jojo laughs, "Do you really like it, Mr. Davis?"

I circle him twice, ogling him from head to toe. "Mm-mm-MM! Mr. Thompson! I might need to walk around you a third time to make sure you're real."

"Oh, go on, boy. Gotta say though," he croons as he gives me a once over with a sexy smirk. "I don't look nearly as good as you do. Looking like blueberry ice cream!"

Blueberry and lemon, what a pair, I think. Then I say as we prepare to hustle out the door, "Well, since we're using food to describe each other, it's safe to say that we are hungry. So, let's hop in the car and go eat!"

Chapter Twenty
A LEGACY OF LOVE

"I'm glad you are finally out of your place. Tell me, how was your first day back at work?" Jojo asks, while we are seated at Carrabba's. Jojo is buttering a piece of oven baked bread from the basket the waitress brought over.

I heave a sigh of playful exhaustion., then reply, "Crazy, but in a good way. I feel good about being back. It's needed and that check I got from VaVoom was just what the doctor ordered."

"How so?" he says, putting the bread down and picking up the water glass to take a sip.

"Well, we can use that to decide on where to go for our honeymoon."

Jojo says excitedly, "That's right! With everything that has been going on, we haven't even chewed on that."

"Well, where is a place you've always wanted to go?"

Jojo thinks a minute. Slowly, he resumes conversation, "You may get a broad answer because there are so many."

"One, Jojo! One place!" I joke, holding up my index finger.

"OK, OK, let me see…"

"And while you are thinking, I'll just eat this," I say, as I snatch the buttered bread from his plate and devour it. Jojo looks at me with his mouth open.

"Yes, I took your bread!" Jojo throws his napkin at me.

"You shady, greedy asshole!" he says with a huge grin.

"And it was good too," I laugh. Then I take another piece of bread, butter it, and look at Jojo. "Open your mouth," I say.

Jojo smiles and obeys. I place the bread on his tongue, and he closes his mouth. Then, with my finger still in his mouth, he sucks on it. *Oh my!* I feel huge attention in my pants! "You are a freaky thing, ain't you?" I say, grinning and retrieving my finger.

"And you love it, don't *you*?" Jojo leers, then winks cheekily at me.

After a nice romantic tension fills the air, I rebound while blushing, "So, you haven't answered my question."

"Hmm… well, I've always wanted to go to Mexico. That Puerta Vallarta trip that Garrett and his family took sounds interesting… even though it ended tragically." Jojo looks downcast for a second. But then he smiles, then points at me. "Same question."

"You already know where I want to go."

"Barcelona?"

"You know it."

"So, which one are we going to go on?"

"Well, I know I said one, but why *not* do both? Puerta Vallarta for the first week and a half and Barcelona on the second."

"That's a good idea. Between your bonus pay and my vacation savings of seventy-five hundred, we should be covered."

"Hold the phone. Who said you had to pay any money towards it?"

"I did." Jojo looks at me, determined. "Come on, Lion. You know that if we are talking about going somewhere for three weeks, that's gonna add up to a lot of money. Why blow a huge portion of your wad?"

"We won't have to worry about that if I talk with Floyd's travel guy. He always gets us a sweet deal."

"Ok, but I insist on paying half. We're gonna do this together, baby."

I kiss him on his cheek… then I tickle him in his side. Jojo cries out, laughing, "Lionel, that ain't right. You know I'm ticklish."

I laugh along with him. "Yeah, that's why I did it!"

"Good Lord. Get a fucking room!" I hear Peep's voice yell out. In a flash, he is standing in front of us, smiling. This is the first time I've seen him since the funeral, but I'm confused. He is the opposite of what Jojo described to me. Peep is dressed in a rust colored cable-knit sweater that hugged his muscular upper body, white jeans that his leg muscles are stretching, and brown dress boots. A tan trench coat and a brown leather messenger bag are slung over his left shoulder. His two-toned hair is coiffed and brushed to a glint. He looks like the Peep I know and love. But in looking in his eyes, I see vulnerability and brokenness.

"What's going on? What'd I miss? Did you order yet?" Peep questions as he sits in the opposite booth.

"Not a thing, and no, we didn't," Jojo says. "We are just talking about where we want to go for our honeymoon."

"Ah, the afterglow of the wedding we have to plan. That's why I wanted to talk to you both. We are two months away from the cruise and we have yet to discuss what you are wearing, what decorations you want to have, and…"

I stop him. "Peep, slow down. We got time for that."

Peep shakes his head, saying nervously, "No no no. You say we got time, but time flies and the cruise date will be here before you know it."

Why do I feel something underlying in his voice? I think to myself. I look at Jojo and I see my concern for Peep mirrored in his eyes. I want to talk with Peep and encourage him to share how he feels, but I resist, saying, "OK. Well, we didn't want anything grand. It's just a simple ceremony."

"Please. A lifetime friendship segueing into partnership *is* something grand. Come on, now. If you are going to tie the knot, let's do it right! Besides, after all you both went through, you deserve this," Peep says purposefully.

I raise my hands, saying, "Ok, I'm cool with that." My mind adds, *But, before we get up from this table, we are going to have a little talk with you, Mr. Bravefront.*

Jojo follows, "Me too."

"Great!" Peep beams. He then goes into his messenger bag and pulls out a binder. "Now, with this being a special case, I decided that your tuxedos need to be custom tailored."

"We could easily buy them from the tuxedo shop."

"Ah, but they won't have that personal touch," Peep replies brightly. He opens his binder to show us sketches of his tuxedo designs, and they are beautiful! "Forgive me for overstepping, but I just feel like everything about this wedding needs to be tailored to fit you both. And I'm not just talking about the tuxedos."

Jojo looks pleasantly mystified, as am I. I speak up, "Peep, I knew that you styled people. But I didn't know you actually designed clothes for them."

"Nobody knows. You two will be the first to wear them out in public and I am going to tailor you. I didn't take those sewing classes with Grandma for nothing."

"Peep, you never cease to amaze us. These are really beautiful, but are you sure you can sew these?"

"Of course, I'm sure. I had been tinkering with sewing for a while now and I got clothes that I've sewn but didn't have the courage to wear them in public. It was actually Jimmy who persuaded me to wear one of those suits for the wedding. Jimmy AND Corey before he..." He stops and I could swear I saw a tear in his eye. He puts it off with a bright smile. "Look, I figured that while I'm at it, I'll sew tuxes for my two bestie brothers, OK?"

Jojo and I glance at each other, then at Peep saying simultaneously, "We're game."

Peep claps his hands excitedly, "Fabulous! Now, for this tux, I'm feeling more of a brocade fabric. It gives it an elegant look..."

*****

Over a two-hour dinner, we plan the wedding and as we do, Peep is feverishly writing ideas down. I called three people. The first two calls were to A.D. and Dean, asking them to be the best men for Jojo and me. The last was to Darrell Alston and he agreed to provide the music in Corey's stead. Peep called Reverend Washington to confirm that he was still going on the cruise. He said yes and that he had a surprise for us.

We chose an exquisite cream tux with red lapels, vest, and ascot, and decided to pattern the decorations behind those colors, along with a splash of gold. Peep said that he would call the cruise line to see if they could provide the balloons, as well as white seat covers and a large canopy structure. How excited his voice became when he offered to go to Jo-Ann's and buy gold satin sashes to tie a bow around the chairs, as well as cream voile fabric to hang on the canopy.

"A canopy with voile drapes would look romantic blowing in the sea breeze. Oh! What time of day did you want to have the wedding? I need to know so I can tell the cruise line to block a portion of the lido deck."

Jojo and I both say without even thinking, "Sunset!" We both look at each other, blushing. We haven't even gotten married yet and our minds are already knitted to where we desire the same things.

"Oh my God, that will be so romantic! The sunset would add a rosy atmosphere," Peep says before writing in his binder. He then sits back, closes the binder, and emits a sigh of relief. Afterwards, he gushes, "Well, this is something more to work with. We will add more as we go along. So, now that we got that out of the way, how have ya'll been? I know it's been a while since..." He stops short, trying to find the words. The table is silent as he looks down at a saltshaker.

"We are fine. Taking it one day at a time," I say. "The question is, how have you been?"

"Oh, I'm fine. Busy as ever. If I'm not personal training, I'm at the bank. And if I'm not there, I'm talking with the lawyer about Corey's..." He halts again, biting down on his lips.

Jojo puts his hand on Peep's, saying, "It's OK, Peep."

Peep looks at Jojo, saying, "What?"

"It's OK to share how you are feeling."

"I'm fine, ya'll. Really," Peep lies, with a tear escaping and falling down his face; a tear that he unsuccessfully tried to blink back. There are new tears pooling in his hazel eyes.

Jojo sees through the paper-thin charade. He says, "No, you are not. You're hurting, Peep. It's ok to feel hurt. But why are you trying to hide it from us?"

"Yeah. You can talk to us. We're your brothers."

Peep can't stop the tears from falling. His head bows as violent sobs shake his body. He lowers his head to the table. Jojo moves to sit next to him and put his arm around Peep's muscular back as I squeeze both his hands. After a few moments, Peep sits up, the river flowing from his eyes. He tearfully sobs out, "Oh my God! This is hard as fuck. I keep hoping this shit is a bad dream and I'm going to wake up at any minute. Then when I'm reminded that it's not, I strain to hear his voice, arguing with me. But I can't. It hurts... Oh God, this hurts!" He bows his head and releases my hand and bangs on the table repeatedly. He then looks out of the window. With a quivering breath, he says, "Ya'll, I loved Corey! I really did! I might not have shown it as much as I should, but I really loved him!"

I rub his hand to reassure him as Jojo rubs his back, "We know, Peep. And Corey knew that too."

"Yeah, you just shared your love in a different way," Jojo reaffirms.

"But in the eighteen plus years that I've known him, I can't count past one hand how many times I actually told him. With all our fussing back and forth and even in all the fun times we had, those three words rarely were said between us," Peep says, as he continues looking out the window.

I say, "Peep, between friends, things are not always said, but they are felt through proof of the love we say we have. People who love you push you to follow your dreams, despite their fear-filled nightmares concerning your life. You practically made him get his ass on a plane to pursue his."

"Yeah," Jojo jumps in. "And you nagged him to get some help after he was attacked. If you didn't love him, you would have let him stay in his pity party."

"I know." Peep laments, looking at both of us in turn. "I'm trying to move past this."

"You are trying too hard, Peep," Jojo says. "And you're doing it alone. But like you told Corey, building walls around yourself is not good for you, especially when you have people who love you. I had to remind this one over here of that." He shoves me on the shoulder.

I look in Peep's eyes, filled with strong emotion. "Listen, Peep. Corey may not be here for you to tell him you loved him. But like I said, he knew. Now, if it bothers you that you didn't tell him enough, then you just make sure you tell somebody else. Give them that same sentiment you wanted to give Corey."

Peep's face lifts and he snorts a laugh. He stands up and hugs us both mightily. Before he can utter the words, we feel them through the beat of his heart and the warmth of his tender embrace. With laughter mixed with affection, he yells out, "I love both ya'll bitches." We yell the same thing, laughing.

The other customers turn to look at us as if we are crazy. Peep breaks the hug and looks back at them, saying exactly as Corey would've said, "What are ya'll looking at? You ain't never seen three men loving on each other before?"

*****

On December sixteenth, Jojo, Peep, Garrett, A.D., Jimmy, and I are seated on posh brown leather seats in the office of Ms. Regina Stapleton, Attorney at Law. We are here for the reading of Corey's will, as we were all mentioned in it. Color us puzzled, well... except Peep. We assumed that most of his estate went to charity, since he had no family other than his Aunt Freida, who flew up for this as well.

Ms. Stapleton had earlier excused herself to check on something with her secretary, so we are waiting on her. The energy is awkward as we just sit and gaze at the pictures and citations that hang on cream walls with oak borders. After a while, Ms. Stapleton- a sixtyish, attractive, buxom, brown-skinned woman dressed in a black suit- comes in with a brown leather portfolio. She seats herself in a tall, brown leather chair behind a huge, ornately carved oak desk, then smooths her salt and pepper bobbed

The Cost

hair into order.

"My apologies for the wait. I hadn't accounted for the office being so busy today."

"It's ok," Jojo assures.

She places her wire-rimmed glasses on her nose and opens the leather portfolio containing the will. "So, we are here to discuss the last will of Mr. Cordell Rodgerick James Kennedy. The first order of business is to confirm that all pertaining parties are present." She reads off our names one by one, prompting us to answer, "Here."

"Darrell Alston?"

"Oh, he is on an Asian tour."

"Very well, I will set up a time with him later. On to the will. Mr. Kennedy has emphatically stated for terms of his last will and testament to be incontestably implemented as follows."

We wait in bated breath for the lawyer to read the contents. As she reads, we are all in complete shock. Corey had four bank accounts: one that totaled beyond two million dollars, money that came from his salaries at the Unity and Love Church, Towson University, and Howard University. From that account, he split nine hundred thousand dollars between Peep, Jojo and me. A.D. was to get the car and he, Freida, and Jimmy each got one hundred fifty grand. The remaining funds were to go to Unity and Love Community Church. The second account was money from royalties, the huge concert, and honorariums from different workshops and tours. It tallied up to four hundred and twenty-five grand and that went to Garrett.

Per their original agreement, Darrell Alston would continue to collect fifty percent of the revenue for the songs he recorded with Corey; as well as for a new single called "Inhale, Exhale, Relax", which they co-wrote, recorded, and released before they went on tour. Already, "Inhale" received notoriety and constant airplay in Sydney and Japan. For all the songs, Corey's half of the royalties were to be directly deposited into Garrett's newly inherited account on a quarterly basis.

I thought Freida would be pissed that she was getting less than us, but she tells us that she understands before saying, "If I had friends who treated me better than my own family did, I would do the same thing." Corey told me in times past that Freida was the one who talked his mother out of aborting him, although she couldn't care for him herself. Her presence in the will was his way of saying thank you to her.

He gave us Fellas specific instructions for the house, saying that he wanted it to be converted to a home for children that were either gay and disowned by their parents, or displaced and left to fend for themselves. They would stay there until they graduated from high school or were adopted by a suitable family, whichever came first. Corey's home had six bedrooms and four and a half bathrooms, so it was large enough. The upkeep of the home was to be funded by the third and fourth bank accounts. The third bank account was opened in Miami by his foster father when Corey was thirteen years old, and the fourth was money bequeathed to him by Rev. Kennedy's main estate. Both accounts matured with interest. Between the two, the amount was well over three point five million dollars.

The name of the home was to be called The Legacy of Love Home for Displaced Adolescents. The age limit was to be between nine and eighteen and they would have to write an introductory essay, as well as sign a contract that in exchange for room and board, they would keep their grades to a "B" or higher and strengthen whatever talents and gifts they possessed.

Upon the conclusion of the will, we thanked Ms. Stapleton and walked out in a daze. Freida went to her hotel to prepare for her flight back to Miami, and The Fellas and I went back to Corey's house. We sit on the stoop to ruminate over what we just heard. After a few moments, I blurt out, "How in the hell are we going to make this work? We have so much to do... so much to pay for... and we have to think of the state codes as well as approval to even run this home."

Peep says, "We have those two big accounts Corey left to cover it, remember? That will get us started at least."

"But that money won't last too long. We've got to pay a staff, and the money has to keep rolling in from different sources."

"You must have forgotten that I'm a financial advisor, Garrett is an accountant, and Jojo is a financial secretary. Between the three of us, we have connections with grant writers, foundations, charitable organizations..."

"But I bet many of them are homophobes who wouldn't throw a red cent our way."

Jojo, who is sitting next to me, puts his arm around my shoulders, saying, "Well, there has to be somebody who may not partake in the life of our community but have heartstrings that get pulled where young castaways are concerned."

"But who is going to run it? We have careers and homes of our own! If we try to do it, we'll run ourselves crazy."

"Well," Garrett thinks aloud. "Both Mama and Rachel have administrative experience, and both are well acquainted and comfortable with the fam at large. Plus, my cousin Mark once ran a group home with an iron fist for seven years. They all might be able to advise us on what direction to take."

"Your cousin, Mark?"

"Yeah. Remember I told you about him. He's fam, too."

"Oh, right. I remember. But would the home be for girls, or boys, or coed?" I ask.

"Coed," A.D. replies. "De house got three flo's, right?"

"Right," we answer.

"Plus, Corey has a finished basement," Jojo says. "We can redesign the space and make that the office and bedroom for dorm counselors that work overnight."

"Good idea," Garrett agrees. "We can install cameras in the upper hallways."

"Not in the bedrooms, I hope," I gush.

"Please, Lionel. Those kids are entitled to their privacy, of course. But we can install them in the hallways, the foyer, the kitchen, and other common areas. We will have counselors walking the floors periodically to make sure everything is alright."

A.D. adds, "An' we kin buil' a control room in de basemen' wit monituhs fuh de counselas tuh check duh halls, win dey ain't walkin' de flo's."

"Right!" Garrett says. "I guess we can leave the living room alone because it's big enough. But let's knock out the kitchen wall and make it bigger. We can upgrade the appliances and enlist the help of Devetra Nash and Ms. Katie in teaching the older kids how to cook."

"We have the second floor, strictly for the girls," Peep suggests.

"And the boys we can put on the third," Jimmy follows.

"What would be the capacity? And what if there is an overflow?" I ask.

"Welp, Corey got three bedrooms on each flo'. Except fuh duh masta' bedroom, mebbe we kin put two beds in each uvum, makin' it ten young'uns in de whol' house. The counslas kin sleep in the masta' suite and dat wud mean we wudn't hav tuh buil' an office or bedroom. We kin buil' a rec room instea'," A.D. reasons.

"And I might be able to help if we have overflow," Jimmy muses. "Mama's house is just sitting on Alto Road collecting dust. We might be able to do the same thing there, just on a lesser scale."

I am still very skeptical about the whole idea. "I know Corey put this in his will, but I don't know about this. None of us have experience with this sort of thing. And would it just be for gay fam? I mean..."

"Bruh," A.D. says, with a comical laugh. "Yuh talkin' like we gone do dis shit tomorra!"

"Right," Jojo reasons. "And you're right, we may not have experience..."

"But Corey never gave a time frame. Something like this is going to require a team of financial backers and a full administrative staff. We can't just write grants or hire folks in one day," Peep interjects. "We are going to do this, step by step, with careful planning and research. It may take us months... Maybe years... But this is an opportunity to help give children a voice, a backbone, a network, and a safe place to call home. That is, if they are willing to work for it. Even if we have those that just need a listening ear or a reliable resource, we can be there for them. And Lionel, it wouldn't just be for gay teens. We can use this as a way to properly and safely educate the straight displaced kids on how to live and get along well with kids that are gay."

"But ya'll are forgetting one thing. This is the same house Corey was killed in. I don't think any kid would want to live here knowing that," I point out.

"Lionel, that is just superstitious bullshit and you know it. You talk as if this is a haunted house. The only one Corey would be haunting is the one who killed him. He can't haunt someone who is already dead," Garrett retorts.

Jojo jumps in, "Baby, don't be so pessimistic. You oughta know by now that when there's something that needs doing, we cannot sit here thinking about all the negative outcomes. We might hit roadblocks and, Lord knows, we have our reservations about how all this came about, but it is crucial that we do this... If we don't, who will?"

Mulling this over, I remember the fear I had when I first discovered I was gay. I was afraid to tell my parents for fear that they would kick me out. I wondered where I would go and what I would do to support myself. I think about Orchid and how she had to go to DC to find a home when she was banished. All these things fly through my mind, pushing out all my fears and doubts. Something like this is not just needed in Baltimore, but in areas abroad.

"OK, I'm in."

"Great!" Garrett says brightly. "Plus, I believe this is also a great way to keep Corey's spirit alive."

"Right," Jimmy agrees. "A legacy."

"Somethin' dat might las' a lon' time, jus' like his music is doin' worl' wide," A.D. adds.

I breathe out a sigh, "So, when do we start?"

Just then, we catch sight of a slight teenager with worn shoes, a dirty t-shirt, a pea coat, and torn faded jeans. He is carrying a cardboard sign saying, "Please help me. I'm homeless."

We all look at each other and say, "As soon as possible."

Chapter Twenty-One
"BEFORE WE SAY, 'I DO'"

It is now February 20th, and I am walking along the beach next to the hotel. We are supposed to board the boat tomorrow for the cruise. Jojo, Peep, Jimmy, A.D., and I got here around noon and checked into the hotel. We decided not to tempt fate this time by getting accommodations to make sure we got on the boat. Last time we went, Corey almost made us late. Dean, Roland, Brenda, Mercer, and the Petersons (sans Mike Jr.) are coming tomorrow. Roland almost said no. When I asked him why, he told me plainly, "I'm not saying that you are wrong, but if I got on there and heard the term 'husband and husband'. I can't help it. I'd just start laughing. That's gonna take some getting used to." He changed his mind after I told him that I needed him there… and that he'd have food around the clock. Ha! Wave food in front of that boy's face, and you'll get him every time!

Listening to the strong surge of the ocean crashing and feeling the afternoon breezes of the warm Florida coasts, I reflect on the step I'm about to take. Marriage. A gay marriage. A marriage that will be viewed as an abomination by the church, a mistake career-wise, and a sickness among the homophobes of the world. In three more days, I will be married to Jojo and I am totally lost as to what to do. I have a huge orb of questions that Jojo and I never explored to find the answers to. My stomach is feeling queasy and I feel a bit lightheaded. This is a new chapter. I will be the first in my family to marry my own sex. Eighty percent of my siblings know and are supportive, but what about the rest of the family? When we have the family reunions and I decide to show up with Jojo, how are they going to treat him? How will they treat me?

I remember going back home for the reunion after Corey had his concert in August 2019. The moment I stepped onto the park, I had family members staring at me with such disdain. All the whispering, the pointing, and the derisive laughter and jokes about me and Jojo were nerve-wracking to say the least. Uncle Timothy even had the nerve to ask me with a self-righteous look on his face:

"Are you still a Christian?"

"Yes," I said.

"Well, I just don't see how that is possible. You are in a lifestyle that angers the Lord God."

Oh God, I thought. **There is that fucking word: lifestyle. Now I see why Corey hates the word. Not only does it inaccurately describe the struggle we all as gays have to go through. Whenever people say the word, they have a look of someone who just smelled a pile of horseshit. Plus, I notice that the only time that word is used is when they are talking about us.**

"Well, Uncle Timothy," I said. *"I believe that all of us are in a constant struggle as to what ultimately angers or appeases God, and none can claim carte blanche as to the absolute knowledge of either."*

He looked at me with scathing condescension and said, *"That sounds like that new age mess. Satan has really gotten you deceived. The Bible speaks against homosexuality and for you to willfully practice it is what angers God."*

"The same Bible that was FIRST translated into English by someone who was proven to have had homosexual lovers?"

"We are not back in the time when the Bible was given in English, so the jury is still out on that claim."

"Nor were you living in the Bible days, so you can't really give credence to God's feelings about us gay folks."

He tried to sidestep that fact by saying, *"Well, so King James had men in his bed. Even though that practice is sinful, it just proves that God can use anybody to carry out His work, even a sissy. It doesn't change that fact that it's wrong and God will send you to hell for it."*

The snarky venom I heard in his voice was enough to kill an elephant. *"You know, you church folk who profess to be like God really sicken me with your double standards. I mean, you spend your Sundays praising God and Jesus but have yet to look in the mirror and watch how your face looks when you encounter someone who is gay. Seems like you all need to police your own house. But then again, you pastors and church folk do use homosexuals... just like you **say** God does."*

"What in God's name are you talking about?"

"Homosexuals direct your choirs. Homosexuals play your instruments. Homosexuals look over your church accounts. Homosexuals spend hours praying

and trying to stay loyal to the churches... and many of them are loyal either because they were taught to be, or maybe they just have that type of heart. But you all don't see that. You just continue to use them until something better comes along, then you send them out to pasture."

"That has nothing to do with me because I don't have any 'sissies' on my church staff!"

"How could you know? You are not around them every second of the day. If you were, one would question your own sexuality as well as whether you have a life of your own. And what is this 'my church' mess? I thought it was God's church."

"You know what I mean."

I thought about something that I read when I was in the library studying different kinds of love. One stuck out to me: Koinonia. Armed with this, I asked, *"Uncle Timothy, do you love the Lord."*

"I can't believe you would ask me that. God is my Savior, my healer, my..."

"That's not what I asked you. I asked if you love Him, assuming He is male."

"What do you mean by that?"

"Just answer the question. Do you love the Lord?"

His eyes darted nervously around the park. *"Of course, I love God."*

"Then, if you love God, why do you look at us with such hatred? Isn't God a god of love? And why would you study and swear by a book that was translated into vernacular by the same type of person you preach against and turn your nose up at Sunday after Sunday?"

His mouth dropped open. Of course, he had nothing more to say. He gave me an icy look, turned, and walked away.

I don't remember all the events of that family reunion, but I remember how strong I felt. I was finally standing up for myself and not hiding who I was. I had other members of the relatives to sling a few other snide gems, and I had an answer for all of them. Like these:

"Um... Who's the man and who's the woman?" Aunt Mavis, my Dad's sister, snidely asked. I remember telling her, *"We share the roles, dear auntie. What about you and Uncle Horace? Who's the man in that marriage?"*

"I don't understand how you can sleep with men when God made Man and Woman," My diaconate cousin, Morrice, said with an accusatory tone. He is one of those closet cases that would kiss his wife in public but has his muscular side pieces fuck him repeatedly under the cloak of night. My answer: *"The same way **you** do it. The difference is I don't have a wife to skip out on."*

I was encouraged not to show up for the reunion THIS past summer.

I am thinking of all this even as I see Peep sitting on a rock in the distance, looking contentedly out into the setting sun. I smile, then saunter over. Peep turns, sees me, and smiles back. I sit on the rock beside him. After listening to the surf, I ask, "What are you doing out here?"

"Just reflecting on things," Peep says with his eyes on the waves. He then turns his head to look at me and ask mockingly, "What are *you* doing out here?"

"Jojo is taking a nap and I wasn't sleepy. So, I came out here to clear my head."

"Oh."

We let the waves and the waters fill the gap of silence, then Peep asks, "Are you thinking about Corey?"

I say after a beat, "Not really. When I am in settings like this, I try not to. I am not at the place yet where I can think about him without getting depressed. This is a time to enjoy and reflect."

Another silence. "Peep?"

"Yeah?"

"Do you think that there will ever come a day when we will be accepted?"

Peep lets his silence linger for about ten seconds, then he philosophizes, "You know, I used to ask that same question. But in thinking about it a little more in the last month, I don't know if I want to be accepted."

"What do you mean?"

"Well, I don't profess to be a complete authority on this. It's just my opinion. For me, being accepted means that you are subordinate or beneath the person accepting you. A better question would be, 'Will a day come when we all can co-exist peacefully?' And my answer is, 'I don't know, but I remain hopeful.'"

A starfish crawling along the sand catches my attention before the tide comes and sweeps it away. I think, then say, "I'm trying to understand what thought process can convince these narrow-minded bigots that it's ok to hate and kill us."

"Oh Lionel, please. They have been hating and killing us off for years… and using interesting and inventive ways of doing it. I would say that these psychopaths are geniuses if it wasn't so sad. And might I point out: some of them are probably asking the same question about us gay folk being ok with loving whomever we deem worthy. But I ask you this: Why worry about hatred that started from the day that humans first learned what hate was?"

"Because the same ones that hated gays back then taught their children that same hatred, and that hatred passed down through the generations… to the point where we, the gays of the present, are killed, preached against, shaded, and humiliated because of it."

"But Lionel, the hatred people carry with them is *their* burden. And the reality is that they will refuse us before they attempt to understand us. I guess that's the reason why Corey wanted to start Legacy of Love; so we can not only house displaced kids, but teach both the LGBT and their straight peers that being gay is just one more agent of diversity and it doesn't define your overall existence."

"I don't think I follow."

"Well, let me put it like this. You are gay. Does that make you less human?"

"No."

Peep punches me playfully on the shoulder before he says, "Lionel, the questions you are asking are probably the same questions that were asked back then. But I'm going to tell you something that Corey once said to me."

"What?"

"He said that half of the people who hate us don't even know why. We know that there are those who struggle with their own attractions, but they would die before they admit it. And the others are just following the rhetoric they were taught."

"That makes sense."

"But we can't be stuck on wondering why the contempt exists. Doing that will put a damper on all the strides we are about to make."

"I guess," I say. "Legacy of Love is really needed. I am still a little apprehensive about the startup of this. How are we going to do it?"

"The way we do everything else: on a wing and a prayer. We may have obstacles but if we can learn anything from Corey's life, it is to keep going, no matter what."

"Hmmm…"

We hear the call of the seagulls hovering over the sea. Peep asks, "So, how are you feeling about marrying Jojo?"

I lift myself from the rock and place my hands in my pockets as I scan the immense distance of the sea. "About eighty percent of me is excited and ready to walk down the aisle to become Lionel Davis-Thompson," I muse, turning back to Peep.

"Oh, so you are hyphenating?"

"Yeah," I say, blushing and smiling. "Jojo wanted us to hyphenate because he thought it 'looked cute'." I chuckle and turn back to the sea.

Peep laughs and says, "Ok, ok. What about the remaining twenty percent?"

After reflecting on my next words, I exhale and reply, "That part has me asking myself if I'm doing the right thing." I go back to the rock to sit back down. "Let's face it, Peep. This is not exactly what I'd call status quo-approved."

"No, it's not. No getting around that. But who cares? Status quo can't hold you at night and make you feel safe and loved. Besides, I assume that you and Jojo have had this conversation long before now?"

"Yeah, but we only talked about how to function as far as our careers are concerned. We didn't talk about society at large."

Peep turns his body towards me. "Let me ask you this. When you proposed to Jojo, what was the word you said stuck out to you the most?"

"Fearless."

"I want you to think about the times you were fearless. Three of them stand out for me. One was when you were at your mother's funeral and walked out when the pastor started ranting. Another happened when you kissed Jojo at Corey's concert and in front of that lady with that god-awful dress. And let us not forget the ultimate third that began it all… when you told your mother that you were gay."

I ponder, then admit, "Those were the times when I followed my heart. If my heart tells me I can do it, I do it without even thinking of fear."

"So, why are you showing that fear now?"

"I don't know."

"I do. It is the pre-wedding jitters. You are nervous about saying those words, 'I do". And because of this, you are replaying negative scenarios. But take it from me. If you really love Jojo, the way you will feel when Rev. Washington makes that pronouncement will chase away any feelings of fear that you may have. Maybe even before that."

I look at Peep. His clear, honest eyes are shining with happiness for Jojo and me. "Are you sure?"

"Lionel, look at Jimmy and me. In April, we will be celebrating sixteen years! We both felt the same jitters, but we knew we were doing right. We followed *our* hearts."

In hearing Peep say the last statement, I smile.

"Besides, you are blessed to have relatives that support and love you.

Focus on **them**. The ones that don't want to coexist with you are of no consequence, dear one."

He grabs my head and gives me a soft head bump. Then he puts his arm around my neck as I put mine across his back. There is a beautiful feeling when you can talk with a close friend who understands and embraces the whole you. I am experiencing that feeling right now.

We let the sea carry on its conversation with the surrounding elements of nature as we watch the sun slowly descend. "Peep?"

"Hmm?"

"Speaking of spouses, did you and Jimmy ever talk about why he was so distant?"

Peep cackles and looks dreamy, "Yeah, we did."

"So, am I to deduce from the twinkle in your eye that the conversation turned out well?"

He looks at me with excitement in his face. "You would never believe this, but he was so distant because he was planning our second honeymoon for our sixteenth anniversary!"

"Get out!" I exclaim. "See? I told you that things would be fine. Where are you two going, and for how long?

"We are headed to Dubai and Argentina for two weeks. Where are *ya'll* going?"

"We are headed to Puerta Vallarta… and I'm finally going to Barcelona!"

Peep rolls his eyes heavenward and laughs. "Thank God! You have had a hard on for Barcelona for years. I'm glad you are finally going so you can shut up about it!"

"Oh, come on, I haven't been that overbearing, have I?"

"I plead the fifth. How much you want to bet that you won't even sightsee Barcelona as much as you say you want to?"

"What makes you say that?"

"Because you and Jojo are going to be in that hotel room fucking all the time, or, more accurately put, you fucking Jojo."

"Who says I'm gonna be the only one doing the fucking?"

"Well, Jojo's a bottom, ain't he?"

I grin as my eyes skip coyly from the ocean, to him, and to the ocean again, but I say nothing. Peep reads the hidden message as his face depicts shock.

"Hell naw! He ate your cookies and slid his sausage in your bun, didn't he?"

"I ain't saying nothing!" I tease.

Peep laughs. "You don't have to! It's written all over your face. Oh, you 'ho!"

"What?" I drawl out.

With another chuckle, Peep says, "Well, like Corey said, it's always the quiet ones that end up being the biggest freaks. Anyway, I got twenty dollars saying that you ain't leaving that hotel room as much as you think you will."

"That will be twenty dollars that you will lose," I say, chortling.

"So, is it a bet?" Peep asks.

"It's a bet," I say as we shake on it. Then I add, "I do take postdated checks!"

*****

It is Sunday evening and we are on the ship. For the umpteenth time, I am trying on the suit that Peep made for me while he looks to see if anything needs to be altered. Peep also organized a day of relaxation which includes a facial, a massage with hot stones, a pedicure, and a haircut by Jimmy.

The process for boarding this year was a lot smoother. Rainbow Pride decided to use Funtown Cruise Ships this year, which was a wise decision aside from the faux pas that caused us to move the sail date. The ship is huge and very opulent with various shops, restaurants, spas, and casinos. We decided to chip in and upgrade to the Villa Suite, which has a living and dining room, three bedrooms, and an enormous deck with a hot tub. The living room has a piano in it, which Corey would have put to good use if he was here. There are six of us occupying the suite: Garrett, Dean, Peep, Jimmy, Jojo, and myself, paired up in that order.

Jojo suggested that for the nights before the wedding, Garrett would sleep in the room with me, while Jojo bunks with Dean. I asked him why and he said, "Because when we are in the room by ourselves, we can't keep our hands off each other. The distance will give you something to look forward to." He grabbed my ass on the last sentence. Damn! Something about the way he grabbed it made me hot! I thought that I was going to be the more dominant force in the bedroom during this marriage because, throughout the courtship, I called the shots and topped him. How quickly things shift!

Though the affection was abundant between us, we have not had sex since that night. And it was not because I didn't want to. After I told him how mesmerizing he was as the penetrator, he came up with a game to play until we finally get married called "Hold Out". The object of this game is to refrain from sexual activity, and we can jack off only once per week. *Ugh!*

"I think I might have made the inseam a little too long," Peep says while scanning me in the suit, his face critically pinched.

"Felipe, you had Lionel try on this suit four times in Baltimore, two times in the hotel, and three times on the boat," Eunetta fusses.

"Yeah," Rachel agrees. "Are you running Jojo this crazy with his suit?"

"Bay-BEE, you know he is!" A.D. laughs out, pulling Rachel to him and kissing her, before patting her behind.

Eunetta sees this and quips humorously, "Young man, what makes you think you can feel on my daughter's ass?"

Rachel replies, "Do you hear your daughter complaining?"

"Umm-Hmm!" Eunetta says with her lips pursed. "I'm counting the days when you two tell me that ya'll go'n haul your asses down the aisle. What has it been, two years and some change? In your words, 'Wha's up wit dat?'" She goes up to him and playfully shoves him.

"'Bout dat long, yeh!" Andre replies, smiling bashfully.

"Rachel, can you go over there and see how the suit looks from a distance?" Peep asks in a musing way as she complies.

"Peep, can yuh relax, puleeze! I wonduh why Li'nel's gittin' married an' you de one gittin' de heart attack?" A.D. jokes.

"Lionel was about to have one yesterday, lest we forget. I was instrumental in calming him down. It's my turn now," Peep says in an occupied tone. He stands back to size up the work. "Well, it doesn't look too bad. How does it feel on you?"

"It feels fine. It looks beautiful. Now, quit worrying," I assure.

"Yeah," Rachel agrees. "You talk like you are getting ready for a fashion show."

"Or a designer's audition for Top Model," Eunetta finishes.

"In a way, it is, y'all. This is the first time that people are going to see these designs. I don't want a string out of place." Peep sizes me up again. "Ok, put the suit back in the bag and please smooth it out and hang it up properly. I don't want wrinkles."

While I am doing this, Peep asks, "A.D., I got the red satin shirts. Did you, Roland, and Dean remember to bring your black suits?"

I turn around to look at A.D. He looks shocked. "Uh-Oh…" Eunetta and

Rachel turn to look at him.

Peep looks exasperated. "What do you mean, 'Uh Oh'? A.D., please tell me that you didn't..."

A.D. starts laughing, "Quit yuh worryin'. I wuz jes' kiddin! We bruhs got tuxes! I got mine in muh bag!"

Peep punches him lightly on the shoulder. "You play too much!"

"You need tuh play mo'!"

After hanging up the suit, I ask Eunetta where Jojo is and she tells me that he is on the lido deck getting something to eat. I take the opportunity to grab a parcel to put in my pocket, then go and catch up with him. After a few minutes, I find him leaning over the railing on the aft part of the deck while staring at the sea. I come up behind him and hug him tightly. I feel his body relax against mine.

"How are you, Mr. Davis?"

"I'm better now, Mr. Thompson. I got you."

Jojo chuckles. "You know, I'm really proud of you. You went through some crazy shit last year."

"We both did."

"So, what have you learned from all this, Mr. Davis?"

I hug him tighter and smile as he chuckles. I tell him, "Well, I learned that things are not always what they seem. Years of turmoil with Mama, and I didn't know her story. But, now that I do, I can concentrate on redirecting my emotions to a more positive place, especially after getting that letter from her."

"That's right. That letter seems to have done you a world of good. I see you looking at things differently than before. But you never told me what happened with her."

I hesitate because this is a delicate subject, with Jojo having survived rape and trauma. But with us getting married, he needs to know. I finally say, "My mother was raped by her father and her uncle. And they were sexing each other while raping her."

For a moment, there is silence. Only the conversations of other cruisers can be heard. Jojo gazes at the blue horizon, then asks, "How did you discover this?"

"Mama kept a journal with details. Anyway, it made me understand more deeply why she held all gay men in disdain. And for Dad to cheat on her with Troy didn't help matters."

"How could it?" He sighs in relief as he snuggles up against me and I kiss his beautiful neck. We gaze at the stars shining like diamonds. "I learned something else too."

"What's that?"

"That I have a whole lot of love around me. I got my friends, I got my family, and I got you... I almost lost you all."

"But you didn't," Jojo turns around and grabs my hands.

I think for a second, then I say, "Come with me. I want to show you something." I lead him over to a large wastebasket filled with discarded food.

"What can you possibly show me in a stinking trash can?"

"I think you will like what I'm going to show you." I reach in my pocket and pull out my parcel: The last two bottles of Alprolozine pills. Jojo sees them and tenses but says nothing. I begin to explain.

"I got these last two bottles of pills on the night I got shot. They had been sitting in my glove compartment so long that I forgot them. When I remembered, I was going to throw them away, but I decided to wait until we got on the cruise. I wanted to let you know before we say I do that I am in this for the long haul. And this is my way of showing you how much I love you."

I open the caps of the bottles and dump the pills in the trashcan. I look up and Jojo is smiling broadly at me. He asks me, "Remember when you asked me if I thought we were ready to get married?"

"Yeah."

"I couldn't have asked for a better confirmation than what you just gave me." He grabs me and gives me a huge squeeze. We then go back to the star gazing spot.

"Jojo?"

"Yeah."

"After the night we made love, I've been wondering."

"Wondering what?"

"How our sex life is going to be."

Jojo cackles wickedly. "Well, we both know how to please each other in the bedroom."

"But I didn't know you had that dominant streak in you."

"Well, whenever we had sex in the past, you were always topping me. But, in the words of the late Ms. Whitney Houston, 'I learned from the best. I learned from you.'"

"And all this time, I thought I was learning from *you*."

"Baby, we learned from each other. It's good to know that we are versatile in the bedroom," Jojo pauses before coming closer to whisper in my ear. "Because I love my man's ass... AND dick." He kisses me with a heavenly softness that makes me shudder. Then he steps back to look at me with love in his eyes and a stunning smile on his lips.

Just then, Jojo's face freezes in shock as he looks over my shoulder. I look to see what the expression was all about, and I see a tall, thick man with coal complexion in a captain's uniform. He sports a salt and pepper cut under his captain's hat. He looks at Jojo with surprise.

"Jojo, what's wrong? Who is this?" I ask, looking at the man, then at Jojo.

He turns to me with an incensed look on his face and says these words, "He's my father."

Chapter Twenty-Two

CLOSURE

Words fail us all as Jojo and the man stand opposite each other, as if in the Wild West fighting a duel. I gaze at the man's nametag, which read, "Cpt. Joseph S. Thompson Jr."

"I'll leave you two alone." I say as I turn to go back to the suite.

"No, Lionel. You don't have to go anywhere," Jojo says as he grabs my shoulder. He then looks into my eyes meaningfully. "I want you here."

I glance back at Cpt. Thompson. The look on his face is apologetic and fraught with uneasiness. He steps forward and says in a deep voice, "How are you, son?"

With hostility, Jojo looks at him before saying, "What can I say? I'm here."

Cpt. Thompson takes off his hat and smooths his hair down. "Joseph... When I came across your name, I couldn't believe it. I saw that you were getting married to... Lionel Davis." He looks at me with an unreadable expression. "Is that you, young man?"

"Yes, sir," I say, holding my hand out for a handshake. Stoically, he grabs my hand and shakes it with a strength that almost cracks my bones. I put a little more strength in my grip because I can tell that he is the type that tests the strength of a man yet knows how to handle that of a woman with disarming elegance. Maybe that is how he swept Ms. Thompson off her feet. There is no denying his fiery sex appeal. He obviously felt the strength I transferred into the handshake because he is smiling broadly.

Without a doubt, he is Jojo's father. Jojo has his smile.

"It's good to meet you, Lionel."

Jojo says to him curtly, "I knew you were a captain of Funtown Ships, but I didn't know you were the captain of *this* ship."

A nervous laugh escapes Cpt. Thompson's lips. He says, "Well, we would have met eventually. Fate is designed for that to happen, whether you got on this ship or not."

"I wonder why fate didn't design you to stay where and when your presence was necessary."

"Joseph, please," Cpt. Thompson emits, embarrassed.

"Well, it's the truth. You know, it irks me that you spent my whole life being a captain of ships carrying thousands of people, and you abandoned the one ship with the only two people that needed you the most, your wife and child."

Cpt. Thompson's face floods, "You don't know what happened between your mother and me. I married her at twenty-seven and we had you..."

Jojo interrupts, "Correction: *She* had me."

Cpt. Thompson looks downward in shame.

"What can you tell me, Captain? That you weren't ready to be a father? That things were harder than you thought?"

"The first two years, yes. They were. I was in my last year of studying for my Master's in maritime engineering when I met her in Yeti. I fell in love with her when I first saw her."

"You fell in love with her? Then why did you knock her up and leave her?"

"I did not knock her up and just leave. I wouldn't have married Michelle if I didn't love her."

I excuse myself and ease back to go to the bar and grab a Pina Colada. Being that the bar is a short distance from them, I can hear their conversation quite well. I just feel that it may be a good idea to fall back while staying in the area in case Jojo needs me. During the conversation, I hear Cpt. Thompson explain his case to Jojo.

"I was optimistic when I married your mother. We both moved to Chesapeake Bay with rose-colored glasses on. I remember nights when we would imagine how wonderful our lives would be. But it didn't turn out that way. After graduating and getting my certifications, reality hit us both hard. By this time, she was eight and a half months pregnant with you. I was studying to take my marine captain's exams and working odd jobs around the Bay to support us. It was a miserable time. We became so frustrated about life's craziness that we began turning on each other… She eventually got tired of fighting and went back to Yeti for a few weeks to stay with her mother. While there, she went into labor. She had her mother call me and I flew back just in time to witness you being born." He smiles as he reflects. After a few seconds, he muses wistfully, "You never saw a prouder father than me. When I first saw you, I beamed. It made all those months of chaos seem worthwhile."

Jojo's face is like stone. He folds his arms and looks at the Captain like he's an annoying mosquito. "If you were so proud of me, why did you skip out on us."

"Joseph, I did not skip out on you. After you were born, we went back to the Bay, not foreseeing that life would get much harder. I aced my exams but was finding it hard to find work. The bills were piling up and the money wasn't coming in. Then just after you had turned one, I got a call for a job on a freight ship in Seattle. It was an opportunity to work my way up to the position I have now. I wanted you both to come with me, but Michelle said no. She said that the ship life is too exhausting and that you needed stability. I told her that I had to take the job to support us, but she wasn't hearing that. She wanted me to stay and find something stationary where we were… Joseph, I did not want you to be without me in your life… but I had to take the job to support all of us. When I told her this, she closed her ears and told me not to bother coming back to her if I left. We had a big fight and I left for Seattle while she moved back in with her mother. I tried to send checks to support her and you, but she returned them then filed for divorce after you turned five. When I got the papers. anger at her replaced my concern for you and I just gave up."

"You didn't just give up on sending support. You gave up on us to go traipsing around the world to follow what YOU wanted," Jojo says bitterly. I turn from the bar to view Jojo's face, and it is filled with resentment. "What happened to 'For better or for worse'? Huh? Something tells me that if you had held out a little longer and took care of your responsibilities, you might have found that same opportunity at the Bay."

For the first time in the conversation, Cpt. Thompson's face becomes stern. "What do you want me to say, Joseph? That I was wrong. Well, I was! I know that. I know I should have pushed through my anger to be there for you. I know I wasn't there to teach you things that men are supposed to know. If circumstances were different, I would have raised you with your mother. You would have grown into a man with a wife and kids of your own… You certainly wouldn't be… marrying another man."

"So, my being gay makes me less of a man?" Jojo says, his face is plum colored with fury.

"I'm not saying that, Joseph."

Jojo steps back and temples his fingers. He then says, "Cpt. Thompson, sex with a woman does not make a man. Taking care of responsibilities and not passing the blame to others does. You have worked practically all your life learning to become a captain. But there was one lesson left unlearned, and it's this: A Captain does not abandon his ship. If it is sinking, he finds a way to save all the people on it; not just himself. To make things easier on Mama, I had to be the man of the house even through my attraction to men. And I went through hell trying to prove myself worthy to be called a man!" Jojo shouts before cutting off, his eyes filling with rage. I go over to him to place my hand on his shoulder. As he calms down, he mutters, "For thirty-nine years, your absence is something I have learned to deal with. You say you tried… but I say that trying is not enough. What you prioritize is what you carry out… and obviously Mama and I were not your priority. Lionel, let's go." Jojo takes my hand and we walk away. I twist my head back to look at Cpt. Thompson… and see the overwhelming look of thirty-nine-year-old regret in his eyes.

*****

We go up to the top deck and stand at the railing, the night breeze blowing lightly. There is silence between us, broken by Jojo. "I know you have something rattling around in your brain about all this shit."

"It's probably the same thing you got in yours."

Jojo blows out a puff of air and looks out at the sea. At length, he says. "I have rehearsed that moment for years. Practiced all the things I was going to say and all the ways that I would say it. Now that I've seen him and got all this shit off my chest, I am lost as to how to proceed with him." He looks at me and asks, "How would you feel if you were in my shoes?"

I shrug my shoulders and say, "I'd probably feel the same way you're feeling."

We let the ocean fill the space of quietness between us. Afterward, he asks half-rhetorically, "What do I do? I've been carrying this hurt in me for so many years. I had to sit there and watch as Mama worked three jobs to support us. Cosmetologist, day care worker, secretary, even housekeeper. She became so worn out that she couldn't even lift her hand. Then she hooked up with Mike and fell for his bullshit, promising her the world and not telling her that all the affection and money came at a cost. When he split, she was worse than she was before meeting him. No money. No job. To this day, I am grateful for your Dad caring enough to help her get that job at his firm. That was needed because there were times when she'd be crying and worrying about where our next meal was coming from."

"I remember you telling me that. I also remember when you took on a few odd jobs to help support."

He looks lost in the memory of those years. I have to call his name a few times to get his attention. He snaps back to earth, saying to me, "I'm sorry… This whole thing is crazy… Thirty-nine years of wondering… Hoping to meet my dad… then becoming angry when those hopes remained unfulfilled. Then when I finally meet him… My God!" Jojo gushes in passionate frustration as he turns his face to hide his betraying emotions. "He comes with all these fucking excuses and lies trying to turn it around on Mama."

I remember what Jojo told me about my own anger with my mother, but how can I convey the same thing to him about his anger toward his father?

Finally, I say, "Jojo, there is no way that you can know what happened between your parents, other than talking with your dad. You were just one year old when they split up. The hurt that you carry is valid, but I think a little of your mother's anger bled into you."

"What do you mean?" Jojo says as he spins around, his face hard.

"I mean that you spent all this time hearing what your father should and could have done but failed to carry out."

"My mother rarely mentioned Dad to me. When she did, she didn't run him down."

"But when my mother and yours were friends, she talked about him to her. I happened to hear their conversation one time and it wasn't all peaches and roses. It was an all-out gripe session about men being dogs."

"You heard her?"

"Yes. But I'm going to be real with you. From what I heard her tell Mama, both of your parents' versions of the story do not conflict each other. As angry as they were with one another, they obviously still loved each other enough to stick with the truth."

"So what? He left me, Lionel. He left us. If he hadn't, things would have been better."

"And you know that for certain?"

"Well, not for certain. But at least, I would be able to say that he was around. Look, the bottom line is that HE took off. I'm just supposed to forgive thirty-nine years of his absence?"

"Thirty-eight. He was around for that first year, remember? I know people whose fathers weren't around at all! And yes; even though it might take a while, you will have to forgive him eventually. Otherwise, you will be making the same mistake both your parents made… and I made with you and everybody who cared about me. Being angry about the situation and making the innocent pay for what they didn't cause."

"I thought you would be on my side with this," Jojo says in a sullen tone.

"Jojo, I'm always going to be on your side. But I am also taking this opportunity to give you a huge dose of the same medicine you spoon-feed to others," Jojo turns back towards the ocean as if trying to glean answers from it. Taking care to soothe my voice, I put my hand on his shoulder. "Babe, you cannot effectively tell me to move on and forgive my mother when you are not prepared to do the same with your father."

"But Lionel, he was wrong for what he did."

"And your mother didn't have a part to play in that?"

"No!"

"Jojo," I say. "Come on now. He wanted back in your life. Surely you must have heard your mother telling someone that."

"Maybe, but she had a good reason for not allowing it. She didn't want us both shunted from one destination to the next on some cruise ship or waiting for months at a time for Dad to come home. She was just watching out for me!"

"But she didn't have to keep him out of your life. Look Jojo," I say, turning him around gently to face me. "Your mother made the right decision by keeping her feet rooted so she could raise you on stable ground. I applaud her for that. But honestly… I cannot begrudge your father for going after his dream. It's just the way he did it that's the problem. The way I see it, *both* your parents have something to answer for… not just your father. They both were wrong, but he is trying to make amends for his part."

Suddenly, I think of a sure-fire way to reel him in. I turn towards the ocean, coyly smiling.

Jojo looks at me, saying, "What's that grin about?"

"Oh, not much. I just seem to remember someone saying that you still have to do what is right with people who treat you foul. Sounds like good advice to me."

I give him a sneaky side-eye as he grants a small smile, then pokes me in my side. "You don't ever play fair, do you?"

"What?" I say, with big eyes and an innocent smile.

"Don't give me that look! You know exactly what you did. Took what I said to you years back and use it to school me!"

I laugh and say, "Well, I'm sneaky like that."

"I'm going to have to keep my eye on you!" Jojo says with mock suspicion, wagging his finger at me slowly. He then wraps his arms around my body. We let the air caress our skins as we engage in a lover's embrace and kiss. When we part, we gaze into each other's eyes while holding hands. Jojo looks contemplative as he says, "Forgiving him is going to be hard; you know."

"Such is life, babe. But you need closure just like I did with Mama. Hey look. If it will make it any easier, remember this. Your father did not hurt you and your mother on purpose. He was young. The youth of yesterday don't always know what the elders of today know. And I am not excusing him. But you both need to sit down and talk. You might be able to get answers from him that you can't get from your mother. Also, he is the only surviving parent you have. Who knows how much time you are given with him? I'd make good on *this* time while I got it."

"And what about what he said about my marrying you."

"Well Jojo, he was speaking from a time when men didn't get married. He's old school but I really feel that honest communication might clear the air. Plus, it will benefit us both to get married without hangups. Come on, just go talk to him... for me... For us... And most importantly, for yourself."

"OK," he says, taking a deep breath. He walks toward the steel stairs headed downward as I turn back toward the ocean. I hear his sweet beautiful voice call my name, "Lionel?"

"Yeah," I say, still looking to the ocean, but smiling.

"Thank you."

"What for?"

"Just for being the strong, stubborn, hard-headed, and sweet husband-to-be that I've dreamed of."

The tenderness and heartfelt emotion in his voice cause tears to enter my eyes and roll down my cheeks. And somewhere in my spirit, I can sense the tears coursing down his face. I feel him wrap his arms around me from behind, causing us both to laugh with the contentment of a couple celebrating their fiftieth anniversary.

"Just reciprocating, baby. Just reciprocating. Now quit stalling and go talk to your dad."

*****

I go to the restaurant to sit, eat, and think. It's funny how fate deals itself in life's game even without being asked to play. Right before we get married, Jojo's dad comes in the picture. It was as if life hurled a test onto Jojo's lap and was telling him, "Ok. You say you are ready to face the world as a gay married man. See what you can do with this." I have a quick word with God, asking for Jojo and the Captain to find some common ground, to forgive where needed, and to move forward.

After eating and walking off the food, I make my way back to the suite. As I walk into the darkened living room, I see Peep and Jimmy on the couch watching a movie, or rather the movie was watching them. They were too involved in each other; just chuckling and kissing the night away… with their muscular bare upper bodies catching the blue light of the TV. I clear my throat affectedly, causing them to turn my way in slight alarm. This is the first time I have seen those two in this type of intimate setting, and it is quite comical. They casually reach for their shirts and slip them on.

I smirk at them, saying, "So, this is what Jojo and I are in for after hitching up?"

"In the beautiful and bona fide flesh, baby!" Peep laughs out.

Jimmy looks at me sheepishly as he turns on a lamp and says, "I told Feli that we should have went to our room… but we got a little hot and bothered."

"No need to explain good loving. It's actually nice to see you two so uh… demonstrative."

"Uh-huh! Where is Jojo?"

I take my time and choose an overstuffed armchair to sit in. Then I say, "You will never guess."

"Probably not, so tell me," Peep quips.

"His birth father is the captain of this ship and Jojo is talking with him."

"Shut your mouth!" Peep says with his mouth dropped open.

Just then, Garrett, A.D., Roland, and Dean come in, just laughing and joking like they have been friends for years. They stop short when seeing us in conversation.

"What's going on?" Roland asks.

After I fill them in on the events of the last few hours, Dean says, "Well

The Cost

I hope Joe and his father are able to patch things up."

"So, do I," Garrett says. "But I wouldn't hold out much hope for it to happen right away."

"What do you mean," Roland asks.

"Welp," A.D. reflects, wisdom shining in his eyes. "Joe spent all 'is life widdowt 'is daddy. It's go'n take a good lil' minit befo' he kin find 'is own peayce wit 'im."

*****

We wait for Jojo to come back, half expecting that it would be a while, given the circumstances that he and his father had to discuss. Finally, just after two a.m., we decide to head to our bedrooms. We were slightly drunk from both the champagne and the gentle swaying of the boat in the sea's breeze. Peep pulls Jimmy into their room, presumably to finish the lovemaking I walked in on. They sure as fuck aren't going to be sleeping, at least until they exhaust each other sexually.

Garrett and I are in our separate beds with the bedroom's sliding glass doors open and the filmy curtains floating in the darkness. But despite the champagne and the promise of slumber it carried, we lay awake for hours talking. We talk about our careers, our families, and life in general. It's much like that first conversation we had on the phone years ago. The exchange is lively and robust but when we start talking about Corey, he chokes up.

"Are you ok, Spades?" I ask him.

"I'm getting there, Blackjack. It's weird being here without my baby."

I breathe in the sweet scent of the sea, then say, "I know what you mean."

"Do you think I'll ever meet anybody like him?"

"No."

"Why not?"

"Speaking pragmatically," I say in a scholarly tone, causing him to chuckle. "Corey and whomever you meet will differ from each other. There may be things about the person that remind you of Corey, but it won't be him."

"I know. I don't know if I'm ready to find the guy anyway."

"Maybe not. You are still grieving, as we all are. This is going to take time, but Corey would not want us to put our lives on hold and *continue* grieving. You do know that, don't you?"

"I know."

A gentle knock is heard, and Jojo pokes his head in. He looks content. "Oh, I didn't mean to wake you both."

"It's ok, we're just up talking about Corey and life," Garrett says.

"Great! Uh Lionel, can I talk to you?"

I remove the covers from me and stand up. I gesture toward the sliding doors to the balcony, "Spades, do you mind us going out here and shutting the door. We'll only be a minute."

Garrett hoots and says with the playful innocence of Mike Jr., "Blackjack, who you kidding? We all know that ya'll are gonna be longer than a minute. Take all the time you need."

Jojo and I step out on the balcony. As soon as I close the door, and turn to face him, I feel his lips on mine and his arms around my body.

"Mmmmm..."

After a minute of kissing, I ask, amused, "What was that for?"

"For reminding me of the lesson that I thought I was teaching you. It seems that I had one coming myself, Mr. Davis."

I laugh and hold him tighter, "So, am I to assume that the conversation went well, Mr. Thompson?"

"It... wasn't half bad. He did explain the remark and confirmed what you said about him being old school but he told me that even if he had been in my life, he would have no viable say as to who I love. He told me I needed to be happy and that he hoped he could be part of that happiness."

"So, are you both going to continue communicating?"

"We have each other's numbers, so we'll see. I still have questions... Still have unresolved issues. But I'm willing to see what happens from this point on."

I hug him with a force that staggers us both. "My turn to say this: I'm proud of you."

We watch as the sun makes its slow appearance on the watery horizon.

I look at my watch, which reads five fifty-nine. "Wow, were we up that long?"

"It looks that way."

I turn him around and hold him from behind. "So, are you ready to be my valentine for life?"

Jojo giggles, "Boy, Valentine's Day been passed."

"My heart doesn't know that." We contentedly look at the horizon again. I pose the question, "Do you think we will make it?"

Jojo leans his head back and breathes evenly. "I think we will have our sunrises and sunsets being married. But even in the darkest nights we face, we will make it."

"How?" I question. Then, Jojo gestures to the sun rising.

"By remembering this moment. As long as we know that there is always a dawn coming, our lives together will always have beauty and longevity."

I smile. "Hmm… Seems I'm not the only poet between us."

Jojo turns with a smile and puts his arms on my shoulders. He says to me before his lips softly caress mine, "Baby, I believe that all our lives are living and breathing examples of poetry. But our marriage is going to be one long, beautiful symphony… one that will make Corey smile, wherever he is in the universe."

"Kiss-Kiss."

"Kiss."

To Continue…

"Lionel?" I hear Jojo nudge me. I come alive.

"What?" I hear titters and giggles among the people viewing the wedding.

"Good Lawd, Li'nel! De Rev'n done asked if yuh gone marry Jojo! Wake up, dude!"

I feel my heart swelling and my head is incredibly light. I feel as if I am floating on a cloud. I practically shout out happily, "Yes! Yes! A thousand times YES!" I see Jojo grinning at me and I am in complete awe. I am ready for this ceremony to hurry up and finish so I can be with my baby.

"About time," Roland shouts.

"You are out in space!" Brenda exclaims. Mercer smiles as he wraps his arm around her. She cranes her head back to kiss Mercer lovingly.

Reverend Washington grins and turns to Jojo. "Joseph Stanley Thompson III, do you…"

"Yes!" Jojo shouts with the same energy. Once again, there is hilarity on the deck.

"Well! I know two men who are eager to get married. Can't even let me finish," Reverend Washington says, chuckling. He calls for Dean to present the rings, then for us to speak our vows and exchange them. He continues:

"Before we proceed with the ceremony, I would like to read a note to the both of you, penned by your best friend and former minister of music at Unity and Love Church, Cordell Rodgerick James Kennedy. He gave this to me at the beginning of October when we were originally supposed to cruise, because there was a possibility that he had to be on tour." There is a reverent hush on the packed deck. All we hear are the winds and the whisper of the waters as the sunset paints our faces a romantic saffron color. Reverend Washington proceeds to read the letter.

To My hardheaded friend Lionel and my Sugar sweet buddy Jojo,

I am so sorry that I could not be there. I gave this letter to Reverend Washington to read in case I could not make it. So, if you are hearing this, it means that I could not come on the cruise to witness this moment. However, I hope this letter can pinch hit, so to speak.

Over the years, I have learned some things about love. I learned that it is not the temporary feeling of bliss felt in a fleeting moment of passion. Love abounded in the many years that all four of us have experienced in the fabulous friendship we had and continue to have. The only difference is that two of us are getting married. I told you that I smelt the wedding coming!

Love means to be adventurous while people around you are afraid of taking chances. I do not believe that half the people in this world really know what love is. But to me, love is sunshine even when storms are raging around you.

Love is like dwelling in the eye of a hurricane. The outer winds and rain may cause unfathomable calamity; but inside the hurricane is peace and calm. Love is kissing and being blithely unaware of the passion you display to a world full of people that frown on our kind. Yet, they are choking on the vine from not having a love of their own.

Love is being fearless and courageous. It means standing up for yourself and for the one you were made to love, even at the mercy of devastation and danger. This love I wish for you. I wish this and much more. I love you both with all my heart and I raise my prayer to God that you have a long and happy life. I will see you when I get back.

All my love, Corey.

P.S. Peep, please hug them both for me. I love you too, with your ornery ass.

Damn. Leave it to Corey to put his mark on the ceremony even without him being here. There is not a dry eye to be found, especially among those who knew Corey well. But between Jojo, Peep, and me, the emotions are most abundant. As Peep cries, Jimmy puts his arm around him.

Overcome with emotion himself, Reverend Washington barely croaks, "At this time, we are going to ask Darrell Alston, Brother Kennedy's music partner, to come and favor us with a song."

With his guitar in his hand, Darrell takes the platform. He grabs the mic stand and sits on the stool provided for him. After adjusting the microphone, Darrell says, "First, I would like to offer my sincerest congratulations to Lionel and Joseph. Corey talked about you both, as well as Felipe. It's obvious that you have a beautiful friendship."

Darrell clears his throat and continues, "The song I'm about to sing is the last one that Corey and I wrote together. If he were here, he would sing it with me… But…" Darrell stops, looking at Peep, then Jojo and me. He exhales to keep from crying. When he finds his voice, he says, "As much as it hurts me to tell you on this special occasion, Corey was killed last October."

Scattered expressions of sadness blanket the deck. A few people lament about the hatefulness of the world. Darrell goes on, "These things we read about every day. Transwomen being killed for having the chutzpah to own their lives. Same gender loving people being abused, maligned, and maimed by bigots. And on and on. But, working with Corey has reminded me that we have the power to change things if we all come together as one."

As he plucks the strings of the guitar and sings with his smooth voice, Jojo and I gaze at each other. I listen to the lyrics of the song and they are so beautiful that I can do nothing but mourn the gift of Corey being taken from this world while I concurrently encourage the gift of Darrell who remains here to bless it.

Come fly with me. Let's soar into sweet freedom.
Flowers and hearts that bloom in every season.
Don't be afraid. Take my hand. If you fall, I got you.

Let's take a chance. Let's build a world together.
Sunshiny days to break through stormy weather.
We waited so long for love sublime. Now I'm yours and you're mine.

The first time I saw you, I saw Diamonds and silver. I heard soft breezes whisper.
In your eyes, my world lies. Although I may not know much, and sometimes my tongue may fail.
This I know. Oh baby. I love you.

As the song is being sung, Jojo and I break protocol and move to embrace each other, We begin to sway to the music, mindless of all the people watching. As we dance, I remember the way we swayed in the snow and listened to the music within us. I remember the way we swayed with grief in our minds.... with Maxwell's voice in our ears. It feels so good to hold him in my arms. I make a silent promise here and now to protect and cherish this man. I will be his strength when he weakens. I will be his shelter of love when the world brings blizzards of hate. I make this solemn vow before all.

Yes, I do.
  Yes, I can.
    Yes, I will!

As Darrell ends the song, we kiss even before the Reverend has the chance to say, "I now pronounce you husband and husband, and I present to the world, Lionel and Joseph Davis-Thompson."

Amid the cheers and the congratulations (and the good-natured schoolboy titters coming from Roland), I embrace my love. I look towards the setting sun and I see a guy there among the sheer, flowing curtains. He was dressed in a white suit and a black and red shirt. He has curly black hair, glowing butterscotch skin, and a huge megawatt smile on his face. He looks like… Corey! I shut my eyes, then open them again. No… it's not him. Just a look-a-like.

He comes up to us and bestows his congratulations, offering his hand to shake ours in turn. The moment his hand touches mine, I smell a whiff of his cologne. Curve! That was Corey's favorite cologne! I stare at him in amazement.

"Is there something wrong?" he asks.

"No," I sputter. "I'm sorry for staring. You just remind me of Corey." I look at Jojo, asking. "I know you see the resemblance. Doesn't he look like him? Even has on the same cologne."

Jojo looks closer. Then, he looks back at me with a shocked expression.

The stranger laughs, saying cryptically, "Well, there's an old saying. 'Those that leave us in body find ways to be there in spirit."

"Lionel, Jojo," We hear Eunetta call us, sounding like both our mothers. We turn toward her direction. "Come on and cut this cake. The folks are hungry and we wanna serve it before your brother eats it all."

"We'll be right there," Jojo says. We then turn back to the stranger, with Jojo saying, "I'm sorry, we have to…" He stops short because the space where the stranger stood is now vacant. All we see are the flowing voile curtains blowing in the wind.

Was he an angel? An apparition? Or was he just a guest that had to get somewhere quickly?

I pull Jojo to me, both of us chilled to the bone, puzzled of the ghostly experience yet hopeful that the encounter proved to be an omen of a bright future filled with wonder and blissful enchantment. It also lent a peace in my heart and mind as well as assurance that Corey is OK, wherever he is.

*****

As my husband sleeps, I sit at my drafting table while writing my thoughts, as always. It's been four months since the wedding, and they were filled with affection, emotion, and new discoveries. After the wedding cruise, Jojo and I hopped on the plane to our dual-location honeymoon.

How was it? Oh, it was fabulous! In Puerta Vallarta, we got on the jet skis for the first time. Jojo tried to show off by trying to pop a wheelie. He could do it on his bicycle when we were kids, but I never could. I tried to tell him that a bike and a jet ski are two different things. But would he listen? Noooo… His ass flew off the jet ski and into the water. It's a good thing the water wasn't too deep. I laughed and kidded him about that the whole time we were at P.V., making him mad. Ha! His fault! Nobody told him to do that shit!

Ok, Ok. Maybe there was another reason he was mad. I did pull a small prank on him. He asked me to mix him a bloody Mary and I did… only I put a little Cayenne pepper and Jalapeno in there to give it a little kick. I laughed my ass off watching as he ran around the hotel room trying to cool his tongue, then diving for the bathroom sink and sucking water from the stream pouring from the faucet.

But you know the saying; *What goes around comes around*. MY comeuppance happened in a Japanese restaurant we went to in Barcelona called Shichiro's. You see, I ordered a Thai dish called kaproaw mu. Jojo recommended it to me, advising me to order it "pet mak". He neglected to tell me that the term meant *very spicy* in Japanese! When that shit touched my tongue, I started clamoring and crying for water. The waiter brought water, but it wasn't enough! When we ran out at our table, I hopped from table to table bumming water from other patrons, crying and flapping my arms the whole time. By the time I got to the fourth table and gulped half a pitcher of water, the heat subsided. I turn my head slowly towards Jojo, who had this huge grin on his face. I walk back to my table, amid the laughter of the other patrons. I sit down to find Jojo laughing as well. Good sport that I am, I began laughing too, saying, "Well, I did have it coming." During our gales of laughter, we called a truce in the war of pranks.

In these weeks of married life, I am living it up! It feels good just to have him near me, cooking delicious dishes together and gazing into each other's eyes while talking about life. Upon renting out his townhome, he sold some of his furniture and moved his personal belongings here. We placed his living room set into my upstairs den, at my behest. I remembered a workshop I attended that emphasized the importance of spouses having their own thinking spot. I have my den downstairs, so it is only fair that he has a space to meditate alone.

I went to see Dr. Banneker shortly after returning to Baltimore. Seated in our regular position, I went on about the nuptials and the wonderful life I found with Jojo (so far). He asked me how I felt now, and I told him this, "I really feel that I have a clear path now, and ironically, Mama's letter helps me when I feel shaky. It's strange that each day after marrying Jojo and getting the message from Mama brings a freedom."

"A freedom?"

"Yes. A freedom to love and care for another and allow myself to be loved and cared for. A freedom to not agonize and overanalyze the way things are but to simply live and love in abundance. I am learning that it does not benefit me to yearn for total acceptance in a world where the hatred for gays and trans grows as the days pass. Instead, I have to find ways to work and survive alongside those who don't understand our struggle and hope that an opportunity presents itself where I can educate them. I may not understand why people hate us to the point of extermination, but I do understand that the way to combat that hatred is by giving myself authentic love… and stretching that love to cover all who are in desperate need of it."

Upon hearing this, Dr. Banneker got up and requested for us to switch seats. The moment I sat in the chair facing the open window, the sun hit my eyes and made me flinch. Dr. Banneker saw this and smiled. He said, "No doubt you've been wondering about the opposite setup of these chairs. Well, when you were facing the door, your path was filled with hard truths: truths about yourself and this world that you felt you couldn't meander through or even stand toe to toe with. But hearing the clarity in your voice as you made your statement, I believe you see the benefit of facing those truths head on that have been hard to examine in the past, just like the sun in your eyes. At first glance, we turn our eyes away because the sun's light hurts them. But here is a concept that should be explored figuratively. If you look at the sun long enough, you will see it for what it is: just a sphere of ever-changing consciousness. When you can do that, it makes it easier to face almost anything." *Go Head, Doc!*

To help my healing along, I went ahead and mailed Troy Matterson the crumpled, yellowed letter that he wrote so many years ago. I thought of sending my letter from Mother but decided to hold off until I felt it was necessary. Five days later, he called me to thank me for sending it, but he initially wasn't sure about what to do with it. But his lover, who worked for the Birmingham District Attorney's Office, pulled some strings to try to find the shotgun that Mama used to shoot Dad. They went to the house and looked feverishly. Finally, the new owners of the house found it in the back shed, wrapped in an old burlap cloth. After rewrapping it carefully, they called Brenda, who in turn took it to the Yeti Police Precinct. They dusted it for fingerprints and discovered my mother's, and not Troy's. They also went to forensics where the original bullet was and matched it with the remaining bullets in the gun. At the time, the detectives told Troy that because no gun was found on the scene, there was probable cause that Troy did not commit the murder. They offered to find the gun but stopped when Troy kept insisting on his guilt. Through all of this, there may be a chance that Troy will be exonerated, although he may receive a penalty for lying to the police in covering up my mother's crime. Still, they may consider the time he served as punishment enough. I pray for his success. No one should have to pay for a crime they didn't commit.

Things at the firm are as busy as ever. We now have clients beating down our doors, especially after the marketing strategy for the VaVoom campaign proved tremendously fruitful. Stores were selling out of the product and the company had to hire a bigger corporation to expand the mass production of the perfume. We just wrapped up the work with the Nesbitt campaign, and my hope is that we can work the same magic with it, as well as the others. The firm is negotiating a deal to lease four floors in one of the buildings in downtown Baltimore. If all goes well, we can move from the large office building in White Marsh to the high rise on 414 Light Street. I hope the negotiations do not fall through. It would be nice to live and work in the same area instead of taking that long drive to White Marsh every day.

Peep and Jimmy just returned from their second honeymoon two weeks ago. After hearing about the awesome time Jojo and I had in Barcelona, they decided to make that one of their destinations. Speaking of which, I had to fork over the twenty dollars Peep bet me, because Jojo and I didn't do half as much sightseeing and exploring the city as I said we would. We went on a few tours. But, most of the time, we were so busy um… exploring each other. Ha!

Oh, guess what. Through the wedding suits he tailored, Peep left such an impression on The Rainbow Pride organizers that they offered him an event to highlight his fashion next year. When I asked him how he felt about it, he said, "I feel ecstatic. It looks like the good Lord is working miracles overtime, with the help of Heaven's newest and bossiest resident, Corey."

My family is progressing. We are doing what we can to keep open communication and it has been extremely healthy. I found out that each of us got a letter from Mama and each letter held a special message of love, apology, and reconciliation, as everyone learned from reading them to each other. Well, everyone except, (you guessed it!) Rhonda. I don't think we will ever know what Mama wrote to her. I will say this though; it must have done her some good. After the house sale, we divided the funds and, for once, Rhonda listened to sound advice. She completed her probation shortly before the house was sold. When the purchase was final and the money was split, she took her share and made a down payment on a nice small house in Birmingham, put the rest in a bank, and got a job as an advocate for an inner-city school while studying cosmetology at the Venice School of Cosmetic Arts. We are still not on the best of speaking terms, but what can I say? I still love her… and that will never change.

After I got my share, I gave a large portion to the start-up fund for Legacy of Love, Corey's vision. The contribution was financially matched by Peep, Jimmy, Jojo, Garrett, Darrell, and A.D. Since Peep's return, he, Garrett, and Jojo have been working hard trying to find benefactors to provide a little seed money to revamp Corey's house. Jojo told me they were seeking contributions so we could hold off on spending money from the inherited accounts. Our first benefactors were Devetra Nash and this affluent LGBTQ organization called The Belvedere Club. Ms. Nash provided two hundred thousand dollars and The Belvedere Club provided four times that amount. Jimmy, Rachel, Eunetta, and I have been researching the Maryland Codes of Safety as well as items to pass inspection. If all goes well, Legacy of Love may begin serving our youth by December of 2022.

A.D. and Rachel? My God! You'll never believe this but, my dear brother that's full of surprises, proposed to Rachel during a beautiful toast at our wedding reception and she happily said yes, as Ms. Eunetta cried, hugged, and fussed at the same time. Like Jojo and I, they decided on a long engagement to ensure their readiness to link up. I tell you; I couldn't be prouder. Plus, I will be gaining Garrett, Mike Jr., and Eunetta as new family members! Ain't that nice! Yes, A.D. is still working at the airport and going to Baltimore City Community College where he is finishing his sophomore year. From what he tells me, his doing quite well and on schedule to graduate in May of 2023. I am still shocked at the confession A.D. made on the plane... and I'm wondering how they are going to play THAT one out in their marriage... seeing as how he said that my future sister-in-law was almost as freaky as my husband. I never would have thought my street-smart, playa-playa brother would have played on both sides of the fence. Go figure!

Garrett is dealing with his grief for Corey in stages. Some days are more challenging than others, but he did tell me that he and Darrell Alston have begun to become close. Sharing their grief at first, they began to see each other as friends, but I have a sneaky suspicion that it may be progressing to more. I cautioned both Garrett and Darrell, whom I have begun a good friendship with, to be careful. "With you both still in the grieving process, a relationship may be risky," I tell them. But the more I see them together, the less I worry.

Mike Jr. is as adorable as ever with his clever view of the world. He is much wiser than his years, yet childlike in his curiosity. I remember a conversation we had when I went over to Eunetta's for dinner. Ms E., Rachel, he, and I were just sitting out on the front porch when he asked me in his sweet caring way how I was holding up after losing "Mr. Corey". I told him that I was doing ok. He asked me, "What's the big deal about gay folks?"

The question took me by surprise. I looked at Rachel, who shrugged as if to say, "Answer the boy." I asked him, "What do you mean?"

"I mean, I hear boys at my school callin' other boys 'faggy'. I see people get crazy when they see two girls even holding hands. One time on TV, I saw this preacher yellin' about 'Adam and Eve' not 'Adam and Steve'. And I wanna ask them, 'Why are y'all so mean?'"

I cleared my throat and told him, "Well Jitterbug, many of them don't understand how love works. That true love has nothing to do with whether you love a boy or girl. The only thing that matters is that you CAN love someone and have others love you in return. People who hate and hurt others have never learned how to love and help."

"I feel bad for those folks. It must be a sad life to go around hating people." He got quiet for a few seconds, then said, "You know what?"

"What?"

"I have these two boys who pick on me all the time. Pullin' on my hair and callin' me names."

"Does that bother you?"

"Sometimes. But I think that they both really like me."

"Why you say that?"

"I gotta be on their mind a lot for them to pick on me so much. Maybe that's the same problem with those people who pick on gay folks."

Hearing this, Eunetta, Rachel, and I burst into loud tempests of laughter. When we calmed down, I said, wiping moisture of joy from my eyes, "Jitterbug, you got more smarts in your little head than most adults have in their whole bodies."

Hilarious as that might have been and as truthful as his view was, I find myself praying for his innocence, intelligence, and resilient nature to remain intact, particularly when I see these gangs on the corners of Pennsylvania and North Avenue smoking, robbing, selling dope, and fighting each other. They do not care who they hurt, whose kids they're recruiting to sling dope for them, or what teenager ends up on a morgue's slab with a toe tag attached. I comfort myself though on the fact that he is getting quality home training and love from his uncle, his grandmother, and his mother. I pray for him, as well as Katie and Orchid, who is graduating in June and traveling to Los Angeles to stay with a friend of Miss Zena's and complete her studies in Criminal Law and LGBTQ Civil Rights.

Oh my God! What turbulence. What harrowing decisions. And yet… what bliss to come from it all. I lost a mother, but I gained understanding and an unaffected ability to forgive. I lost a friend through senseless violence, but I gained more appreciation for the ones I have left as well as the need to be of help to others. I thought I lost my self-worth, but with the help of friends as well as reconnection to family and faith in the Creator and myself, I realize that my worth was always there… yet it was waiting to embrace me when I acknowledged its presence.

I have also learned that for everything that looks good to the eyes from pills to prosperity, a price must be paid. But we are always given options before the cost is revealed, and it pays to root out the price from every clever scheme that paints rosy pictures of the options. Then, we must weigh every option on the scales of life to see what we can surely gain, as well as what we are fated to lose.

I have no more blank pages in this journal, but I did buy another notebook, which is sitting in our nightstand. Blank pages of lines waiting to be filled with words of life. The one I am writing in now is full of things I've said out loud, as well as thoughts I've pondered intently. Some entries are questions about the complexities of what exists, and others are answers to those questions based on my own logic.

Hmmm… Maybe I will lay my journaling aside for a while to focus on my worth, my husband, my career, my family, my friends, and the healing memories of my departed mother, Lynetta, and dearest brother, Corey. Then again, who knows what new adventures the years ahead will bring? Perhaps, another entry to this saga I call my life. Anyway, whether I continue writing or not, I will take every available opportunity to forgive wrongs done to me, to admit to wrongs I've done to others, to listen more without making harmful assumptions, and to finally have peace with all that has troubled me.

To end this narrative concerning this part of my life, I acknowledge that I have made decisions both right and wrong, but I like to think I am learning from them, and gaining enough wisdom to ask the questions:

Are the costs behind my decisions too steep for me to pay?

And will each decision yield favorable results… or cause devastating regrets?

THE END

is not yet here.

The struggle to coexist harmoniously continues…

DISCUSSION QUESTIONS

There are no right and wrong answers, as some see things differently than others. These questions serve merely to encourage discussion.

1. Do you think there is an influx of doctors of all practices that do not take the health of their patients seriously? What do you think could be the reasons that doctors lose their empathy?

2. Jojo, Peep, Corey, and others have tried to tell Lionel about the things dragging him down, but Lionel rejects their warnings. Why do you think it is hardest for many to hear caution from loved ones, whether they are friends, natural family, or both?

3. In remembrance, Peep lied to his grandmother about his sexuality, even though she said she loved him no matter what. What do you think might have happened if he told the truth?

4. In different parts of the novel, Lionel expressed that unresolved issues people possess have potential to morph into life threatening ailments. Do you share his view? Why or why not?

5. Lionel confessed to Jojo about his encounter with Ben Longwood. What do you think of Jojo's reaction? What would you have done?

6. What roles do you think Floyd, Katie, and Eunetta play in Lionel's life? How about Mike Jr, and Orchid?

7. Do you see a parallel between Corey and Floyd in what they were trying to teach Lionel?

8. What are your feelings about the lesson the Davis siblings decided to teach Rhonda? Do you think she deserved it?

9. In your opinion, are there a lot of families that resemble the dysfunction of the Davis family, excluding the murder of Lionel's father by Lynetta's hands? What could be some reasons for the dysfunction?

10. Regarding what happened to both Lionel and Corey, what are your thoughts on how hatred motivated the attacks. Do you feel angry, sad, indifferent?

11. Throughout the novel, there are examples of hatred and religious disdain for the LGBTQ family. What are some other examples that might have happened to you? How did you feel during the occurrence?

12. What are your feelings concerning Jojo's father? Do you think both his parents could have work things out and stayed together or co-parented separately? Was Jojo's father wrong for taking the job and moving to Seattle?

13. Regarding Sonny Daniels, it is obvious that he nurses destructive hostility toward gay individuals which inevitably became his downfall. What is your theory on why homophobia exists and what are some things we can do to conquer it or lessen the effects on us as a community?

14. What are your feelings about what Floyd was trying to convey to Lionel both in the restaurant and on the getaway?

15. Though we read very briefly about the presence of cannabis (marijuana) at the getaway, do you personally feel that partaking in "the medicine of the earth" is beneficial? Note: *We deal with mixed company in discussion groups. Some partake and some do not. This is not to determine moral validity, but to encourage healthy discussion.*

16. In contrast to the first novel of The Fellas' series, this novel focused more on Lionel's family. Lionel began to see them in a more positive light than he did before. Do you think that sometimes we let the closeness and comfort of extended family blind us to the good coming from our natural families?

17. In contrast to the last question, do you believe that there can be an entire family that exhibits opposition to an individual who is gay, trans, or just plain "different"? Do they benefit the individual mentally? Is such a family best loved from a distance?

18. This question can be answered in open forum or personal reflection. Is there any part of this book that you can relate to?

Thank you for reading the book,

THE COST

Follow the author, Eros Da Artiste, on Facebook, Instagram, and Twitter.

Made in the USA
Middletown, DE
28 May 2023